THE WALKAWAY

KU-365-034

Praise for *The Walkaway*

'Phillips is a stylish, laconic writer and *The Walkaway*, in pulling off his merging of two time scales, never falters for a moment. Terrific...'   *Observer*

'Essential reading'   *Literary Review*

'This is dark stuff – the way noir should be'
Metro London

'*The Walkaway*, with its shifting narrative and off-centre approach to lowlife culture, will most certainly count amongst the year's best crime novels'   *Crime Time*

'*The Walkaway* stands on its own legs as a complete work of art'   *Chicago Tribune*

Praise for *The Ice Harvest*

'Delightfully mean-spirited, this is a razor-sharp slice of low-down Americana with a gothic vengeance both gripping and touching'   *Guardian*

'Like the film *Fargo*, *The Ice Harvest* oozes atmosphere. The ice and snow throw a blanket of calm over everything, but beneath the smooth veneer it's all kicking off . . . The writing is simple and stylish and the detail's perfectly observed. Oh, and you won't be asking for your money back'   *Mirror*

'[A] funny, craftily malevolent first novel . . . An ice-pick-sharp crime story that sustains its film noir energy all the way to an outrageous whammy of an ending'
New York Times

'Scott Phillips's real-time thriller hooks us from the first chapter with funny, profane prose and sure-fire "In-a-minute-sweetheart" suspense . . . Whatever you do, don't start this book at the beach without applying a day's worth of sunblock before'   *San Francisco Chronicle*

'[This] funny, tough first novel felt like it was written by an old pro, an Elmore Leonard we've never heard about'
Richard Russo

'Descended from the gritty Depression tales of James M. Cain, as filtered through the darkly humorous cynicism of Jim Thompson . . . Sharp . . . Intriguing'
Los Angeles Times

Scott Phillips's first book, *The Ice Harvest*, was a finalist for the Hammett Prize and the Edgar Award, and winner of the Commonwealth Club of San Francisco Silver Medal. In the UK he has been shortlisted for the CWA John Creasey Award and the Macallan Dagger for Fiction Award, for best debut crime novel. He lives in Southern California with his wife and young daughter. Scott's third novel, *Cottonwood*, will be published as a Picador hardback in 2003.

Also by Scott Phillips

THE ICE HARVEST

THE

SCOTT PHILLIPS

WALKAWAY

PICADOR

First published 2002 by Picador

This edition published 2003 by Picador
an imprint of Pan Macmillan Ltd
Pan Macmillan, 20 New Wharf Road, London N1 9RR
Basingstoke and Oxford
Associated companies throughout the world
www.panmacmillan.com

ISBN 0 330 48145 2

9 8 7 6 5 4 3 2 1

A CIP catalogue record for this book is available from
the British Library.

Typeset by SetSystems Ltd, Saffron Walden, Essex
Printed and bound in Great Briatin by
Mackays of Chatham plc, Chatham, Kent

To Anne, again,

and this time to Claire, too,

with all my love.

THE WALKAWAY

PROLOGUE

29 DECEMBER, 1979

The farmhouse hadn't been painted since Gunther had seen it last, and curled paint chips littered the decaying wooden porch where it met the outside wall. He rapped on the door with the back of his fist and waited. A week's worth of frozen newspapers lay in various spots between the front door and the steps, still folded with rigid, brittle rubber bands around their middles. He picked up yesterday's, which he'd missed. The headline was below the fold:

TWO SOUGHT IN STRIP CLUB SLAYINGS
Pair Were Associates of Victims

He skimmed the article until a tiny old man opened the door and squinted up at him. His clothes were dirty and too big for him. 'Yes sir?'

'Mr. Gladwell, I'm Gunther Fahnstiel. Remember me?'

'Sally's friend. Uh-huh.'

'My old dog Pal died and I'd like to bury him out near the quarry, he liked hunting out there so much.'

'Uh-huh. You ain't been out here hunting in a while, have you?'

'Been a while, yeah.' Twenty-five years, in fact, but he didn't say that. 'Pal was a real old dog.'

'How's the girls doing?'

For a second Gunther thought he meant his daughters, both of them married and in their forties now, then realized Gladwell wanted to know about the girls from the cabin.

'Sally's off in Cottonwood, got married a few years ago. Frieda got into some trouble with narcotics and went to jail for a couple years at least; never heard what happened to her after that. Sonya and her husband moved away somewhere, KC or St. Louis maybe, about '60 or '61. Last I heard she was going to try and set up a raffle there.'

'How about Lynn?'

He'd been hoping he wouldn't ask about Lynn. 'Shot herself in '67. Something to do with a fellow she was going with. That's what I heard anyway.'

Gladwell nodded sadly, whether at Lynn's end or at his own sorrow at not having them around his place weekends any more Gunther wasn't sure. 'Go ahead if you want,' he said. 'It's hard digging out there, you know. Especially when it's frozen.'

'Rented a backhoe.'

'You want to come in out of that cold for a minute or you want to get started digging?'

Even here on the porch the stench from inside was enough to get Gunther breathing through his mouth. 'Better get started, I guess. Thanks.'

He stepped off the porch, and Gladwell shut the door

behind him; if he thought there was anything strange in burying an old hunting dog with a backhoe in a gravel pit he didn't show it. Gunther really had had a dog named Pal once, back before he got married for the first time; Pal was buried in back of his mother's old house on Emporia, unless someone had uncovered him landscaping or putting in sprinklers in the intervening fifty years. That burial had required only ten minutes and a shovel.

Crossing over the rise behind Gladwell's house he hiked back through the brittle, three-day-old crust of snow to the quarry where the backhoe sat waiting to be unloaded from the truck bed. The cabin's foundation was still there, marked by a crumbling stone chimney and half a charred beam standing out black against the white ground.

He opened the splintered wooden lid of the duck-blind. It stank the way a duckblind usually does, and from the body inside it, too, despite the cold. He pulled out the briefcase first and set it down, then climbed down into the blind. He got hold of the canvas and gave it a good heave. It went halfway up, bent over at the middle, and he got under it and shoved it up the rest of the way.

He picked a spot in the gravel and unloaded the backhoe. Even with the instructions the rental man had given him, it took him three hours to get the hang of it. When the hole was finally dug he rolled the canvas package into it, mumbling an apology of sorts to the corpse it contained, and then filled it up again.

He put the briefcase into the cab of the truck, opened it, and spent a minute or so looking at the money; he didn't count the bills, and when he snapped the case shut he knew for sure he was keeping every last one. He got out, loaded the backhoe onto the bed and secured it. Then he drove down the old familiar path to the county road, the truck bumping and jolting all the way. He didn't suppose he'd ever see the place again, and that was all right with him.

CHAPTER ONE

TEN YEARS LATER

This was the day the barber came to Lake Vista to give the old men haircuts, but Gunther wasn't there to take advantage of it. If he'd been thinking about it, he would have stayed around another day; as it was, he had become so preoccupied by the missed haircut that he decided he had no other choice but to part with the three-fifty or four dollars or whatever it was up to by now. Wincing at the thought, he touched his right hand to the back of his neck and pinched a lock between his thumb and forefinger to get a sense of its length. No, a haircut was the first order of business. Another week and it'd start to curl.

Walking west up the street, his sleeves rolled up to his elbows and his clothes damp and heavy with sweat, he saw very little that was familiar to him; most of the buildings he had known had either been torn down entirely or taken over by new businesses, and he was slightly cheered to see Ray and Cal's battered old barber pole rotating placidly on the rough orange brick wall next to what had always been Simmons's watch repair shop, occupied now by a forlorn and unhygienic-looking frozen yogurt store. He watched it turn for a minute, its red and blue stripes faded to pink and baby blue, then yanked open the door and stuck his head through it into the yogurt shop for a moment, startling the morose teen manning the counter.

The boy regarded him with mute wonder, as though the arrival of a potential customer was the most puzzling development of his day so far. Gunther looked the place over disapprovingly, the sweat on his face and neck and in his hair going cold in the breeze from the ancient box air conditioner buzzing and rattling in the window behind the counter. The yogurt store couldn't have been there long, but, with its bare walls and the worn-smooth formica countertop left over from the watch repair shop, the air inside it was already thick with failure. He knew that there would be no point in asking the kid what had become of old Simmons, so without a word he slammed the door shut and descended the half flight of concrete steps to the barber shop.

*

Inside it was way too bright. Half a story underground, Ray and Cal's had always been gloomy, even by barber-shop standards. Now the dark wood panelling had been pulled down, the walls painted a pastel yellow, and the dim incandescent lighting overhead had been replaced with fluorescent tubes, which were also mounted around the frames of the mirrors. Two women and one young man were stationed behind the chairs, and all three of the customers were women, their clothes protected by shiny plastic sheets of dark grey. Gunther had never seen a woman in Ray and Cal's before. All six of them looked at him expectantly, and the young man's eyes narrowed.

'You're going to have to leave now, okay, sir? I'm very sorry,' he said, stepping out from behind his chair and, for the benefit of the women, making a show of taking charge of the situation.

'What the hell are you talking about?'

'I'm very sorry.' He was young, thirty or less, and when he put his hand on Gunther's shoulder Gunther removed it calmly and deliberately, his eyes locked on the young man's, gauging his resolve. The young man took a step away from him without making another attempt.

'Where's Ray and Cal? I need a haircut.'

'I don't know who you're talking about, sir. Now as I said, you're going to have to go.' The young man's voice was artificially low and soothing like a goddamn orderly's, and the tone made Gunther want to smash him one right in the snotlocker.

'Wait a sec, Curt.' The older of the two lady barbers spoke up. Her face was pretty and her eyes friendly, but her greying hair was shaved close on the sides like a man's, and the combination made Gunther vaguely uneasy. 'Ray passed away a couple of years ago, sir.'

'Oh. Sorry to hear that.'

'Cal's still around, though, out at the Masonic home.'

'Cutting hair?'

'I don't think so. Just living there.'

'What do you know. So it's a beauty salon now, huh?' He looked the young man up and down. He didn't seem to Gunther like a fairy, but you couldn't really tell any more just by looking.

'No, sir, it's unisex,' she said, and the word threw Gunther off for a second. 'I'll be glad to cut your hair if you like. I'm almost done here and my two-thirty cancelled on me.' The woman sitting in the chair in front of her stared at Gunther, in curiosity more than annoyance at the interruption of her haircut. He took a good look at her for the first time, a tall, plumpish woman of forty or forty-five with large, dark eyes, short, wet hair and a lot of makeup. Her legs were so long they stuck out from under the plastic sheet a good six inches above the knee, and she reminded Gunther of somebody he couldn't quite place but was pretty sure he liked. He was staring back at her so intently he forgot to answer.

'Sir?' The lady barber's voice was louder this time, but he still didn't respond. He tilted his head to the left, trying to think of who she reminded him of. One of the nurses? An old girlfriend, maybe, or a teacher from school? No, he never saw any of his teachers' legs up that far, not in those days.

'Oh. My. God,' said the other lady barber, stifling a laugh. 'The old bastard's getting a hardon.'

'All right, pal, enough's enough. Let's go.' Curt's voice had lost its unctuousness, and Gunther resented him a little less for it.

'I'm going.' He turned and pulled the door open. 'Sorry I was staring at you, Ma'am. You look like somebody I used to know.'

No one spoke as he left. Once the door closed he stood for a minute or so at the foot of the concrete steps, waiting for his erection to deflate. It was his first in a while and he was sorry to see it go.

*

A quarter mile or so up the road he stopped at a pay phone in front of a Stop 'n' Rob. In the Yellow Pages under 'Hair' he found a listing for Harry's Barber Shop, which sounded like the kind of place where he'd be safe from any lady barbers or customers. It was about two miles west, close enough to get there before the end of the afternoon if he hurried, so he tore out the page and started walking again. He thought about going into the store for a soda, but his cash was tight and he hated to pay convenience store prices. He wasn't all that thirsty anyway. It was humid without being overwhelmingly hot, the sky was a dark, orangey gray, and sniffing the warm afternoon air he could smell rain before sundown. If he made it to Harry's Barber Shop in time he might be able to wait out the storm there.

It felt good to be outside and unsupervised. Earlier he'd been thinking how much simpler things would be if he were in a car, but he was happy now to be on foot and decided he wouldn't even mind being rained on a little, as long as there wasn't any lightning. As he got closer to the center of town the proportion of familiar, intact landmarks began to increase. He passed a used car lot where he'd once bought a 1946 Hudson Super Six with 35,000 miles on it which had ground to a permanent halt less than two years later as a result, his third wife had insisted, of his never having once changed its oil. Gunther had never known or cared much about cars, and he maintained that the postwar models didn't need their oil changed all that often; the ensuing fight had been one of the marriage's last. He wasn't sure what had become of her after she remarried and he didn't have to send her any more alimony. He didn't know what had happened to his first wife either; the one in between them was the mother of his two daughters and they'd kept in touch over the years through the girls and the grandchildren.

A couple of doors further west was a diner with thin plaques of fake marble mortared to its brick facade. Through the plate glass he saw a waitress he recognized, bored and loitering next to the cash register. She was a lot heavier now, her face gone round and slack with deep creases running from her nostrils to her mouth, but her hair was as thick and luxuriant and black as the last time he'd seen her. She gave a little start at the sight of him and beckoned him to come inside. Eager as he was to get to the barber shop before it closed for the day, he figured he had time for a cup of coffee.

'Gunther!' She had him in a bear hug as soon as he got through the door, and feeling her warm and soft against him Gunther couldn't help thinking that her increased girth was probably a good thing. 'How long's it been? Long time, seems to me. Hey, Jimbo, get out here and see who it is.' When she turned her face away from him to yell at the kitchen he snuck a glance at the nametag pinned to the polyester above her substantial left breast: IRMA. That seemed right.

A tiny, wizened man, who looked decades older than Gunther felt, came out of the kitchen scowling and wiping his hands. He brightened at the sight of Gunther and held out his hand to shake.

'Well, I'll be dipped in shit. What's a penny made of, copper?'

It was only at the familiar salutation that he recognized the old man as the diner's proprietor, about a foot shorter and thirty pounds skinnier than Gunther remembered him, as though a good part of his physical being had been siphoned off into Irma. 'How you been, Jimmy?'

'I been getting older. Looks like you have, too.'

'Sit down and have something,' Irma said.

'Guess I got time for a cup of coffee,' he said, taking the stool nearest the register. The stools looked new, and in fact most of the fixtures seemed to have been replaced since he'd been in last. Shiny chrome along and behind the counter, new naugahyde on the booths and stooltops, unscarred red and white checkerboard linoleum on the floor. He wondered where Jimmy had come up with the money for a remodel; there wasn't another customer in the place.

'Have something to eat if you want.'

'I just had lunch,' he said, though in fact he hadn't eaten since breakfast: some fruit salad he could tell was from a can and part of one of those pressed sawdust oat muffins they gave the old folks to make sure they all crapped like clockwork.

She poured him some coffee. 'I'll make a fresh pot for you here in a sec. So how's old Dorothy?' Jim went back into the kitchen.

'She's fine,' Gunther said.

'Give her my best. You'll have to bring her in some time.'

'Yep.'

'So how long since we've seen you?'

'Not long after I retired, probably.'

'So I guess that means you don't know Jim and I got married?' She held up her left hand, palm inward, to show off a wedding band and what looked to Gunther like a pretty expensive engagement ring. Jimmy must have been squirreling it away for years, unless he was just spending himself into the poorhouse out of love.

'Congratulations.'

'Thanks. It was a long time in coming, I'll tell you that. Look, we even changed the name.' She held up a menu with 'Jim and Irma's' printed on the cover. 'We had to throw out all kinds of menus and pens and guest checks marked "Jim's",' she said, and pulled a framed photo off the wall behind the counter and handed it to Gunther. It was a wedding picture with Jim and Irma surrounded by a group of children ranging in age from toddler to about ten.

'Nice looking bunch of kids.'

'Three of 'em are mine by my oldest daughter Nina, the others are Jim's son's kids. You got any grandkids?'

'Six, all of 'em grown,' he said, though it was a guess. It was close to that, anyway. 'One or two got kids of their own now.' He found himself distracted by the smell of frying onions.

'You don't have a picture to show me, do you?'

He reached for his wallet, thinking he didn't. Inside, though, were pictures of a little boy and girl of about five, taken separately, and another of the little boy, slightly older, with a girl of about two. There were also high school pictures of two other girls and another boy. He pulled them out one by one and gave them to Irma.

'The one girl's my granddaughter Cynthia's first, Cynthia's expecting her second in November. The brother and sister are my other granddaughter Tammy's. My grandson Steve isn't married yet, but there's nothing wrong with him. These three older ones are Tricia and Amy, and the boy's Danny. They're Dot's boy Sidney's kids. None of them's done with school yet.' The litany of names and relationships had poured out so fast and effortlessly he wondered where it had come from. For the first time since he'd left Lake Vista it occurred to him that people might be worried about him.

Irma studied the photographs with great interest as she emptied out his coffee cup and refilled it from the fresh pot. 'They're beautiful, Gunther.'

'Yeah.' He took a sip of hot coffee. It was the first caffeine he'd had in a long time, and he could feel himself starting to get a little jittery by the time Jimmy came out from the kitchen holding a plate with a cheeseburger and fries on it.

'Told you I didn't want anything to eat.'

'I was going to throw these fries out anyway, and you never used to come in here without eating a cheeseburger.' He set it down in front of Gunther, who was too hungry to be stubborn.

'I'd hate to see it go to waste,' he said. He poured some ketchup on to the plate for the fries, then some more on to the onions on top of the patty and took a big bite out of it. Jimmy's had never been his burger of choice, but this was better by a long shot than any he'd had since taking up residence at Lake Vista, and five minutes later burger and fries were a memory.

'You sure you don't want something for dessert, Gunther? Piece of pie, maybe?'

'Guess I'd better not.' He took another sip of his coffee and took out his wallet as he got up off the stool. 'Going to get my hair cut this afternoon.'

*

One block up was a bar that Gunther knew from an armed robbery one afternoon in the late sixties when the owner had gunned down the would-be thief who turned out to be armed only with a starter's pistol. Gunther remembered congratulating him, both of them marveling at the poor dead shit-for-brains on the floor next to them trying to rob a bar in mid-afternoon on a Tuesday, when the till must have had less than twenty-five dollars in it. Peering into the dark, empty bar through the glass pane set in its front door, he was trying to remember the owner's name and coming up blank when he heard the horn honking behind him. He turned to see a late model silver Caddy pulling over to the curb, its passenger side window rolling smoothly and effortlessly down. The driver scooted over to lean out.

'Excuse me,' she said. With her hair fluffed and dry, it took him a second to place her as the woman he'd been ogling back at Ray and Cal's. She was prettier than he'd thought before, more carefully made up than most of the women he saw lately. Since he found large women attractive anyway, he appreciated the fact that they often worked extra hard to look nice, although in her case he thought she might have overdone it a little around the eyes. 'I didn't mean to embarrass you back there.'

'That's okay,' he said, surprised that he rated an apology. 'Didn't mean to stare.'

'The thing is, after you left? When you said I reminded you of somebody?'

'Probably my imagination.'

The woman looked at him doubtfully. 'Is your name Gunther?'

'Who's asking?'

'My name's Loretta Gandy. It used to be Loretta Ogden.'

The first name meant nothing to him, but the second resonated somewhere in the back of his mind.

'Sally Ogden's my mom,' she added.

The name gave Gunther a jolt, though he wasn't sure why. It was a good bet, though, that this Sally was the woman she put him in mind of, and he relaxed a little. 'Oh.'

'Do you need a lift? I'd be glad to give you one.'

'Which way you headed?'

'Whichever way you need to go.' She unlocked the passenger door and pushed it open, sliding back into the driver's seat.

'Thanks a lot,' he said, and as he got in the first few warm drops of rain started falling, spotting the reddish dust on the windshield. She set the wiper to the slowest speed, smearing the drops into mud and necessitating a shot of wiper fluid as they pulled out. 'Harry's Barber Shop, on Cowan and Second.'

She nodded and continued westward on Douglas, and for a while they were silent, though it seemed she was waiting for him to say something. Since he didn't know what she was expecting, he kept his counsel.

'So don't you want to know how my mom is?' she finally asked.

'Sure,' he said, though *who* she was might have been a more pertinent question than *how*.

'Well, pretty good, at least as good as you can expect. She buried old Donald last year.'

'Was he dead?' He was instantly sorry he'd said it, but the old censoring mechanism had never been too sharp to begin with; now it seemed to be completely shot. She held her breath for a second, then looked over at him with her mouth wide open, stunned. He was about to apologize when she let out a loud laugh like a seal barking.

'That's a good one. Guess you didn't have any reason to like him much, huh?'

He guessed that he probably hadn't; the list of people he liked much was a short one.

'They moved back to town five years ago. I've been here since college. I don't think she ever sees any of her old friends.'

'Probably they didn't like Donald,' he said, still not knowing who Donald was.

'Probably. He was pretty good to her, though, you got to give him that.'

'I guess you do.'

'You were, too. She always said so.'

He turned away from her to look at the passing streets,

and she suspected he was trying to hide a tear. In fact, he was just trying to figure out what it was he was supposed to have done for this Sally. In an odd, indirect way it seemed to Gunther to be connected to his money and where he'd left it.

*

Gunther recognized Harry's Barber Shop when he saw it. The front of the building faced the streetcorner, and an uneven old sidewalk bisected a triangular lawn, a week past its mowing time, from the intersection of the sidewalks along Cowan and Second streets, in a mostly residential neighborhood. Inside a lone, elderly barber stood bathed in ghostly, greenish fluorescent light, looking out of a picture window at the sprinkling. By now the sky was so dark Loretta had put her headlights on.

'Here we are. Cowan and Second. That must be Harry in the window.'

'Must be. Thanks for the ride.' He tried to think of something else to say. 'Give my best to your Mom.' He pushed the door open slightly.

'Hey, Gunther . . .?'

He pulled the door almost shut.

'How are you fixed for money?'

'I got plenty of money. I just can't get to it, that's the problem.'

'The thing is, I know Mom owed you some money, 'cause I've heard her talk about it . . .'

He couldn't tell if she was lying or just nervous about offering him money; in either case he normally would

17

have been insulted. But right now he needed the money badly, and he was certain he'd be able to pay it back in a timely manner.

'Maybe so, it's hard to remember. Don't worry about it.'

She pulled open her purse and dug excitedly through it. 'No, no, Mom'd never forgive me if she knew, now hold on . . .' She pulled out a billfold and took out a pair of hundred-dollar bills, then a business card. She wrote something on the card, then handed it to him along with the bills.

'You take this, and if she owed you more than that you call me, okay?'

'Thanks.'

He got out of the car and as she watched him marching up the sidewalk to Harry's she worried that she hadn't given him enough. She knew it had been hard for him to accept the money, and she was sure he'd never call to ask for more. This was likely her only chance to do something for him.

She rolled down the window just as he reached the door.

'Gunther?'

He turned and squinted at her, his hand braced perpendicular to his forehead to shield his eyes from the rain. Offering him more now would only embarrass him.

'Call, okay?'

He nodded, turned away and entered the barber shop. As she drove away it struck her that no trace of a smile had crossed his face since she'd first seen him, an oddly endearing trait that accorded with her own vague memories and her mother's occasional drunken anecdotes about him.

*

Gunther didn't feel much like talking, and Harry couldn't seem to stop. He went on for a while about the local triple A Baseball team, which Gunther thought had folded years ago, then moved on to the subject of his kids, grandkids and great-grandkids. Having listed them all, he waxed philosophical about the business of barbering, and Gunther let it wash over him, enjoying the luxurious sensation of being in a real barber chair again. When Harry was finished cutting, he applied lather to the back of Gunther's neck and sharpened a straight razor with a leather strop hanging from the counter.

'Why don't you give me a full shave while you're at it.'

'Sure thing. Not many go for a shave any more, they got their Norelcos and their Brauns and they think that's the same as a real shave.'

'Uh-huh.' The sight of the slightly curved blade jogged something. 'Did you have an accident in here with that once?'

'It was no accident. You're showing your age. That was in forty-seven.'

It was coming slowly into focus. It had been a big story at the time. 'Some old time vaudeville comedian, right?'

'That's right, Jimmy Cavendish of Cavendish and Carlisle. He was from around here, raised on a farm outside of Shattuck.'

'Yeah, I remember him.'

'Carlisle played the hayseed and Cavendish was the

19

city slicker, just the opposite of what they was in real life. They was big in vaudeville in the teens, then on Broadway, after that they made some movies. Last one they did had Martha Raye in it.'

Once he'd finished shaving the back of Gunther's neck he brushed warm lather on to his face and began carefully and systematically drawing the razor down at the side of his ear.

'He used to come back to see the family. His nephew Jack was a great friend of mine; we were in school together. I was just starting this place up, fresh out of the army, when Jack brings in his uncle for a haircut. His partner Carlisle had just died, and he was in kind of a funk. He wasn't a young man any more. Younger than you and me today, 'course, but remember back then a man of sixty was old.'

Gunther nodded. 'Mm-hm.'

'Anyhow, right after I lathered him up he says in this real quiet voice, "I'm not going to make it to supper, Jack, tell your mother I'm sure sorry," and by God if he don't grab the straight razor right out of my hand and slash it right acrost his throat.' He moved the razor quickly under his own chin to illustrate.

'Yeah, I remember now.'

'Cut so clean for a second I didn't think he'd really done it, then I seen the blood start coming in a straight line through the lather; pretty soon it was all over the sheet and everywhere. Bled to death right in this chair, and it was brand new at the time.'

'Huh.'

'I was scared it'd hurt business, but it sure didn't. Put

me on the map is what it did. Once I had the chair reupholstered I had all the business I could handle. I'm sure as hell sorry he killed himself, but he really did me a favor, doing it here in my shop.' Harry finished up the shave and pulled the sheet off Gunther. 'Still raining. Your daughter coming back to pick you up or what?'

'My daughters both live out of state. That was just somebody who gave me a ride.'

'Well, okay. How you getting home?'

'Don't know.' He wasn't sure where home was, anyway.

'Well, you can sure sit it out in here. I close up at six.'

'Thanks,' Gunther said, and he sat looking out the window while Harry talked, not thinking about much of anything except the rain.

CHAPTER TWO

WAYNE OGDEN: 14 JUNE, 1952

The train got into the station east of downtown at four-fifteen in the morning, which suited me fine. I hadn't made any effort to adjust to American time; most of my business here would be at night anyway. At that hour the station was crawling with porters and railroad workers, passengers disembarking or boarding for the second half of the train's eastward crossing, people manning the newsstand and the candy counter, an elderly midget hawking the early edition of the morning paper. I left my duffel bag at the baggage claim and stuffed the claim check in my pocket. 'Twenty-five cents a day or part thereof,' the solemn attendant said as I walked away.

The coffee shop downstairs from the platform was open so I took a seat at the counter and grabbed a mimeographed menu from a little wire rack next to the napkin dispenser.

'Hey, Sarge,' a gaunt, rheumy-eyed old man said, taking the stool next to mine. 'How about a little grubstake for a fellow vet?' He wasn't too dirty, and he'd shaved recently, but his shirt collar was frayed and so were his cuffs. His pants had long, oval holes worn through above each knee, and his slight vocal tremor gave him away as a rummy, probably a step or two away from sterno. Clean as he was, he probably lived at one of the transient hotels a few blocks toward downtown, the last stop before permanent residence on the sidewalk.

I was about to tell him to go piss up a rope when the counterman came over. 'All right, Chester, I told you for the last time. You bother the customers you're back on the street. Out.'

'Chester's eating with me,' I said. 'I'll have the K.C. Strip and eggs, over easy. Give him whatever he wants.'

'Same as him, only scrambled.'

The counterman waited a second before writing it down, glared resentfully but powerlessly at me, and then turned away to put the orders in.

'Look at him. He wanted to tell you where to shove it, but he's still scared of noncoms.' Chester ran his fingers nervously through his hair, and I noticed how much of it was still dark. My first guess had been the Spanish American War, but looking closer I could see he wasn't much past fifty.

'AEF?' I asked.

'Yep. Belleau Wood.'

'So was my old man.' I was lying, but so was he, probably. 'Thomas McCowan, Master Sergeant.' Another lie; this was the first time I'd used McCowan's name, and I found that it amused me to introduce myself that way.

McCowan would be apoplectic if he knew about it, even more so that I'd downgraded him from a Lieutenant to my own lowly noncom status.

'Chester Bemis, Corporal First Class. Pleased to meet you.'

'You want to go get a drink after breakfast?'

Chester beamed. 'You're shittin' me.'

'Not at all. I haven't been around for a while and I wouldn't know where to go myself. Commanche still open?'

'Sure is. Not this late, though. Inside the city limits they shut down at two. But you know the Hitching Post, out on 49th? They'll be open.'

'Sounds good to me. Maybe we'll go pick up on some whores, afterward.'

'Fine with me, if it's on your nickel. There's usually a few hanging around the Hitching Post, if you're not too particular.'

The counterman came back with coffee cups and filled them without addressing either of us, and we fell silent in his presence, Chester studying my uniform. When the counterman left again Chester leaned forward with his elbows on the counter.

'Quartermaster Corps, huh?'

'That's right. You got a sharp eye.'

'I got fucking trenchfoot is what I got, almost killed me, thanks to the goddamn Quartermaster Corps.'

I knew what was coming, but I asked anyway. 'How do you figure that?'

'Rubber goddamn boots. Every goddamn supply sergeant in Europe had 'em, but not on the front, not where men was fighting and dying in trenches full of pigshit and muddy water. The whole Quartermaster Corps can go fuck itself as far as I'm concerned.'

'Hey, buddy,' I shouted. The counterman came over slowly, a dishrag tossed over his shoulder. 'I'll be eating that second steak and eggs myself. Chester here just talked himself out of some free booze and pussy, too.'

'You hear that, Chester? Hit the pavement.'

He got up off his stool. 'I'd rather eat shit by myself than steak and pussy with a supply sarge,' he said, but there was terrible regret in his eyes and a choke in his voice. He left without an argument, turning around once as if to apologize. He didn't, though.

A couple of minutes later my two plates of steak and eggs came and I tore into the first, suddenly realizing how hungry I'd been. I'd awakened at midnight, and there was no food service on the train at that hour. It was a good thing Chester had come along; I was still ravenous when I finished the first plate, and as I started in on the second steak a middle-aged couple entered and sat down a few seats up from me. I'd seen them the day before on the dining car, elegantly dressed and looking out at the passing scenery rather than talking as they ate.

This morning the man, heavy and slow on his feet, looked exhausted, but the woman was cheerful and wide awake. He was wearing an expensive grey suit, well cut, and she had on a brown silk dress with a diamond pin at the left shoulder. If it had been even a little cool I was certain she would have been wearing fur.

'Morning, Sergeant,' the man said.

'Morning.'

They studied their menus and the husband stretched, cracked his knuckles and yawned extravagantly.

'Edwin. Don't yawn, and don't crack your knuckles either. You're in public.'

'I can't help it, it's the middle of the goddamn night.'

'Don't curse, either.'

He ignored her and stuck out his hand to shake. 'Ed Brenner, Brenner Agricultural Insurance Company, Ventura, California.'

'Master Sergeant Thomas McCowan, United States Army. Pleased to make your acquaintance.' I was pleased with how smoothly the name came off my tongue. 'What brings you folks to town?' I asked.

'Visiting her family. Mine's up in Chicago.' The man didn't sound happy about either fact. 'How about you?'

'I'm on a ninety-day re-enlistment furlough. Just came back to see the old hometown, spend a little time with the family.'

The conversation dried up when their food came and we were all three shoveling it in, and I didn't speak again until it was time to pay the check. The counterman shook his head when I asked for it.

'Your meal's taken care of, Sergeant.'

The couple smiled at me over their breakfasts.

'I can't accept that, thanks . . .'

The man cut me off, as I'd expected. 'Forget about it. It's already taken care of. Now have a nice visit home.'

I pretended to consider it for a moment, then flashed my most charming grin. 'Thanks. God bless you folks.'

I picked up my hat, put it on, and walked out briskly without exactly marching.

*

Outside the station there were no cabs. Presumably they'd picked up whatever passengers there were on the four-fifteen and then dispersed, and the next passenger train didn't come in until half past six, so I went over to a pay phone and called for one. I stood waiting for it to arrive, feeling good about saving a little money on breakfast. I felt a little bad about old Chester, though; I thought I might give him a little change if he was still around, but he was nowhere to be seen.

The cabbie must have been cruising around down-town, because he was there in less than three minutes. He was a burly guy with hair on his neck and a particular slow, droll way of talking I hadn't heard since I'd left this place. 'Where you headed, Sarge?' Three days in the U.S. and I'd already had about a belly full of civilians calling me 'Sarge.'

'The Hitching Post, out on 49th.'

'If you're looking for a whore, I know where there's better and cheaper.'

'I bet you do. The Hitching Post is where I'm headed.'

The driver shut up and headed west through down-town, then north. Hard to tell driving through it at five in the morning with the sidewalks empty, but the main business district seemed not to have changed much, at least physically. The town's population was about double what it had been before the war, though, and when we started heading north I could see where it had grown.

Tract after tract of cheap houses that hadn't been there when I left lined the road until we got well out of town and into the county.

I could see the neon sign for the Hitching Post half a mile before we got there; I remembered it from '46, when I'd spent an ill-considered year back here as a civilian. The sign featured an immense caricature of an inbred moron with enormous feet, ears and nose, wearing a torn straw hat and threadbare overalls, his gigantic, misshapen thumb hooked through a moonshine jug marked 'XXX.' A single buck tooth jutted up out of his lower jaw, and another downward from the upper. An overwhelming proportion of the Hitching Post's customers were yokels themselves, up from Arkansas or Oklahoma to work at the aircraft plants, but none of them seemed to mind, or to think that the sign referred in any way to them. The parking lot this morning had six or eight cars in it, and when I got out of the cab one of them lurched from its space and with a metal-buckling crunch hit another, parked a good fifteen feet away. I heard laughter from the first car as it roared away, the taxi following it at a timid distance back to town.

Inside hillbilly music played on the jukebox, some yodeling hog farmer's lament about a woman who'd walked away with some other, presumably non-yodeling hog farmer, and I took a seat at the bar. 'What's the best scotch you got?' I asked the bartender.

'Bourbon.'

I put down half a buck. He poured me a shot and a beer chaser and I took a look around the room as I downed it. Eight guys, three of them dancing with three girls, all of whom I took to be pros. One of them, a short, thick-torsoed brunette, was practically humping her partner right there on the dance floor. Two more guys were seated at a table, and two more were playing pool. The eighth guy was sitting by himself, staring at the dancers, and I thought he was probably waiting for one of the girls to get free. The room was dark, most of the light coming from a mismatched set of table lamps strategically located from front to back. There were three ceiling fixtures but they'd been equipped with red bulbs and provided little more than what passed for atmosphere on 49th Street.

I turned my attention to my beer. There was a good chance one or more of these guys had come off the second shift at Collins, and if I didn't act too interested I might be able to get one of them to spill a little.

'Well, looky there,' someone said behind me. 'Looks like a war hero. Coming in here in uniform and all.' At the small of my back, in a pocket I'd paid a German civilian tailor to add to my class A uniform trousers, I had a set of brass knucks. As I spun to face the speaker I surreptitiously pulled them on. Covering my right hand with my left, I found the loner standing a couple of feet away from me. He was loaded, and there are lots of ways to disarm a drunk without resorting to violence.

'Don't want no trouble, now, Elishah,' the bartender said slowly and calmly.

'I don't want no trouble, either,' the man said. He sounded like he was from Arkansas, maybe, or even Tennessee, though his accent was undoubtedly thickened with alcohol, and while my first impression of thinness still held, I saw now that he was wiry rather than scrawny.

His nose had been broken more than once, and his teeth were false. The pool tables were watching us now, and the dancing couples. I tried to judge their interest in him, and whether they'd come to his aid if a fight broke out.

I stood up and gestured with my head to the empty stool next to me, my left hand still hiding the knucks. 'Sit down, buddy, and let me buy you a drink.' If there was trouble, I wasn't going to get the information I wanted tonight.

'What you want to buy me a drink for, faggot?'

In this kind of place those were fighting words if ever there were; my options had narrowed to one.

'No sir, you misunderstood me,' I said in a very concil-iatory tone. Then I suckerpunched him in the gut so hard I could hear the air rush out of his lungs, the brass digging deep into his entrails. All eyes were on the downed man for the moment, and I took advantage of it to slip the knucks off and into my front pocket. The pocket of a Class A uniform is too tight to conceal anything effectively, but putting them back into the hidden pocket would have been too conspicuous. In a few minutes I'd head for the john and make the switch there. Elishah rolled around on the floor, curled up in a ball with the dry heaves, and I looked up at the bartender first to make sure I wasn't about to be eighty-sixed. The urge to finish what I'd started and kick the shit out of my floored opponent, starting with his face, was powerful, but I resisted. 'Sorry about that.'

Around then I noticed the laughter of the other men. One of them was clapping.

'Yay, Sarge.'

The bartender rang a bell suspended over the backbar. 'Congratulations, Sergeant, you just bought the house a round.' He started making drinks and pulling out beer bottles, and a couple of his drinking buddies helped the coughing, retching hillbilly into a chair at one of the tables. I pulled a ten-dollar bill from my sock and laid it on the bar.

'Keep 'em coming,' I told him.

The song was over now and one of the girls was sitting on the high barstool next to me. She wore a short blue dress with a very low neckline, and she leaned forward to let me get a good look. 'You are a very handsome man.' She made it sound like she'd never seen a handsome man in the flesh before. 'My name's Beulah. You in town for long?'

'Depends,' I said. She had a remarkable figure, large breasts and wide hips accentuated by an extremely narrow waist, and her legs were long and nicely shaped. Her face, though, seemed to belong on another body altogether: slightly wall-eyed, with a freakishly small nose and an equally tiny, seemingly lipless mouth over the biggest lantern jaw I'd ever seen on a woman. She'd caked on the makeup and piled her black hair in an elaborately woven mound atop her head in a valiant attempt to compensate. She was one of the homeliest women I'd seen in years, and yet it was all I could do not to start running my hands up and down her body right there at the bar. It had been close to a week since I left Japan and all the free pussy I could handle.

'Depends on what?'

'I guess it depends on the kind of reception I get while I'm here.'

She laughed like that was the funniest thing anybody'd ever said and lit a cigarette. 'Anybody beats the shit out of Elishah like that's gonna get a pretty good one around this place,' she said. Urban upper midwest, I guessed, harsh vowels and a nasal quality to the voice overall, maybe Detroit or Flint. I wondered how she'd ended up down here.

'I like to see a man in uniform. My husband was in the army,' she said. 'Don't worry, he's dead.' She smiled coquettishly and leaned forward, placing her hand incidentally on my thigh and giving it a little squeeze. I followed suit, placing mine at the hem of her dress. Nobody seemed to care; one of the women punched in another hillbilly song on the jukebox, over which could be heard the howling denunciations of the wounded man.

'I'm off at six,' she said. 'Maybe you'd like to come over and have a little party.'

'Maybe,' I said. Jesus, she was ugly, but when I looked at the body underneath the face I knew I was up for it. 'Sure.'

Her hand moved up my thigh and touched my groin, then slid unexpectedly the other way, toward my front pants pocket. Before I knew what she was doing, she was waving the brass knuckles over her head.

'I knew it!' she cackled. 'I fuckin' knew it!'

Elishah's friends started moving in to the bar. Once again I found myself reviewing my options. Since I didn't have a car they seemed limited: take a beating or talk my way out of one. Before I could open my mouth I felt something hard collide with the back of my head, and I turned in time to see one of the other whores holding a pistol and then someone turned me around and slammed a fist into my belly, and then someone was holding my elbows, and then came the first of the blows to my face.

I must have passed out for a minute, because I don't know how we got into the parking lot. The next thing I remember is a kick to the ribs as I lay on the gravel, my right eye swollen shut, and the bartender stepping out the front door.

'You might as well know, I just called the Sheriff. If you're fixing to leave, do it now.'

I heard car doors opening and slamming shut, engines turning over, gravel crunching. Somebody kicked me again, most likely Elishah, then got into a car and drove away. After a few moments of silence I became aware that someone was watching me. I opened my eye again and saw a pair of blue high-heeled shoes two or three feet away. Beulah lowered herself to a squat, balancing with one hand down on the ground. Her short dress and slip rode up well past the tops of her stockings, and I saw in the dawn's early light that she wasn't wearing any underwear; funny how after all my years of pimping I was still so affected by the sight.

'I'm sure sorry it got out of hand like that,' she said. 'But you ought to know better than to use brass knuckles in a fair fight.'

I murmured something that must have sounded like humbled assent.

'Good. Now you see? You're all even-steven, and as far

as we're all concerned you're welcome back here any time. Maybe some morning you'll come home with me after all.'

She got up and walked back into the Hitching Post, and I managed to raise my head up from the jagged gravel. The neon idiot glowed like an inbred cartoon ghost against the still-dark sky to the west; for the first time I noticed that he had eleven fingers and the same number of toes, and I laughed a little through the pain. I felt my cash supply still in my sock, though they'd all seen that I kept my money there. It hadn't been as bad a beating as I'd expected, either; maybe they figured Elishah deserved what he'd gotten. I dragged myself to a sitting position and took a deep breath. I was pleased to confirm my suspicion that no ribs had been broken, and I let the breath out slowly. The air was cool and moist, and in the distance I heard a siren getting closer.

It was the first time I'd been home in six years.

CHAPTER THREE

Sidney McCallum sat in unwittingly menacing silence across from the director of the Lake Vista Elder Care Facility, listening to his mother piss and moan about lax security procedures and lawsuits. The director, a small, nervous man named Mercer, was considerably less afraid of the old lady's threats of legal action than of Sidney suddenly diving across his desk and choking him to death, an option to which the bigger man, fists clenched and eyes angrily fixed on his Adam's apple, appeared to be giving due consideration. When Sidney began absently smacking his right fist rhythmically into the palm of his left hand, the man's blink rate increased perceptibly, as though a fan were blowing directly into his eyes.

'On the up side, Mrs. Fahnstiel,' he said, 'apart from his blood pressure your husband is in excellent health for a man of seventy-seven, and he's not on any medications he can't afford to miss for a few days.'

Sidney finally spoke. 'He just doesn't know what fucking year it is, is all.'

Mercer swallowed hard. 'Those are, of course, the sort of patients who pose the greatest risk for elopement.'

'Elopement, shit. I can't get into the Memory Impaired Ward without passing the front desk and signing in, same thing goes when I leave. How does a senile old man pull off a jailbreak like that?'

'Mr. Fahnstiel, this is one of the finest elder care facilities in the state. To compare it to a jail—'

'My name's McCallum. Gunther's her second husband,' he said, jerking his thumb at his mother. 'Anyway, weren't you supposed to be putting some kind of house-arrest bracelets on all the head cases?'

'These head cases, as you call them, are human beings, Mr. McCallum, and some of them have been reluctant to wear the devices,' he said with a hint of tension-induced vibrato. 'We've found it's better to let them get used to the idea gradually—'

'Listen.' Dorothy Fahnstiel said in a voice solid enough to stop Mercer in mid-phrase. She leaned across the table. 'It costs twenty-five thousand dollars every year to keep him in this shithole, and I have a right to expect better than this.'

Sidney turned to his mother and addressed her for the first time since their arrival. 'The police pension pays twenty-five big ones a year?'

'Yeah,' the old woman said. 'It's a hell of a pension plan.'

Mercer slid his index finger down to the pertinent figure on the page before him. 'Actually, the pension pays about a third of it.'

'Then who's paying the other sixteen grand?'

'We'll talk about it later,' the old lady snapped, and she

stood up. 'Come on, I want to be home in case he shows up.'

Mercer escorted them to the lobby, and as they passed the security desk outside the Memory Impaired Ward Sidney's mother pointed at the nameplate on the desk and shouted, 'Security Director! That's a hot one.'

A tall man with a square face and slicked-back black hair that smelled of Brylcreem, the Security Director gave no indication that he'd heard her.

A number of elderly residents and visitors stared at them as they crossed the spacious, leafy atrium to the front door. 'That's right, folks, I'm the old lady whose husband they let just up and walk out of here. He doesn't know who's President of the United States, but he was sharp enough to get past these assholes.' She shoved the door open with her shoulder and Sidney followed.

*

'Where's the money coming from, Mom?' They were running across the parking lot, neither of them having come prepared for rain.

She failed to respond as he opened the passenger door and helped her into the seat. He crossed over to the driver's side slowly now, letting the light, warm rain soak his hair and enjoying the smell that it seemed to draw from the asphalt, aware that any answer he might eventually get would be hard won.

He turned the key and tried again. 'I'm talking to you. Where's that money coming from?' He backed out of the cramped space and cruised slowly through the parking lot.

'I told you, the pension.'

'I'm not Gunther, Mom. I don't forget things people said five minutes ago. Pension pays a third of it, according to the doctor. Where's the rest of it coming from?'

'Doctor,' she snorted. 'That doctor crap is strictly for the rubes. Mercer's a Ph.goddamn D. "He's not on any medications he can't afford to miss for a while." Well, how about his goddamn blood pressure meds? Mercer don't know shit from shinola about medicine.'

'Where's it coming from, Mom?' He pulled the big car slowly on to the street.

'Just take me home,' she snapped. 'Did it ever occur to you that I might not want to talk about this right now?'

'I'm always offering to help you out with anything you need. You always refuse. And now I find out you got a sixteen thousand dollar a year nursing home bill . . .'

'Just take me home,' she said, and she sounded so tired and scared and sad that for once he let her have the last word and drove her home in silence.

*

Ed Dieterle tossed his overnight bag into the hatchback of his little one-lung Japanese model, the best the rental agency could do on such short notice. He hoped no one he knew saw him at the wheel; he would have prefered to drive the LTD up from Dallas, but there wasn't time. Gunther's granddaughter Tricia had phoned around noon, right after she'd heard, and he'd thrown a couple of changes of clothes into his bag and headed straight for the airport.

The rain in Wichita had delayed the flight's takeoff and arrival, and he'd be too late to interview anyone at Lake Vista today. He sent Gunther occasional letters and postcards there, and Gunther usually wrote back, too, his letters seemingly lucid but with only a vague apprehension of recent events. He knew Ed had retired, for example, but each letter expressed fresh surprise at his relocation to Dallas. Sometimes he still sent his love to Daisy.

Heading east in the feeble remnants of what must have been a real gullywasher, he listened to the news on the radio. Wichita in summertime was as lush and green as it ever had been, but it had changed physically in disorienting ways. New commercial developments had appeared up and down both sides of Kellogg, leaving the occasional familiar landmark intact but surrounded by empty space or strange new buildings and robbed of its context. He felt as though he'd been gone for decades.

Lake Vista was far to the east, practically at the city limits in an area that had been mostly undeveloped when he'd left town. Slightly further on and across the freeway was the Highlander Seven Motel, new to him but with a marquee offering a free continental breakfast and cable TV for only $24.95, with the promise underneath of an even better AARP rate, and he swung across the freeway and through the nearly empty parking lot into the carport next to the office.

*

Loretta pulled the Caddy into the detached garage, preoccupied with Gunther; she should have offered to come back and get him after his haircut. She didn't even know if he had a place to stay, but her gut instinct was that he didn't.

She ducked under the garage door as it lowered and cautiously crossed the slick cement to the house. The rain had all but stopped, just a few stray drops splashing her face as she opened the back door, and the sky was so much lighter now it felt earlier in the day than it had when she'd dropped Gunther off.

Inside the kitchen, she grabbed the phone book from the shelf above her desk and looked up Harry's Barber Shop. Harry answered testily after ten rings.

'I'm closed. Open tomorrow at nine.'

She licked her lips. 'Uh ... Harry?' Her throat was dry and scratchy.

'That's me. Who's this?'

'My name's Loretta Gandy. I dropped off a friend there a while ago, and I just wondered if he was still around.'

'You talking about Gunther?'

Her spirits rose for a moment. 'Yes. Can I talk to him?'

'Nope. He left in a cab about half an hour ago.'

'Did he say where he was going?'

'No, he didn't, and my dinner's waiting for me at home getting cold. Good night, miss.'

He hung up on her. At least she knew Gunther had the two hundred dollars; maybe he'd call when it ran out.

The red light was blinking on the answering machine and she pressed the play button. After the beep came the fuzzy, indistinct sound of Eric's voice raised over the white noise of a crowded bar-room, and even on a Thursday she knew what her husband was going to say before he was three words into it.

'It's me, I'm working late. Gonna grab a bite at Ruby's with Blake and the guys.'

'Fine with me,' she said aloud. The knowledge that he was probably on a date bothered her very little, and scanning the fridge for dinner she remembered she had one last load of laundry to dry. Before work that morning she'd put in a full two hours of cleaning; not enough to stay ahead of it, really, just enough that she didn't have to come home to a messy kitchen.

She poured herself a glass of white wine, drained it, poured another and took it downstairs to the basement. She clicked on the light in the big room and could barely stand to look around as she passed through, appalled as ever at the expense of finishing it when Tate and Michelle were both on the verge of going off to school. Now they were out of the house and Eric, as she'd predicted, never used the place. The massive, grotesquely expensive pool table he'd insisted on buying sat untouched, like the wet bar he'd installed with the dubious and unappealing claim that it would keep him home nights. She resented the pissed-away money all the more for the fact that despite earning a substantial portion of it she still seemed to have no say in its disbursement.

In the tiny laundry room she pulled a handful of damp panties, a lingerie bag full of pantyhose and a couple of bras from the washing machine, threw them into the dryer, and after a long, satisfying pull from her glass of wine turned it on and went back upstairs.

She ate a turkey pot pie in the living room while she watched the last fifteen minutes of an old movie with Clark Gable and William Powell and that woman who always played his wife, whose name she couldn't quite summon at the moment. Gable died in the chair in the end, which came as a surprise to Loretta, and as the credits rolled she picked up the phone to call her mother and tell her about running into Gunther.

*

Gunther's plans on leaving the nursing home that morning hadn't evolved far enough to include thoughts of where he'd sleep if he didn't reach his goal before nightfall. If it hadn't been raining, he might have slept under the stars, but it was still coming down in sheets when Harry had asked him where he lived and made him realize he was going to have to find a bed for the night. Without the two hundred extra dollars, he would almost certainly have gone looking for one of the old welfare hotels west of Union Station, having forgotten that they'd all been shut down over the course of the last decade or so, replaced by men's shelters and the sidewalks. With the options the unexpected windfall presented, he decided to treat himself to a taxi ride and a good night's sleep in a real motel: not one of the fancy places out by the highway but one of the nicer cheap ones south of downtown. By the time he'd left Harry's the rain was tapering off and the sky to the south and west had cleared to a bright yellow-white above the trees and beneath the thunderheads, which had stopped rumbling and whose undersides had become wispy and light gray against the dark main mass of cloud.

When the cab let him out twenty minutes later in front of the All-American Inn the rain had stopped. As he paid and stepped across the crunchy wet gravel of the motel's parking lot he saw a very thin, greasy-haired young woman in a black and yellow halter top with STRYPER written across its front approaching him with a lewd smile. 'You looking for a date, Grandpa?'

'Jesus Christ,' he said, startled at her brazenness. 'You're a hooker,' he added helpfully.

She was unfazed by his lack of discretion. 'You a policeman?'

'Used to be. Not any more.'

'In that case I sure am a hooker. Are you a customer?'

'I'm a customer of the goddamn motel is what I am. I'm just looking for a good night's sleep.' Mercifully, his censoring mechanism kicked in just in time and he didn't add that he'd sooner lie down with a yellow dog. She was among the most bedraggled prostitutes he'd ever seen, even for a streetwalker. Their lids caked blue with eye shadow, her eyes looked like they never closed; below them, generous amounts of flesh-toned makeup failed to conceal the dark lines flaring from the bridge of her nose toward her ears.

'A customer of this motel here?' She cracked a couple of knuckles on her left hand, then rubbed her palms together nervously.

'Just looking for a place to lay my head for the night.'

'You know what you want in that case, then, is probably the Stars and Stripes a couple doors down. This one don't really specialize in long-term rentals, like overnight.'

He nodded. 'Thanks. If I run into anybody looking for a date I'll be sure and send 'em your way.'

She turned her attention back to the passing cars. As he walked to the Stars and Stripes he stopped to look at her once again, something nagging at his consciousness. Why had he been surprised to see a hooker here? South Broadway had been the city's principal redlight district for twenty years or more, a major trouble spot since well before his retirement. When he'd started out as a patrolman in '39 the streetwalkers had all been north of downtown and in the old tenderloin, and when development and do-gooders chased them away they'd settled here.

The man at the desk of the Stars and Stripes was younger than Gunther but not by much, and spoke with a mellifluous foreign accent which Gunther took to be Indian. He had on a big pair of plastic framed eyeglasses and a bright yellow cardigan despite the heat.

'Can a fella get a room for overnight on this street anymore?'

'Certainly, sir. Just fill this out.' He handed Gunther a form, which Gunther examined with a puzzled look. 'Print your name and permanent address, and the license plate for your car.'

Gunther continued to scowl at the form, baffled.

'It's a state law, sir. You must fill out your name and so forth.' Just as the man was starting to wonder if anything was wrong with Gunther, something seemed to kick in and he began to fill in the blanks.

'Neighborhood sure has changed.'

'Yes, sir. It's getting better.'

'Better? You call this better? Jesus, I remember when

these motels used to cater to traveling salesmen and families on vacation.'

'Ah, I see what you mean. But it is changing back, bit by bit. Just one year ago, when my nephews bought the Stars and Stripes, it was called the Bide-A-Wee, and the rooms that weren't being rented by the hour to the ladies of the street were occupied by drug addicts and dealers, all of whom had to be evicted with great difficulty. Now look – a perfectly nice family motel.'

'The Bide-A-Wee, huh? That rings a bell.'

'I'm sure you remember it from its happier times, before the decay of the neighborhood.'

'No, I used to be a policeman. I'm sure it was something bad, whatever it was.' He handed the man the form and took his key and left the lobby.

As he filed the form, the man happened to glance at the address, and was mildly interested to note that it was a local one: 1763 Armacost Street. He had no reason to suspect that this was a house Gunther had owned and inhabited with his third and least favorite wife from 1946 to 1950, after which it had belonged to her. Having put the form in its proper place the man picked up the phone to make a call; if he had turned on the lobby television to the news, as was his habit in the early evenings, he would have seen Gunther's face staring back at him.

*

Sidney sat looking up at a picture of Jesus on the wall next to his office manager's desk, swiveling and tapping his fingers on a crude flyer he'd drawn up with magic marker. He had planned to print up a few hundred of them on the copier, but after finishing the lettering he'd realized he'd given the police the photo of Gunther he'd intended to use.

Now he was trying hard to remember the married names of Gunther's daughters. One was a nurse in Minneapolis and the other a housewife in Florida, and unless their financial situations had changed since he'd last heard it didn't seem likely that they were the source of the extra money.

He opened an enormous Rolodex, a relic from an earlier incarnation of the business when it had consisted of a single strip club in midtown called the Sweet Cage. Half the cards in it were useless; interspersed with entries for his own friends, family and associates were cards for those of the previous owner, dead ten years now, and Janice had been trying to get him to weed out the outdated cards since her first week on the job. He shrugged and started with a card for Brennigan Vending Machine Service, which had once serviced the jukeboxes for the Sweet Cage and its sister club, the Tease-o-Rama, both now equipped with expensive, DJ-operated PA systems.

He tossed the card into the trash; eventually he'd stumble across Gunther's daughters this way, trimming part of the Rolodex and making his office manager happy in the process. After Brennigan was Bristol, Janice, herself; then Castle Beverage Distributors, and then a card that made his stomach muscles clench: Cavanaugh, Victor. One suburban address out west was crossed out and another, this one in Forest Hills, scribbled beneath it in his dead boss's odd, square foreign handwriting. He plucked it from the Rolodex, crumpled it and flung it into the wastebasket, then flipped ahead to see if there was an entry for Bill Gerard, Cavanaugh's boss. There was, with business and home phone numbers and the notation EMERG. ONLY next to the latter in block printing he also recognized as Renata's. The day after Christmas Sidney had opened up the Sweet Cage to find Bill Gerard lying dead on the office floor; several hours later the police found Renata dead on her hall carpet. Vic Cavanaugh, widely presumed to be the killer, was long gone, and now Sidney knew why he hadn't ever gotten around to editing the Rolodex.

*

Three days after Renata's death Sidney was on the couch of his old house on Twenty-third, looking without much hope through the Eagle-Beacon's classified section for a bartending job. He answered a knock at the door and found Gunther standing alone, gloveless hands in his pockets against the cold. Gunther had never come over without Dot before that he could remember, and he surprised Sidney by saying that if he didn't make an offer on the club he was a fool. After the old man left, Sidney phoned Mitch Cherkas, a bank officer whose sole interest outside banking seemed to be a series of painful, unrequited crushes on strippers. Mitch thought it was a great idea, and they set about raising the down payment. When he told Gunther this two days later, he surprised Sidney again by handing him a cashier's check for twelve thousand dollars, almost the exact sum they needed to raise. Thus at the age of thirty-six Sidney McCallum – bartender, bouncer, part-time cab driver and occasional holder of illicit goods – had been reborn as a businessman. Within three years they'd expanded into flea markets and car shows, bought up a rival strip club outside the city limits and started promoting oldies concerts with a local radio station, and he found himself making more money than it had ever occurred to him to hope for.

*

He had no idea, then or now, how Gunther could have afforded to loan him twelve thousand dollars, but when he'd tried to pay it back Gunther actually denied having given it to him in the first place. He thought about that for a minute, then picked up the phone and dialed Mitch's number.

'Cherkas residence, Mrs. Mitchell Cherkas speaking.'

'Francie, I need to talk to Mitch.'

'Hi, Sidney. Just a sec.'

While he waited Sidney scribbled on a sheet of scratch paper. He had doodled an entire dog by the time Mitch got to the phone.

'Hello? Sidney?'

'Mitch. I need six grand right now.'

'Six *grand*? From *me*?'

'I'm gonna put up a reward for Gunther, goose people a little. Six each.'

'In *cash*?'

'We owe him and you know it. I want twelve grand in the bank tomorrow.'

'Can I send you a check?'

'Bring it in person.'

Sidney hung up on him and started going through

the Rolodex again. He was up to Trusty Bail Bonds and the Rolodex was twenty cards lighter when the phone rang.

'McCallum Theatrical Enterprises. Sidney speaking.'

'Daddy? I called Moomaw and she said Gunther ran away?'

'Hey. Amy. I'm glad you called. What's Ginger's last name?'

'It's Fox.'

He thumbed his way backward. 'Fox. Got it. Thanks, honey. I gotta call her now, she doesn't know about this yet.'

'Call me when you know something, okay?' she asked, disappointed, and he felt guilty for trying to rush her off the phone. His eagerness to get hold of Gunther's daughters was only part of it; Amy was in college in Wyoming, majoring in Women's Studies, and their conversations tended lately to center on the exploitative economics of his business. The last time it had come up he'd testily reminded her that nude dancing, whether she approved of it or not, was paying for her courses in GynEconomics and Herstory, and of course he'd felt like an asshole the moment he'd said it. The worst part was that she'd halfway convinced him she was right.

'Don't worry, he's gonna be fine.' He hung up and dialed Ginger Fox's number. What a great name for a stripper, he thought, and the mental image of sturdy, short, serious Ginger onstage and stripping brought forth a laugh and a small shudder. On the fourth ring a machine picked up.

'This is Sidney McCallum calling. We have kind of an emergency here. Call any time, as soon as you get this.'

SCOTT PHILLIPS

He left his number and decided it was best not to get more specific. He hoped he could get Ginger to call her more volatile sister Trudy with the news. Both sisters loved the old man to excess, just like the grandchildren did, both Gunther's own and Dot's, and like Dot for that matter. How, he wondered as he locked the office up for the night, did a man as tight-lipped and glum as Gunther inspire so much devotion from women and children?

*

The main room at Ruby's was an atrium overlooked on all four sides by offices on the third and fourth floors of the former Hammerschmidt hotel downtown. The building dated back to the 1870s, and it was believed that its original owner lay beneath the cement floor of the basement, murdered by his very young second wife and her lover in 1887, shortly before the start of the renovations that occasioned the laying of the new floor. Even on slow nights the room's acoustics made everything loud, and Eric Gandy had to raise his voice to be heard over the easy listening pseudojazz, as well as over all the other voices trying to be heard over it at the same time. It was a few minutes before ten o'clock and Eric was flirting with a woman fifteen years his junior, a reporter from one of the local TV stations. She hadn't invited him to sit down yet, but she had allowed him to buy her a vodka tonic, and a Stoly at that.

'You know, Lucy, we ought to pull on out of here and head over to the Brass Candle and get some prime rib.'

'You're married, aren't you, Eric?' she asked, though

52

she didn't sound as if the answer meant much to her one way or the other.

'It's just dinner.'

'I have a basket of cheese fingers coming.'

She was very slender for a consumer of deep fried cheese. Her immaculately made up face was quite round, though, more noticeably so for being surrounded by a frothy blonde semicircle of hair. He felt an urge to reach over and lightly caress its brittle, shellacked surface; aware that this would not advance his cause, he resisted and pressed on. 'That's not dinner, that's just to keep people from getting shitfaced too quick.'

'Be that as it may,' she said evenly, 'they're coming.'

The need to urinate, which had been building in him again for a good ten minutes, was suddenly too powerful to ignore, and he straightened up, gesturing at the men's room.

'I'm gonna hit the john, and when I come back I want to hear all about that story you did – the kids at that school, with the little kid in Africa they adopted with their allowance money.'

'South America.'

'That's it.' He was already maneuvering through the crowd toward the men's room, and by the time he got there what had seemed merely an urgent need had revealed itself to be an emergency situation. There was no one at either stall, and he unzipped with the speed and grace of a virtuoso and let loose his stream on to the minty urinal cake. On the back of the basin someone had pasted a 55MPH – *PISS ON IT*!! sticker, grey and tattered from long and steady use as a urinary bullseye, and tiny flakes in its center shivered in the current.

The comics pages were tacked up on a pair of cork bulletin boards at eye level above the urinals, and Eric reread the current episode of 'Mary Worth' for the fourth time that evening. She was mediating between an estranged couple, the husband domineering and cruel, the wife addicted to pills because of it. 'Mind your own business, you nosy old bitch,' he drawled into the ether, then the sound of a flush came from the sitdown stall, followed by the click of its latch unlocking. Glancing over his shoulder, he saw a woman of about thirty-five push her way out of the stall. She stared brazenly at his prick, its flow momentarily interrupted, flaccid in his right hand.

'Line in the ladies' room. I didn't feel like waiting.' He didn't know her name, but she worked at an accounting firm with his friend Gary Halloran, and he remembered flirting with her at a Christmas party at Gary's house a couple of years earlier. She had on a short white knit dress with a V neck that night, and tonight she wore a burgundy dress of more or less the same design but cut from a lighter weight material and affording a still better view of her breasts.

He put his organ back in its place and zipped up, more or less finished anyway. 'Who likes to wait?' was all he could manage as she pushed the men's room door open.

'Let me know if you need a designated driver later,' she called to him as the door floated shut.

When he got back to the table Lucy was gone, her change untouched on a small black plastic tray. The almost-full drink and untouched basket of cheese fingers on the table suggested a hurried exit, which most nights would have pissed him off; tonight, though, he had a better option to pursue.

She was standing by the bar, openly watching him, and he decided that, once he subtracted the undeniably arousing factor of his having seen Lucy on television, this woman did more for him than she did. She gestured to him, whatever her name was, jerking her head in the direction of the door. Eric nodded and signaled for the waitress, who brought him his tab. He paid it, then followed the woman to the front door, flush with victory. He hadn't even had to buy her a drink.

CHAPTER FOUR

GUNTHER FAHNSTIEL: 14 JUNE, 1952

I was in Jack's Riverside Tavern for a beer after I got off duty. My knees hurt from eight hours sitting at the wheel of a prowlcar and I didn't want to listen, but Jack kept talking anyway.

'I'm gonna buy the whole goddamn building, Gunther,' he said. 'Take that empty space next door, knock down this part of the wall here and put in some pool tables.'

'Gonna have to move the bar, then,' I told him. It ran along the wall he wanted to remove.

'Not at all,' he said. 'I'll knock out a passage on this side, and I'll put a pass-through back here, so the bartender can see into the poolroom.' He was wearing a seersucker suit. He was skinny and five six, but he had a low, growly voice that helped him handle drunks and high school kids trying to talk their way into a beer.

'You ask the bank about this yet?' Jack had a daughter in college, and I knew he didn't make that much off this place. He made a little book on the side, but that still didn't amount to a great deal.

'I got me a real friendly banker. He owes me a thousand dollars, personally, and I'm graciously allowing him to pay it off in bits and pieces, no interest, just because I'm a nice guy. So when I went to him for a loan he was anxious as hell to give it to me.'

'A grand? Didn't know you were taking in that size bet.'

'I gave him credit for a few months. Twenty dollars here, fifty dollars there.'

'I never heard of you giving anybody credit, even for a beer.'

'Giving credit for beer's illegal, you know that. I gave him credit because he works at the bank, and I already had this idea in the back of my head. He was real surprised when I showed him my black book, boy. He hadn't been adding it up, thought it was maybe two hundred, two-fifty. 'Cause he was winning a little every once in a while, and he started to feel like a winner.'

'Who is this banker, anyway? Anybody I know?'

'Dave Atley, over at Third National.'

'Maybe I ought to go see him about a car loan for Ginger.' My daughter was about to turn sixteen.

'He don't owe you anything. Don't fuck up my sweet deal here, Gunther.'

'Yeah.' I finished my beer and he poured me another one. He was smart to expand, because as it was he could barely serve a dozen customers at a time. It was the tail end of a dogass hot afternoon, and he had the door wide open with the screen door closed to keep the flies out and a couple of big Vornado fans blowing at full speed. There was no crossdraft, though. The windows were painted over and nailed shut, and it was hot as hell.

'Might be a little cooler if you pried up the nails from the windows and opened one of 'em up.'

'That's what the beer's for, to cool you off.'

Behind me the screen door opened and pulled itself shut with a hissing sound. 'Howdy, Jack. Gunther.'

It was Ed Dieterle in his suit and tie. He'd made Detective Sergeant three months before, and he thought I was pissed off at him since I was still in uniform. I wasn't, though. I wouldn't make sergeant without some big changes I wasn't planning to make any time soon.

Jack poured him a beer and set it down on the bar. 'Fifteen cents.'

'Put it on my tab,' Ed said.

'You know I don't keep no goddamn tabs, Ed. It's against the law in the State of Kansas to sell beer on credit.'

'It's illegal to make book, too,' Ed said with a wink, and he put a quarter on the table. 'Been looking for you, Gunther.'

'I didn't come in here for a lecture.'

'Didn't come in here to give you one. Sally ever hear from that ex of hers?' Ed asked me.

'Wayne? They're still married.'

'You hear anything about him coming home?'

I shook my head and took a swig of my beer.

'Because I was down at the hospital this morning and a couple of deputies, Fallon and what's his name, the big dumb looking one, they brought this soldier into the emergency ward; he got the shit kicked out of him over at the Hitching Post out on 49th. I only met him once, but I'd swear up and down it was Sally Ogden's husband.'

'He's in Japan, far as I know.'

Ed shrugged. 'Just thought you ought to know, in case he's back looking for trouble.'

'Sally says he's never coming back here.'

'Well, next time you see her, ask. Because it looks like this guy started a big fucking brawl.'

'What about?'

'Fallon said nobody was talking. He had some horseshit story about getting jumped in the parking lot, but he still had his cash on him. Nobody saw anything, one of the whores just found him when she stepped outside for some fresh air.'

It wasn't Sally's husband. 'Thanks, Ed.'

He nodded. 'Taxi picked him up from the hospital and took him away. Might be worth checking the dispatch. He gave his name as Master Sergeant Thomas McCowan, U.S. Army. Claimed to be on furlough and Fallon said his papers looked okay.'

I nodded.

'Something else I got to tell you about. I was talking to Hawkins the other day, he was telling me he got a call last month from some guy, got beat up while he was staying at a cabin with a couple of gals. Thought the guy who shoved him around might have been a cop.'

I nodded. 'He got rough with Lynn and she blew the whistle. I backhanded him one and let him know the weekend was over.'

'You know how much trouble you're going to be in if one of those guys files a complaint and points to you?'

'He didn't, did he?'

'He backed down when he realized he'd have to file it in his own name. His wife thought he was duck hunting. But someday there might be a guy who's single, or stupid or just doesn't give a shit.'

'He hit Lynn. While he was fucking her.'

'You don't understand, Gunther. Whether you were right or wrong doesn't matter. The point is what were you doing there in the first place?' Ed was getting loud, and I wasn't going to say any more.

'How's about you boys find something nice to talk about,' Jack said, and we got quiet.

'How's old Daisy doing?' I finally asked.

'Fine,' Ed said, and he looked away. I didn't want him to do me any favors, and he couldn't stop trying.

'How's Jeff?'

'Fine.'

'How old's he, now?'

'Three.'

I shut up and drank my beer. Pretty soon a guy came in and placed a bet with Jack on a fight, and all four of us started arguing about it, and pretty soon me and Ed were pals again. The thing was still between us, though, and I didn't plan to quit anytime soon.

*

Afterward I drove over to my mother's house to do some fixing up. Since I couldn't do it most weekends I came by evenings after work. Her eyesight was going and she had a bad hip, and living alone was getting to be too much for her. My brother and his wife invited her once to move into their house, but she had the sense to say no. I didn't want to think about what was going to happen when things got really bad.

'Ginger tells me you're buying her a car,' she said. I was nailing a new gutter to the edge of her roof.

'Used.'

'I never heard of a sixteen-year-old with her own car.'

'She's going to have to drive her sister around, and then when Trudy's sixteen they can share it.'

'You are spoiling those girls rotten. Do you know they have a television set in their house now?'

I knew. That was part of why I was buying the car. My mother would never own either; she didn't know how to drive, and the television was Lucifer's playhouse.

She slunk back into the house to listen to the Gospel Hour and sulk. She wasn't being mean. She just wanted the best for me and my daughters, but she was a country girl and the modern world scared the hell out of her. Lately she was interested in flying saucers, since one of her radio preachers had said they were visitations from heaven, sent down by God to warn the wicked. The older she got the more she liked to listen to the fire-and-brimstone type of sermon on the radio and the less she worried about whether one of us drove her to Sunday mass or not. She wasn't born a Catholic, just converted when she married my father, and I wondered if it ever really took.

She wasn't my real mother, either, though I thought

of her that way. I was eight years old when she came to our house, two years after my first mother died of the flu. I hadn't prayed a lick since that happened so I didn't much care whether our new Mama was Catholic or not, but it was strange thirty-two years later to watch her listening to these programs, nodding her head and saying 'uh-huh' and 'praise Jesus' like a holy roller.

I finished the gutter and passed through the living room on my way out. It was almost dark outside but she had all the lights off.

'Want a lamp on?'

'I don't need any. Thank you.' The radio dial next to her was about the only light in the room.

'I'll be back tomorrow to fix the bathroom sink.'

'Why can't you come Saturday?'

'Got a security guard job lined up. All weekend.'

'You ought to be spending weekends with the girls. If you can't live with them you at least ought to be seeing them once a week.'

'I know, Mama.'

'I don't care how much you're making, the girls are more important, even if the money's for them. They'd rather see their Daddy than have a new jalopy.'

'I know.'

I left then and drove home. She was right about the girls, but the money wasn't the only reason I worked every other weekend.

CHAPTER FIVE

Dot and Gunther hadn't stayed in a motel since buying the RV ten years earlier. He'd always loved motels, though, ever since the first time he'd stayed in one. It was 1932, his first honeymoon, and he and his new bride were on their way to Hot Springs, Arkansas. Although they could have made Hot Springs by dusk, at three in the afternoon they'd stopped at a motor court. It was brand new and smelled of cedar, and ever since then that smell had always taken him back to that night. Gunther was twenty, his bride nineteen, and he was under the impression that it was her first sexual experience beyond a little heavy petting in the back seat of the used Ford he'd bought upon becoming engaged. The marriage hadn't lasted six months – the range of her experiences was actually rather vast and after they returned from Hot Springs she resumed collecting them with a variety of partners – but the sweet memory of that night in the motor court persisted fifty-seven years later, even with so many others seemingly irretrievable.

This room wasn't bad, considering what it must have been like a couple of years back. It was clean, the bedspread cheap but new. The bathroom fixtures looked new, too, and there was a painting on the wall of a mountain lake. It wasn't very skillfully painted, globs of bright color slapped on in what looked like a hurry, but he found his gaze repeatedly drawn to it, as if a fresh glance might reveal something he'd missed before.

For dinner he'd eaten most of a pepperoni pizza the man at the desk had helped him order, and he sat now on the bed watching the Shopping Channel with the sound off.

He was getting sleepy, and he crawled under the covers gratefully; he'd been afraid it would be one of those nights where he just sat up until dawn, barely able to close his eyes. As he lay there, feeling himself drift closer to sleep, he tried to picture Sally Ogden. He had a vague idea that she resembled her daughter, and he knew her face was there in his head somewhere, but he couldn't call it forth. If he could, he might remember who she was.

*

At that moment Sally Ogden was on the phone with Loretta, who had been trying to get through to her for several hours while Sally chatted with her sister-in-law back in Cottonwood.

'I got my hair cut today,' Loretta said. 'Really short in back, a little more body in front.'

'Oh.' Sally didn't like short hair on women, it seemed to her a waste of a natural feminine resource. She was certain most men felt the same way, but knew better than to say it.

'I thought Eric might even notice, but of course he's not home.'

Sally was in a relatively good mood, and didn't want to spoil it with a discussion of her son-in-law, so she pretended not to hear. 'Look nice?'

'Three hours ago I thought it did. Now I think I just look like a fat lady with short hair.'

'Now quit that.' Sally hated to hear her talk that way, particularly since she outweighed her daughter by seventy pounds or more. She'd been considered quite attractive at Loretta's age and size; of course today you couldn't turn on the television or open a magazine without seeing some young woman, skinny as a little boy, no tits or ass or curves of any kind, supposedly representing the feminine ideal. Seeing Loretta fall for such a pile of crap made her want to puke.

'Oh, hey. I almost forgot why I called you. Guess who I saw today? Gunther! What was his last name again?'

'Oh. Fahnstiel.'

'You don't sound too excited.'

'I am. How'd he look?'

'Pretty good. He seemed a little confused, you know? I ended up giving him a ride to the barber shop.'

'That's nice.' She could hear the enthusiasm in Loretta's voice, but she couldn't fake it in her own. She'd stopped wondering about Gunther a long time before.

'Did you guys have some kind of falling out or something?'

'No, sweetie, we didn't, but, you know, time passes. Gunther's a good man.'

'He seemed real interested in you.'

'That's nice. Is he still married?'

'I didn't ask. He was on foot when I ran into him.'

'That's probably a good thing. He's got to be pushing eighty, and he wasn't the greatest driver forty years ago.'

'Wasn't he the one who drove us when we moved to Cottonwood?'

'Listen, Loretta. I don't want to talk about Gunther any more, okay? I'm glad to hear he's still kicking, but I don't want to talk about those days.'

'Okay,' Loretta said, her tone just a shade higher than a whisper.

'Oh, shit, don't get your feelings hurt. I'm sorry.'

'It's okay.'

'Why don't you come over and spend the night? Give Eric something to wonder about when he comes home.'

'Except Eric might not come home and probably wouldn't notice I was gone if he did. I think I'll just get in bed and watch the first part of Johnny Carson.'

Upstairs as Loretta undressed she turned on the television news. She half-watched a report about local elementary school students sending money to support a little boy in Peru, then went into the bathroom to brush her teeth. She was rinsing and spitting, insulated from the sound of the television by the running water, when the newscaster read a brief message about Gunther, a photo of his grizzled face floating behind the anchor desk. Over the water she did hear the phone ring faintly, but she ignored it, assuming it was Eric, and after ten rings it stopped.

*

Eleven miles away Sally sat holding the receiver and wondering what to do next. She debated calling the number the newscaster had given for anyone with information on Gunther's whereabouts, but Loretta was the one with that. She told herself he'd be fine until morning, and she believed it. Senile or no, he was about the toughest bastard she'd ever met.

She hadn't thought about him in a while, which was funny, because lately she'd been thinking about Wayne. The thoughts came unbidden, often in the context of something Loretta did or said, or one of the grandkids now that they were more or less grown. Especially the boy, Tate. He didn't have much of Wayne's personality in him; he wasn't a liar, a thief or a cheat as far as she knew, and he didn't have the obsessive need to win at any cost that Wayne had. In his moments of triumph, though, he'd get a cocky, off-center grin that was pure Wayne, just like when she'd first known him in high school; at that age there didn't seem to be anything screwy about Wayne, either, at least not to her. President of the Student Council, Captain of the track team and the debate squad, crack door-to-door salesman in the summertime, he looked to her like the biggest go-getter in town, the kind of kid people thought of as a future President of the United States, or even better, U.S. Steel.

They were married in 1940 after he got his business degree, and a year later he was assistant office manager in the sales division of Collins Aircraft, the youngest manager in the whole company. After Pearl Harbor he volunteered for the army over the company's objections, and nothing was quite the same after that. He came home after the war

69

a Master Sergeant and spent a year working at Collins, treating Sally like the only mistake he'd ever made and trying to think up better, faster ways to make money. She was two months pregnant with Loretta when he stunned her by quitting the job at Collins and re-enlisting. Opportunities in the peacetime army were good for a man like him, he said, and he didn't want her traveling in her delicate condition; he'd send for her once the baby was born. He never did, and though he dutifully sent half his pay home every month – at first, anyway – it was years before she saw him again.

A couple of weeks earlier she'd found a picture of him in his uniform, a hand-tinted 8x10 taken when he got home in '46. She'd studied the portrait for a long time, trying to find some trace of the real man somewhere in the face of the friendly, smiling soldier.

She hoped he was burning in hell. What she'd done, she'd done for Loretta, and for the sake of having a little fun, a pretty scarce commodity for a woman with a small child and no husband around and a full-time defense plant job, and she wasn't sorry for any of it. Not for one goddamn minute of it.

*

Gunther found himself standing next to the lake in the painting. It was all wrong, too much of a lake and not enough of a big rocky hole in the ground, and that mountain behind it should have been just a gently sloping rise, but he knew more or less where he was. It was dusk, the start of a warm summer evening, and he made his way around the shore and up a path through a clearing to the cabin: two bedrooms, a kitchenette and a living room. A dim yellow light shone in one of the bedroom windows, and before he looked inside he knew what he'd see: Sally Ogden with her feet in the air.

And there she was, thirty years old again and making that loud, throaty sound of hers, a skinny little freckle-faced guy propping himself up on top of her with his skivvies around his ankles and Sally's red fingernails on his hips, eyes rolled back in his head as he pumped away. Sally looked like she always did, like she was enjoying the hell out of herself.

Gunther wasn't jealous. He just wanted to ask her a question, and he could wait until they were done. He admired her as he waited, her long black hair undone and splashing all over the pillow, her lovely soft belly, those legs that looked like they could have pinched the scrawny fellow on top of her in half if she wanted. Abruptly she turned to Gunther and looked straight at him as she cried out with unfeigned and unashamed joy.

He opened his eyes. His second erection in as many days was fading, and the front of his shorts was wet. There was a thin white line of light visible under the window-shade and the digital clock on the desk read 6:17, as good a time to get up as any.

It seemed crazy now that he'd ever forgotten who Sally Ogden was, and it made him wonder if Dot hadn't been right to put him into the home. He put his clothes on, wishing he'd thought to bring a change or two with him, and was dismayed to realize he couldn't retrieve the question he wanted to ask Sally in his dream. From his shirt pocket he pulled a business card with Loretta Gandy's picture on it in black and white above a business address and phone number, and her home address and phone scribbled on the back. It might embarrass her if he showed up at her place of work in his current state; better to go to her house and wait.

*

He walked out of the room and across the parking lot, leaving his door open. The ground was still a little wet from yesterday's rain, but the sky was clear and blue with rosy tinges at the horizon, and the morning air was already warm and humid. As he passed the Stars and Stripes heading toward downtown he spotted the hooker from the night before, still on duty. She gave him a friendly three-fingered salute. 'Hey there, Grandpa. You get a good night's sleep?'

'Uh-huh. Your shift about over?'

'Yeah. I shoulda gone home a while ago. Guess I just wasn't sleepy.'

'I bet you hardly ever are,' Gunther said.

'Hah. You got that right. Plus it was so nice out after that rain.'

'See you later.'

'Okay. Don't do anything I wouldn't do,' she said, and as Gunther moved on he pondered what that could possibly include.

*

Dot had been awake since before dawn, listening to the radio, drinking coffee and smoking cigarettes. The news didn't mention Gunther, which grated her, since the announcer droned on and on about some incomprehensible finance bill in the Senate or the Congress and how the President was expected to do this or that about it, and who gave a shit anyway? The DJ didn't even know what it meant, she could hear in his voice he was just reading it off a page. After that he gave the farm prices and last night's baseball scores, and then he mentioned that the temperature at the airport was seventy, with today's high expected at around a hundred and five and humid as a greenhouse. If you're going outside today, he said, now's the time to do it. She looked out the window and thought it looked nice out on the back porch, the morning light still soft and diffused and even a slight breeze stirring the branches. A little dewy, maybe, but she could put a towel down on one the old metal chairs. She'd leave the door open so she could hear the phone.

Outside it was gorgeous. She sat at the table, drinking from her mug and finding herself comforted a little. The mere absence of the sound of the country station was unexpectedly pleasant, and she realized that the DJ's deliberately upbeat twang had been jangling her nerves.

She watched a robin pulling a worm up out of the ground and thought of Sidney, aged five or so, watching the same thing one morning and wanting to rescue the worm, running at the bird with his arms flailing and crying furiously, fists clenched, when the bird flew away with the worm in its beak.

He'd been a serious and solitary little boy, and he wasn't much different as a man. His last girlfriend was gone now and Sidney hadn't wanted to talk about why. Gunther had seen it coming, though, even with his memory gone south on him; she's an educated person, he'd said, she wants someone she can introduce at her college reunion and say here's my husband the dentist, or professor, or lawyer, not here's my husband the nudie show tycoon.

The robin finished extracting the worm, then flitted into a tree in the yard behind hers where its nest must have been, and as she watched it go the phone rang. She was inside so fast she had it before the third ring.

'Mrs. Fahnstiel? Dr. Mercer. Just checking in.' His voice was cheerful and soothing.

She looked at the clock. It was seven-fifteen in the morning, too early for any but an emergency call as far as she was concerned. 'Mister Mercer. Where the hell were you brought up that you call people for no reason before eight in the morning?' That she'd been up since four-forty-five was irrelevant; it was a question of manners.

Despite yesterday's skirmish he'd clearly been expecting a friendlier greeting. 'I'm sorry . . .'

'Sorry doesn't cut the mustard. Call me when you get my husband back.'

She slammed the receiver down, then filled her mug and went back outside. It was a little warmer already, the sky a little bluer, and she wondered what Gunther was doing right then. The worst thing was the deep, gnawing suspicion that she knew where he was headed and the impossibility of telling anyone about it, even Sidney. Especially Sidney.

*

Eric was roused from a deep but unsatisfying sleep by a hand on his shoulder and an angry voice an inch from his ear.

'Get up. Goddamn it. Come on, I have to get to work. Get up, *now*, or I'll call your wife.'

It was the woman from the night before, wearing a slip and nothing underneath, and he reached his hand up between her thighs, warm blood beginning to lengthen his sticky organ. She slapped her hand around his wrist.

'Don't. I'm late as it is.'

'You got time for a quick one.'

'Not even as quick as last night. Come on, out of bed. Get your clothes on.'

Pretending he hadn't caught the insult he lay back on the pillow, hands behind his head, and beamed at her as she ran around the room putting on her clothes.

'Listen, asshole, this is how fucking late I am. I am not taking a shower. I have never, in eight years at this job, gone to work without taking a shower.'

She had on her underwear and was buttoning her blouse at this point, and he grabbed her by the wrist as she passed by on the way to her dresser, to try and pull her back down on to the bed. She yanked the hand away effortlessly and with the other gave him a very solid slap across the cheek.

'It's seven-thirty. I have a shitload of stuff to do today and a bitch of a hangover.'

He looked her up and down in wonderment as she adjusted her skirt, the left side of his face still hot from the impact of her open palm. She didn't look hung over, looked in fact far better than anybody had any business looking at this hour of the morning, with or without a hangover.

'Where are my clothes?' he asked, beginning to sense defeat. He saw his jockeys lying in the corner of the room.

'They're in a path from the front door to here.'

'Look. Why don't you take a sick day, we'll knock around and have a few laughs?'

She glared at him like a drill sergeant. 'If you ever want to fuck me again, Eric Gandy, you will put your clothes on right now and march out the front door with me. Understand?'

He put on his shorts and started down the stairs. On the upstairs landing were his socks and on the bottom two steps lay his shirt, twisted into a spiral as if by a whirlwind. He had a vague recollection of whipping it around over his head like a lasso the night before, and he unfurled it to find it wrinkled like an immense golden raisin. His pants were nowhere in sight, but he saw his shoes next to the door.

'Where's my pants?' he asked as he pulled the shirt on.

'You took them off at the top of the stairs and threw them down into the living room somewhere,' she said, standing in the bedroom door looking like she was heading for a job interview: makeup immaculate, clothes pressed and perfectly coordinated, hair tussled in a way that looked not only deliberate but carefully worked at. 'Over by the fireplace, maybe,' she said, adjusting an earring.

He found the pants between an expensive, low-slung

coffee table and the hearth. He put them on, then grabbed his shoes and they walked out into the morning. Stopping on her front step for a second he tied his shoelaces, then followed her to a black BMW vaguely familiar from the night before. When he stepped around to the passenger door she looked at him like he was crazy.

'What do you think you're doing?'

'I thought you could drop me off at my car. At Ruby's.'

'You've got to be kidding. I'm late, and that's the wrong direction.'

'I thought you worked downtown.'

'You thought wrong.' She got in and backed out, rolling down her window as she waited for a space in the morning traffic. 'Talk to you soon,' she called out, suddenly and surprisingly cheery.

He started down the sidewalk, heading east toward downtown. From his shirt pocket he pulled a five-dollar bill along with a scrap of paper. It was a deposit slip for Belinda Naismith, her phone number circled in red ballpoint.

*

Lester Howells yawned like a giant redheaded baboon, his eyes clenched shut and his head thrown backward, his teeth bared and his tongue rolled back, one hand clutching his desk as his spine arched, the other thrusting into the air above him, opening and closing. 'Sorry, Ed. Pulling a lot of those late nights this summer, still got to be up at five regardless.'

'Been up since five myself. Went over to Maple Grove and saw Daisy before I came down here.'

77

'Pretty there in the morning, isn't it? I go early mornings sometimes and visit my folks.'

'Yeah. My nephew and his wife come by every other week, I guess. There were flowers, anyway.'

As they talked Ed examined a xeroxed list of all the places Gunther had been spotted, looking for a clue to his thought processes and finding none. Maybe he'd just wanted a haircut and a cup of coffee.

'Well, I'm glad you're here. Wish you didn't have to be.' Howells draped one calf across the top of Ed's old desk. 'Why couldn't that son of a bitch have wandered off in the spring or the fall so I could spare someone full time?'

Ed waved him off. 'I know how it is in this kind of heat.'

'You going to go out to Lake Vista today? You might look in on old Rory Blaine if you do.'

'I thought he was in that place out on Twenty-first.'

'Nah, they moved him. He more than likely won't know who you are, but it's nice when he gets a visitor.'

'I'll give him a holler.' Not much chance of Rory forgetting me, he thought.

'Probably Gunther'll just turn up at Dot's wanting dinner like nothing's up at all.'

'That'd be just like him,' Ed said. He stood up. 'I'm sure I'll talk to you before I leave town.'

'Hope so. Give my best to old Dot when you see her.'

He took the elevator downstairs. City offices were just about to open and the lobby was filling up with city workers and citizens, most of the latter looking aggrieved. He stepped into the press room and found it full of strangers, one of whom, a young woman wearing a hat decorated with flowers, looked up at him. 'You looking for parking fines? Third floor, right across from the elevators.' He nodded, thanked the woman and left.

*

Sidney had been up since five-thirty; by the time Janice got there at eight he'd already been on the phone for more than an hour and a half, talking to the police, to the nursing home, to Ginger Fox and to Gunther's other daughter Trudy in Florida, Ginger having been too distraught to do the job herself.

'Hey, Sidney,' Janice said. 'Heard about your stepdad on TV last night. Find him yet?'

'If they'd found him, I wouldn't be getting here before you.'

'My great uncle Rudy wandered off one time, walked from his house to a bus station five miles away, said he wanted to go to New York City. We couldn't ever figure out why, he'd never been further than fifty miles away from the house where he was born.'

She picked up the flyer. He hadn't run it off yet, but he'd attached another photo of Gunther to it.

'What did you do, Sidney, go out to a kindergarten and get the kids to letter this?'

'It doesn't have to be pretty, just readable.'

'It's neither one of those, believe me. Let me do it on the computer. I'll make it nice and eyecatching, and we'll get them printed up in color over at Printco.'

'It's fine the way it is.'

'I'm not going to argue about it, Sidney. This is for your

stepfather's sake, let's do it right and don't get all prideful on me.'

'Fine, do it your way, I don't care.' He rose to let her take her seat. 'I want to print up about five hundred. I'll go start putting them up soon as they're done.'

'Why don't you get Larry and Bill to do it?' They were the college kids who went around to the supermarkets, schools, churches, shopping centers and anyplace else with a public bulletin board, putting up posters and flyers for the car shows, flea markets and oldies concerts the company produced for twenty-five cents per flyer posted.

'They're only half done putting up the flyers for the car show.'

'They can do both at the same time. Duh.'

The phone rang and Sidney headed for his office. 'I'm only here if it's about the old man.'

He sat and opened his morning paper, and within twenty seconds the intercom buzzed. 'Sidney, that's Dennis on line one. There's some kind of problem with the new lighting at the Sweet Cage.'

'Tell him I have other things on my mind right now.'

'That's what I told him you'd say.'

'You were right.' The new lighting system in the Sweet Cage had been, up until yesterday around noon, his most time-consuming problem. He missed the sleazeball atmosphere of the clubs before he cleaned them up; ten years ago the idea of a professional theatrical lighting system for a strip joint would have seemed ridiculous. But once in charge he'd modernized, offering edible food and getting a full liquor license when the club laws finally changed, even wincingly adding the laughably ambitious phrase

'A Gentleman's Club' to the marquee. In the end he'd succeeded in attracting the crowd he'd aimed for, young executives who couldn't stop whooping and high-fiving one another and generally behaving like a beer commercial brought to life.

He hated them, but they brought in a lot of money; between improvements to his other club and moving the Sweet Cage out to a new facility west of town his overhead had increased considerably. He had also stopped hiring the druggy, dowdy, inexpensive, hard-luck-case dancers who had long been the mainstay of both clubs, bringing in instead the kind of sleek, hard-muscled dancers he'd seen at clubs elsewhere. His account books proved that he was in the minority on this score, but how these skinny, silicone-injected hardbodies with their cold looks, artificially enhanced cheekbones and big spiky hair could make anybody horny was beyond Sidney. He found he couldn't bring himself to fire any of the old dancers, and it took attrition nearly eight years before Francie, the last and oldest of the old girls, quit to marry Mitch Cherkas.

The phone rang again and a moment later Janice stuck her head in the door. 'For you. Some lady, says she saw Gunther.'

He punched line two. 'Sidney McCallum.'

'Mr. McCallum? My name's Loretta Gandy. I just spoke with a Captain Howells and he gave me your number.'

He stared out the window at some kids in the backyard of one of the houses behind the building. They sat listless in the shade, the sun already too hot for play, waiting to be brought inside. The house next door to it had a flagstone back patio with a glass-topped table, at which an old man sat in a checkered bathrobe reading the paper and drinking from a mug. As he listened to the woman talk about picking Gunther up and taking him for a haircut Sidney spotted Gunther's picture on the man's newspaper.

'I gave him some money when he got out,' she said.

'And he took it?'

'Yeah.'

'Doesn't sound like Gunther.'

'It was him all right. I thought he was the nicest man when I was little. He took me and my friend Sandra to the Shrine Circus when I was about five. I threw up my lime Coke all over him as we were leaving and he was so sweet about it. My mom would have smacked me.'

Sidney leaned back in his chair and watched the kids' mother trooping them back inside their house like a vanquished, retreating army, listening to the woman rattle on. Another gal who thought sullen old Gunther was the greatest guy she'd ever met. 'Yeah, he's got his good points.'

'Could you do me a favor and call me when you find him?'

'Sure.'

He took her number and hung up, and despite himself the picture of the little girl throwing up on Gunther made him laugh. That was one thing about the old man, it took a hell of a lot to get a rise out of him.

CHAPTER SIX

WAYNE OGDEN: 16–17 JUNE, 1952

The Sheriff's deputies had questioned me and the bartender and Beulah and the other two whores for half an hour or so to no effect, and when I left with the deputies I knew I had redeemed myself in the eyes of the Hitching Post staff. I would be welcomed back, and I intended to return as soon as possible. No hillbilly moron and his peers would get the better of Wayne Ogden for long.

The deputies had insisted on a stop at the emergency ward to make sure I hadn't broken any bones or ruptured anything crucial, and to give them a chance to grill me a little bit more. When they saw I wasn't going to get any more specific about who'd licked me they let me go. A taxi drove me by the station to collect my duffel bag and then dropped me off here at the Bellingham. I had only stayed at the Bellingham once before, on my wedding night in 1940, when it had seemed to me and my bride the height of luxury and elegance. Having kicked around a little more in the years since, I still had to admit that for a town this size it was a pretty nice place to hang my hat for a few nights.

A couple of days with an icepack on my face had made it presentable again, if not an object of beauty. My eye was still purple with black and yellow striations, but the swelling was mostly gone and I could make jokes about walking into a door without getting the horrified or nauseated looks that had kept me mostly sequestered in the room since my arrival. It was noon, and I went downstairs to the lobby, where I found the day manager, Mr. Nash, taking a reservation over the phone. When he was done he looked up at me and gave the eye a quick once-over.

'Well, Sergeant. I see you're healing nicely. Going to take some air?'

'I need to buy a suit. What's the best haberdasher in town?'

'There's the Thistle Men's store, downtown. Much better than any of the department stores, and it's walking distance, too.'

'I remember it. Thanks.'

'It is expensive, of course, but one's paying for the best.'

'Only the best,' I said, ignoring the implication that it might be too pricey for a non-com.

'It's a beautiful day for a stroll, I almost wish I could go with you.'

I'll bet he did, too. 'Thanks for the tip.'

It was indeed beautiful out, in the upper seventies with a few clouds that made the sky seem an even deeper blue, and a very slight breeze that cooled my face as I walked east over the bridge to downtown proper. I stopped half-way across to watch the river flow past for a minute, muddy brown and wide and slow as ever. I had a vivid memory of a drowned man being pulled from it when I was a kid, of the muffled excitement of the crowd that had gathered, waiting to see who it was. I seemed to recall a vendor selling popcorn and candy apples, but that might have been a nostalgic embellishment. When they got the body out of the water he was nobody anyone knew; a bum, judging by his clothes.

The Thistle was a few blocks east, and before going in I checked my reflection in the mirrored glass of a nearby building. I'd never allowed myself the indulgence of buying clothes there before, not even when I was a young man on the rise at Collins and took care to look prosperous, and I wanted to be treated with respect when I walked in now. It was lunchtime, and the sidewalks were bristling with office workers heading for cafeterias and restaurants and sandwich stands; once I'd satisfied myself with my own image I watched them in the glass, marching and shuffling and trotting in different directions at different speeds, all of them after the same quick bite to eat before heading back for an afternoon just like the morning.

My thoughts were interrupted by a stationary reflection in the glass next to mine. I turned to face a chubby, red-faced man about my own age, grinning to beat the band.

'Holy cow. Wayne Ogden. What do you know?' He held out his hand for me to shake, and I took it.

'How've you been, Stanley?'

'Oh, just great. I'm working for Donner Peatman Hapner now. I'm a Vice President as of last month.' He seemed delighted at the prospect.

'Very impressive,' I said, though I had no idea who or what Donner Peatman Hapner were, what they sold or did or brokered or baked. Stan and I had played football and baseball together in high school, and we'd been partners on the debate squad. He wasn't a bad guy, and he wasn't stupid, but one look at his face and I saw that he didn't know the score any more than he had when we were kids.

'I married Louise Neville, remember her?'

'Sure. Nice gal.' I wondered if he knew about Louise blowing me behind a barn on a high school class picnic in 1937, while unbeknownst to us six or eight guys watched from the hayloft. She really seemed to enjoy sex, not like some girls who cheerlessly accommodated you just because you were captain of this team or president of that club; Louise had in fact provided me with an initial glimpse of the female orgasm one night that same year in her parents' bedroom during my very first session of cunnilingus, an experience I found unexpectedly arousing. If she was half as sexually enthusiastic as she'd been back then, Stan was either a lucky fellow indeed or a cuckold many times over.

'Got three kids, a fourth on the way.'

'That's great. Congratulations.'

'You finally muster out, or are you just on leave?'

'Mustered out.' Why not?

'My Louise tells me she sees your wife Sally once in a while, and your little girl. I bet they're glad to have you home.'

My stomach turned. This grinning imbecile was ready to fuck up my whole operation; I should have thought about the possibility of running into someone I used to know before I decided to take a leisurely stroll downtown. 'Listen, Stan.' I looked at him sideways. 'They don't know I'm here yet. I'm trying to get a day or two in as a civilian before I let them know, get back on a stateside schedule. So do me a favor and don't tell anybody you saw me, all right?'

'I get it. Sally's got a surprise coming.'

'That's it exactly,' I said, and he waddled off to his midday meal, happy to have a secret to keep.

In the Thistle they treated me like the King of goddamn England. I'd brought along a pretty good roll and I ended up spending most of it on a suit with two pairs of pants, a houndstooth sportjacket, a pile of casual shirts and pants, and a couple of neckties, one conservative and one loud, and two hats. The clerk, a tall, prematurely bald man of about thirty, marked the clothes for alteration and seemed very pleased as he wrote up the sale. When I asked if the alterations on at least the casual pants could be done by that evening he brought the tailor out to meet me. He was a small man and looked far too old to be working.

'Mr. Chancellor, this is Sergeant McCowan. He was wondering if he could get some of his alterations done in advance of the usual schedule.'

He looked me up and down. 'Your uniform fits better than most.'

'I'm in the Quartermaster Corps, so I know some of the tailors personally. I also know good tailoring when I see it.'

'Okay, I'll move you to the front of the line. I got a boy

87

just got back from Korea myself. Made PFC when he was over there.' That he could have a son young enough to be a private seemed incredible, but I was grateful for his indulgence.

'Can I show you something an Army tailor who's a buddy of mine did?' I showed him the pocket inside the back of my trousers. 'It's a good place to hold bills, safer than a wallet or a sock. If I came back later do you think you could alter these that way?'

'No need to bring them later, I'll do it when I do the hems.'

I thanked him and arranged to have at least one pair of pants delivered to the hotel that evening and asked the clerk to call me a cab. When it came I asked the cabbie where he thought was the best place in town to buy a cheap car.

'Welker Brothers' Used Cars. They won't cheat you too bad.' He was missing his top left canine and whistled a little when he talked. 'Long as you look like you know what you're doing.'

'Let's go, then.'

The Welker Brothers' lot was one of six or seven along the same stretch of East Douglas, none of which were fighting off crowds today. It was done up like a carnival with bunting and balloons and little red, white and blue triangular flags, and like its neighbors it was empty when I got out of the cab and walked on to it, glad for the chance to nose around a little and see what was on offer. I examined a black '47 Packard at $795 and a green '49 Chevy Fleetline with '$995!!! RADIO + HEATER' soaped on its windshield. I had a vague notion that I wanted a Ford but I didn't see any, and now I wanted a salesman so I could get an idea of how much leeway there was in the pricing.

'Howdy,' a voice called out from the sales office. 'Bill Crenshaw, Welker Brothers' assistant manager. Sorry, I was just closing a deal over the phone.' He was about my age and had on a brown suit that hadn't been pressed recently. He held out his hand, and we shook; his was slightly wet and cold, as though just washed and not quite dried enough.

'You're off to a bad start, Bill. You weren't on the phone, you were in the crapper.' I said this with a hint of a smile.

He managed a chuckle. 'You got me there, friend.' I noticed sweat stains on his hatband and thought maybe I could make a good deal after all.

'Thomas McCowan, Master Sergeant, U.S. Army.'

'Pleased to make your acquaintance.' He was uncomfortable around a man in uniform, and my guess was he'd sat out the war for one reason or another. Whether it was his own choosing or not, that could work to my advantage. 'How can I help you this afternoon?'

'Well, Bill, I'm looking for something serviceable I could drive for a few months around the country while I'm on furlough, then turn around and sell when it's time to go back on duty.'

'Furlough, huh?'

'Something with some resale value. No sawdust in the transmission and an odometer hasn't been messed with.

I'm sure you don't have anything like that on the lot anyway, but if you do you can save it for the shit-shovelers.'

He chuckled again, a little more uncomfortably. 'Well, how's about this '46 Plymouth?' He showed me over to a red four-door. 'Six forty-five and she's all yours.'

'Six even, more like,' I said.

'I could go as low as six thirty.'

'How about the two-door?' Right next to the red Plymouth was a black one, another '46.

'Five ninety-five.'

'Five fifty.'

'It's got a radio and a heater.'

'I'm not going to be driving it come winter time. Five fifty.'

Half an hour later I drove a two-door 1946 Plymouth off the lot and over to a garage downtown where I asked the mechanic to give it the old once-over. An employee of the garage would drive it to the hotel for me while I slept, and if the mechanic's report was unsatisfactory I would personally take my $550 out of Mr. Bill Crenshaw's hide. I called another cab and took it back to the hotel, where I ate my supper at four p.m., pulled the curtains in my room and settled in for a good night's sleep.

*

I'd asked Mr. Nash to leave word with the hotel staff not to bother me or enter my room for any reason between the hours of four and eleven p.m., and I woke up at ten-thirty feeling rested and recovered. My eye looked a little better still, and I was looking forward to the evening's entertainment.

Outside my door was the breakfast I'd ordered: bacon, eggs over easy, link sausage, and coffee in a thermos, and I set the tray down on the desk. My room overlooked the river, and as I ate I watched the headlights of the cars going over the bridge below. There weren't many of them this time of night, but in less than an hour second shift would end at several of the plants and the roads coming and going would be jammed.

After breakfast I phoned the front desk and asked the bellhop to bring up the clothes. I was pleased to see that it was all ready except for the suit. I showered and put on a new pair of pants, a crisp white shortsleeved shirt and the houndstooth sportjacket, then headed downstairs to find out about the Plymouth.

'Good evening, Sergeant McCowan,' the night manager said. I didn't know his name; he was a great deal more reserved than Mr. Nash, and didn't seem any more interested in me than in any other guest. The mechanic's report on my Plymouth was waiting for me; he gave it a passing grade, and in the envelope were the keys to the car.

The night was as lovely as the day had been, warm but with traces of the afternoon's breeze, the sky clear except for an enormous vertical bank of clouds in the distance illuminated by the moon. It might have meant a storm, but the wind didn't feel right for it. The Plymouth sat there in the guests' lot, looking as anonymous as I'd hoped it would among the cars of all the weary salesmen, vacationing families and furtive adulterers staying at the Bellingham.

I handed the keys to the attendant, and when he brought her over I gave him a quarter and slid in behind the wheel.

I rolled down the window, turned the engine over and pulled out of the lot. Rather than wait for a chance to make a left I merged into the flow of traffic, swinging in and out of lanes, sailing through the Hudsons and Pontiacs and Buicks and Chevys. A middle-aged man in a late-model Ford, driving with the dome light on, snarled something incomprehensible but unmistakably nasty at me through his open window, and I accelerated past and in front of him, making a U-turn at the first intersection and heading back downtown, where I made a left at Broadway and headed north all the way to 49th.

There were five cars at the Hitching Post, all of them parked along the row of trees that marked the edge of the property, and I assumed they belonged to the bartender, maybe one or two to the whores and the rest to the early customers of the evening. I parked next to a light blue convertible and waited. After a few minutes the thick-bodied brunette from my previous visit emerged laughing, hanging on to the ham-thick arm of a gigantic, balding man who wasn't too steady on his feet. She was leaning on him so hard she almost knocked him down before they got to his car, but they both managed to get in and after a couple of failed attempts he turned the engine over, and the car moved off the lot and headed south toward downtown. It was twelve midnight on the dot.

I was a little surprised when less than fifteen minutes later they returned and went back inside, the big man looking dejected and the harlot making plainly unwelcome consoling gestures. I doubted he'd be staying much longer. In the meantime a half dozen cars had parked between me and the front door of the club, and if I didn't get what I wanted in another half hour I'd move on to the Commanche for the night's second order of business; I'd have to work fast in any case, and if the lot got much more crowded the risk would be too great.

I only had to wait another five minutes. A late-thirties model Oldsmobile chugged in off the street and parked nearer to the neon hillbilly than I would have liked. Out stepped Elishah, instantly recognizable but looking quite different than he had the night we met. In the hazy multicolored light of the sign his motionless facial features suggested despair rather than anger, and the bitter thinness of his face looked like years of bad luck and hard work instead of just backcountry meanness. It didn't make the slightest difference to me, though.

Once he was inside I made my way in a crouch to the Oldsmobile and opened the door. Taped to the steering column was the information I required: Elishah Jack Casper, 1565 Lincolnshire Street. I strolled casually back to the Plymouth.

As I neared it I heard the club door open, hillbilly music spilling out into the perfect night air and damn near ruining it. I got down behind another car when I saw that it was Beulah. A minute later somebody followed her, a guy in an old army jacket she didn't seem much interested in talking to. He whispered something in her ear, though, and she smiled and followed him to another car and they took off.

*

Lincolnshire Street was a considerable distance south and east, and number 1565 was a small house made of brick that in daylight must have been dark red. There was nothing in the front yard but grass, no trees or shrubs. I drove past it once, parked around the corner and strolled casually to Elishah's back door, which was unlocked.

The whole house smelled sour, as if he'd been cleaning it with vinegar. I went from room to room, taking inventory. I noticed that there were no pictures of family or girlfriends or ex-wives or any of the kinds of photographs that people usually have up on their walls, especially people living alone and far from where they were raised.

I wondered if he and Beulah were lovers, or if he was just a customer. Maybe a little of both. She was the one he was staring at as she danced that night, and it made him so mad he'd started a fight with a stranger, and a soldier at that. If he had some sort of claim on her, his attacking me made sense; he couldn't have confronted the man dancing with her, a potential paying customer.

I turned on a lamp in the bedroom and looked in the closet. Hanging next to the shirts and pants were several dresses, three blouses and a black skirt, and beside a single pair of work boots were three pairs of high-heeled pumps, two black and one white. The white pair had little bows at the heel. In the closet was a dresser; in one drawer there was a stack of boxer shorts and half a dozen pairs of socks, and in the next one down were panties and brassieres of various colors and styles, and in the one below that garter belts, stockings and various other pieces of women's intimate apparel. Either Elishah was keeping a big secret from the world or he was sharing the place with a woman.

Next to the double bed was a battered nightstand with chipped paint, its drawer empty except for a matchbook from the Hitching Post with a single match left standing, the hillbilly caricature on its cover mocking Elishah right there in his own bedroom. I checked behind the nightstand, too, and found nothing, and then I dropped to the floor to check the slats of the bedframe. I had eliminated, I thought, all the other obvious places to hide a gun: if Elishah had one I wanted to be holding it when he came home. There was none. What there was, balanced on a slat halfway down the frame, was a little case with a broken lock. Inside was a syringe and a rubber hose and several needles. I didn't think our boy was a diabetic, and I guessed that in the kitchen I'd find most of the spoons scorchmarked. There was no dope with the rig, nor anywhere under the bed, and I had a funny feeling there wasn't any in the house at all.

I sat down in a tattered easy chair in the living room, and it creaked beneath me, a gust of that sour smell wafting up from it. For about an hour I listened to the occasional car passing by, and to a dog that started barking every fifteen minutes or so until its owner stuck his head out the back door and told it to shut up. I thought about doing the whole neighborhood a favor and blowing the dog's brains out, but the whole cycle – barking, shouting, silence, barking again – amused me. Anyway, that wasn't what I'd come for, and I didn't want to attract attention before I'd done what I came to do: jump Elishah and beat the shit out of him. Cripple him, maybe.

The more I thought about it, though, the less sense that made. Elishah was addicted to opiates, and if I could keep them from him I could get even and get a little free labor from him besides.

I rose and went to the back door. It was still only one o'clock, time enough to get to the Commanche and have a drink before closing. If I was lucky I might run into someone from the line at Collins with a story to tell about what a wild and wooly place Wichita in general and Collins Aircraft in particular had become since I'd left.

CHAPTER SEVEN

At eight-fifteen Gunther sat at the bus terminal lunch counter finishing up a rotten breakfast; the scrambled eggs, though drowned in ketchup, still tasted like burnt grease, the bacon was undercooked and chewy, the toast blackened yet so cold the paper-thin butter patty on each slice retained its sharp edges.

He'd seen his face in the newspaper machine and knew he was going to have to lie low. Here he more or less blended in: an elderly man in rumpled clothes, more recently shaved than the others, maybe, eating in morose silence. Chewing joylessly, he pondered getting to Loretta's house. There was the bus, but he might sit down next to some do-gooder and then there he'd be, heading back to the goddamn old folks' home emptyhanded. He didn't know the bus routes anyway, and he wasn't the kind to ask for help. By now the cabbies would all have his picture. He wondered suddenly if Loretta herself might come pick him up, and he moved to the pay phones along the wall, fishing in his pockets for a dime.

The phone cost twenty cents, which seemed like an odd amount, but he put in two nickels plus the original dime and dialed the number scribbled on the back of Loretta Gandy's business card. He thought he remembered her now, a quiet little kid, scared of everything; he was glad to see she'd turned out okay, with a brand new Caddy and a house in a nice neighborhood.

'This is the Gandy residence,' Loretta's stiff, pre-recorded voice said. 'We're not here. Leave your name and number and we'll call you back.'

He'd have to remember to tell her it wasn't safe to say they're not at home on the outgoing message. 'Loretta. Mrs. Gandy. This's Gunther Fahnstiel. Sergeant.' He nearly left the number of the police department and his old extension, and when he stopped himself he couldn't think of anything useful to add. 'I'll talk to you later.' Might as well start walking, he decided, before it gets too hot.

Heading back to his half-eaten breakfast he saw that one of the other old guys at the counter was looking at the paper, and it occurred to him that Loretta had probably seen it, too. He was sure if he could explain himself she wouldn't turn him in, but he'd better hurry up and get there. He paid and left without anyone seeming to recognize him.

A few blocks in the direction of Loretta's neighborhood was a military surplus store, already open at a little after eight-thirty, and he thought it might be wise to buy a hat. He pushed open the front door and stepped inside, setting off a warning buzzer somewhere in the back. Only a third of the overhead fluorescents were on, and large sections of the musty interior were bathed in shadow. Behind the counter sat a middle-aged man with a military haircut.

'Welcome to the Quartermaster. You are under video

surveillance. You are also under my personal surveillance. Shoplifters will be dealt with,' he barked in a drill sergeant's cadence without looking up from his issue of *Soldier of Fortune*.

Down the middle aisle Gunther found the mess gear section. Having abandoned his breakfast in mid-meal he was starting to get hungry again, and he wondered if he should get a mess kit, or at least a canteen. They sold good metal ones with green cloth covers like when he was in the army, not those goddamn goatskin things his grandkids took when they used to go camping. Too much to carry, he decided, and at the end of the aisle he confronted a back wall covered with tools, shovels and axes and saws. He turned up another aisle and found gloves, winter coats, rubber raingear and heavy sweaters. No summer clothes, though. When he got to the front of the aisle the door opened again, activating the buzzer behind him. The woman who entered got no warning from the clerk, and she approached Gunther with a pleasant smile, her head cocked to one side.

'Good morning, sir. My name's Lena. Is there anything I could help you find?'

She was sixty or so, plump and shapeless, with a mop of equally shapeless curly hair of indeterminate color.

'Looking for a hat to keep the sun off my head, but all I see is winter stuff.'

She beckoned him and turned down another aisle and stopped at a big cardboard box filled with floppy hats.

'We have khaki or camouflage, whichever you prefer.'

Gunther reached down and pulled out a camouflage hat. When he tried to put it on his head it wouldn't go.

'No, that's a child's size, here...' She grabbed one in khaki and put it on his head. 'Perfect. You want camouflage?'

'Khaki's fine, I ain't trying to be pretty.'

The woman took the hat up to the register. 'Jim, you want to ring this up for this gentleman?'

'Three fifty-four,' he said.

'Three fifty-four what?' Lena chirped.

Jim looked like he wanted to punch her, but she kept smiling. 'Three fifty-four please, sir,' he said in an absurdly cheerful, high-pitched voice. Lena either missed the sarcasm or chose to ignore it.

'See? Isn't that nicer?'

Gunther handed Jim five dollars. 'You get a lot of shoplifters in here?'

'Damned few on my shift anyway,' Jim said. 'I was a cop after the army.'

'Until he got fired,' Lena offered cheerfully.

Now Jim looked like he wanted to take one of the shovels down from the back wall and brain her. 'I was placed on administrative leave and during that time I chose to resign.' His voice was level and quiet.

'Jim, this gentleman doesn't care one way or the other. Anyway, if you were still on the force you wouldn't be working here and we'd have never met.' She kissed Jim on the mouth, to Gunther's surprise, and Jim kissed her back, which surprised him even more.

'You want a bag?' Jim said, looking no friendlier or happier for his moment of bliss.

'I'll wear it.'

Gunther stepped out into the sunlight and headed

eastward. He didn't guess Lena and Jim had much of a future together; he'd spent too much time as a referee not to think that someday her inability to sense his resentment would lead to something bad. About the best you could hope for was that it would be non-lethal, and that Lena would have the sense not to forgive him and take him back.

Nearly a mile further east he reached Bleeker's drugstore, and outside it he stopped to look at his arms, whiter than they'd ever been in the summertime but already getting pink from yesterday's exposure. If the goddamn rest home would just let him spend more time outside he'd have had a tan already. He decided he'd better get some Coppertone if he was going to be walking very far in the sun today; if it hadn't gotten so cloudy before the storm yesterday he'd have had a bad burn.

Bleeker's looked completely different inside than he remembered, full of name-brand junk and lit up like a goddamn Christmas tree. 'Where's the suntan lotion?' he asked the young woman behind the counter, who was busy filling in a clip-out form in a magazine ad.

'Sunscreen, aisle seven A.'

'Where's that?'

She looked up, annoyed, and pointed to the sign at the end of aisle seven. 'It's right between aisle six B and aisle seven B.'

He walked over to where she'd pointed, grabbed a squeeze bottle and headed back to the counter. The woman who used to manage the front desk would have fired the girl for that kind of smart talk, he thought. Mrs. Perkey was her name, a nice, polite churchgoing woman with a round face. She had worked here until 1954, when her husband Albert died outside a roadhouse, having fallen down drunk in its parking lot behind a Cadillac belonging to Everett Collins, founder of Collins Aircraft. Collins, only a hair less drunk than Perkey, had backed over the poor bastard with his rear tires and then his front and then, wondering what the thumping sound had been, had shifted into first and ran him over again getting back into his space. He climbed out to see if he'd damaged his tires and saw Perkey lying there, presumably dead already, and he pondered his options: going forward would take him into the wall of the roadhouse, and backward would involve running Perkey over again. He chose the latter option, and this time somebody saw him as the Caddy's tires bumped over Albert Perkey for the third time, tail fins sashaying from side to side with each impact. A squad car arrived a few minutes later, and once they realized who they were taking in the arresting officers apologized but took him in just the same, and Gunther remembered seeing Collins being led that night to the holding cell that would serve as his private drunk tank.

'This is going to cost him a fucking bundle,' Ed Dieterle said as Collins passed by them, handcuffed and blubbering. Just keeping it out of the papers was a major undertaking for Collins's lawyers, and Mrs. Perkey turned down flat an initial offer of fifty thousand dollars, demanding that amount plus a substantial chunk of stock in Collins Aircraft Corporation. In the end the police report recorded that the driver of the offending vehicle had driven away without having the courtesy to identify himself, and Mrs. Perkey quit the drugstore. Two years later, having passed out in the middle of one of the company runways, Collins was himself nearly run over by a twin engine Collins Perfecta coming in for a landing, and six months after that he dropped dead in the same roadhouse. A squadcar dropped his body off at his house where, according to the newspapers, he had died after a brief illness.

Outside the drugstore Gunther applied the lotion to his arms and face and neck, and tried to pursue a train of thought. Something about Sally and Mrs. Perkey? They didn't go together in his mind; maybe something to do with old Collins. Probably he'd think of it on the way.

*

Eric Gandy was unexpectedly enjoying his long walk home. Once he'd managed to orient himself, he'd realized his wallet was gone and so were his keys, presumably lying somewhere between Belinda's stairs and her fireplace. He had the five-dollar bill, though, more than enough for breakfast at a tiny, dismal doughnut shop that caught his eye after a couple of miles of walking. The screen door swung shut with a loud slap as he walked in and sat down at the counter.

The counterman looked like he lived on the things, and in fact in the half hour he was there Eric saw him remove and consume four glazed doughnuts from the case. He looked about thirty, with short shiny black hair and skin so pale it was almost blue. He was so fat he could barely move, and got up off his stool only when there was no other option. His entire body moved sideways with each step, and a ten-foot trip across the backbar to get some half and half had him wheezing so alarmingly that Eric almost regretted having asked.

He picked up a paper from the stool next to him with the vague idea he might like to go out to the track and watch the greyhounds that night. There was no sports section, though, and he glanced at the national news for a moment before tossing it aside.

'You ever go out to the dog track?' he asked the counterman.

'Nope. In my church we don't believe in games of chance.'

'Dog racing's not a game of chance. It's who the fastest dog is. Nothing random about it.'

'It's gambling.'

'Yeah, but you're betting on your own handicapping skills.'

'Not me. Jesus says no gambling, that's good enough for me. Ought to be enough for anybody.'

'Hard to argue with you there.' He'd lived his whole life among the devout and knew that arguing over matters of doctrine was pointless. He had been raised Lutheran and couldn't remember any proscription against gambling ever being mentioned there, but that didn't mean there wasn't one. Apart from weddings and funerals he'd hardly been inside a church since his kids were little.

'Want some more coffee?' the counterman asked. Eric didn't, but he wanted to see the self-righteous bastard walk again. The wheezing wasn't as funny the second time; he swigged the coffee and stood before the man had made it back to his stool.

'Keep the change,' he called over his shoulder. It was appreciably warmer than when he'd walked in, the sky was a brilliant blue and the humidity hinted at what was certainly destined to be a miserable afternoon. By the time he got to Loretta's office the real scorching wet heat would be starting, but by then he'd have her Caddy.

*

Sidney hadn't eaten breakfast, and by the time he took off for an early lunch he was in such foul spirits he didn't announce to Janice that he was going, just stormed through the reception area and slammed the door on his way out. She warbled 'See you' at the closed door.

It was too hot for a walk already, over ninety degrees at barely eleven in the morning. Slowly he passed hair salons, mail box rental facilities, credit unions and used record stores. Halfway to his destination stood ten rows of small warehouse spaces set perpendicular to the street and containing a variety of small businesses ranging from aircraft parts to artificial limbs to a beanbag chair outlet. Feeling the heat of the sidewalk bleed through the soles of his shoes, he started worrying about Gunther keeling over from heatstroke.

Walking had been a big mistake, he now realized, but he was almost there and ravenous. His shirt and hair were drenched, his scrotum felt prickly and he was very conscious of the material of his trouserlegs rubbing against each other with each step, sticking to the insides of his thighs.

He stopped at the pay phones outside the front door of the restaurant, dropped two dimes and called Janice.

'I'm at Harold's. Anybody calls about Gunther, you call me here right away. Nothing else, understand? I don't want to hear about the fucking lights at the Sweet Cage.'

'Have a nice lunch,' she said with a chirpy sweetness he would have taken as sarcasm from anyone but her. When he finally pushed through the inner door of Harold's he just stood there in the air conditioning for a minute with his face turned upward toward the vent, letting the heat drain away from him. After thirty seconds or so he felt a hand around his upper arm. 'Hi, Barbara,' he said without opening his eyes.

'How'd you know it was me?'

'You're the only waitress who touches the customers.'

'I don't touch all the customers. Just my regulars.' Barbara was forty-five years old and working her way slowly through a community college business degree, and Sidney had been nursing a mild crush on her since she first started working lunches. She led him to a booth in the non-smoking half of the dining room, chatting merrily at him over her shoulder on the way. 'You know people actually keel over and die walking in heat like this, don't you?'

He didn't even watch her behind, swaying in off-orange polyester as she headed for the coffee station. She was back a minute later with a glass of water and a pitcher of coffee.

'Drink the water and I'll give you some coffee.'

'I don't want any,' he said. He was thirsty as hell, but he couldn't stand being told what to do.

'I'm not kidding, you're sweating like a whore in church and I'm not serving you anything until you drink this. You're gonna get dehydrated if you don't.'

Sheepishly he drank; it felt good going down and knew she was right. Once the glass was drained she poured some coffee into his mug and set the plastic carafe down on the table. 'Atta boy. I'll be back in a sec.'

She took off again and he looked out the window at the parking lot at a man and a woman arguing in front of the Sure Foods. She was wearing a Sure Foods apron, and whatever their conflict was it appeared to be escalating. They were both about thirty and he guessed they were a couple because it looked so serious, more serious anyway than an argument between strangers over a cash register error or a dent in a station wagon from a grocery cart. The guy looked like a grad student, short hair and glasses and a short-sleeved button-down shirt, and he was big. People were watching from their cars or stopping their carts to listen, and the couple seemed oblivious to them.

'You know what you want, Sidney?'

Sidney kept staring at the couple, surly at having acquiesced to Barbara's bossiness. 'Short stack and scrambled eggs.'

'You okay?'

'I'm fine,' he said. The couple had begun yelling so loud he could hear them through the plate glass, though the words were indistinct.

'You don't look okay.'

'I'm fine,' he repeated, aware that if she said one more thing not directly related to the ordering or preparation or serving of his food, he would snap something at her that he would feel sorry about later.

'Boy, look at those two. Wonder what's the matter.' She slipped into the booth and pressed herself into his side, leaning across his chest to get a better look. 'I bet she's sleeping around. Check out the look on her face. She's yelling too, but you can tell she's on the defensive.' She put her hand around Sidney's shoulders and gave the right one a pat. 'Sometimes a gal just isn't getting what she needs at home, Sidney. Sad but true.'

He turned to look at her, halfway thinking he'd heard it wrong, but she was already sliding out of the booth and speeding away with his order. This time he watched her rear until it disappeared into the kitchen.

*

A yell from the grad student brought his attention back to the story unfolding in the parking lot. He now had the woman's wrist in his hand, his teeth bared. She wrenched her arm, yelling back at him with equal vehemence and disgust, and by the time the man raised his fist Sidney was out of the booth and heading for the door.

The moist noontime heat radiated upward from the lot's asphalt like steam, burning his face as he strode toward the continuing conflict, its participants oblivious to him. The man's fist was wavering under her chin.

'Go ahead and hit me, big man. Tough guy. Prove what a fuckin' hardass you are. Stubdick.' Droplets of spit flew from her lips, shimmering, and she didn't seem to take any notice as Sidney came up directly behind the grad student.

'Throw that punch and it'll be the last thing you do with that arm for about a year,' he said quietly, his mouth two inches from the man's ear.

He turned to look at Sidney, amazed and infuriated at the intrusion into what he obviously still considered a private matter, and in the confusion he let go of the woman's arm, at which point she ran back into the safety of Sure Foods. He stared after her, then back at Sidney, unsure of whom to hate more.

Sidney's bouncer days were ten years behind him, but from time to time he liked to step in and throw a belligerent drunk out of one of the clubs himself, just for old times' sake, and as the guy raised both fists in a pathetic attempt at a boxer's opening stance Sidney started getting that good, electric feeling in his belly.

'You wanna dance, man?' the grad student said, going into what he probably thought was a pretty convincing bob and weave, and Sidney laughed despite himself at the movie-tough-guy line.

The laugh, more derisive than Sidney had meant it to be, spurred the man to take a swing, which failed to connect as Sidney took a single step back. He was mentally preparing his left and starting to weave move in when the icy cascade hit his head and shoulders from behind, tiny freezing projectiles and cold liquid, the shock knocking the wind out of him with an audible huff, and he struggled for a moment to regain control of his chest muscles and refill his lungs. He looked across at his opponent and saw that he, too, was wet and standing there dumbfounded.

'Didn't you hear me calling your name?' He turned to face Barbara, an empty water pitcher in her right hand. The small crowd that had gathered began applauding her. Sensing motion from his sparring partner, he pivoted in time to see the grad student dive for an old Datsun, get in and drive away.

'Come on inside, he-man, you got a short stack and scrambled eggs waiting.'

He followed her as though in a trance, the water cool on his shirt and beginning to evaporate even before they got back inside.

*

Ed sat across from Janice, his jacket folded across his arm. His sweaty shirt embarrassed him but not to the point where he was willing to put the jacket back on.

'He's having lunch over at Harold's. Shouldn't be much longer if you want to wait.'

'Don't think I will. Just wanted to touch base with him.'

'You have a number where he can call you when he gets back?'

'I'm over at the Highlander Seven.'

'Ew. Out on Kellogg? You know there was a drug murder there last year?'

'Hadn't heard that.'

'Cocaine buy gone wrong,' she said knowingly, leaning forward a little. 'You want something to drink?' She opened a half-sized refrigerator without leaving her chair.

'Pepsi'd be fine.' She tossed a can to him and he opened it slowly to control the spray, then reached out for a flyer from a stack on the corner of her desk. 'Twelve grand, huh? Didn't know Sidney thought that highly of the old man.'

'He certainly does,' Janice said, taking offense.

'Sidney put the reward up himself?'

'Him and Mitch together. It's what Gunther gave them for the down.'

'Beg pardon?'

'After Sidney's boss passed away ten years ago—'

'She didn't pass away, honey, she was blown away.'

'Well, after whatever you want to call it, Gunther gave Sidney some money for the down payment on the Sweet Cage.'

'Gunther gave him twelve thousand dollars?'

She nodded. 'There's a lot more love between those two than you'd think.'

He examined the strangely cheerful image on the flyer, less concerned about the amount of love involved than about the source of the money Gunther had provided Sidney. He saw no way, then or now, that Gunther could have had twelve grand in cash lying around. He had a thought, then rejected it as absurd, shaking his head. 'No,' he said aloud.

'No, what?' Janice asked.

'Nothing. I just thought something stupid.' He stood up and headed for the door.

'You got a message for Sidney?'

'Just let him know I'm in town. I'll catch up with him.'

*

Dot sat in Gunther's old living room chair, drinking a big glass of iced tea and wondering how the carpet had managed to get so ratty in such a short time, with a path worn into it from the front door to the kitchen and back into the bedroom, too. They'd put it in the same time as the air conditioning, about six months after they came into the money. Jesus, that's nine years, she thought, and it seemed like a long time after all: almost a decade of not worrying about money. The house was paid for and the RV too, though they'd ended up selling that for a fraction of what it would have fetched if Gunther had only taken better care of it mechanically; they'd taken trips and bought things for the grandkids, and when Gunther's medical troubles had come along they'd been able to put him into a seemingly quality facility like Lake Vista instead of the Veterans' Hospital. Now that her lifelong money worries were back they were worse than ever, as though her short span of prosperity had worn away all the toughness she'd acquired from the Depression and the war and close to thirty years married to Fred McCallum.

So she'd broken down in front of Gunther; she hadn't meant to say anything, but it was one of those mornings when he seemed just like his old self, and before she knew it she was crying and saying she was goddamned if she was going to put him in the fucking Veterans' Hospital. He was quiet after that, even after she regained her composure and tried to reassure him that nothing was wrong, and it seemed to her now that his thoughtful demeanor for the rest of the visit should have served as a warning.

Once he came back she'd just have to swallow her pride and ask Sidney to lend a hand. She'd get a settlement out of Lake Vista, too, at least enough to finance a couple of years of double occupancy in another nursing home, one that wasn't run by jackasses. By God, they owed her a couple more years of peace of mind.

CHAPTER EIGHT

ED DIETERLE: 18–19 JUNE, 1952

Daisy didn't mind me working late now that I'd been promoted, but if she knew I was running around on my own time trying to help Gunther out I'd be sleeping on the goddamn lawn. She used to like him, and in her day she was a little bit wild herself, but she'd started getting religious since our boy was born. These days unless I could find a good excuse I found myself staring at the back of a pew every Sunday, squirming like my three-year-old son did; the way Daisy saw it, Sally and Gunther had gone from free spirits to sinners without much of a transition.

Funny thing is, it was her idea to fix the two of them up in the first place. When Gunther finally had enough of his crazy third wife we had a little party and invited him and Sally both, intending to throw them together if necessary; it wasn't. They left the party together a few minutes after Gunther's arrival, and at the time Daisy was elated.

Now I was standing in the lobby of the nicest hotel in town at nearly midnight, trying to keep the two of them out of trouble.

Gunther wasn't taking Sally's husband seriously, so I had to. The cabbie that picked Ogden up at the hospital reported dropping him off at the Bellingham, and I determined that he'd checked in, still using the name Thomas McGowan. I hadn't been out to the Hitching Post yet; if he had friends there I didn't want him to find out anybody was interested in what he did.

The staff at the Bellingham didn't like him. He was a big spender and a flashy dresser, one of those guys who demands a certain amount of brownnosing from those he considers his inferiors; compensation, maybe, for kissing all those officers' asses all those years. Whatever the reason was, he had alienated the night manager, Mr. Reynolds, to the point where he didn't need to be coaxed or threatened to cooperate with me. He described Ogden's car and predicted he'd be taking it out before long.

'Sounds like he's still on Jap time. Any idea why?'

'None.'

'Any idea where he goes?'

'No. Although when you see him you'll notice he's got a shiner. My daytime counterpart found it pretty alluring.'

While we were talking the phone rang and Reynolds picked it up.

'Yes, sir, Sergeant McCowan. I'll see to it. I'm sorry about the eggs; I'll leave word for the day manager to speak to the cook personally.' He hung up. 'Eggs weren't runny enough. He's coming down shortly; he just asked for his car to be made ready.'

*

I waited outside in my own car a half a block east, hoping he wasn't going to buck the traffic and head in my direction; turning around would be easy, but the traffic was so light he'd know he was being followed. He turned right instead, and I waited a minute for him to get into the flow before merging. I stayed a few cars back and watched him. He drove like an idiot for a couple of blocks, cutting off other drivers, accelerating suddenly, refusing to let anybody change lanes in front of him. He looked like he was spoiling for a fight.

He turned north on to Broadway, and I thought he might be headed for the Hitching Post again, but he turned right, headed east on Twenty-first. Traffic was so thin I didn't dare follow, but I played a hunch and continued on three more blocks and beat him to Washington headed north. The traffic was heavier here, but I could see the Plymouth three cars behind me on the left, driving more or less normally, and sure enough when we got to the Commanche he turned into the parking lot. I continued on for a block and then doubled back.

He was going in the front door just as I pulled into the lot. I drove slowly across it, gravel crunching underneath, and parked at the far end next to a tree.

*

The Commanche was still hopping, but only for a couple more hours. It was past twelve, and if the city was prepared to allow it to flout the liquor laws provided the right palms got crossed, the two a.m. closing time was still rigorously enforced. City government liked to give the impression it had things under control at these roadhouses, which it didn't. You could buy a little reefer here if you wanted, and various other drugs could be procured off the premises with a discreet word to the bartender. There were striptease acts on the weekends, brought in from as far away as Chicago and New Orleans, that consistently crossed the line from raunchy to obscene. Naturally there were whores, and if you were looking for a poker game, high or low stakes, the Commanche was a good place to start asking. There was a guy at the bar all weekend and most weekdays making book on sports, and he'd sell you a deck of pornographic playing cards if you asked. None of this was any of my business, since I didn't work vice, and the guys that did were well taken care of.

I went inside and sat at the bar. The bartender wasn't particularly glad to see me, but happier than he would have been if I'd pulled out my badge for all and sundry to see. I ordered a beer and looked around. For a weeknight it was pretty crowded, I thought. I didn't spot Ogden right away and didn't want to be too obvious about looking, so I took a sip. Almost immediately I was joined by a pretty, full-figured girl with a pouty little smile.

'What's a girl got to do to get a drink around here?' she asked. The bartender shook his head at her but I waved him off and let her order a Bloody Mary. I didn't know if she was a B-girl or a hustler, and I didn't care; this way it looked like I was there to pick up a girl and not to spy on anybody. Her name was Lena, or so she said, twenty-two years old and a student at the university. She wanted to be a lawyer, and I laughed when she said it. She got her nose a little out of joint over it, and for the first time it occurred to me she might not be working for the house.

'Sorry about that, you just caught me kind of off-guard.' She looked away from me, and I noticed she was tugging at her bare ring finger. 'First night out on the town without hubby?' She snapped her head around at the accusation, but she took pains to keep her cool.

'He works midnight to nine. Why should I have to stay around the house listening to the goddamn radio all night?'

'You have a point there, miss.'

'It's not what I got married for, if you know what I mean.' She leaned over toward me, arching both eyebrows meaningfully. 'Spending the night alone.'

In the corner of the room I finally spotted Ogden, sitting and talking to a couple of drunks in coveralls. One of them was so far gone that even sitting down he was weaving, looking from his buddy to Ogden and then around the room and back to his buddy again, all the while with a big goofy smile on his face, and my guess was it wasn't just alcohol producing the euphoric grin. Before Lena could elaborate any further on the injustice of her husband's third shift job and the hardships of sleeping solo, I felt a hand on my shoulder.

'Ed Dieterle, you old hound dog.' It was Frank Elting, and he must have sensed I was working, because he didn't bellow out 'hey flatfoot' the way he usually did. 'Stepping out on the old lady, huh?'

'Just out for a drink and a little conversation. Lena, I

need to talk to Frank, here. Why don't you take your drink over to a table.'

'I don't want to. I want to talk to you.'

'No you don't, because if you do you'll just hear what I think about married women who go trotting around behind their husband's backs. There's a word for 'em where I come from.'

She got down off her stool, more annoyed than wounded. 'Thanks for the drink, Reverend.'

Elting watched her go, shaking his head. 'Pretty sweet caboose on her. You got kind of rough there, didn't you? Somebody told me you got religion.'

'I just wanted to get rid of her. How come you're by yourself?' Elting almost always had a girl with him, unless he was working.

'Gal I came with ran into somebody she knew and took off. She'll be back in an hour or so, probably a little more bowlegged than before. So what brings you here? No shit.'

Elting might be helpful, but he might just as easily fuck things up. 'Just having a drink.'

'Horseshit, it's after midnight and you're not much of a drinker, and you don't chase skirt. Unless your marriage is busting up, you're not here for fun.'

'It's not and I am. You think you goddamn know everything.'

'Don't you usually work in pairs?'

'Exactly.'

'I don't suppose it has anything to do with the guy with the shiner in the houndstooth jacket, came in right before you did?'

'Which guy?'

'The guy you're watching out the corner of your eye. He came in last night about forty-five minutes before closing time, asked a bunch of questions about Collins.'

'Is that so.'

'According to Bill Ketcham, he was asking what the situation was. He just got out of the Army, he's looking for a job, wanted to know if there was any action out there. Like specifically if there were still a lot of good looking women on the line. How loose were they.'

'That's interesting.'

'Shit, he all but asked point blank if there was a pussy raffle going on. Made Bill real nervous; he didn't say anything, but that doesn't mean somebody else didn't. What Bill figures is, he's some kind of state cop, or maybe a fed.'

'That could be.'

'Well, for fuck's sake, Ed, give me a little something back.'

'I just came in for a drink.'

'Come on. Give me something. You know I wouldn't do anything to fuck up Sally's operation, but if the state's going to do it anyway I want to get there first.'

I shook my head. 'I have nothing to say about it.'

And I didn't, either, not until I saw one of Ogden's companions urgently waving somebody over. It was Amos Culligan, and Elting saw him too.

'Now that's interesting, Ed. I bet you old Amos is going to tell that fellow there everything he wants to know and some more on top of it. Now you can't go over there, seeing as Culligan knows you're a cop. I could, though, if I knew who that guy was and what he was doing.'

'He's Sally's husband,' I allowed.

Elting rubbed the back of his neck. 'I thought she was a widow. Or at least divorced.'

'She's still married. Master Sergeant Wayne Ogden, U.S. Army Quartermaster Corps.'

'What's he doing back here, you figure?'

'Spending money. He's got a room at the Bellingham, paid for a week in advance. Bought a car day before yesterday, and I'm betting it was a cash transaction.'

'So he's crooked. Where's he stationed?'

'Japan, since '46.'

Elting nodded. 'Dressed like a pimp. Think he's through with the Army? Things are changing fast over there, with the Occupation finished.'

'His story is he's on a three-month furlough, re-upped for three years and he's taking it all at once. But his papers are in a phony name.'

'Sounds to me like a man who ain't going back,' Elting said.

I nodded. It sounded that way to me, too, though he had a lot to lose by deserting. He had to have extremely pressing reasons if that was the case.

'Sally know he's back?'

'I don't know. Gunther does, but he doesn't seem inclined to do anything about it.'

'You're here as a private citizen, then.'

'That's right.' Elting was strictly looking out for his own interests here, but in this case I thought his and mine coincided as much as they were ever likely to. 'I don't think anything's going to come out of this that's going to be suitable for newspaper publication. Even in the *Beacon*.'

He shrugged. 'You never know, do you? I just like to keep things stirred up.'

I went back to my car, delighted to be leaving the Commanche. It was a clear night, and despite the weatherman's prediction it hadn't rained that day.

At home I looked in on Jeff, sleeping peacefully. In our room I undressed and got into bed next to Daisy, who stirred but didn't wake, and I went right to sleep and started dreaming about my Navy days. I was in the engine room talking to a recruiting officer trying to get some leave that was due me. We were yelling back and forth over the sounds of a battle, the ship's guns going off repeatedly, their echo deafening in the hot, damp bowels of the ship, and then we took a hit and the big turbine started burning, with thick greasy smoke roiling out of it, filling the air and making it hard to breathe, and the bastard still wouldn't let me have the shore leave. I was about to go for his throat when I woke up with the feeling that the house was on fire. When I'd managed to reassure myself that it wasn't, I looked at the clock. It was two thirty-five; I'd been asleep less than an hour.

CHAPTER NINE

Loretta arrived at the office at ten-thirty and made an appointment for an early afternoon showing, then spent most of the morning on paperwork on a pending sale. At eleven-thirty Steve Blasik stepped into her office.

'You got Bill Dearden's number handy?'

'I have it, hold on...' She opened her Rolodex, wrote the number down and handed it to him and went back to her papers. At the clearing of a throat she looked up and found Steve still in her doorway.

'Are you free for lunch? Around twelve-fifteen?'

'Sure,' she said, and again she returned her attention to her work.

Ten minutes later the receptionist buzzed her. 'Loretta? There's a guy here, says he's your husband.' She sounded dubious, and before Loretta could answer she heard the receptionist yelling. '*Stop, goddamn you*! Loretta, he's heading your way. You want me to call the cops?'

Standing in the doorway was Eric, looking worse than she'd seen in a long time, his hair dusty and matted into a wedge on top, his clothes half-soaked with perspiration. 'That's okay, Anita, it's him after all.'

'That bitch actually wanted me to pull out my driver's license.'

'So? Why didn't you?'

'I left it somewhere. Look, I need to take the Caddy.'

'What for?' she asked, although she knew it didn't matter; she was already thinking about the quickest way for her to rent something nice enough to show her afternoon listing in.

'Because I can't get to my car until tonight.'

'And why is that?' she said flatly, feeling a little throb of defiance; she was angry with herself even though the part where she gave in hadn't arrived yet.

'It's in a parking garage that doesn't open until six.'

'That's a funny way for a parking garage to operate. How'd you get all that dust in your hair?'

He touched his hand to his dirt-stiffened hair and looked surprised. 'I don't know, I was cutting across an open lot and the wind kicked up. Look, are you going to give me the keys or not?'

'I need my car for my job, Eric, I can't just hand it over every time you get so drunk you can't remember where you parked yours.' She said it with such force and speed she hiccupped slightly and had to take in a deep breath afterward.

'Look, I have places to be and you're wasting both our time arguing about it. So how's about you hand over the fucking keys?'

'It's my car. Would you give me yours if I showed up at your office looking like shit and just demanded it?'

'I have a very important meeting about funding the Trade Mart, and I'd like to get home and get cleaned the fuck up before I have to walk into a roomful of bankers to ask them for money; you think that might be a good idea?'

His voice was rising again, and Steve Blasik appeared in the doorway.

'This guy bothering you, Loretta?'

'No,' she said, almost feeling sorry for Eric. She could see skin on his side where his shirt wasn't all the way tucked in, and there was a small patch of dried, crusted blood on his knuckle, the blood obscured by more dust. 'Steve, have you met my husband?'

'Do you mind?' Eric said quietly, and Steve moved along. 'Look, I'm sorry I yelled. Just give me the keys, all right?'

'I need my car this afternoon.' The words caught her by surprise even as she spoke them. 'Why don't you get a cab?'

'A cab?'

'Or you can walk. Suit yourself.'

'It's almost noon. Take me home on your lunch hour.'

'Can't. I'm having lunch with a colleague.'

He looked away. 'I'll take it,' he said quietly.

'Take what?'

'I'll take the goddamn cabfare. Make it ten.'

She opened her purse and pulled out a twenty. 'I'll call the cab company.'

He grabbed the twenty out of her hands and left without looking at her. She felt a little mean as she watched him walk away through the office, a tight grip on the twenty, but mostly what she felt was exhilaration.

*

125

Ed parked next to the front door and stepped out, ignoring the PASSENGER LOADING ONLY – FIVE MINUTES sign. The hot, heavy air outside burned his exposed skin, even in the shade of the carport, and stepping into Lake Vista's overcooled lobby was a relief. It was full of plants and bright with sunlight, designed to give a happy first impression of the home to prospective residents and, more importantly, their decision-making family members. A thin, crabbed looking woman seated behind an enormous low-slung desk looked up from a fast-food taco as though she thought he might snatch it from her hand.

'You a spouse?' she asked through a partially chewed mouthful.

'Wait 'til you swallow. Nobody wants to look at that.'

She looked hurt, chewed fast, and gulped. Her curled-too-tight platinum blonde permanent looked wet and gave off a powerful chemical odor, and her attempt at a smile suggested that she'd never seen one, only heard them described. 'Yes, sir. How can I help you? Would you like some information about Lake Vista?' Her voice had a practiced, sunshiny quality that her face gave lie to, and she tried to hand him a brochure, which he ignored.

'I want to talk to whoever's in charge. Who would that be?'

'That'd be Dr. Mercer. Was he expecting you?'

'Where is he?'

'He and his wife are out looking at houses.'

'When's he coming back in?'

'Probably before five-thirty. His office hours are 'til six and he likes to be around at the end of the day in case any of the residents need his attention personally.'

'I bet he does,' he said, bewildered at the lack of concern. Probably their liability insurance covered whatever Dot might care to sue them for. Come five-thirty he'd set this Mercer straight. Househunting, for Christ's sake. 'I'll come back. Where's Rory Blaine?'

She consulted a piece of paper, squinting. 'Mister Blaine is in 513.'

'How's he doing?'

'I don't know anything about him one way or the other except his ID number.'

'Can I go back and see him?'

'That's the Memory Impaired Ward, so you'll need to check in with security.'

'Where's that?'

She pointed to a desk where a bored-looking guard with a crewcut and a dark green windbreaker sat looking sullen and disappointed. Normally Ed didn't like the phrase rent-a-cop, since lots of private security guards were off-duty or retired officers, but this one really did look like he'd rather be home drinking beer and jacking off to the Sears catalogue.

'Here to see Rory Blaine.'

The guard roused himself with some difficulty and hauled a clipboard out of a desk drawer. 'Fill this out. Also I'll need to see a driver's license or other form of state-issued picture ID, no credit cards or Social Security cards or school IDs accepted.'

As he filled in his name and address he handed the guard his Texas driver's license.

'Well, there, Mr. Dee-treel, looks like you're about ready to check in yourself.'

With some effort he managed to look into the man's eyes without changing his expression as he handed the clipboard back to him.

'Be real careful coming in and out the doors. They may be space cases in there but some of 'em's pretty crafty when it comes to breaking out.'

'That's what I hear,' he said, the remark partially drowned out as the lock on the door buzzed then clicked open.

The corridor he entered was white and brightly lit with greenish fluorescents, and the first person he ran into was a tiny, shriveled woman doing a little dance of exultation at the sight of him. She grabbed his arm, grinned salaciously and started walking alongside him, leaning into his side, feeling as weightless as a hospital gown full of goosedown.

'So who do I have to blow to get out of this dump, old man?'

'Beg pardon?'

'You heard me,' she said, her voice wispy and dry. 'I'll do pretty much anything you want if you'll take me out of here.'

'Afraid I won't be much help on that score, ma'am.' She might have been a hundred.

'Anything. Fucking, sucking.' She put the back of her hand beside her mouth and looked at him sideways. 'Even up the back stairs, if that's what you go for. I don't mind, I had a beau who was a merchant marine up in Seattle.'

An attendant appeared at the end of the hall. 'Mrs. Halliburton, I hope you're not making them nasty suggestions to our visitor.' The attendant was a large woman in a white uniform, and she smiled indulgently at Mrs. Halli-burton, whose sunny demeanor had instantly switched to pokerfaced nonchalance.

'I was just asking him for a light.'

'Sure you were,' she said, leading Mrs. Halliburton off with a firm hand on the shoulder.

At the end of the corridor, in a small room without windows, he found Rory sitting up in his bed, watching television. At the sight of Ed he jumped out and pointed at him, standing easily on one foot.

'You! Ed!' Rory hopped over and crushed him in a bony bear hug. Though he hadn't retained much of his former bulk he was still stronger than he knew, and thoughts of broken ribs filled Ed's mind as the hug got fiercer.

'You retired and moved to Dallas,' Rory said when he finally let go, as if reciting. 'Your son lives there.'

'That's right.'

'Gunther got out of here, you know.'

'I heard. You know anything about that?'

'He just up and walked away. I got to wear a bracelet now.' He raised his pajama leg to show Ed an electronic bracelet above his slipper, and it was only then that Ed saw that Rory was standing on one foot because the other was gone. 'Gunther ought to have been wearing one too, but he wouldn't.' Rory laughed at the thought. 'Gunther just does as he pleases.'

'He does at that,' Ed said. 'Sorry to interrupt your movie.'

'That's okay, I seen it enough times.' It was *The African Queen*, playing on a VCR. The buttons on the player with their abstract symbols had all been marked with a label-maker: PUSH ME TO PLAY THE MOVIE, PUSH ME TO GO BACKWARD, PUSH ME TO STOP THE MOVIE.

'That's a good one.'

'Uh-huh.'

'What happened to your foot, Rory?'

'They had to take it off. Diabetes. That was a while ago, right when I got in here.'

Rory seemed happy, as he usually did. His dementia was due to head trauma, not his advanced age; he'd been hospitalized for decades now, since his mid-thirties, and the scars on his scalp still shone pink and terrible despite the greyness of his skin in general.

'When'd you move in here, anyway, Rory?'

'While back. I was in another one in between. My boy pays for it. He sells insurance now, he's all grown up.'

'Costs a lot to be in here, huh?'

'I guess it does.'

'I don't guess Gunther's pension covers the whole nut,' Ed said, not really expecting a response.

Rory looked blank for a second, then piped up, 'Gunther up and walked away from here.'

*

What Gunther wanted most right then was a drink of water, and seeing the hospital where Dot used to work he was heartened to realize that he was just four or five city blocks west of Loretta's street. Then he'd get his water, and maybe something to eat, too, though Loretta seemed to be one of these modern career girls, and he was led to believe they didn't cook much. Probably there'd be something in the freezer, pizza rolls or tater tots, or maybe some ice cream. Glancing over at the hospital he watched an ambulance pull up in front. When he'd met Dot in '42 it was a single building in the middle of a city block, surrounded by a vast lawn; now the whole block and more was taken up by the hospital, and he wondered if that original building was intact somewhere within the concrete and steel of the new facility.

Four blocks later he stood at the end of the street and consulted the business card again. Number 249, on the opposite side of the street, a nice big two-story house, bigger even than he'd pictured, built of dark brick and with old trees lining both sides of the property and a couple more in the middle of a nice big front yard. He walked up the driveway and peered into a detached garage under the shade of a big oak. He knocked on the back door and got no response; the doorknob didn't give, but he knew there'd be a key somewhere around. He looked on the ledge outside the window, under the mat and under a large round rock before he found it above the doorsill. He'd have to lecture her about this, too, he thought as he opened the door and stepped into the cool air of Loretta's kitchen, though he did replace the key in case someone was counting on its presence. Slamming the door behind him he felt odd about what technically amounted to breaking and entering, but he couldn't wait outside in the yard without being noticed. Besides, he told himself, I'm doing everybody a favor if I get a shower and wash my clothes. He was acutely aware at that moment that he was less than scrupulously clean; he and his clothes, his shorts in particular, were beginning to ripen, and the passing of the afternoon, even in the air conditioned splendor of Loretta's house, could only make it worse.

He moved to the sink, turned on the tap and stuck his face under it, washing away the heat and grease and dirt with his hands before opening his mouth and drinking the cool water down in big, slurping gulps. He wiped his face on a dishtowel next to the sink and looked around. It was a big kitchen, and on one wall hung various family pictures. There were a number of photos of two children at various ages, a boy and a girl, several of them with Loretta, a picture of Loretta getting some kind of award, and finally one that gave him a real jolt: a snapshot of Sally as a young woman.

It was a flattering snapshot, all right, but she didn't need any help looking good. God, she was a pretty girl, maybe the prettiest he'd ever seen in person. Big sweet eyes and a wide smile that was smarty without suggesting any meanness, though you found out about that quick enough if you got to know her.

He studied the photo closely, a black and white candid shot out at Lake Bascomb or someplace. Or maybe it was out at the quarry; it was hard to make out the background very well except that there was a blurred body of water surrounded by trees. It looked like about the right period for the quarry. Hell, he might have taken it himself, and he thought he remembered the blouse she was wearing in it, started thinking about unbuttoning it, about the way her breasts felt in his hand under the blouse through the silky fabric of her brassiere, and then about snaking his hand under the cup to the nipple. Her skin where it wasn't tan was white as Niobara chalk, soft and smooth to the touch, and it was as though he could really feel it against his fingertips, the memory as vivid as his presence in Loretta's kitchen. He realized that he once again had an erection, and he let his hand stray down just to make sure, without ever leaving that place where he was undressing Sally, and by the time she was wriggling out of her panties he was experiencing his second orgasm in the last twelve hours. It was a dry one this time, which came as something of a relief even if he was about to wash his clothes. Its aftermath felt good, loosening his stiff muscles and calming his brain, though he suspected a little sadly that it would be a while before his next one.

*

When Sidney got back to the office he stopped at the stack of flyers on Janice's desk. He was surprised by the vividness of the color; Gunther's baseball cap shone a brilliant red against the light background, and his skin was only slightly ruddier than in real life.

'Larry and Bill grabbed a few hundred each, they're already putting them up all over town. I'm going to church tonight and I'll give some away there, ask people to put 'em up wherever they can. And Mitch came by with a check for six grand.'

'Good.' Sidney pulled out his checkbook and started writing. 'I'm going out, I'll probably end up at the Sweet Cage or at my mom's. Can you make it to the bank with this? Probably ought to open an escrow account or something.'

Janice took his check. 'I already talked to Noah over at Bank Three about it, it'll be set up by close of business this afternoon. And Ed Dieterle came by looking for you.'

'Ed's here? What for?'

'What do you think? Looking for your stepdad.'

He stepped out the door and went downstairs to his car, trying to understand what brought a 75-year-old man four hundred miles from home in this kind of heat.

*

When Ed walked in Howells was writing something down with his right hand and manipulating a sandwich with his left, all the while listening to someone on the phone balanced on his left shoulder.

Ed wandered over to the wall and started looking at photographs. On the left end at eye level was a picture taken twenty-five years earlier at Howells's bachelor party. The three of them were wearing Beatle wigs and Ed and Howells looked pie-eyed, but Gunther stared straight into the lens as though daring the photographer to find anything funny about him.

Finally Howells hung up. 'What's the good word?'

'None, so far. Hey Lester, is Hank Neeland still working?'

'Fell over dead last year.'

'No kidding?'

'No kidding. His wife asked him to go to Safeway and get some eggs, he collapsed right in front of the dairy case. Dead before he hit the ground.'

'Jesus. Sorry to hear that. How about Connover?'

'Retired, moved to Colorado.'

'Shit. You remember who else worked on the Renata Forsythe killing?'

'I did, a little bit. Not her case exactly, but the Kansas City guy got killed in her club the same time. Gerard.'

'What's your gut feeling about that money?'

'Well, first of all, nobody ever conclusively proved there was any.'

'Come on. What are all these scumbags killing each other over then, baseball cards?'

'All right, I guess Vic Cavanaugh took it, or that lawyer, whatsisname. They're the only two unaccounted for.'

'You don't think somebody might have killed them, too?'

'Never found a body for either one, and the others were pretty much left to rot where they fell. Shit, that Gerard really stunk that place up. He'd been dead a coupla days before anybody found him.' He set the last quarter of his sandwich down on its wax paper wrapper. 'So what's so damned interesting about that?'

'What do you think about Gunther's boy Sidney buying the place right after?'

Howells shook his head. 'Doesn't mean anything. He's the one found Gerard and hell, he was pretty much scared shitless. Anyway, he's Gunther's son. Stepson, rather.'

'Where do you think he got the scratch?'

Howells shrugged and picked his sandwich back up. 'That partner of his, Cherkas, he was a banker before.'

'You know this Cherkas character?'

'I stop into the club now and then, just to make sure everything's on the up and up.'

Ed nodded. 'Hey, I saw Rory. He seemed pretty good, considering.'

'Yeah, considering.' Howells's father had been a police-man, and as a boy Lester had known Rory the way he was before his accident. He was the only cop of his generation who likely gave him any thought, in fact probably the only on-duty cop who even remembered Rory at all. 'I gotta make it down and see him. Maybe next weekend.'

The phone rang and Howells picked it up and started talking again, and he nodded when Ed waved a silent goodbye.

*

If the lunchtime hostess at Lupe's hadn't known Eric she never would have let him in. She strongly suggested a trip to the men's room when he arrived, and once inside he was shocked at what stared back at him, grimy and unshaven, from the mirror. The shift in dynamics between him and Loretta lost some of its mystery. After tucking in his shirt, washing his face and combing his hair he looked passable, he thought; at least freshened up enough to be served alcohol.

He'd been at the bar now for an hour, munching down chips and salsa and swigging crappy generic margaritas. At another restaurant he might have ordered a little food, but Lupe's was part of a big chain and the burritos were worse than the prefabricated drinks. Eric signalled for his fourth margarita, all he had money for. As the bartender brought it to him he sensed a presence at his side.

'Hey, Eric. How's it going?'

He looked up to see Skeeter Garcinich, a tall, cadaverish man who always looked hungry and angry at the same time. 'Hey, Skeeter.'

'You want to have lunch?'

'Just had it,' he said. 'Hey, can you lend me twenty? I'm stuck without my wallet and my checkbook.'

Skeeter fished out a twenty and dropped it on the bar. 'There you go, man. Think I might join you for one of them margaritas.'

'How's business?' Eric asked without really giving a shit. Skeeter had done a lousy job last time they'd worked together, and he wouldn't be using him again, no matter how low he bid or what he kicked back.

'Can't complain. How's things going with the Trade Mart?'

'Great. Still in the backing stage.'

'Well, I'd sure like to be considered for the plumbing when it happens.'

'Oh, yeah. You will be, don't worry.'

'You keep me posted.'

'I'll do that.' He swigged the margarita. Office workers now swarmed around the bar waiting for tables and Eric didn't much want to be there any more, particularly with Skeeter at his side pestering him about the Trade Mart. 'Guess I'll see you later.'

Skeeter followed him out into the lobby. 'I'll be just about done with Quail Cove by the time you get going.'

'Sounds perfect,' he said. How bad are you fucking up the toilets in Quail Cove, he thought. As he reached the front door Skeeter called out to him, halfway through the open door of the dining room.

'Hold on, man. Check this out. It's Loretta. With a guy.'

'It's a business lunch.'

Skeeter shook his long, narrow head. 'They ain't talking real estate, my friend. Take a look.'

He looked in, around Skeeter. The dining room was full, the waitresses speeding from table to table to wait station in their low-cut South-of-the-Border uniforms. 'I don't see her.'

'Over there, in the booth. Where the waitress with the monster tits is headed.'

For a second he thought Skeeter had the wrong woman, then he recognized her underneath the new haircut he'd failed to notice when he was trying to get her to part with her car keys. He felt slightly dizzy, from the alcohol or the aftereffects of the heat or the impossible sight of his wife holding hands across a small table with the same yuppie asshole he'd seen in her office before.

'You going over there or what?'

Clearly Skeeter expected him go over and make some kind of a scene to save face, but he suddenly felt very drunk and tired, and Loretta had already bested him once that day. 'Nah, I'm going home.'

Skeeter couldn't believe what he was hearing. 'Man, you know as soon as they leave here they're gonna hop off somewhere for a fuckin' nooner.'

'Which I do about three times a week, Skeeter.' Including, a couple of years back, every Tuesday with Skeeter's then-wife Lacey. 'I gotta go.'

As he pushed the heavy oak double doors open and stepped into the parking lot he patted the crisp twenty in his shirt pocket and decided to stop at the Chimneysweep, which was just a couple of blocks' detour on his way home and so dark no one would see how dirty he was. It seemed like a good day to get shitfaced.

*

Gunther was thoroughly impressed by the Gandy's master bathroom, upon whose toilet he was now seated. The fixtures were new and shiny, the towels fluffy and thick and the same color as the wallpaper, and the tub looked big enough to float a canoe. Once he was done with the toilet and had his load in the wash he might just treat himself to a bath. He and the old woman had a nice house, and paid for, too, but this one had it beat all to hell. Expensive as Sidney's house, he bet, but not as modern or uncomfortable. What Sidney needed was a wife to make that place more like this one, a real woman's house. His best guess was that Loretta was divorced, as the only adult male on the kitchen wall photo gallery was clearly the little boy in the other pictures grown into a young man. From where he sat there wasn't any sign of a man's presence in the bathroom either.

When he was finished he went straight downstairs to the basement. It was finished and somewhat more masculine in feel than the upstairs, and Gunther wondered if this was the lingering effect of an absent husband or if this was simply where he'd been banished. There was a pool table that looked like it didn't get much use, a big screen TV and a well-stocked wet bar. In the refrigerator were a couple of six-packs of expensive foreign beer, the same kind Sidney drank. He didn't picture Loretta as a beer drinker, but then eleven of the bottles stood intact.

The washer and dryer were next door in the utility

room, which was finished to match the rest of the basement. Out of habit he emptied the pocket of his shirt before taking it off; in it were the receipts for the suntan lotion and the hat, as well as Loretta's business card. Stripping naked he stuffed his clothes, including the hat, into the machine. He grabbed a box of detergent from a cabinet above the machine and poured out what seemed like about the right amount, then pulled the knob without bothering to reset the dial from its current position, figuring he'd probably get it wrong anyway. He was fairly proud of himself when he heard water running into the drum; he hadn't done a load of laundry since before he and the old woman had got married, and even back then he'd usually sent it out.

As the cycle got under way he looked around the utility room. Hanging on the off-white wall above a stack of plastic laundry baskets was a framed poster advertising some art show at some museum he'd never heard of. A painting of a bunch of apples and oranges in a bowl, it reminded him that he was hungry, so he climbed the stairs to get something to eat.

For a minute he stood stark naked in front of the freezer, trying to decide what to make from the bewildering variety of frozen foods stocked in it. When he felt his scrotum begin to shrink in the frigid breeze, he grabbed a box of pizza rolls and set the oven to 450.

While he waited for the oven to heat up the phone rang. After four rings the machine picked up, and he heard Loretta's voice again saying they were out. Might as well have mentioned where the key was hidden and where the good silver was. If he knew how to record a new message he would have done it himself.

'Hello? Eric? It's Teresa. I really need to talk to you before I do payroll. If you get this before you come in give me a call.' There was a pause, and the woman sighed dramatically on the other end before she hung up.

He found a cookie sheet, emptied the whole box of pizza rolls on to it and looked at the oven. He decided it was probably almost hot enough and stuck them in, then set the egg timer next to the stove to twelve minutes.

I'd sure like to live in a house again, he thought as he stood there waiting for the light on the oven door to go off. He'd spent the twenty-two years between his third and fourth marriages living in bachelor apartments and efficiency studios, sad dark rooms with murphy beds and hotplate kitchens he never used. He had a sudden flash of his old nightstand in one of those apartments, crowded with pictures of his daughters, of his mother and his stepmother, and a good sexy one of Dot in her nurse's uniform, looking sidelong at the lens with a sly, horny smile. She'd given it to him before he left for the war, though she was mad as hell at him for going, and years later when they got back together she was surprised to see that he'd kept it. That one was on the wall at their house, and the ones of his daughters and his stepmother, too, but he wondered what had become of the picture of his mother. Maybe his sister Gertrude had it, or one of his daughters. In the picture she was seated on a swing in a photographer's studio before a painted garden back-drop, her head tilted so that her curls fell to her left shoulder, smiling sweetly and looking exactly as he remembered her, maybe because the photo was the main source for the memory. He was six years old when she died of the flu, right at the end of the war, only twenty-three and already the mother of three tiny children.

Grethe had immigrated with her parents at fifteen, married Gunther's father at sixteen, and given birth to Gunther three months after her seventeenth birthday. She didn't know much English and never spoke it at home, and whenever Gunther thought of her he thought in the simple German of a small child. Just a few months after her death his little sisters wouldn't speak it with him any more, even with their father out of earshot. The elder Fahnstiel disdained the language of his parents, and after Grethe's death he decreed that German was no longer to be spoken in his house. Gunther's name was thereafter pronounced exclusively Gunn-ther in the American manner, a pronunciation he remembered his mother mocking. She had called him Günther, the vowel in its first syllable narrower and sweeter to his ear than anything in English; it was more than twenty-seven years before he heard that sound again, from a German woman trying unsuccessfully to trade a blow job for half a loaf of bread. He was an MP then, the war just over, and when she saw she wasn't getting anywhere she asked him his first name.

'Gunn-ther,' he had replied, though they were speaking German. Even to him it sounded strange in that context.

She asked him to repeat it, and then spell it, and when he did she laughed. 'Günther!' she said, and she sounded so much like his mother he went ahead and gave her the bread for nothing.

Two years after Grethe's death the family moved to Cottonwood, a slightly larger town thirty miles to the east where his father, a stonemason, had found a regular position with a chance for advancement. By then he had remarried, and despite himself Gunther still thought of his stepmother Nellie as his mother most of the time; when he did think of Grethe it was with sorrow and shame at having allowed another to eclipse her in his affections. He was trying to remember the German word his mother had used to refer to his baby sisters when the egg timer went off and, looking in through the oven window, he saw that the pizza rolls were leaking their sizzling insides on to the cookie sheet.

*

Dot had expected she wouldn't feel much like eating, but when the time came she found that she was ravenous. She heated up the electric skillet and fried four strips of bacon, carefully removing them at just the point when the fat and lean parts were equally chewy, before the lard disappeared into the skillet and the meat got crumbly. She toasted and buttered two pieces of white bread and discovered that she had neither lettuce nor tomato in the fridge. She slapped a little mayonnaise on to the top slice and put the sandwich together, leaving it whole. Standing at the sink she ate it from the corner inward, washing down every other bite with a mouthful of iced tea.

She lit a cigarette and wondered if there was any way she could find the rock quarry herself. How many of them could there be, after all, in this part of the state? She didn't know how to go about looking for it, though. She'd awakened from an uneasy nap just as Gunther was getting back from hiding the money and burying the man they'd run over. Ten years gone by and she could still hardly stand to think about that, even knowing what she knew about the young man who'd stopped to help them that morning.

There was a knock on the front door and it opened before she could ask who it was. Her granddaughter Tricia tossed her purse on the couch.

'Hi, Moomaw. I thought you might like some company,' she said.

Truthfully Dot would have preferred to be alone, but she knew Tricia wouldn't understand that. 'Thanks,' she said. 'You want a bacon sandwich?'

Tricia smiled politely, or tried to; her expression was more akin to a grimace. 'Actually, no thanks. Got anything lower fat?'

'Christ on a crutch, look at you! You're skinny as a rail. Why are you worried about calories?'

'It's the saturated fat, Moomaw, and the cholesterol and the nitrosamines and the sodium, not the calories.' Tricia sat down on the arm of the couch, a maddening habit her grandchildren all shared that she forced herself not to comment upon.

'I know what it's got in it. I'm not asking you to eat two of them for lunch every day 'til you're my age, I just wanted to know if you wanted one right now.'

'No, thanks.' Tricia was still making that face, though less severely.

'Anyway, what about protein? It's lousy with protein. Don't forget I was a nurse for goddamn near forty years, and I still know a thing or two about nutrition.' She took a long, ostentatious drag on the cigarette, daring Tricia to make a comment.

'You're right. Sorry. You want to play gin rummy or something?'

She thought for a minute. 'What I'd really like is to get out of the house for a few minutes.'

Tricia shrugged. 'Sure. What if Gunther gets here while we're gone, though?'

'He won't. If he does he'll wait around. Come on. How'd you like to drive me out to the mall?'

*

Steve Blasik sat across from Loretta in the dining room at Lupe's doing his best to make her want to go to bed with him, a possibility she'd never entertained before and wasn't entertaining now. He leaned across the table, maintaining constant eye contact, talked about her and not himself, wondered how things were going at home -- Eric's visit had provided him with an excellent opener there -- and discreetly complimented her changed appearance, though he was quick to add that he'd always found her attractive.

By the time drinks were served he was holding her hand across the tabletop. She felt herself redden, debated yanking the hand away and decided not to. She enjoyed being the object of public affection, something she hadn't experienced in a long time. When their appetizers came his hand had moved under the table, where it came to rest gently on her knee, stroking it lightly until she removed it a millisecond later, giving no other indication that she'd even noticed its presence there.

Now she felt the conversation developing more explicitly in the absurd direction of their sleeping together, maybe even that afternoon. She was discouraging that turn every way she knew how when she looked up to see Skeeter Garcinich, his thin nostrils pinched in anger, arms folded across his chest, his face as red as hers felt.

'Hey, Skeeter.' She couldn't think of anything else to say. Two years before Skeeter had shown up at the house early one evening and angrily informed her that their spouses had been having an affair. By that time Eric's infidelities no longer qualified as news, and she saw that her attitude of resignation disappointed him. That Lacey would ever do such a thing was clearly a shock to him, and though Loretta failed to dissolve into the emotional, weepy mess he'd apparently been expecting, he went ahead and suggested that they exact revenge by sleeping with each other.

The multitude of reasons she'd had for turning him down started with the fact that his entire motivation seemed to be paying Eric and Lacey back, rather than any actual interest in her; also working against him was her suspicion that, despite his self-righteous anger at his unfaithful wife, he was at least as promiscuous as Eric. Finally there'd been the problem of that name; it was impossible to imagine herself moaning 'Skeeter' in a passionate moment without laughing.

Steve pulled his chair back, prepared to stand but clearly hoping he wouldn't have to. 'What seems to be your problem?'

'My problem is this paragon of virtue here. You know Eric saw you a minute ago? Holding hands with your boyfriend here? You have any idea how hurt that man was?'

'Not very, I bet,' she said, though the idea delighted her. She looked at the surrounding tables, relieved and, to her surprise, slightly disappointed to see no faces she recognized among those pretending not to eavesdrop.

Steve was on his feet now. 'Time to go, pal.'

Skeeter ignored him. 'What's so fuckin' special about him? What the hell's he got?'

'We're just eating lunch, Skeeter,' she said.

'Lunch,' Skeeter said, his upper lip curled as though reviling the very concept of a midday meal.

'You leaving or what?' Steve said, and mentally Loretta tried to handicap a fight between them. Steve was younger than Skeeter, thirty-five at the outside, and in good shape besides, but her money would have been on Skeeter, who was mean and, according to Eric, without scruples.

Skeeter dismissed Steve with a millisecond's glance, then turned his attention back to Loretta. 'I never wanted you anyway. I was just trying to make you feel better about Eric trying to fuck every other woman he meets.' He turned and stomped away in the direction of the front door.

Before sitting back down Steve stood next to her and touched her shoulder. 'You okay?'

'I'm fine,' she said. 'Sit down.'

He kept standing there, rubbing her back from side to side as though reading an inscription in braille on her brassiere. 'You sure you're okay?'

'Sit down, Steve,' she said, and it was a command this time. He took his seat, looking like he'd just guessed correctly what the outcome of today's lunch would be. Most likely he wrongly blamed his failure to seduce on Skeeter's interruption and the accompanying shift in mood.

'Who was that, anyway? Some friend of your husband's?'

'Yeah. He made a pass at me once.'

'Some friend,' he said, and his contempt for such behavior seemed genuine.

CHAPTER TEN

WAYNE OGDEN: 19–20 JUNE, 1952

I was driving the Plymouth through miles of empty space, or what seemed empty to me. Actually every plot of land I passed was planted with something or other, wheat most likely, although they might as well have been fields of banana trees or venus flytraps for all I cared. To be honest I didn't remember what they grew around here, exactly. I was a full-fledged city kid, and I never gave a damn about agriculture. All I'd cared about growing up here as a boy were airplanes, both the flying and building of them, which now occupied a rung of my consciousness just above sorghum and barley; all I cared about now was making a living. At the moment I also cared about getting laid, but that would evaporate soon enough.

I'd gone way north on Washington up to 49th street, then headed west toward the Hitching Post. I'd just spent a couple of hours at the Commanche, mostly talking to a certain Amos Culligan, who claimed to be Sally's shop steward and who split a third of the monthly take between the union and himself. I was taken aback to find such a talker at the center of such an enterprise; in my operation he would have been long gone before he had a chance to blabber anything to anybody. I was glad to have met him, though. He gave me a lot of information I expected to have to work hard for over the course of several nights. He was about forty, and not stupid, really, just one of those guys who got that way every time sex entered the picture. The occupation army was full of guys just like him, or rather it had been.

In the Plymouth's passenger seat sat a young woman named Lena. She was talking about Senator Taft, who she thought ought to be President.

'Damn Democrats got us into two wars in a row, and Eisenhower's not likely to do any different,' she said, failing to consider that from my perspective a desire to keep the U.S.A. out of another war might be a drawback in a presidential candidate.

Her slur was considerably more pronounced than when she and her friends had introduced themselves to me and the shop steward earlier. The girl she'd come in with had latched on to a fellow who worked for the *Beacon*, and I noticed that Culligan clammed up about Sally's deal when he came around. He probably thought of that as being extra cautious. When last call came the girls conferred and Lena announced to me that I'd be driving her home. She was young, younger than twenty-five anyway, and married to somebody who pissed her off by working for a living. I thought I'd take her to the Hitching Post and see how things stood there, have a drink or two and then head for her place. She was so drunk we could probably have done it in the backseat in the parking lot of the Commanche, but I felt like the luxury of a bed, and I didn't want her to know I could be found at the Bellingham.

She was still on the subject of Taft when we parked at the Hitching Post. She laughed at the neon hillbilly and held on to my arm going in. She was a nice looking, slightly heavy girl, prettier than any of the whores inside, and nicely dressed, too. I had on my new clothes and intended them and her to be as provocative as my uniform had been a few nights earlier. If I wasn't on solid ground here, I'd find out fast.

The Commanche had been jumping, but the Hitching Post was having a slow evening. Elishah's car wasn't there, and he wasn't inside. Beulah was sitting at the bar, though, and the same bartender was on duty.

'Well, look who's back, and dressed to beat the band, too,' she said. 'I was afraid those boys'd scared you away.'

I pulled out a thick roll of bills and made sure Beulah saw it; I knew she'd made a note of my cash supply the other night. 'Bourbon,' I said, and the bartender waved the wad of green away.

'You still got most of a ten in credit from the other night.'

What do you know, I thought, a bartender who's on the square. 'Bourbon for me, then, and whatever the lady wants, and another round for the house.'

Lena asked for a Bloody Mary and settled for a beer, and as the bartender poured the round and rang the bell I spotted a couple of the guys from the other night, both of whom nodded at me as they came up to get their drinks.

Neither seemed unfriendly; a little sheepish, maybe, the way you might get if somebody you'd beaten up bought you a drink.

'I like a good sport, Sarge,' Beulah said. She had on a green dress cut pretty much like the one she had on the other night. 'Who's your friend?'

'Beulah, this is Lena.' My new friend was having trouble just looking at Beulah without staring at her face, something Beulah was clearly used to.

'Pleased to meet you, Lena. You sure have snagged yourself a fine handsome man here.'

'I'm married,' Lena said, the way a child might suddenly announce 'I'm five.'

'That's nice.'

Somebody put a nickel in the jukebox and a hillbilly record started playing.

'Mind if I snag your fella for a dance?' Beulah asked, and Lena seemed not to have heard. A minute later I was dancing with Beulah, a close, slow dance completely unsuited to the idiotically jumpy tune.

She murmured into my ear, and I could smell the perfume behind hers. 'I'm glad you came back, Army Man. Even if it is with a pretty kid like her. Where'd you meet her, a high school hop?'

'She says she's in college.'

'Uh-huh. Well, once you drop her off at home you feel free to come back in the wee hours of the morning, maybe we can have a party of our own.'

'Maybe tomorrow.'

'Suit yourself. I may be spoken for tomorrow, who knows.'

She was completely sure of herself, ugly as she was. Maybe that self-confidence was part of the attraction; in any case by the time the song ended I was pressing a full-blown erection against her belly. Another song started and the tall, balding man I'd seen in the parking lot the night before cut in. I found Lena at the bar nursing a grudge against Beulah.

'Two of those yokels asked me to dance,' she said.

'So how come you didn't?'

'Because I came with you. Come on, let's go over to my house and have some fun.'

I was all for that. I waved at the bartender and a couple of the regulars and we headed out. I was glad to see that I was still welcome at the Hitching Post as promised, and once I was done screwing Lena I might head back.

She lived in a little house near the river. She had me drop her off, then park around the corner and walk in the back way as quick as I could to reduce the risk of the neighbors seeing me go in.

It was a little brick house with a low fence enclosing a tiny terrace in front. Around back was a yard with some big old trees in it, and that reminded me of the white cottage Sally and I had rented before the war. As soon as I got into the house Lena held up her face for a kiss, and before she got the lights on we were in the bedroom.

'You're only the second guy I've cheated on Doug with,' she said matter-of-factly but slowly, concentrating too hard on the suddenly difficult task of unbuttoning her blouse. I told her I had to go to the bathroom and as I pissed I wondered who the first guy was, feeling a little sorry for poor Doug.

When I opened the bedroom door, she was passed out on the bed and snoring; it looked like we weren't going to be having any fun after all. I covered her with a blanket and went into the living room. It was filled with books, most of which appeared to predate the marriage, having either his or her name written on the flyleaf. His interest was history, whereas her specialty was English Literature, and I thumbed through his copy of the Byrd translation of Procopius's *The Secret History*, wishing I could still read it in the original Latin. Of course if I really wanted to there was nothing to stop me brushing up on it.

I could still hear her snoring as I stepped out the front door. I'd noted her phone number on the dial, and if things got slow maybe I'd call her some evening.

I drove back to the Hitching Post, where the first thing I noticed was Elishah's Oldsmobile, parked in that same spot next to the sign. It was close to four in the morning when I walked in, and once again Elishah sat at a table all by himself, staring at Beulah as she danced with some other guy. I switched to beer for the duration of the evening, and as the bartender served me he nodded at Elishah. 'He's in about the same mood he was in the other night.'

Elishah didn't seem to have spotted me, and when the song ended and Beulah came over and sat next to me he looked at me with no sign of recognition.

'So you slipped it to your college girl and you're calling on old Beulah for seconds?'

'Didn't get a chance. She passed out on me and I put her to bed.'

'A gentleman on top of it all. What more could a girl ask for?'

I tensed up as Elishah rose and moved toward us, but he was fixed on her and not me. 'Beulah, I was wondering if I could have the next dance.'

'Elishah, I'm talking to someone right now. We'll dance later, maybe.'

He looked closely at me now. 'Okay,' he said without much hostility, and he went back to his table to stare off into the distance.

'He doesn't seem to mind me as much tonight,' I said.

'It was your uniform set him off before. Most likely he doesn't realize you're the same guy.'

'What's he got against soldiers?'

'He didn't get to be one. He volunteered right after Pearl Harbor and got turned down, and you know how that was for some guys. He's had a chip on his shoulder since I've known him.'

The door opened and a woman stumbled as she crossed the threshold with a blond-haired, freckle-faced guy with front teeth so big they looked fake. If you dressed him in overalls and a straw hat he could have been the inspiration for the hillbilly on the sign outside. Beulah nodded at the woman, whom I hadn't seen before; her hair was hennaed red and her lips painted orange to match, and she sat the bucktoothed guy down at a table by himself before coming up and sitting on the other side of Beulah.

'Bernice, this is Sergeant McCowan. I'm gonna knock off at five-thirty since I didn't take a break, and Sergeant McCowan and me are going back to my crib for a party.'

Bernice looked at me carefully, or maybe it was at my new clothes. 'Sometime maybe the three of us could have a little party, if you want.'

I danced with Beulah a few more times and so did Elishah, and the whole time they spun around on the floor he was talking to her quietly, maybe pleading, I thought, and she closed her eyes, listening to the song on the jukebox and acting as if she couldn't hear a word he said. When five-thirty finally came, I was ready for trouble, but he just silently watched us go, looking more sad than angry. Something about him right then reminded me of a greasy haired, emaciated Duke of Windsor.

'Where exactly are we heading?' I asked, leading her to the Plymouth.

'I live at the Crosley, downtown. You know where that is?'

I did. When I was a kid it was a nice hotel, about half residential, but during the depression it had been sold, and its new owners had allowed it to deteriorate physically; by the time I'd left town it had developed a reputation as a den of iniquity, populated by whores and dope fiends. It hadn't started renting by the hour yet, but it was heading in that general direction.

As I pulled on to the road she pulled the last cigarette out of a pack. 'I hope you got smokes on you 'cause this is my last.' She lit it, crumpled the pack and tossed it out her window.

'Offhand I'd say old Elishah's a little smitten with you.'

'Smitten.' She giggled, a sound that didn't sound right somehow, coming from her. 'Listen to you. Yeah, Elishah's carrying a torch. He doesn't like to see me go off with anybody else, but shit, what's he think I do for a living?'

'Doesn't he want any of the other girls?'

She shook her head. 'See, every once in a while I take a liking to a fellow, and I start giving him special treatment. You know, freebies. Hanging around together off hours. It was that way with Elishah for a while, and then . . .' She shrugged. 'I'm taking kind of a liking to you.'

'That's good.'

'I'm still on the clock, though,' Beulah said. 'You left with me from the club, so I'm gonna have to collect.'

'I was planning to pay anyway.' The idea that fucking Beulah would be free of charge hadn't even entered my mind; I knew exactly what she was really taking kind of a liking to.

The sky to the east was getting to be a lighter blue now, the clouds in the distance orange and faint pink, and for an unsettling moment I had to think whether it was a sunrise or a sunset. My sense of day and night, of today and tomorrow and yesterday, was completely out of joint now, a disorienting but not altogether unpleasant sensation. It had been that way when I'd first arrived in Japan; the difference this time was that I was making no attempt to get synchronized with the locals. My conversation with the shop steward, Culligan – had that been last night, or was that tonight? Was it the next day already, since the sun was coming up, or had the new day started when I woke up at the hotel? What time was it in Japan, anyway?

I parked in the Crosley's small, weedy lot and we went inside. In the morning light the lobby looked like the nice

157

hotel it had been once; it was only when you looked closely at the wallpaper or the carpet, or took a deep sniff, that it was clearly at the tail end of a steep decline. There was nobody at the front desk, but she had her key in her purse, and we climbed the stairs to the sixth floor. The hallway wasn't as bad as the lobby. It was clean, and though the carpet was worn down the center it was intact. A tall old woman came out of one of the other rooms wearing a bathrobe and slippers and glared at Beulah. When she was safely down the stairs Beulah looked over her shoulder and grinned. 'Mrs. Grenwald. She lived here back when it was nice, and she doesn't like anybody else who's moved in since. Sometimes I like to introduce her to whatever fellow's with me, just to get a rise out of her.'

She opened the door and I was surprised to see a clean, comfortable looking room with a nice view of downtown to the south. The light coming through the window cast long shadows, and she reached up and started unpinning her hair. When it came down, past her shoulders, the effect was startling. Framed that way, her face wasn't half as bad as it looked in the bar. You wouldn't call her pretty, but it did a lot to balance out that jaw.

'Would you like me to strip, or do you want to undress me?' she asked. 'I'm ready for anything. And I mean anything you can think of.'

*

At that point all I wanted was a straightforward missionary-position screwing, and after a little of the old soixante-neuf to get us warmed up we went at it. It lasted longer than I had expected, given my recent bout of celibacy; every time

I was on the verge of ejaculation I thought about my lost money back in Tokyo, which was distraction enough for a nice long roll. It was good to be fucking a big-bodied American girl after such a long time in Japan, and when I finally did finish I clung to her for a minute, my hands cupped on her shoulders from underneath, not moving, my body still tensed with the final inward stroke, relaxing slowly before I rolled off her and into a sitting position with my feet on the floor.

By that time the sun was all the way up, the sky blue and cloudless, and the downtown traffic was getting heavy. She smiled as casually as if we'd been dancing and bummed a cigarette. Once it was lit she got up and limped into the bathroom, and instead of washing her off my raw, reddened dick in the sink in the middle of the pathetic kitchenette I went to the tiny closet and quietly opened it. In the bathroom I could hear the water running as I took a quick inventory. There was an ancient and badly painted dresser inside, like the one in Elishah's closet, and quietly opening the drawers I found exactly one brassiere, three pairs of panties and one pair of stockings. Hanging from the bar was a single dress, orange, cut in the same style as the two I'd seen her wearing, a single blouse, white, and a skirt, black. There were no shoes. The dresser was three or four inches from the wall, and running my hand up the back of it I found taped to it a small glassine envelope containing a fine white powder. I wet my pinkie and tasted a minuscule amount, then closed it back up and replaced it. There wasn't a track mark anywhere on her, I knew that much.

I shut the closet door, lay back down on the bed and

fired up a Lucky, staring at the ceiling and wondering for some odd reason what was happening back in Tokyo. For years I'd been waiting patiently for the end of the occupation, for that moment when all the rackets would be in the air and up for grabs: girls, gambling, narcotics. I had no room to bitch; I'd done well during MacArthur's time and even better afterward. A smart operator now, though, would be in a position to set himself up for life, and if I ever got my hands on the Frenchman who fucked me out of it, I was going to kill him and resurrect him, then kill him again.

I'd only been able to take three thousand dollars American in cash with me when I left, and even that much was a risk; greenbacks were strictly forbidden, and if I'd been caught with it on my way out of Japan it would have been confiscated on the spot and I'd have been jugged. I had another twenty thousand bucks or so stashed away in various spots, but by now the Criminal Investigations Division had their hands on most or all of it. The rest was in scrip and worthless outside Japan, and by the time it was safe for me to go back it'd be worthless there, too.

Apart from the money, though, the timing had been perfect; I'd just learned that I had business at home to take care of. I knew how to skirt channels, too, and by the time the intrepid Lieutenant McCowan got wind of the fact that I'd even applied for my furlough I was already out of Asia with a duffel bag full of legitimate-looking papers, some of them in his own name.

I pulled my nailclippers out of my pocket and started cutting my fingernails, letting the clippings pop into the air and on to the floor. I was already done with my left hand by the time Beulah stepped out of the bathroom, still naked, and sat down on the bed next to me. 'You gonna wash up? If you want to catch a little shut-eye you can. Maybe you'll feel like some more afterward.'

I knew I would, but right now I was bothered by her lying. I stood up and went into the bathroom and soaped up my joint. 'So how long you lived here, Beulah?'

'In town? I got here in '47.'

'Here at the Crosley.'

'Since my husband got killed, in '49.'

'How'd he get killed?'

'This guy I was seeing shot him.'

'No shit.'

'Jimmy'd pulled a knife on him. They said it was self-defense.'

Rinsing myself off, I admired her ability to lie without registering anything on her gruesome pan at all; her husband was alive and dependent on her to feed his narcotic habit. I decided to crowd her a little. 'You ever feel like something bigger than this? A little more space? Something for two, maybe?'

'I hope you're not suggesting a shackup after one quick fuck.'

As I re-entered the room I got another good look at that body of hers, soft here and firm there, and glad to do anything that came into my head.

'I just thought of something else,' I said, feeling myself stiffen. She leaned back on to her elbows, arching her back.

'Tell me about it,' she said softly.

'Roll over,' I said, and she raised her ass compliantly

into the air as she did so. Screwing her the second time, it struck me as funny that this ten-dollar whore thought she and her hillbilly consort Elishah were putting one over on the likes of Master Sergeant Wayne Ogden, and I started laughing so hard that she gave me a troubled look over her shoulder.

'What's funny, baby?' she asked.

I didn't break stride, just kept going at it and laughing. I could tell it was annoying the hell out of her, but after a while she started moaning and carrying on and pretending it was the greatest boning she'd ever had. Beulah was nothing if not a professional.

CHAPTER ELEVEN

The parking lot at the Sweet Cage was three-quarters full when Sidney got there, not bad for almost two o'clock in the afternoon on a weekday. Inside there was a bachelor party in progress around stage two, its participants in red or yellow power ties and suspenders, their jackets draped over their chairs, all of them doing those high-pitched rebel yells that seemed to be an essential part of the striptease business; at least it meant they'd probably been buying drinks.

Stage one was doing lighter business; a few regulars and some yuppies who weren't part of the bachelor party, breathlessly watching the athletic, elaborately choreographed moves of Tyfannee, a small, wiry woman with a wild mane of bleached hair and no visible fat on her body. Her breasts stuck straight out from her chest like pink and brown antigravity devices, each one looking as supple and soft as a bag of Gold Medal flour. Her nose was half its original length and width, her lips so densely packed with collagen she actually had trouble speaking, and Sidney wondered, as he often did on seeing Tyfannee, what she must have looked like in her natural state. Midway between her carefully trimmed pubic hair and her navel – which, she had told him during her initial job interview, she'd had surgically converted from an outie to an innie – was a tattoo of a tigress, leaping at the viewer. 'Springing out of the bush, get it?' Tattooing was another element of the business that had changed over the years; there had always been a higher incidence of tattoos among the dancers than in the general population of midwestern women, but when Sidney had started out they were mostly of the jail-house variety, drawn with faded blue ink, simple in design and not too different from the tattoos men wore – skulls, dragsters, the signs of the zodiac, the occasional cross. Now they were multicolored and professional-looking, another supposed improvement that left Sidney cold.

Dennis was nowhere in sight so he stopped at the bar, where a single tall bartender, ponytailed and balding, was working frantically to keep up with the bachelor party's considerable demands.

'Where's Dennis? Where are the lights?'

The bartender shrugged. 'How should I know? I'm totally fucking swamped back here. If you see him tell him I need help.'

On his way to the office a woman he didn't know in a bikini approached him carrying an empty drink tray and scowling.

'You just get here?'

'Yeah.'

'Heading for the can?'

'Maybe.'

'You have to order a drink first,' she snapped, sounding like she'd caught him at something. She had the ubiquitous fake tits and a hard expression to go with the body, and she stood blocking his path, feet planted firmly and palm held out like a traffic cop's to stop him.

He could have gently or even curtly explained to her that he was the owner, but he decided to press the conflict on. A customer in this situation might have left in a huff, and Sidney didn't like customers walking out before they'd spent lots of money.

'No I don't.'

'House policy. One drink minimum. What'll you have?' She was still scowling at him. He hoped she was a great dancer, because she was the worst fucking cocktail waitress he'd seen in twenty years.

'I won't have anything.'

'Then get your ass out of here before I call the manager.'

'Better call him.'

'Dennis,' she yelled, her tone rising sharply, along with the volume, on the heavily stressed second syllable.

If he's down to serving as his own bouncer, Sidney thought, we've got worse personnel problems than I thought. Dennis came out of the office looking harried, and before he had a chance to say anything the woman shrieked at him. 'I just eightysixed this cocksucker and he won't leave!' Her voice was shrill and loud enough to be heard over the Van Halen on the PA. On the other side of the club the bachelor party took note, craning their necks to see who the troublemaker was and hoping to see a fight.

'That's Sidney, Bambee. He's the owner,' he said in a wearier drone than usual. 'Don't antagonize him.'

Bambee looked back at Sidney resentfully, trying to decide whether Dennis was fucking with her or not.

'Give me one reason I shouldn't fire her ass right here on the spot,' Sidney said.

'Sidney, meet Bambee. Bambee, Sidney. Here's two right off the bat. If she doesn't finish her shift, we don't have anybody to serve drinks.'

'How about you?'

'I don't think I'd make much in the way of tips with this chest here.'

'What's the other?'

'She's a hell of a dancer with a very loyal following that we don't want to lose to the Classy Lady.'

'Get back to work, then,' Sidney said, and she turned away expressionlessly and marched to the bar.

'What'd she do? Usually takes a lot to set you off with the girls.'

'She needs to improve her people skills.'

'As a matter of fact, I'm reliably informed that her people skills are pretty extraordinary,' Dennis said. 'Which probably accounts partially for that loyal following.'

'Yeah, well, make sure she keeps a low fucking profile on that score or she's out the door. That gets to be common knowledge and we've got big-ass troubles, and not just with the cops, either.' Three years before Sidney had been obligated to let a couple of dancers go after an angry local entrepreneur called on him in person to inform him that the pair were turning tricks in the parking lot of the Tease-O-Rama after hours. One of them went to work at the Classy Lady and the other joined the payroll of the entrepreneur who'd blown the whistle on her.

'She knows that, Sidney. I've been drilling it into her head since the day she got here. Discretion.'

'Well then you need to drill in something else about not pissing off the clientele.' He handed Dennis a dozen or so flyers. 'Here, put these up, would you?'

Dennis squinted at them. 'Twelve grand? I may start looking for the old coot myself.'

'Good luck,' Sidney said. He nodded at Bambee on the way out, a conciliatory gesture that she met with a scowl.

*

The Arlington Home for the Aged was a low-slung brick building extending from either side of a central reception area. Behind the receptionist's desk was a picture window through which an indoor commons could be seen, and waiting for the Home's director Ed watched the old folks through the glass; some were reading, some playing board games, and three couples danced to music from a record player. He was watching a pair of men, both about ninety, engaged in a tournament of arm wrestling. The smaller of the two had just won his second fall when the director opened the door to his office and invited Ed in.

The office was cramped and unadorned except for the director's medical diploma and the facility's license to operate, and styrofoam coffee cups filled the trashcan. One sat on the director's desk; he took a quick sip, grimaced and spat it back into the cup without embarrassment or apology.

'I don't know how much information you're allowed to give out without a court order,' Ed said, watching the other man's face carefully, 'but I need to know the dates when a patient named Rory Blaine was here.'

The director touched his black eyeglasses and smiled, not bothered at all by the implied legal threat. 'Not a problem at all, Mr. Dieterle. Hold on just a minute . . .' He swiveled his chair to a filing cabinet and opened the top drawer. 'Blaine, Blaine, Blaine . . . Bingo, Blaine. Mr. Blaine moved out on the third of September of eighty-six.'

'Right around when they opened Lake Vista.'

The director looked over his glasses at Ed. 'Exactly. He had been with us since February twelfth of nineteen eighty.'

'His monthly fees were how much?'

'All I'm at liberty to tell you is they were less than Lake Vista's.'

'Taken care of by the Police Officers' Pension Fund?'

'Now we're getting into the realm of what you'd need a court order for.'

Ed stood up. 'Thanks for your help.'

'Mr. Blaine is doing well at the other facility?'

'As well as you could expect,' Ed said, and he thanked him as he left. He noted that the arm wrestling continued in the commons, and had drawn a small crowd.

*

It was already too late to take advantage of the Chimney-sweep's dollar Bloody Mary Special, which ran from 8 to 11 a.m., so Eric ordered another margarita from the elderly, unfriendly bartender, who didn't know him and didn't care whether this was the way he usually looked or not.

Even in the forgiving light and casual ambience of the Chimneysweep it had been a tossup when he walked in the door as to whether he'd be served or not, and only the intervention of the owner's brother-in-law, sitting at the far end of the bar, gained him admittance and the right to order a drink.

The brother-in-law's name was Rex, and he was in every day to make sports book. 'No offense, Gandy, but old Freddy's got a point. What the hell happened to you?'

'I got stuck without wallet or keys all the way across town and I had to walk back.'

'In this heat? Jesus Christ. You coulda gotten heat stroke, you know that? Especially drunk. You get all dehydrated like that and next thing you know—' He slapped his hand down hard on to the bar and lolled his head over to the side, eyes bulging out and tongue hanging out the side of his mouth.

'I'm not all that drunk.'

'You sure smell like you are. So how's business? I hear that Trade Mart of yours is gonna be the next big thing.'

'Yeah. Still working on the financing.' He signaled for another margarita.

'You know who you ought to talk to is old Danny Orville, over at South Kansas Federal.'

'Met with him last week, they're crunching the numbers. Waiting to hear.' Freddy sat the second drink in front of him, and with a single swig he drained half of it.

The phone rang and the bartender picked up, then signalled to Rex, who picked up a Princess phone next to his elbow.

'Uh-huh. Gotcha.' He hung up, pulled out a small notebook and wrote something down. 'You want some action while I got this out?'

'You take dog bets?'

Rex stared contemplatively into the distance. 'Hm. Greyhound racing. Is that some kind of sport with an unpredictable outcome?'

Eric knew he was being mocked, but he didn't want to alienate Rex. He nodded. 'Sure.'

'Then I guess I take dog bets.'

He had fourteen dollars left. He was almost ready to go; between the heat and the long walk, daytime drinking wasn't as much fun as he'd thought it might be. He was still disoriented from the sight of Loretta and her lover, too, and he knew he was just a few drinks short of getting melancholy. One more margarita would leave him eleven to bet. He reached over Rex for the sports page of the morning paper and looked at the racing page. Not much in the way of handicapping information, but he knew a lot of the dogs, and sometimes just the trainer's name was enough for him to go on.

'I like Rusty in the eighth.'

Rex nodded. 'Win?'

'Five to win, five on an exacta with Prince o' Chincoteague.'

Rex noted the bets and replaced the notebook in his hip pocket. 'Best of luck.'

Eric could feel his head begin to swim, and he ordered his last margarita. When Freddy served it Eric gave him three of the four dollars he had left, slipping the leftover bill back into his shirt pocket; old Freddy sure as shit wasn't getting a tip out of Eric Gandy.

*

Dot sat watching the passing cross streets from the passenger window of her granddaughter's car and mentally retracing as much as she could of the route to the quarry, but she'd been asleep for most of it. All she knew for sure was that it started out southbound on the turnpike, which is where she'd fallen asleep, and then once you got close there were a bunch of turns on a series of dirt roads.

'Are you okay, Moomaw?'

'I'm fine. What were you saying?'

'Nothing, just talking about school.' Tricia was starting med school in the fall, and her intelligence mystified Dot as much as her sweetness; neither was in great supply at any recent point in her family tree. 'I applied for a semester abroad program at the medical school in Heidelberg. That'd be in two years.'

'Well, if you think that'd make you a better doctor.' Dot didn't think it would; Tricia had spent one semester over there already, which she and Gunther had helped pay for, and that seemed like enough. 'Sure is nice that a girl can grow up to be a doctor now,' she said.

'It's not a new thing, Moomaw. There've been women doctors since the turn of the century or before, even.'

'Well, excuse me, miss, but I can promise you in my day it wasn't considered an option.' She knew she shouldn't be snapping at the girl, who'd been nothing but obliging to her since she'd shown up. Tricia kept driving and didn't seem to notice. 'I'm just real proud of you, is all, honey. Me and Gunther both. We'd always hoped we'd be able to help send you off to school, but with Gunther in the home now, you know...'

'Moomaw, that's okay. I don't think Daddy's having any trouble coming up with it. I appreciate your wanting to help.'

She was polite as hell and gracious, too, more traits that set her apart from the rest of the family. Must have skipped a couple or three generations, she thought, her own grandmother being the last such personality type to show up in the family line. If both the girls and the boy hadn't looked just like Sidney when they were babies she would have suspected they weren't his.

God knew their mother was capable of such a thing. When the girls were about two and six years old and the boy four it had become clear to everybody that she wasn't fit to care for them any more, and she still remembered the day she was babysitting because Sidney had to work and Christine was off who knew where and little Tricia had found a drawerful of drug paraphernalia. 'What's this, Moomaw,' she'd asked, some kind of vile narcoticky-looking thing dangling from her six-year-old hand, all blown glass and rubber hoses. She'd read Sidney the goddamn riot act that evening when he got home, and though in her heart she was certain he would never use drugs himself, she certainly blamed him for looking the other way while his wife ran wild. By the time they split up for good, Christine had been arrested and was on probation, which according to Gunther she'd been lucky to get. Even then she couldn't stay sober for the custody hearing, all jumpy and irritable and unable to restrain herself from sassing the judge, who'd awarded Sidney full custody, with only monthly supervised visits for her. She reminded Dot back then of a doctor she'd once worked with who, it was whispered on the ward, had become addicted to amphetamines. She thought maybe it was cocaine Christine was using, though, since that seemed to be the drug everyone was talking about back then.

'So what's this book you're looking for, Moomaw?'

'Not a book. A map.'

'Of what?'

'The state. Or the county if they have one.'

'What for?'

She almost snapped at her again, then made herself answer nicely. 'Just thought it might soothe me to look at a map.' In the distance she spotted Sears, at the far end of the mall and a full story higher than the rest of it, and she thought about how there used to be nothing out this far west of town but wheat fields and vacant lots, and how nice that had been.

*

On his way to Dot's house Sidney passed by the old Riverside Zoo and decided to stop. Gunther had always loved the zoo; Sidney remembered clearly how put out he'd been when the new one opened outside town, and it seemed like a decent bet he might end up here. He parked on the street and walked in; there were a few people milling around in the shade of the big old trees, but he saw no one he could ask about putting a few flyers up. He went over to the old Monkey and Lion house and taped one to its padlocked front door. It was an imposing brick building decorated with ornate masonry. Inside it was bare concrete with cages on either side: monkeys to the right, lions to the left, all gone for decades.

Turning away from the door an odd memory fragment surged forward: he was about five years old and a couple of teenage girls were fussing over him while their dad talked to his mom. He was someone she knew from work, and Sidney reluctantly went along with the girls to look at the bear cages, terrified his mother would forget and leave without him.

He taped a flyer to each outer wall of the now-empty bear cages and went back to the car. Slowly, hanging his left arm out the window, he drove through the neighborhood to his mother's house, thinking about the girls. Delighted at the prospect of a few minutes' worth of babysitting experience, they tried hard and failed to cheer him up. He vaguely recalled that their father had bought him some popcorn afterward, at their insistence, which he'd eaten in the car on the way home, and that his mom had asked him not to tell his dad who they'd seen at the zoo.

There was nobody in his mother's living room when Sidney walked into her house, the sudden cold of the air in her front room stinging his eyes and chilling his sweaty shirt, and checking the wall thermostat he found it set to fifty-eight degrees, forty-five or fifty degrees cooler than the air outside. I'd love to see their electric bills sometime, he thought, and then it struck him.

He made a furtive check of the rooms of the house

before he found the note from Tricia on the kitchen counter:

> DADDY:
> Took Moomaw to Towne West for a
> change of scene. Back soon.
> Love
>   Tricia

Five minutes later he was going through their bank statements and bills, and while he saw no indication whatsoever of what was paying the balance of Gunther's nursing home bill, he noted that they hadn't been paying a mortgage for a long time, and that the paperwork on the sale of their RV indicated that they had owned it outright on the date of sale.

In the living room he heard the front door open, and his first instinct was to replace the paperwork and deny everything, but instead he called out 'I'm in here.'

Tricia and Dot appeared in the doorway, and he still had a bank statement in his hand. He stared straight at her, daring her to lie about it or yell at him for digging into her private business. Instead of acting like she'd caught him at something, though, she folded her arms across her chest, her face as closed as he'd ever seen it, and said, 'It's the police pension, I already told you. You're wasting your time.'

*

As his bathwater ran Gunther rummaged through a cabinet next to the tub and found a bottle of Mr. Bubble, enough of which remained to produce copious suds. After scrubbing himself thoroughly he sat back in the warm, foamy water and relaxed until he guessed that the washing was done. He pulled a big, fluffy towel down from the rack and dried himself off, feeling physically and mentally better than he had in years.

The wash cycle was indeed finished. Pleased at having got it right on the first try, Gunther opened the dryer and found to his dismay a dry load of lingerie. He debated for a moment what to do – unloading it would involve handling Loretta's intimate garments, which seemed to him an indecent invasion of her privacy – and decided to throw his wash in with it. He slammed the dryer door shut and pushed the start button, then went back upstairs and started going through drawers to pass the time.

In the boy's room he found a baggie full of dope hidden under a bunch of *MAD* magazines, then put it back. He didn't approve, exactly, but he didn't think it was worth getting hysterical about, either, the way Dot had done when she found a waterpipe at Sidney's house a few years ago. He'd rather arrest a pot fiend than a drunk any day of the week; nobody high on a reefer had ever taken a poke at him. Usually the worst that happened was they'd get to talking and couldn't stop.

Not unlike that barber last night. Gunther looked in the boy's mirror at the haircut. Pretty sharp, he thought, though the shave was all gone to hell and back; he should have had another one that morning. There was no razor in the boy's bathroom – presumably he was off at school somewhere – but Loretta would have to have one, wearing those short dresses like she did, and he headed for the master bathroom.

The delicate pink razor was in the first drawer he opened, and he wondered if women used shaving cream on their legs or just soap, or some other mysterious feminine product entirely. In the big medicine cabinet he found an abundant supply of men's toiletries: shaving cream, razors and blades, aftershave, cologne, deodorant, toothbrush and paste, athlete's foot powder. Maybe her husband had died. No, she'd have pictures up. A boyfriend, maybe? It was a lot of stuff for someone who wasn't a fulltime resident, but if the husband was still around he didn't otherwise leave much of a spoor. Gunther replaced Loretta's razor in the drawer, inserted a fresh blade into the man's razor, and lathered up. It wasn't a really first-rate shave like last night's, but it would keep him presentable until Loretta got there.

Afterward he went back down to check the dryer. The cycle was done but the wash was still damp, his clothes and Loretta's formerly dry undergarments intermingled in a way that, his cheeks burning, made him wish he'd been brave enough to take them out and put them into a basket. He hit the switch again and as the clothes started to spin he decided to play a little pool in the next room. The table, balls and cues were all virtually without wear, and he marveled at the waste of money – it was a good table, sturdy as you'd find in a pool hall – as he racked up.

He broke and began shooting stripes, knocking the straight shots right in and having a little trouble with his bank shot. Once he'd finished with the solids he racked

177

up again, but before he had a chance to break a second time he heard the muffled sound of a door slamming upstairs. He moved to the bottom of the stairs and listened. Someone was in the kitchen, the footfalls too heavy for a woman.

Holding the business end of the cue he crept as quietly as he could up the stairs, and at the top he heard the man, whoever he was, going up the other staircase to the second floor. Maybe it's the son home from college, he thought. He tiptoed across the kitchen and over to the staircase, where he heard the man open the door to one of the bedrooms. He flattened himself against the wall of the stairwell and moved slowly up, thinking maybe it was the husband after all as he stepped into the master bedroom.

*

The man he found going through the dresser was clearly a transient. He was dirty, sunburned, and moving like a drunk; Gunther could smell the booze on him halfway across the room. He wished he had his service revolver with him, but he gamely raised the cue and used his command voice for the first time in a very long while. 'Hey!'

The drunk turned, startled, and looked at Gunther.

'You just broke into the wrong house, partner.'

'I used the key. I live here.' Failing to take his own nudity into account when assessing the man's reaction to him, Gunther took his uncertain tone of voice as evidence of a lie.

'Uh-huh. Looks to me like you haven't slept under a roof in a year.'

'I had a rough night.'

'You live here, huh? Show me some ID.'

The drunk began improvising, always a bad sign. 'I left it at a friend's house.' With a move he no doubt meant to be a surprise, he tried to grab the cue from Gunther, who surprised him with a solid blow across his left temple from the heavy end. The drunk crashed dizzily to his knees, his hands on his head, squinting at the pain.

'Jesus! Who the fuck are you?'

Gunther maneuvered to his flank. 'Did you hear me? What are you doing here?'

'I told you this is my house...' He tried to struggle back to his feet, one hand on the bed and the other on the carpet.

'Lady owns this house is a friend of mine, and I'm damned if I'll let a goddamn dirty bindlestiff like you waltz in here fresh off a fuckin' boxcar and claim he's her husband.'

Gunther slammed the cue into the drunk's left kidney, and as he went down again, eyes closed, hit him hard in the right temple. He lay there, face down on the carpet, and Gunther, once he had verified that he was still breathing, dragged him into the closet. He propped a chair against the door and took the cue back downstairs where it belonged.

CHAPTER TWELVE

GUNTHER FAHNSTIEL: 20 JUNE, 1952

The phone rang at eight a.m., and I let it ring ten or twelve times before I finally got out of bed and answered. I was off duty until four p.m. and didn't want to get up until nine, so I guess I didn't sound too friendly.

'This is Gunther, what do you want?'

'It's Ed. I need to see you this morning. How about Cliff's?'

'I'm off duty, Sergeant.' It was going to be more grief about Sally and how I was wrecking my own life, and I didn't want to hear it.

'I got some bad news about a friend of ours. Real bad, maybe. I'll see you there in half an hour.'

He hung up on me, and I threw on a shirt from the clean clothes pile over the back of my easy chair and pulled on my pants from the day before. When I finally found my shoes I put them on and strolled out the door.

I decided to walk; since I hadn't bothered to shower or shave I'd still be there before he was. There was all kinds of traffic around the park, people headed for work in offices and stores, and I felt lucky for having a job that kept me outside so much of the time. The zoo wasn't open yet, and walking by I saw the keepers feeding the animals and hosing the cages and sidewalks down for the day·to come. School was out so they still had a lot of visitors even on weekdays. Jack's Packard was sitting outside the tavern, shined up as usual, and next to it was a shiny new Ford pickup truck with a bedful of construction materials. Jack stepped outside with a cigarette in his mouth.

'You sure look like shit this morning,' he said. He was in his seersucker suit again.

'You start that work already?'

'I got a man looking the place over, taking measurements, but shit, how smart can he be? This's a brand new truck, here. Look at this. Got boards and a toolbox right there, unsecured and scratching the paint on the bed.'

'It's his truck, not yours.'

'Of course you wouldn't care. You're not a detail man, Gunther, but I am, and I want my new place looking nice and new, not like I just took a goddamn sledgehammer and knocked down some plaster.'

I moved along, and I could still hear him grumbling a couple of doors down, where a man sat in a chair on his front lawn next to the sidewalk, reading the paper.

'Howdy, Mr. Blake,' I shouted, since he was hard of hearing. He was a veteran of the Spanish-American war, eighty-some-odd years old and married to a good-looking woman in her early forties. They had a son, Ginger's age, who'd started looking exactly like the old man from the age of twelve or so, jugeared with a nose like a gherkin, which put the lie to all the things people had said about Mrs. Blake's honor and Mr. Blake's virility.

'Morning, Officer,' he shouted back, though I was in civilian clothes. He'd left the first three fingers of his left hand on San Juan Hill, and he held the front part of the paper delicately between his thumb and pinkie. 'Fucking Reds are taking over the whole cocksucking Orient and there's nothing we can do about it. Not a goddamned thing.'

'Hope you're wrong about that,' I said, and didn't stop. I liked Mr. Blake, but those loud conversations with him were hard to get away from, and I wanted to get to Cliff's to read a little of the paper before Ed got there and started his usual speech about me ruining my life. Ed's butting his nose into my business didn't bother me as much as him treating me like a greenhorn and a moron. I tried not to be mad – I knew he was just trying to look out for me – but I couldn't help it.

I bought the morning paper from the man outside Cliff's and took it inside. I sat down at the counter and started reading about the Korean situation that rankled old Blake so bad, the presidential election and a whole lot of other stuff that didn't interest me much. I was just getting to the sports section when Ed walked in and stood behind me.

'Let's get a booth,' he said. There were eight of them, all empty except for the one in front. An old man sat there talking to himself over a cup of coffee the way he did almost every day. Sometimes when he went he'd let out a loud yell before he got up and left, and I never once saw him pay his check.

I took my coffee over to a booth toward the back and we sat. 'How's Daisy and Jeff?'

'Dandy. Listen. That Sergeant I saw out at Wesley?'

'It's not him, I already told you.'

'It goddamn well is. I saw him last night at the Commanche, and he was getting real friendly with Amos Culligan.'

'You followed him?'

'I sure did. He hasn't made any effort to contact Sally?'

I shook my head, trying to figure it out. 'Not as far as I know.'

The waitress came over right then, and all of a sudden I wasn't sure I wanted to eat. I ordered ham and sausage anyway, and pancakes. Ed got scrambled eggs and toast and reminded her to bring a ketchup bottle.

'Wonder how much Culligan spilled.'

'Probably all of it. I need you to tell Sally about this. You think she'll call this weekend off?'

'I doubt it.'

'I could threaten a raid,' he said. 'You think she'd cancel then?'

'Not a chance.' She'd see right through the bluff, and Ed knew it just like I did.

The food came and we ate without saying much more. He'd done this on his own time, and if he'd left it up to me who knows what would have happened. I wanted to thank him for it but I couldn't, so I picked up the check when we left and he didn't stop me.

*

Sally was at work, and what I had to tell her could wait until her shift ended at three. I didn't want to monkey around at the front gate at Collins, since I didn't have an employee identification tag or an appointment to see anyone. I could have flashed my badge and said it was police business, but lots of the guards are retired cops. If I chanced on one of them he'd know it wasn't a plainclothes officer's shield and I'd have a lot more questions to answer.

So I got into my broken down old Ford and headed to the hospital. The chassis rattled every time I hit thirty-five miles per hour, and there was a shimmy every time I braked over forty. I'd been gypped, but I hated to admit it so I didn't gripe. I wished I'd taken better care of the Hudson, but Mildred would have gotten it in the divorce anyway.

One of the doctors on duty in the Emergency Ward had been there and remembered him from the other morning. He talked to me in an examination room while he treated a little boy who'd bent his thumbnail backward playing football in the house. The thumb was all swollen and full of pus, and the doctor was heating up a bent paper clip, and the boy and his mother were watching the end of it get red.

'Charming fellow. Said he'd been jumped after he left some dive out in the county, two or three guys he'd never seen before. He took it pretty philosophically.'

'How bad was he beat up?'

'I've seen lots worse,' the doctor said, 'but he was knocked around pretty well. No broken bones. One eye swelled shut.' By now the hot paper clip was glowing orange on its end, and without any warning the doctor held the boy's hand down and burned a neat little round hole in his thumbnail. The boy hollered, but it was already over, and he just watched and sniffled a little while the doctor squeezed the pus out the little hole like toothpaste coming out of a tube. I thanked the doctor and left.

As long as I was at the hospital I had something else I wanted to do. I went upstairs to the obstetrics ward, where the admitting nurse squinted at me, puzzled at seeing me out of uniform.

'Your wife didn't have a baby, did she, Gunther?'

'Haven't had a wife for a couple of years now. If I'm lucky I won't have one again ever.' I meant it to be a joke, but I guess I looked so serious it came out mean. 'I'm just funning, Constance. Mrs. McCallum on duty today?'

'Oh. She is, just let me check.'

She paged her like nothing was odd, but she was dying to know why I wanted to talk to Mrs. McCallum. I was too jumpy to make small talk, and if she wanted to know what the story was she could ask just about anybody else on the ward.

After a minute Dot popped her head around a corner. 'Five minutes,' she said. 'I rescheduled my break.' Then she disappeared. I wandered down to the nursery and watched the families waving through the glass at the nurses holding the babies up. I was still there when she crept up beside me in her white uniform, all business and no fun, the way she always was now when we were face to face. Behind the stern look, though, I thought she was happy to see me. Not that it would ever do me any good.

'I didn't know you were coming.'

'I was here for something else. Hadn't talked to you in a while, thought I'd come up and see if you had a minute. You want a cup of coffee?'

She looked at me funny, like I must be up to something with this coffee business. 'Come on,' I said. 'It's your coffee break.'

I could tell she wanted to smile, even if it wasn't there on her face. 'Let's keep it brief. I don't want to start any tongues wagging around here.'

Tongues around that place hadn't stopped wagging on the two of us since 1942, but I kept my mouth shut. Since the hospital cafeteria was usually full of nurses and cops we wandered across the big green hospital lawn and jaywalked over to Rudolf's coffee house. We took a booth and ordered coffee, with a danish for her. Her starched white uniform made her seem even smaller than she was, and her hair was pulled up so tight under her cap that from the front you couldn't really tell she was a redhead. Sitting across the booth from her it was impossible to imagine her laughing, or driving out to the lake on a weekend. She was still pretty but doing everything she could to make it not matter.

'So how's he doing?'

'He's fine. Having a big summer at day camp.'

'That's good. School year went okay?'

'Fine. Mostly Bs again. Teacher said he'd do better if he didn't daydream all the time.'

'Bs are okay. Hell, I was happy when I got Cs.'

'Not to hear Fred tell it. If he doesn't bring home As it's because he's not trying, or because he's stupid.'

My jaw clenched up and I had to work it around in a circle to get it relaxed again. 'And how's Fred?'

'He's fine, still having that trouble with his elbow.'

'I'm not asking after his health. I want to know how he's treating you and the boy.'

'Fine.'

'Still drinking?'

She looked at me for a second before she answered. 'He drinks.'

A year earlier I'd run across him at a roadhouse, stumbling drunk and surly, and watched him try to pick a fight with a guy with a goddamn pegleg. Fred was mad and itching for a fight with somebody who couldn't fight back, which I figured would end up being Dot or the boy when he got home. What I wanted to do was knock his fucking head off his shoulders, but instead I called dispatch and had Tommy Carlisle and Rory Blaine wait outside the roadhouse for him to leave. When they pulled Fred over he got lippy and tried to shove Rory, which gave him and Tommy the perfect opportunity to beat the crap out of him. Rory's nightstick cracked a bone in Fred's arm at the elbow, and though I'd never owned up to it, somehow Dot had always known it was my doing.

'You know what's gonna happen if he lays a hand on either one of you.'

'You've told me.' She was scowling now, the way she always did when we talked about Fred. I hadn't meant to bring the whole business up for that very reason, but the truth was I liked her better pissed off than blankfaced.

'I'll be in touch with his teacher come autumn, just like

I was with Mrs. Bleecker last year. She sees any sign there's trouble at home and I'll be all over Fred.'

'Our hero,' she said. Her face was pinched and even paler than usual. 'Anything else before I go?'

I didn't answer, and she stood up just as her danish and coffee arrived. She walked away, and as I watched her go through the door and across the street I thought about how nice things used to be before I fucked everything up by joining the army.

*

I walked into the lobby of the Bellingham a little before noon and introduced myself to the day manager, Mr. Nash. He didn't look too happy, and he sighed out loud when I told him Dan Hardyway of Vice said to say hello. He didn't like informing on hotel guests, and to tell the truth I didn't much like strongarming him that way, but neither of us had much choice.

'I hear he paid cash for a week in advance. That true?'

'It's true. But it's not as unusual as you might think.'

'He's traveling with a lot of green, though, wouldn't you say?'

'I wouldn't know.'

'He paid cash for a Plymouth at Welker Brothers.'

'I doubt he paid more than five or six hundred dollars.'

'That's a lot of cash. And he bought a whole bunch of nice clothes over at the Thistle.'

'You obviously already know this. What do you want me to tell you?'

'I want you to let me into his room.'

189

Mr. Nash was shocked. 'I can't do that.'

'And if he comes back while I'm up there you ring the phone three times so I can get out quick.'

'I told you I can't do that.'

I leaned forward. 'Three arrests, all in the small hours of the morning, all in the park.' I was talking real low, but he still raised his finger to his lips and shooshed me. 'Indecent exposure twice, solicitation once. Charges dropped because it's good to have an inside man at a big hotel. If you don't want to play ball any more you better call Dan Hardyway and tell him. Otherwise give me the key and remember it's three rings if he shows up.'

Mr. Nash handed me the key looking like he hated my guts. The elevator operator stood at attention the whole ride up to the sixth floor, and when I got off he said, 'Have a pleasant afternoon, officer,' even though I was still in my civvies.

*

Ogden's room was more of a suite. There was a duffel bag on the folding stand next to the bed, and his civilian shirts were in the top drawer of the dresser. His class A uniform was hanging in the closet along with some expensive civilian clothes, all of them with the Thistle's label. I looked out the window at the bridge below and the river, and I wondered what the hell was so great about army life that he'd left a woman like Sally for it.

In the duffel bag was a packet of letters tied together with a rubber band. The top letter was worn, as if it had been read over and over, and at least once it had been crumpled and then smoothed out again. The date at the top of the page was less than three months ago; the page had been unfolded and refolded so many times it was hard to read around the creases. It was on Collins company stationery, with the name Cecil Wembly on the letterhead:

March 29, 1952

Dear Wayne,

Perhaps you remember me. We were in high school together on the debate team. I always remember your quickness and off-the-cuff wit when I am called upon to make a presentation here at Collins. For you see I have followed in your footsteps and got myself a job here in the Public Relations Division. Several people here have spoken highly of you, including Mr. Collins himself. You will no doubt be glad to learn that he still comes in every morning rain or shine, and he has asked me to convey his belief that you have a future here when your service to our country has run its course.

But it is not to tender an offer of employment that I write you. What I speak of here could destroy your future with this company, even with this city! I do not relish the prospect of passing on the terrible knowledge I am about to. Every man who weds carries with him into that blessed state an image of his wife as a pure and sacred being, and I well remember your own Sally from our high school days, when she was both admired for her beauty and cherished for her

I couldn't see a second page and my time was short so I dug through a bunch of ratty civilian clothes to the bottom of the bag, where I found a blackjack, an eight-inch hunting knife and a cardboard box full of ammunition for a .38. I put them back where I'd found them and left.

*

Getting off the elevator on the ground floor, I asked the operator his name. 'Roger Lantrain,' he said. He wasn't much over twenty, with a smirk on the corner of his mouth.

'Okay, Roger. Word gets around that I was up there and I'll shut your little operation down real quick.'

His smirk didn't disappear, but he had to work to keep it up. 'What operation?'

'Sneaking bottles and call girls up into the rooms. A little reefer sometimes, too.' The bottles and whores were a sure thing in a big hotel, but I was just guessing on the reefer. I had him, though. That smirk was gone.

'Yes, sir.' He damn near saluted when I stepped out of the cage.

I hadn't found any cash in the room, either, so, unless he had his whole wad on him, he must have put it in the safe. Mr. Nash wasn't too keen on the idea of me searching the safe, either.

'I don't want to search it. I just want you to show me what he put in it.'

He led me into the hotel office and opened the safe, then pulled out an envelope and handed it to me. It contained the title to a 1946 Plymouth and one thousand six hundred thirty dollars in cash. I handed him the envelope back and he replaced it.

'That's all for now, Mr. Nash.' He didn't answer, just

went back to his paperwork and pretended he couldn't see me any more.

As I was walking out, a guy with a fading shiner passed me on his way in. I stopped at the lobby tobacco stand and pretended to study the headline on the *Beacon* while he talked to Nash at the desk. Something he said made the man blush, and as soon as Ogden was in the elevator on his way up I stopped back at the desk.

'Yes, that was him,' Nash said.

'What'd he have to say that got you so flushed?'

'He said he just fucked the ugliest prostitute in the world, and he did it four times.' He couldn't help laughing a little, and neither could I.

*

I still wanted to see Sally before reporting for duty. It was two-thirty, and she'd be getting home in an hour or so. On the way I stopped in at Welker Brothers and went up to the sales office. I didn't see the salesman who'd unloaded the piece of shit old Ford on me. Probably he'd gone on to something more legit, like selling fake magazine subscriptions door to door. The man who'd sold Ogden his car was there, though, and once I flashed the badge he was happy to talk, maybe even relieved.

'Sergeant McCowan accused me of cheating him before we'd even exchanged names,' he said. 'There was definitely the implication that if he wasn't treated fairly something bad would happen.'

'So you treated him fair and square?'

'Sure.'

'Must have felt good for a change.'

'I don't mean I ordinarily wouldn't have.'

'Look,' I said. 'See that Ford out there? The black one? I bought that here less than six months ago and it's a real pile of shit. Nothing but trouble. Won't start half the time, stalls in traffic.'

He was starting to get nervous. 'You should've brought her in when you had trouble.'

'Warranty stopped after thirty days. Didn't start to go bad until day thirty-one.'

He was sweating, from the heat or from the idea that they'd sold a cop a lemon. 'You're a police officer. Why didn't you tell us that when you bought the car?'

'What makes you think I didn't?'

'We never would've...' He stopped himself and shrugged. 'We might've made you a better deal, is all.'

'All right.' I got up. 'I'm coming back in next week and if it's not running like a goddamn top when I take it off the lot I'm trading it in for the full purchase price, understand?'

'Yes, sir.'

'And if you see this character again, not a word about my coming around.'

'Yes, sir.'

I got back into the Ford and headed for Sally's. I was glad I'd come in. The bastards had skinned me, and I wanted it put right. Maybe I'd get some satisfaction after all. Maybe I'd even go back and buy Ginger's car there.

I stopped at a phone booth to make sure Sally was going home. After six rings the babysitter answered.

'Mrs. Ogden will be home around three forty-five, and

then she'll be taking me home.' Which meant she wouldn't be back home until four-fifteen, probably, and I was on duty at five. 'Would you like to leave a message?'

'Just tell her Officer Fahnstiel called.' I hung up and went back to the car. I'd make a stop later, when I was on duty, or in the morning before I went to work. Whatever her husband was doing back in town it wasn't charity work, and I wasn't going to let her do anything this weekend that would give the creep an opening. She wouldn't like it, but that was how it was going to have to go.

CHAPTER THIRTEEN

Tricia had made her way all the way through the front section of the paper to the funnies and her father was still trying to pry something out of her grandmother. As was her habit she had tuned out of the argument and was only vaguely aware of the source of the dispute. Dot had finished the Jumble and done enough of the crossword to ruin it, and there seemed to be nothing in the house to read except the preceding month's Silhouette Regency Romances. She needed something to keep her mind off the bickering or it would give her a stomachache, and she thought about walking around the corner to the drugstore for *People* or maybe a cheap paperback more to her liking than the Silhouettes.

'All right,' Sidney said, no closer to getting his mother to talk than when they'd walked in on him. 'Let's say you're playing it straight. You paid off the RV and the mortgage—'

'Who says we paid off the RV?'

'The bill of sale says so. Let's say you paid that off, plus about twenty years of a thirty-year mortgage, plus you installed air conditioning and God knows what else, on social security plus a cop's pension and a nurse's on top of it. Just for the sake of argument.'

'That's what we did.'

'Then how'd you eat? How'd you buy shoes? You didn't have any savings when the old man died.'

Tricia stood and moved for the door, waiting for an opening in the conversation where she could announce her departure. Her stomach muscles were starting to tighten and she considered leaving without saying anything. Probably they wouldn't even notice.

'And just how exactly would you know that?' Dot snarled.

'Because the VA paid for the funeral and I know you'd have paid for it yourself if you could. Hell, I'd have paid for it *my*self if I'd had the money back then. Would've been my pleasure.'

'Just getting him in the ground was pleasure enough for me.'

Tricia shot a disbelieving look at her grandmother. Surely she'd heard wrong.

'Yeah, hard to see how it could've gotten any better than it already was, just knowing he was dead.' They both chortled in a similar, furtive way.

'What are you guys talking about? About Grandpa McCallum?'

Dot and Sidney looked at each other guiltily, and Sidney drew in and let out a deep breath. 'You never knew him, sweetie.'

'You were glad when he died?'

Sidney shrugged. 'I don't know about glad, exactly. I sure as shit wasn't sorry.'

'Listen, honey,' Dot said, putting her hand on her grand-daughter's shoulder. 'We're just kidding. Your Grandpa had a lot of nice qualities, too.'

'That's a laugh,' Sidney said, which earned him a sharp look from his mother. 'Okay, then, give me something nice to say. If you can honestly come up with one nice thing to say about the old bastard, I'll say it right back to you.'

'He loved that old hunting dog of his,' she said, after a long pause.

Sidney nodded. 'I guess he did.'

Dot thought for a second, then chuckled again. 'That's about the best I can come up with.'

'I got one,' Sidney said. 'He was always kind to his drinking buddies.'

'He never crashed his car into anybody else's house but ours.'

'Good with his hands when they weren't shaking.'

When the phone rang in the kitchen Tricia slipped out quietly to answer it. It was for her father, a woman's voice she didn't recognize, and she went back to the living room, happy for the chance to interrupt. 'It's for you, Daddy.'

Tricia looked through the kitchen at her father as he picked up the phone and started talking, trying to make sense of this unprecedented lack of respect for poor dead Grandpa McCallum, about whom she had never before heard an unkind word. In fact, though, she hadn't ever heard him discussed much at all; he'd died when she was in diapers, and she supposed the reason he didn't come up much in conversation was sensitivity to Gunther's feelings. Her grandmother turned to her, still laughing.

'Sorry, sweetheart. I always tried not to talk that way in front of you kids.'

'You're full of surprises today, Moomaw,' Tricia said. On the way home from the mall Dot had insisted on stopping at St. Luke's Catholic Church, where she went in and lit a candle for Gunther's safe return home. It was the first time Tricia had ever been aware of any member of her family besides her crazy mother willingly entering a church.

'Now keep your damn mouth shut about that business.'

'I didn't say anything.'

'Well, don't.' She was whispering now. 'I don't want Sidney to know, and I particularly don't want Gunther to ever find out.'

'I won't say anything, don't worry.'

Sidney came back out of the kitchen. 'This lady in College Hill got a weird phone message from the old man who thinks he may have been at her house. I'm gonna check it out.'

'You call me, you understand? I don't like sitting around waiting.'

'I'll call you, don't get your bowels in an uproar. And don't think I'm forgetting about the money.'

When he was gone, Dot sat down at the kitchen table with her map, and when Tricia sat down next to her she didn't seem to notice.

'Why don't you tell me what you're looking for? Maybe I can help you find it.'

Dot looked up at her. 'You know how to read a map?'

*

Sidney took the freeway east toward Loretta Gandy's house, feeling guilty about talking the way he had in front of Tricia, then wondering what was the problem with them knowing the truth about his old man, dead before Danny and Amy were born and before Tricia had any idea who he was. They were all adults now, and God knew as tiny children they'd seen worse with their own mother.

He couldn't deny his share of responsibility there. It had been at his urging that Christine had first sampled some coke he'd reluctantly accepted in lieu of cash for a football bet from a customer, in violation of his own strict policy of cash up front. He was head bartender then at a club called the Sporting Life, long since closed, and between his salary, his mostly undeclared tips and his share of the gambling action he'd been making a good living, even with three kids to feed. Suddenly, though, it wasn't enough.

By the time the marriage was over she was shacked up with her connection, a squirrely little guy who wore a big knit beret and thought he looked like a white Superfly. Shortly after she moved into his house he got busted and Christine along with him, and he ended up getting fifteen years. She ended up with four years' probation, a sentence so light in comparison that many observers believed a deal had been struck. Her good fortune had not lessened her appetite for coke or love of a good time, however, and Sidney had been raising the kids by himself with barely a hello from her for almost five years when she abruptly decided she wanted them back. She'd married the owner of the very club where Sidney had scored that original packet of coke, and since she was living in a spacious home in a trendy suburb she thought she might as well have some kids to complete the picture.

It might have worked if she'd bothered getting clean beforehand, but this judge liked her even less than the first one had, and Sidney's lawyer hadn't even had to bring up Christine's status as a recent probationer or her new husband's involvement in the coke trade. He'd had to work two shifts for a year after that to pay off his legal bills, though, and he resented every extra shift bitterly, popping white crosses just to stay on his feet. She was married to a fucking millionaire, but she wasn't interested in supporting the kids financially unless she had custody.

Now she'd been divorced again, joined NA and found Jesus. For their sake and not hers Sidney told the kids they should be nice to her, which as far as he was concerned was more than she deserved. His small measure of revenge was his refusal to allow her to make amends to him, which she kept trying to do. She'd been trying to get him and the kids to attend family counseling sessions at the goofball holy roller church she belonged to. Tricia had attended a couple of sessions – Amy and Danny had refused categorically – and he'd gone to pick her up afterward, waiting outside the mobile home the church had set up next to it, watching people showing up at the church's cinderblock main building. The session had been timed, he realized, to end just as a service was starting. Tricia came out of the mobile home, followed by Christine, and then a youngish man in a robin's egg blue suit with a badly sculpted helmet of hair hurried out to beat Tricia to the car. Sidney rolled the window down and gave him the look he used to give troublemakers at the Sweet Cage, the look that usually preceded violent expulsion. The man none the less stuck out his hand, which Sidney ignored with childish satisfaction.

'Mister McCallum? Jeff Lorrell. Tricia and her Mom are fixing to attend services, I hope the change of plans doesn't put you out too much. In fact we were sort of hoping you'd join them.'

'Tricia,' Sidney yelled, and as she started to move forward the minister motioned her to stay back for a second.

'Mister McCallum,' the reverend began, lowering his voice to an intimate near-whisper, 'what I'm learning from these sessions is that part of the problem seems to be lack of involvement by the family in any church based activities. Tricia tells me her and her brother and sister have never had any kind of religious training, is that right?'

The reverend seemed unintimidated by the glare, but Sidney kept it up.

'Tricia. You ready to go?' Tricia started to come again, but her mother was saying something to her and looking very emotional and she stayed to listen.

'I think there's a real need in your family, Sidney, that's not being met.'

'Don't call me Sidney.'

'Sorry. Mr. McCallum, I'm talking about the need for salvation.'

'Yeah, I pieced that together. Tricia, you want me to come back and get you when the tent show's over?' Unlike her brother and sister Tricia was softhearted enough to come to the counseling session for her mother's sake, but he sensed she'd about hit her limit for the day, and Sidney wasn't surprised when she kissed Christine on the cheek, raced to the car and dived in without a farewell to Pastor Lorrell. Sidney rolled his window up with Lorrell in the middle of a sentence and they drove away.

'How was it?'

'Shitty. He was trying to get me to forgive her, and I told him I already had, a long time ago, and he wanted to know how come I wouldn't join the church then, and he started talking about Mary Magdalene and how sinners could be forgiven, even the worst ones, and he was sort of calling Mom a whore.'

'Hah!' For a second Sidney wished he'd gone after all.

'And I told him again I'd already forgiven her, but he just kept coming back to the same thing: if I'd really forgiven her for being a cokeslut then I'd join their weird little church.'

'So how'd it end up?'

'Finally I said if that's what it takes, then I guess I couldn't forgive her.'

'Good for you, honey. I'm proud of you.'

'I was feeling a little sorry for her, then I thought, hey, she left me when I was eight. It won't kill her to go to church all by herself.'

*

'Moomaw?' Tricia was leaning against the doorframe, half in and half out of Dot's kitchen. 'I don't think we're going to find anything as small as a rock quarry on this map, and even if it was there I wouldn't know what to look for.'

She was right; it looked to Dot like a big abstract

painting with names and numbers and lines pasted in at random. 'Don't suppose I would either.'

'Want to go to the WSU library? There'd be better maps and librarians who know how to read them.'

'Maybe we should. You still got a library card?'

'Don't need one, we're not checking books out. So are you gonna tell me what it's about or not?'

She was going to have to tell somebody, because somebody was going to have to drive her there, and she'd rather it was Tricia than Sidney. Before she made the decision there was a knock at the door and Tricia went to see who it was.

'Uncle Ed!' Tricia's voice rose to a squeal and Dot's stomach got tight. 'Moomaw! Uncle Ed's here.'

'He's not your uncle,' she said quietly, and she stood and gave him a smile anyway as he stepped into the kitchen. Ed gave her a little hug and patted her consolingly on the shoulder.

'Sit down, sit down,' he said. 'What you looking at? A map?' He put his hand on the table to steady himself and leaned down to look at it. His sportjacket was off, but he was sweating hard. Those tiny, perfectly round blue eyes glistened and protruded like marbles from the orbits even while he was squinting at the green map.

'You like something to drink, Uncle Ed?'

'I sure would, sweetheart. Hot as the hinges of Hades out there.'

Tricia opened the ice box and poured Ed a glass of iced tea. 'You can cuss in front of me, Ed. I'm twenty-two.'

'I never cuss, honey. Gunther's pulling your leg if he ever told you any different.' He took the iced tea and drank half of it in a single swig. 'That's good, thanks. Jeepers, it's hot out there. Nice and cool in here, though.' He looked around, trying to spot the source of the cold air. 'You got central air?'

'Uh-huh.'

'Seems like I remember Gunther griping about the heat in the house.'

'Didn't have AC when we moved in, just central heat.'

'Huh. When'd you put the condenser in?'

'Eight, nine years ago. Sidney bought it for us,' she lied, knowing he was leading up to a remark about the expense of installing an air conditioner.

'What do you know.' He peered up at a vent as if he were trying to figure out how the whole process worked, then turned to her. 'How you holding up, Dot?'

She shrugged. 'Okay, I guess, considering.'

'You got any idea what might have made him walk away like that?'

'Well, he's in the zombie ward of the goddamn old folk's home, and he doesn't want to be. How's that for a start?'

'Did he talk about wanting to get out?'

She gave a little grunt. 'How about every goddamn time I spoke to him.'

'Anything else? How's his health?'

'Apart from being half senile, pretty good. Blood pressure's high but he's medicated. 'Course he left his meds behind. No aches and pains to speak of, not compared to me anyway, or you either, probably.'

'Money?' He said it casually and quickly, and she knew he'd been saving it for last.

'Money's fine.'

'Moomaw, what were you just talking about with Daddy? The pension?'

If it hadn't been Ed standing there she would have snarled at the girl. 'We were just discussing Gunther's pension and mine.'

'How much of the nursing home bill does it pay?' Ed said.

'All of it.'

He nodded and didn't pursue it any further. She knew he didn't believe her; he had the same goddamn pension, after all, a captain's and not a sergeant's, and he knew just how far his own went.

'You have any idea where Sidney might be? I was kind of hoping I might find him here.'

'He was headed back to some lady's house, she got a message from Gunther.'

'You know where?'

'Huh-uh. He was going to call here when he was done.'

'Okay. I'll be on my way, I guess. Still lots to do. I'll be in touch.'

Tricia gave him a little kiss on the cheek, and he left the kitchen and headed for the front of the house.

'Moomaw, you should say thank you,' Tricia said quietly.

'He has his reasons.'

'Moomaw! He came all the way up here to help us.'

Dot stood up and peered into the living room as he opened the door to leave. 'Ed?'

He turned to face her, halfway out the door already. 'Yeah?'

'Thanks,' she said with as much enthusiasm as she could generate.

He gave her a friendly little salute and left.

*

When he opened the closet door Gunther found the drunk asleep. He pushed him with his foot and got no response. He put his head to his chest and determined that he was breathing regularly, then shook him again.

'Hey. How's the dryer work, Jasper?'

If he knew it would be an indication that he was who he claimed to be, and then Gunther could ask him where Sally lived. Nothing suggested that the man had heard him, though, and he didn't imagine this guy was much more familiar with domestic appliances than he was. He closed the closet door and replaced the chair.

Downstairs he examined the dryer's control panel carefully. Delicate. Cotton. High heat. That sounded like what he needed. He set it, turned it on and went upstairs to the kitchen. He was hungry again, and before long he'd have to leave.

He was halfway through his second olive loaf sandwich when a small black ring binder sitting on the kitchen desk next to the phone caught his eye. Sally's address was under M for Mom; he copied it out slowly on to the pad of scratch paper and was about to tear it off when he realized that for the moment he had no pocket to put it into. As he took the last morsel of sandwich into his mouth he saw taped to a cubbyhole in front of him the Gandy family Christmas card, a recent one judging from the size of the kids. Standing behind them and next to Loretta was the drunk from upstairs, cleanshaven and dressed in a suit and tie, and still looking like somebody who had no business with a nice girl like her.

Downstairs he shot a little more pool until he heard the dryer shut itself off. He opened the hatch and pulled out his hat, almost too hot to hold, then gritted his teeth and unloaded, pulling his clothes out as quickly as he could and doing his best not to touch hers at all. He was pleased with himself for having conquered the dryer, and as he put on the warm clothes he grappled with the transportation problem. He'd been lucky so far, and it wouldn't last; he needed something reliable and anonymous. Maybe Loretta would lend him a car. He squirmed; something felt funny and hot against his nutsack. He unzipped his trousers, reached into his shorts and extracted, to his horror, a toasty pair of silky white women's drawers, which he threw back into the dryer with its mates, wiping his palms against each other in embarrassment.

He climbed back up the stairs to the first floor. Outside he heard a car pull up and stop. He pulled the edge of the curtain and saw a black BMW parked out front with Sidney at the wheel.

He took the stairs two at a time up to the bedroom, put the chair back in its proper place and opened the closet door. The drunk was still asleep, his mouth open and his tongue on the carpet, and Gunther closed the door from the inside.

Downstairs the kitchen door opened and closed again.

Loretta's voice, indistinct, floated up, punctuated by the sound of high heels on the hard floor. Sidney's voice filtered up too, and his heavier steps now thumped alongside hers.

'Eric?' Loretta's voice echoed through the house.

*

'Somebody had a big lunch,' Sidney said. On the counter were an empty box of pizza rolls, a loaf of bread, half a package of olive loaf and an open jar of mayonnaise.

'Probably my husband.' She turned the oven off, put the bread and mayo up and threw the box away along with the olive loaf, determined for Sidney McCallum's benefit not to let loose a sigh of pained resignation.

She led him to the living room, which was unoccupied. 'We keep a key over the door. It's just possible Gunther could have come in.'

'You want me to check upstairs?'

'Good idea, I'll check downstairs while you're at it.'

*

When the bedroom door opened, he tensed up. It sounded like one person, though the carpet made it hard to tell if it was a man or a woman. The bathroom door opened, and Loretta's voice came from downstairs.

'Nothing down here.'

'Nothing up here either.'

Sidney left the room, and Gunther stood there in silence until the door slammed downstairs.

'All right, Jasper, I'm going to let you out of here,' he said, opening the door. 'You shouldn't drink in the daytime,' he told the unconscious man on the floor and as Gunther dragged him toward the bed, Gandy's over-worked bladder gave up the fight, warm urine soaking his already dirty pants. 'Jesus H. Christ,' Gunther muttered, not unsympathetically. 'Like being back in the goddamn old folk's home.' He picked him up under the arms, careful not to let the urine stain his own clean clothes, and laid him with some difficulty on top of the bed. He would have turned it down and tucked the poor bastard in if not for the urine and the dirty clothes.

He moved carefully to the window. Both cars were still there, but Loretta and Sidney were standing talking like they were about to go, and when they had he'd call a taxi. There were risks involved, but the driver would assume he was picking up a Mr. Gandy at home, and he was confident he could talk his way out of it if he needed to.

*

'Well, we gave it a shot,' Sidney said. 'At least we know he was alive and kicking some time this morning.'

She stood next to the Caddy inside the open driver's side door, without appearing terribly anxious to leave. It seemed to him an odd choice of vehicle for an attractive woman her age. As soon as she'd stepped out of her car he had been riveted by the length of her legs, and not staring required a conscious effort; in her heels she was almost as tall as he was. Whoever her husband was, he was a lucky bastard.

'Nice car,' he said. 'Roomy.'

She looked down into it as if to verify its roominess. 'I

SCOTT PHILLIPS

just keep kicking myself for not offering poor old Gunther
a place to stay last night.'

'You didn't know he was on the lam.'

'I could have asked.'

He had a strong, sudden urge to make a pass at her,
which he knew was a bad idea. Instead he pulled a couple
of tickets from his wallet. 'I'm putting on a car show this
weekend. Is two enough? You have kids?'

'They're both at KU. Two'd be fine, maybe I'll take my
mom. Thanks.'

He handed her two passes, noting that she hadn't
mentioned the husband as a possible companion. 'See you
later.'

*

He headed out of College Hill in the direction of the hair
salon. Lester Howells had given him a rundown of all the
places Gunther had been spotted, a rough trajectory that
extended from the hair salon westward to a diner, skipped
forward several miles to Harry's barber shop, and then
picked up again at a motel south of downtown.

Pulling up to the curb next to the salon he recognized
the space as that of Ray and Cal's old barber shop, where
he used to get his hair cut as a little boy. He went down
the steps and looked inside. It was dark, and a sign on the
door indicated that they were closed Friday afternoons.
Even with the lights out, the place bore little resemblance
to Ray and Cal's, and he climbed back up to the street and
got back into the car, wondering what had happened to
old Ray. The watch repair place was gone, too.

Down the road at the diner an obese, elderly woman

with dyed black hair looked at him quizzically as he entered. There was only one other customer, seated at the far end of the counter. An old man in a new-looking brown suit, he didn't look up from his cheeseburger and french fries, which he was eating quickly but methodically.

'Counter okay?' the woman asked.

'Counter's fine with me,' he said, but he remained on his feet. 'Just coffee. I wanted to ask you about Gunther Fahnstiel.'

'I know you,' she said, brightening. 'Gunther's boy.'

'Stepson. Sidney McCallum.'

'Well, I'm Irma. Hey, Frank,' she called out to the fat man, who didn't respond. She threw a packet of sweetener at his head and he looked over at her, adjusting a hearing aid.

'What?'

'This's Gunther's boy.'

The man raised his eyebrows and nodded, chewing. 'Frank Elting. Glad to meet you. Sorry about old Gunther.'

'Frank used to work for the *Eagle*.'

'*Beacon* before that, back when this was a two paper town,' Frank said, his attention partially back on the cheeseburger. He squinted and cocked his head, studying Sidney. 'You the one was married to that gal, had all that cocaine trouble?'

'That's me.'

Frank looked pleased with his powers of deduction. 'Gunther never told you what he did, did he?'

'I don't know, what'd he do?'

'Had her arrested, her and that pusher she was keeping company with.'

Sidney shook his head. 'That wasn't any of Gunther's doing.'

Frank nodded emphatically. 'Sure as hell was. Gunther thought she was gonna get custody of your kids, and he knew the courts back then about as well as anybody, I guess. He made a coupla phone calls, next day there was a raid.'

'And this is a mother of how many kids, now?' Irma asked.

'Three,' Sidney said, dazed. He finally sat on the stool.

Frank saw that he'd struck a nerve, and he was happy to supply more privileged information. 'He was pretty worried. First, 'cause he still sort of liked her despite it all. Second, he was afraid you'd find out about it and get sore at him. Are you?'

'Just surprised,' he said, and he became aware of his heart thumping furiously. He'd been so preoccupied at the time he didn't remember ever discussing the situation with Gunther. The woman started pouring him a cup of coffee, and he looked at it without picking it up.

'Well, I hope you find the old reprobate,' Frank said, turning his hearing aid back off.

Sidney took a drink of his coffee.

'So do I,' Irma said. 'Just between you and me, though, I'm not sure I believe that about him being out of his mind. He seemed just fine to me, and I see crazy people every day.' She gave Sidney an ostentatiously wise look, then put the pot back on the burner.

CHAPTER FOURTEEN

I parked the Plymouth in the dirt in front of the farm-house, which must have been nice when it was new, with rounded dormers on a curving roof and an ornate iron railing around the top of it, a widow's walk a couple of thousand miles from the nearest ocean. There was a porch big enough to hold twenty people standing, and an old swing lay pathetically beneath the spot where it had once hung. The faded white paint was flaking away, and the wood beneath it was dried out, dark grey and splintering between the chips. I stood back far enough from the ripped screen door to be seen clearly through the glass, cracked of course, of the front door; the oak door itself, massive and ornate, was the only part of the porch that seemed intact. I leaned forward and knocked loud three times, then brought my hands back into plain view at my sides; I was on the verge of knocking again when the door opened and a small, odd-looking man of about fifty in a pair of ancient, filthy overalls and nothing underneath

215

them stood inside looking at me in mute wonder. His tiny, glistening eyes were a watery blue.

'Mr. Gladwell?'

'Uh-huh?' His white hair was cropped close to his head, too raggedly to pass army inspection but just as short, and I saw that I had surprised him in the act of shaving. The right half of his face was still soaped up, the beard under the lather thick and tough-looking, and on the left side among the small patches of beard he'd missed were three pieces of toilet paper, each red in the center. Beneath his chin a small, untreated nick still bled feebly.

'Name's McCowan. I just wondered if I might go take a look around your property.'

His disinterested expression didn't change. 'How come?'

'I'm interested in buying it.'

'Ain't for sale.' He frowned. 'Anyway it ain't worth nothing. Can't farm it. Can't dig for no more gravel even if they was wanting it still. Quarry flooded up a long time ago.'

'My friend Amos Culligan tells me there's some pretty fine duck hunting over there.'

Gladwell brightened, revealing with a grin a mouthful of yellow, broken teeth. 'Ol' Amos, huh? Well, there's lots better duck hunting other places. But if you was interested in leasing it for part of the duck season, I might.' He had a slight lisp, and Amos came out *Amosh*. 'Problem is I got other people using it, at least on weekends.' He watched me carefully, wondering how much to let out. 'They don't want no company.'

'Oh, yeah, Culligan's deal. Well, I wouldn't necessarily

want it on weekends. Wouldn't want to mess up a good thing.'

The grin widened. 'It sure is a good thing. Well, if you want to go take a look, go ahead. There's a trail out back of the house, that's the straightest way to get there.'

He went back inside, presumably to finish his hebdomadal shave. I stepped off the porch and walked around the back of the house, following a trail in the overgrown grass. There was a considerable rise, topped with a grove of cottonwood, that obscured the view of the quarry. Once I got to the top of it I could see a clearing, with a decent sized body of water to the west of it, surrounded by gravel. A few dozen feet to the left of it stood a small cabin, somewhat roughly constructed but in infinitely better shape than the farmhouse. I sauntered over to it and peered in the window; inside it looked pretty swell. Next to a large fireplace was a padlocked cabinet which I assumed was a wet bar; next to it was a kitchenette, and in the center of the room were several big, comfortable looking armchairs and a dining table with four wooden chairs. There was an open door revealing a bathroom, and on either side of it two closed doors, which I assumed led to bedrooms. Behind the house I looked inside and verified it; here's the room where my wife screws other men for money, I thought, and I laughed out loud. I noted the number of windows and the locks on the front door – a deadbolt and a cheap knob lock, both useless since the door itself looked thin enough to smash into splinters with a token effort. I walked back toward the house, trying to figure out where the cop stayed. Most likely he camped at the top of the rise, among the cottonwoods. There was also a duck blind next to the shore which might serve as a discreet vantage point for surveillance of the cabin, but when I pulled up its plywood cover I found nothing inside but a bench and some foul-smelling water.

I hadn't intended to stop at the house on my way back, but as I exited the trees at the top of the rise and approached the Plymouth Gladwell leaned out his window and hollered at me. 'Hey, mister. Come on in for a minute.'

By the time I was up the porch steps he was holding the door open. He'd finished shaving and had put on a black suit that must have predated the Depression and fit him as if he'd shrunk half a size since buying it. He had added three scraps of toilet paper on the right side of his face to match the left, and his feet were bare. He didn't seem concerned about whether or not I was going to lease the quarry. 'You like a drink?'

'Sure,' I said. I didn't want to seem too interested in what went on here on weekends, but I'd be glad for any information he was willing to volunteer; I was also curious to see if the interior of the house matched the exterior's decay. I stepped through an entryway into what had once been a parlor and was not disappointed; it was knee-deep in old farming bulletins, newspapers and magazines, some of them from the same era as the suit. The same sort of paper detritus covered all the furnishings, along with old and deteriorating clothing of all kinds and from several different decades; a lady's hat from the turn of the century with an ostrich feather curling up from its brim lay atop a pile of what appeared to be worn-out men's work shirts, and sitting on a threadbare but finely made wing chair was a pair of army boots from roughly the time of the First

World War. They were covered with dried mud, as was the chair's seat fabric. The vertically striped paper was peeling from the walls, waterstained a yellowish brown on the bottom and so mildewed I nearly retched at the smell. A well-worn path led through the debris to a staircase, toward which he gestured.

'I mostly do all my receiving upstairs. It's a little bit neater.'

At that point I was tempted to make an excuse and go, but I wanted to hear what he had to say, and even more than that I had a strange desire to see the squalor of the upstairs. So I followed him up, conscious of the weight of the brass knuckles at the small of my back.

'This here's my bedroom,' he said, nodding his head at a room whose sour odor, a bachelor's stink of perspiration, skidmarked shorts and masturbation, kept me at a distance. He closed its door and we continued down the corridor to another bedroom in shockingly good condition.

'This one here's my Mother and Dad's room. They're both dead now, going on twenty years.' The big bed was made neatly, nothing was out of place, and with its window open the smell was almost pleasant, if slightly mildewy. On its dark green walls were framed photographs from early in this century and late in the last, and on a fine old oak dresser stood a vase with a fresh sunflower in it. The strange sensation of having traveled back to the year 1910 evaporated when he pulled a pint of Top Hat from the top drawer of the dresser and took a long drink, his adam's apple pumping in rhythm as though his heart had migrated to his throat. He handed the bottle to me without wiping off the neck and, hiding my distaste, I took a swig.

'This is where I do most of my sinning. You like girls?' he asked.

I nodded, happy I'd brought the knuckles. 'Sure,' I said.

'I guess you know what old Amos Culligan and them get up to out there at the cabin.'

'I have a rough idea.'

He nodded, grinning. 'You know how Culligan and them pays me my rent?'

'Nope.'

'I get forty bucks a month in cash and every two weeks on Friday I get a visit from one of them gals.' He beamed with pride. 'You know. A little sex action. Intercourse,' he added, in case I hadn't picked up on what he meant by 'sex action.'

'Sounds like a good deal.'

'Sure is.' He swept his hand down from chin to waist, indicating the suit. 'That's how come I'm so fancied up today. I don't ever pay for no hoors no more.' He shook his head. 'Don't have to.'

I resisted the temptation to point out that by accepting sex in lieu of additional rent, he was indeed paying for the sex with that lost income. 'Good for you,' I said encouragingly. I wondered if my own lovely bride ever paid this part of the rent herself, and had to chase the image of the two of them screwing from my mind for fear I'd burst out laughing and hurt his feelings.

'Thing is, I got an idea. An idea on how to make some more money.'

'What's that?'

He took another long drink and handed the bottle back to me. 'That's all I'm gonna have. Get too drunk and my pecker won't stand.' He went over to the dresser drawer and pulled out a pile of glossy photos, some of them 5x7s and some 8x10s. Mostly they were studio shots of plain girls in their underwear or naked, with a few more lewd than the rest. In the drawer were several more neat stacks of glossies, and another stack of the carefully preserved brown envelopes in which they'd arrived.

'You think those are okay?'

'Sure, they're all right.'

'Okay, then.' He picked up another stack and handed them to me. These were sex shots: similarly homely gals, many of the same ones as in the first batch, blowing and screwing a variety of unsavory looking characters, a high percentage of whom had left their socks on, suggesting a poorly heated studio or an odd sort of modesty. I'd sold photos just like them in Japan; in fact, I recognized one series featuring a peroxide blonde with a hairy upper lip as coming from the Wilkerson Photographic Studios of Urbana, Illinois. 'How do you like those ones there?'

'They're swell.'

'So, you know what I been thinking? I been thinking if I got a fella with a camera in here every other Friday I could make me some of these pictures and sell 'em in the back of *True* and *Argosy* and such.'

'Sure you could.'

'Hoor wouldn't even have to know about it, if I took 'em on the sly.'

'I guess not.'

'See, I had this idea a while ago. Now look at this.'

He pulled the dresser out from the wall and revealed a peephole. Through it was the next room over, empty of furniture and strewn about with yellowed newspapers and worn out clothes like the parlor downstairs.

'Now see, I'd just have to have a fellow on the other side with a camera.'

I looked around the bedroom. Even with the curtains pulled at high noon, the bed wouldn't have been very brightly lit. 'Awful dark in here for that,' I said. 'Maybe you just ought to tell the girl about it and use a flashgun.'

He shook his head. 'Nuh-uh. I'd use one of them spy cameras. You ever seen one of them?'

Outside I heard another car coming up the drive, and I wondered if it might be Sally. 'Sure have,' I said, and on impulse I pulled out my gold cigarette lighter. 'Ever seen one of these babies? Looks just like a cigarette lighter, don't it?'

'Sure does.' He pushed me out of the room, hand on my shoulderblade. 'Get on in there now and I'll move the dresser so she don't see it.'

'Better put your shoes on. Sounds like your gal's pulling up outside.'

He shoved the dresser back into place, a little to the right of its former position to allow a clear view through the peephole. 'Don't think I will. Be taking 'em off pretty quick if I did.' He looked out the window. 'It's Lynn this time. That's good, 'cause she'll do things Sonya won't.' His eyebrows moved up and down suggestively, as if the names should have meant something to me, and then he went downstairs.

I moved into the next room and took my place at the

peephole, its view limited pretty much to the bed itself and the window beyond, and I heard first voices downstairs, then footsteps coming up the staircase and down the hall. I admit to a certain disappointment that the woman wasn't Sally, and I decided I'd go as soon as they were going at it hard enough not to notice my departure.

'Goodness gracious, Lester, this would be the most beautiful house if you'd only just clean the rest of it up like this room here,' the woman's voice said.

'Guess I'm used to it that way,' Gladwell answered like a man who'd heard the same observation once or twice before.

'I'd even come early some Friday and help you. I bet I could talk Frieda and Sonya into it, too.'

'Don't believe I will, thank you kindly.' It was a firm refusal and she didn't press it as he helpfully steered her right into my sightline on the other side of the bed.

'When'd you get that Plymouth?' she asked him.

'Long time ago, usually I got it in the barn.'

'What you want me to do this time, Lester?' Lynn asked. She wasn't bad to look at, with blonde hair in a permanent wave and big tits and a face that wasn't pretty, exactly, but with a lopsided smile that seemed to suggest a good time could be had by all. She did look a little hard-ridden for her age, which I estimated at about thirty.

'Strip down to your shorts and like that,' he said, his throat slightly constricted.

She winked and started undoing her dress in back, undulating and shimmying her way out of it until it slid to the floor. She put her hands to her hips. 'You want the slip on or off?'

'Just your silkies and the other thing.' He cupped his hands in front of his chest, supporting a pair of apparently gigantic imaginary breasts.

'My bra?' she asked, her slip going over her head. 'You like to look at that, Lester?' She had on a pair of black panties with a matching brassiere and a white garter belt.

He nodded. 'Mm-hm.'

'Shoes and stockings on?'

'Yes ma'am.'

'You want to see my titties, Lester?'

'Not yet,' he said, looking straight at me, and I realized I was supposed to be getting shots of her stripping. I placed the lighter against the peephole and flicked it open and shut again with a click, not far enough to spark a flame.

'You hear that, Lester?'

'Uh-huh. I got mice in here. Gonna get me a cat one of these days. Okay, now let's see them bosoms.'

Five minutes later they were both naked and writhing on the bed, changing positions much too quickly to allow for any sort of satisfaction for either of them; ten seconds or so after each switch I'd click the lighter again, the snap of the imaginary shutter his signal to withdraw, turn her over and try something new.

After a click from my phantom Minox ended a very brief session of cunnilingus, he very gently held her hips and rolled her on to her stomach and removed a jar of petroleum jelly from the nightstand, at which point I decided I'd seen enough of these two lovebirds. What red-blooded reader of *True* or *Argosy* wouldn't feel cheated when his brown 8x12 envelope arrived in the mail and out slid pictures of the old farmer's scrawny buttocks pumping away at this tired harlot? Quietly I left the room and its stench behind and went downstairs, and as I got to the front door she began to moan, and as I stood there it progressed to a yell. I don't know what he thought about my taking so much longer to get snapping on what he must have considered one of the most commercially viable positions of the afternoon.

'Oh, my god, Lester, I'm so dirty I'm so dirty I'm so dirty,' I heard her cry as I opened the door, missing the dispiriting sight of Lester and Lynn violating Kansas state law. I hoped he wouldn't be too disappointed about the pictures and drove back to town feeling pleased with the afternoon's labors, hot air blowing through the open windows of the Plymouth. It was a long way back to town and the radio didn't work so I watched the fields roll by, separated by rows of big old trees as wind breaks, the solid expanses of green occasionally punctuated by the appearance of a farmhouse. I felt a brief wave of nostalgia wash over me, though I'd never lived on a farm myself and never wanted to. Then I recognized that the pang I felt was for Japan, and I cursed my own greed and my shitty timing.

*

A French soldier had approached me about getting some uniforms; I didn't know what his racket was and didn't want to either. I sold him the uniforms and had my own tailor fit him out as a corporal and a couple of Japanese gangsters as privates and thought I was done with the whole business.

Maybe three weeks later I read in *Stars and Stripes*

where someone had knocked over a bank in Osaka. There was nothing particularly original about the robbery, and had it happened in the States not much ink would have flowed, but it was the first modern bank job in Japanese history and the press there was all over it. So was the Criminal Investigations Division of the United States Army. There was disagreement amongst the various witnesses as to the nationality and descriptions of the robbers, but one element was consistent in all their accounts: they were wearing United States Army uniforms. As soon as I read that, I started preparing for a possible hasty departure, and a couple of weeks after that Lieutenant McCowan showed up to ask me if I'd ever been approached about selling uniforms. I told him hell no, I would have reported it so fast it'd make your head swim, but McCowan didn't look as stupid as I needed him to be. I was gone before he had a chance to come around again, leaving the party just as it was about to go into full swing. I was lucky, I guess, that I had a place to go and a goal to work toward.

*

Finally I was off the dirt roads and on pavement, and getting close to town. I pondered what to do with the rest of the day; for the first time in my life I was on no one's schedule, not even my own. I decided to drive around and look at the old hometown in the rosy light of the setting June sun.

For some reason I got stuck on the idea of seeing the house I'd grown up in. I hadn't been inside it since high school; my mother moved shortly after I left home, and since then I'd had no urge to relive my childhood. When I pulled up in front of it there was a crewcut guy in Bermuda shorts mowing the lawn with a beer can in his left hand. He was about thirty, his limbs thin but with a gut billowing over the top of his shorts, and though the evening was mild as summer ones go in Kansas his face was red and dappled with tiny drops of perspiration. I lit one up, got out and leaned on the side of the Plymouth, watching him for a minute until he finally noticed me and asked what the hell I was looking at.

'Just waiting for you to stop for a second. I didn't want to interrupt.'

'So what do you want?'

'I was just wondering if I could take a look inside. I lived here when I was a kid.'

'You got another coffin nail on you, there?'

I took out the pack of Luckies, lit one off my own and handed it to him. He took a deep long hit and I looked around the lawn. It was the color of a green olive in the shade and that of a green grape where the low sun hit it. He wasn't friendly, exactly, but he was glad to have an unexpected excuse to take a break. The job was about half done, the grass high enough to make pushing the mower a major physical effort. He swigged down his beer and beckoned me to follow him.

Inside, naturally, it was smaller than I remembered. Shabbier, too, though that might have been due to the passing of the years and the neglect of subsequent residents rather than a failure of childhood memory. The front room was a mess, with magazines scattered all over the coffee table and the floor around it, mostly of the confessional or movie star scandal variety, and ashtrays awash with butts, divided pretty evenly between those with and without lipstick. I looked into the smaller of the two bedrooms, which had been mine, and found it full of ham radio equipment. My parents' old bedroom was down the hall past the bathroom, and I asked his permission to look before I opened the door. It wasn't much neater than the front room, and the unmade bed rested against the wrong wall, beneath a large wooden crucifix that would have appalled my rigidly Baptist mother. I closed the door and was about to thank him for his kindness and go when he called out from the kitchen.

'You want a beer?'

I went in and sat down at the table and he brought over two cans of Hamm's. He opened his own and passed the churchkey to me.

'You aren't Masterson's son, are you?'

'Never heard of him,' I said.

'Landlord.' He seemed relieved. 'He's a prick with ears.'

'Must have been the guy who bought it from my folks.'

'Raised the fucking rent two years in a row, but you try and get him to fix the goddamn water heater and he's nowhere to be found. Had a guy come out and fix it end of March, sent him the bill and he goddamn ignored it. I got half a mind to deduct it from the rent, except the cocksucker'd probably evict us.'

'Can he do that?'

'Shit, yes. Law's completely on his side.'

'I wouldn't know, I've hardly ever been a renter. Been in the Army since the war except for one year right after.'

'Goddamn Army. There's sure times when I wish I'd never left.' He looked at his can of Hamm's for a second, drained it and went back to the ice box for a replacement. 'You want another one?'

'I'm doing okay, thanks.'

As he closed the ice box I heard the front door open and a second later a woman's thin voice tore through the air of the little house. 'I thought I told you I wanted to see that fucking lawn mowed by the time I got home.'

A nice-looking young woman with short blonde hair, six or seven months pregnant, leaned against the frame of the kitchen door, barely registering my presence except as an explanation for her husband's failure to complete his chore. She was dressed nicely, for an office job most likely, and she stared fiercely at my new buddy.

'Hiya, honey, just sitting down for a beer,' he said with deliberate good cheer.

'I can see that. What happened to the lawn?'

'About half of it got mowed.'

I stood up. 'Sergeant Thomas McCowan, U.S. Army Quartermaster Corps. Sorry to have distracted your husband, but I lived here as a boy and I wanted to see the old place again.'

'Great. Now you've seen it.'

I was a little taken aback; the polite, apologetic soldier routine usually worked wonders with lady civilians. I was about to elaborate when the woman stomped out and into the bedroom, where the door slammed as loud as a cheap, lightweight one can.

'Like I said, there's times I wished I'd stayed in the Army. I better get back to mowing while we still got some daylight.'

We went outside. The sun was very low, turning the

house the color of a ripe peach, and he started pushing the lawn mower again. I got behind the wheel and sipped at the beer, considering where to go next. Sally wasn't far from here; there wouldn't be any harm in me driving casually by just to see the lie of the land. In the sideview mirror as I pulled away my new, nameless friend pushed away like Sisyphus.

*

She still lived in the same house I'd bought in '46. The sun was lower and the pretty warm twilight was gone from the lawns, replaced by the cool blue shadows of the houses and the trees. Like my childhood home, ours looked shabbier than I remembered, and she'd painted it brown, something I never would have allowed. The chainlink fence appeared to be the same one I'd put in myself when we moved in, warped now and rusted in spots, and the lawn was spotted with dandelions and crabgrass, showing up dark green and tall against a field of sickly yellow.

Parked in the driveway was a Cadillac convertible, a hatchet-faced slick in a houndstooth sportjacket dangling halfway out the driver's side door, leisurely perusing the front section of the afternoon *Beacon*, one loafered foot on the cement. I didn't want to stop, so I drove around the block for a second look. I thought he might be the cop Amos Culligan had mentioned, the former boyfriend who provided security on weekends, and if he was I wanted to get a good look at him. As I passed he looked up from his paper at the door and then at his watch, and shortly thereafter came a couple of short blasts from the horn. On my third pass a woman stepped out the front door and strolled toward the Caddy, dressed like a rube's idea of a movie star in tight pants, a bright red scarf and, despite the fading light, a pair of catseye sunglasses. Sally stood framed in the doorsill saying something to the back of the woman's head and looking as ripe and lovely as I'd ever seen her.

The pendular rolling motion of the glamor girl's ass looked at least semi-professional, as did the practiced smile she gave the man at the wheel; I was certain now that he was a boyfriend or a john and not a cop, at any rate not the cop in question. Getting into the passenger seat she turned back and said something to Sally, and by then I had passed the house again. I would have liked to swing past a fourth time, but that seemed unwise and I turned left at the intersection, heading west on Douglas, asking myself what she was doing with all that undeclarable income if she wasn't spending it on home repair.

*

There wasn't much traffic downtown, and I made it to the Commanche before the last traces of pink and blue had drained from the sky. It was busier than I'd anticipated, though not like at midnight. Half of this crowd would be home and asleep by that hour, the remainder still here and plastered. These slightly more genteel ladies were exhilarated by the notion that merely by being there with their beaux or husbands they were doing something naughty, whereas the women who closed the place down mostly came with the intention of breaking one or two commandments. I vaguely hoped I might see Lena, and if I did I'd keep her reasonably sober.

I didn't see her, but I did see her friend, whose name I couldn't recall. She was with the newspaperman again, and when I'd been served I took my glass over to their table.

'You sure made an impression on Lena,' the girl said. She had a short hairdo and a sweet face that I suspected was misleading. 'She won't say what happened, but she sure looked like it was something good.'

I contented myself with an enigmatic smile and took a sip of my drink.

'Sorry, but I forgot your name,' the reporter said.

'Tom,' I said.

'Did you tell me you were in the Army? In Japan?'

'Just got out.'

'Ha,' the girl said. 'I suppose they've rolled out the red carpet for the reds already.' She laughed. 'Ha! Red carpet, get it?'

He looked at her a little cockeyed. 'What are you talking about?'

'You ought to do more reading and less writing and you'd find some things out. The commies are taking over all our allies by democratic means, starting in Europe, and nobody's going to do anything about it.' She gave him a significant look, then got up and wobbled toward the ladies' room.

'Jesus,' he said. 'She's a Bircher, but she's a terrific lay. I'm just wondering how much I can take before I have to tell her she's out of her fucking mind.'

'Don't tell her, just keep screwing her.'

He nodded thoughtfully, as if the thought of fucking without intellectual communion was new to him. 'Hey, since she's gone I ought to tell you, that girl Lena's married.'

'Yeah, she told me that before she told me her name.'

'Just thought you should know in case things turn ugly.'

We didn't have much else to say to each other. A few minutes later the girl came back from the bathroom. 'Lena's alone tonight at home,' she said. 'I know she'd be happy to hear from you.'

Maybe she would at that. At the very least I could get my ashes hauled again and it would kill a couple of the long hours before the weekend, when I could take care of my business and get out of this goddamned town forever.

*

I drove straight over without calling. Lena let me in the kitchen door and I declined her offer of a drink as she led me to the divan in the living room.

'Well, I'm having one,' she said, already several doses into her drunk for the evening. She was nude under her peignoir, which to her badly feigned consternation managed repeatedly to work itself open. 'I like to feel a little loose when I'm socializing,' she said, stumbling back into the kitchen.

'I'm loose enough already,' I said, which sent her into an idiotic, whooping laughing that made me glad she was out of my line of sight. The prospect of spending the rest of the night sober in the company of this drunken thimblewit made me sick, and I resolved to screw her as quickly as possible and leave, just to get sex off my mind for the rest of the evening.

I stood and moved over to where she was pouring herself three fingers of Old Grand-Dad into a highball glass, still giggling to herself. I came up behind her and slid my hands through the opening of the peignoir and cupped her breasts. She stopped laughing and let out a long, rapturous sigh, then grabbed my right hand and guided it down between her thighs. I worked my fingers there for a minute, letting her guide them exactly where she wanted. I looked up at the naked bulb in the ceiling fixture; she started bucking against the pressure of my hand and the next sound I heard was the kitchen door opening. Her eyes stayed closed, and mine met those of a man not much older than she was. He stared at us with his mouth open for a few seconds, holding the door open, and when she finally looked at him she didn't stop moving or moaning. He didn't look hurt or angry so much as stunned, and I pulled my hand away from her. He slammed the door from the outside and walked away.

Now she pulled the peignoir shut and ran out the door after him. 'Doug!' There was shrill, culpable disbelief in her voice, as though she'd just awakened from a dream of sex to find herself actually engaged in it. I didn't hear Doug's response as I picked up his copy of Procopius from the living-room bookshelf and walked out the front door, though as I walked to my car I could still hear her apologetic gulps and hiccupping in the distance, carried through the moist air like the cries of a rutting animal. I got into the car and headed for the Bellingham, where I would spend the rest of the evening in the quiet, sage company of a good book.

*

Approaching the tenderloin a few blocks east of Union Station it hit me that I wasn't far from my father's old office. It was at his insistence that I'd studied the classics in the first place, and *The Secret History* was one of his favorites (though I hated to think how disappointed he would have been to know I was lazily resorting to a translation). The block had been in decline in his last years there, and the slide had continued in his and my absences; in the doorway that led to the offices on the second and third floors lay a souse, marinating in a puddle of urine and flopsweat and snoring like a consumptive walrus. On one side of the door was a pawn shop, whose signage indicated it was now run by the sons of the man who'd owned it in Father's time; on the other side was a discount leather goods store, the cheap valises and briefcases in its display window dusty and cracked. Grabbing the handle I found the door unlocked and made my way up the dark stairs, each creaking with its own ghostly timbre as if to warn my father's hardworking shade of my arrival.

His one-man bookkeeping office had been there on the second floor for thirty-seven years, looking out diagonally across the intersection on to Union Station. He didn't marry my mother until he was past fifty; his first wife had, luckily for me, died of a botched appendectomy a couple of years before, and he was dead himself of heart failure before I graduated high school. Until this afternoon's visit to my childhood house I couldn't remember the last time he'd come to mind.

The office was occupied by a firm by the name of Cuthbertson Imports. What they imported wasn't clear looking inward through the glass of the door, but the room looked much the same as it had during my father's tenancy. In the diffuse glow of the streetlamp outside it even appeared that the large desk against the east wall was his own, and perhaps it was; I couldn't remember moving it out after he died.

At the foot of the stairs the stew bum raised himself up on to his elbow as I pushed past him on to the sidewalk. 'Peggy?' he blubbered, his voice full of hope.

'Sorry, no,' I said.

'Fuck 'er,' he growled, then rolled back over.

I was almost to the car when a scrawny little guy crossed my path. ''Scuse me, sir, I was just hoping you could see your way clear to letting me have a quarter.'

'Sure thing, Chester.' I opened my wallet and pulled out a ten-dollar bill, and he looked at me real hard, trying to figure out how I knew his name.

'That's funny, I'm pretty good at faces ...' His voice drifted off as he got a good look at the ten spot, which would have paid his seventy-five-cent room for a week with enough left over for a real pants-pissing bender and a meal afterward.

'What was that you said the other night, something about you'd rather eat shit than steak and pussy?'

'Oh,' Chester said. 'The supply sarge.' He nodded and turned away, looking heartbroken.

'Hey, Chester, come back.' I really did want to give him that sawbuck.

'No, sir.'

'I got ten bucks here for you.'

'I meant what I said, Mister.' He walked away with his

head down, and it got to me. I caught up to him and put a hand on his shoulder.

'Chester, come on, take the ten, I'm in a rare generous mood.'

He shook away and kept walking.

'How are you going to feel tomorrow morning, waking up with the screaming meamies and knowing you turned down ten simoleons?'

He ignored me. When I put my hand on his shoulder again he tried to shake it off, and I spun him around to face me. Without really planning to, I backhanded him across the face, and he fell backward into the plate glass window of a shoe store, which vibrated ominously but didn't break.

'Big man, beating up an old drunk half your size,' he said, rubbing his cheek, and I grabbed him by the front of his shirt and backhanded him again, hard this time, my hand in a fist. I did it again and again until my knuckles were sticky, and then I let him drop to the pavement. I jaywalked over to Union Station and washed the blood off my hands in the men's room, then went to one of the phone booths and had the operator connect me with St. Francis.

'Better get an ambulance over across Douglas from Union Station,' I said. 'There's an old guy here's had the piss taken right out of him.'

I crossed the street to my car and went back to the hotel. I read until seven in the morning, then I went to sleep.

CHAPTER FIFTEEN

Gunther was in the back seat of a cab, wearing a pair of gold wire-framed sunglasses he'd found in a kitchen drawer. The cabbie called him Mr. Gandy, and the first thing he did after Gunther gave him Sally's address was ask him if he'd heard about the old man who'd escaped from the rest home the day before.

'I heard all about it,' Gunther said. 'They say on TV he's so senile he can't talk in whole sentences.'

Sally lived in a new subdivision out west that Gunther hadn't ever heard of whose street names all had to do with aviation, or more precisely with airports: Windsock Lane, Runway Terrace, Tarmac Road. Sally's ranch style house was on a cul de sac called Control Tower Place. A light was on in the entryway and a single lamp was visible through the living room curtains even though the sun was still up. He paid the cabbie and rang the doorbell, and receiving no answer went around back. Before he started looking for the key he tried the door and found it open. The carelessness of it irritated but didn't surprise him, and he stepped into Sally's kitchen to the sound of central air blowing full blast.

'Anybody home?'

There was no answer. The kitchen was neat and the house new, though not as nice or homey as her daughter's. He opened the refrigerator and after a moment's browsing pulled out a cold chicken, intact except for a missing wing and leg. He sat down at the kitchen table and started eating it with his fingers, pulling it apart piece by piece and gnawing it down to the bone. When he had eaten all the meat he pulled the traces of the sweetbreads from the bones and popped them into his mouth, and then he stood up to wash his hands.

He started down a hallway lined with photos, including lots of pictures of Loretta and her two kids and several of an old fat woman with a slightly crooked nose who, on close examination, turned out to be Sally. In two or three of them she was posing with a man slightly older than she was, thin and dyspeptic looking, wearing glasses with lenses so thick you could hardly see what his eyes looked like. He wondered how it had been, being married to Sally; not a happy thing to contemplate, though maybe she'd calmed down a little bit passing seventy.

At the end of the hallway was the master bedroom, neatly made up, and he started going through its cabinets and drawers. At the bottom of her dresser he found a framed photograph of Wayne Ogden in his Army uniform, his face hand-tinted an artificial pink and his eyes bright blue. He was a little surprised to find the picture around, even hidden, although he supposed she'd kept it for the child's sake. No reason she had to know her old man was a louse.

*

Nothing that met Sidney's eye upon entering Harry's barber shop seemed to predate 1965. The floor was a checkerboard of worn, mismatched linoleum, black squares marbled with mint green next to salmon ones accented with cream, with triangular patches of blackened grout where some of them were missing corners. On the wall was a photo of a serious young man and the legend THE JFK, which confused Sidney until he realized it was the name of a haircut; similar photos hung on the other wall, labeled THE CREWCUT and THE BUSINESSMAN.

The client in the chair was roughly the barber's age, and both men looked at him with some annoyance as he walked in. 'Go on, sit down, I'm almost done with old Clyde here,' Harry said.

'Actually I wanted to ask you about something.'

'I said I'll be done in a few minutes.'

Sidney shrugged and took a seat. Harry was taking more time with Clyde's cut than Sidney thought necessary, since all the hair the old man had left was a thin, yellowish white crescent that stretched from ear to ear around the back of his head. Most likely he came in once a week just for the conversation; Sidney seemed to have interrupted a discussion of the Russian situation.

'Shit, my daughter was telling me just the other day "Isn't that great?" like they're our pals all of a sudden, a country with about a half a billion reds in it, just because they said so on the TV.' Clyde was ruddy complexioned with rheumy eyes, his voice surprisingly deep and strong. He shook his head in disgust and Harry pulled his scissors and comb away.

'Damnit, don't move your head. How many times have I told you that?'

'About once every two weeks since 1955.' Clyde grinned at Sidney, who smiled politely in return. 'Anyway, it was your old pal Ronnie Reagan who started the whole thing, kissing up to that Gorbachev.'

'Don't talk about Reagan, now,' Harry said as he whipped the sheet off him. On the floor there wasn't enough hair to sweep, and after Clyde left Sidney took the seat.

'How do you want it?' Harry wrapped the tissue paper around his throat and threw the sheet over his clothes.

'I don't know. Short.'

'How short?'

'Like that one.' He pointed at the wall. 'The Businessman.'

'That's a lot shorter than you got now. You sure? Won't be curly if I cut it that short.'

'Change is good. I wasn't really planning to get a haircut when I came in.'

'Oh, no?' Harry said without much interest, since as far as he was concerned the haircut had started as soon as the big man had sat down in the chair.

'I just wanted to ask you some questions. I'm Gunther Fahnstiel's stepson.'

'I already told the cops everything and I don't like to repeat myself. You still want a haircut?'

The old man was clearly a talker, and maybe he could get him to volunteer something, so Sidney nodded.

'Don't move your head. A man once bled to death right in this chair.'

*

Marty Blaine worked in a brand new office park off Kellogg, not five minutes from Lake Vista, and Ed listened
carefully to his calls while ostensibly reading a month old
copy of *Newsweek*. Marty bullshitted and told jokes, but
at the heart of each call was some sort of business transaction, a new policy or a renewal or a discussion of
increased coverage, and each call was short. When he
had finished with a fifth, he hung up and apologized.

'End of the week, you know, tying up a few loose ends.'

'That's okay, Marty. You remember me at all?'

'Sure,' he said. After his old man's accident the boy had
been taken on as a group responsibility by Rory's friends,
a situation that lasted until his mother, having divorced
her debilitated husband, remarried and made it known
that cops weren't welcome around her son any more. Ed
doubted that Marty remembered him particularly, but he
was a good enough salesman to pretend.

Ed leaned back. 'Just saw your dad this morning.'

'Oh. How'd he look?'

'Well, I hadn't seen him since he lost his foot, so it was
kind of a surprise.'

'That's been a while. Diabetes.'

'Right after he moved into Lake Vista, if I'm not mistaken. What made you decide to move him?'

'The pension plan moved him.'

'Both times?'

He seemed to be calculating. 'Yeah, he was in that
place out on Twenty-first for a little while.'

'And nobody asked you either time?'

'They just called to let me know.'

'You remember who that might have been?'

'One of his old cop buddies, I don't remember who exactly.'

Ed nodded. 'I don't mean to get too personal, but is anybody helping you out with him?'

'What do you mean, helping me out?'

'I don't know how much you're putting up a month, but Lake Vista's a pretty expensive facility . . .'

Marty shook his head. 'I'm not paying anything. Pension fund pays it, and I think his Veterans' Disability pays some.'

'Oh. Sorry, I guess I was misinformed.'

'Is that all you needed to know?'

'I guess it is.'

'Well, glad I could help.' He stood up and held out his hand, grinning. 'It's real good to see you, Ed.'

Ed shook his hand. 'Go visit your Dad,' he said.

*

Eric opened his eyes slowly, thinking he was hung over. No hangover he knew, though, could account for the pain on the outside of his head, both temples throbbing with every heartbeat and threatening nausea. The pain was asymmetrical, too, slightly higher up on the left side than on the right, and stronger. Glancing at the clock radio he was surprised at the lateness of the hour. His memories of the afternoon were vague after Lupe's, but he remembered making a bet with Rex at the Chimneysweep.

As he sat up the nausea started to build, and he held his breath and counted to ten. Just as he reached nine he had a vision: a memory of a horrifyingly lucid nightmare about being attacked by a naked old man wielding a pool cue. Christ only knew where that one had come from. He got up off the bed and looked down at himself. He needed cleaning up badly.

He showered and changed clothes and put some lotion on his sunburn, which was worse than he'd expected. Loretta kept an emergency twenty-dollar bill taped to the underside of a kitchen drawer, which would pay for a cab ride to Belinda's; he'd get his wallet and car keys back, and they could head for the track. She seemed like the kind of woman who'd enjoy the races, and he could put a few more dollars on Rusty.

He verified the presence of the bill and called the cab company.

'Oh, it's Mister Gandy,' the dispatcher said when he gave her the address.

'How'd you know who I was?'

'Recognized the address. Just sent a man out there an hour or so ago. Didn't he get there?'

Shit. Had he ordered another cab and forgotten about it? 'It got here, I just need another one.'

'Okay. He'll be there in about ten minutes.'

He hung up and absently picked up Loretta's address book, in which someone had emphatically circled his mother-in-law's address and phone with a blue ballpoint pen. He went outside to wait for the cab without giving it any more thought.

*

The building that had been the Sweet Cage's first home was on the way to the Stars and Stripes Motel, and approaching it Sidney decided to stop and put up a flyer;

he was curious as to what the new occupants had done to the place to take away the stripjoint atmosphere. A new wooden sign hung where the old one had been:

FIRST CHURCH OF THE END TIMES
REV. Q. LEFLIN, PASTOR

A single car sat in the lot, a rusted Dart with bumper stickers plastered all over its rear. He parked next to it, studying the side of the building. It had needed work when the Sweet Cage moved out and it hadn't happened yet; big chunks of plaster had fallen off and lay nestled in the weeds in the narrow strip of dirt between the building and the parking lot.

Pulling the front door open he had an odd feeling of comfortable familiarity, almost as though the building were welcoming him back. It was hot as hell inside, almost as bad as outdoors, and he wondered what had happened to the air conditioning. He'd forced the landlord to install a new condenser two years before they moved out and even if it had broken down it was under warranty.

'Hello? Anybody here?'

Even without any lights on in the front room he could see that it was dirtier than it had ever been when it was a nudie bar. The carpet looked as if it hadn't been vacuumed since the church took it over, and the dust on the linoleum around the stage was thick enough that someone had fingered a little cross in it with the words 'Jesus Loves You' written above it, like 'Wash Me' on a grimy car. The only physical changes he could see were an enormous plywood cross held to the east wall with baling wire and a matching plywood lectern at the front of the old stage, both of which looked like they'd been made in a junior high school woodshop. They hadn't even bothered to take out the bar.

A small man of indeterminate age in a shortsleeved white shirt, black tie and black pants came out of the back room, apparently in use as an office again. He had close cropped black hair and a somber demeanor, and he seemed nonplussed to see an outsider in the building. 'Can I help you?'

Sidney held out one of the flyers. 'I was wondering if you'd let me put this up on your bulletin board.'

The man looked at the flyer. 'Okay.' He walked over to a water-damaged, tattered cork message board opposite the lectern and tacked it up. In the shadows it was barely visible from where Sidney stood.

'I used to work here, before it was a church. You know, that air conditioner on the roof is practically brand new.'

'Electric bill,' the man said. 'Nothing in scripture says we have to be comfortable when we worship.'

'Would you mind if I had a look at the back room?'

The man held out his open hand and swept it back toward the office. 'Be my guest.'

The office was laid out startlingly as it had been ten years earlier. The desk was in more or less the same position, and his sense that the building was welcoming him back now felt sinister. The office was dark, with no light coming in from the painted-over window on the south wall. He ignored an urge to bolt and took a long, deep whiff. The odor was still there, faint but unmistakable; how did the preacher stand working in here?

'Ever notice a smell?'

'A smell?'

'In here. A funny smell.'

'No, sir.'

He stepped out of the room and stood behind the bar. Replace the roughhewn lectern and cross with a jukebox and it might be 1979, with Sidney on afternoon shift. It wouldn't take much more than that for the display of genitalia to become the building's central function again. The sensation of time travel brought with it an instinctive urge to straighten the place up before Renata showed up and started bitching, and he knew it was time to go.

'Thanks for putting the flyer up.'

'You're welcome.' The minister, if that's what he was, headed back to the office, apparently with no interest in making a convert of Sidney.

'Hey, reverend.' The man turned back to him as he pulled out his wallet and took out a couple of twenties. 'There's a little something for the collection. Good luck.'

'Thanks,' the minister said, stuffing the money into his shirt pocket, and went back into the office as Sidney made his way to the front door in the stifling heat.

*

The late afternoon sun was obscured in Sally's living room by heavy, bluish green curtains. There was an inviting La-Z-Boy in the center of the room that must have been the husband's base of operations, and across from it was a pretty good sized idiot box. Against the wall was a big blue-green couch covered with green throw pillows, and above it a picture that reminded Gunther of the one in his motel room the night before, though the only similarity between them was their painters' lack of skill.

This one was a brightly colored cityscape with a crowd drinking at an outdoor cafe. He stepped on to the couch to get a better look at it, tottering from side to side on the surprisingly firm cushion. In the picture's righthand corner it was signed 'Pablo '68,' and in the background, behind the cafe, loomed a huge white onion-shaped dome that made him think of Russia or India. The longer he looked at it the more it called to mind the other picture and his dream, which calmed him.

He stepped down and pulled a book from a built-in shelf, one of a set of identically bound leather volumes on medicine and nutrition. He wondered for a moment if Sally hadn't eventually found her calling in health care, but according to the title page it was published and distributed by a manufacturer of nutritional supplements. He flipped through it and stopped to read a page at random; it was a rant against the medical establishment in general and the Food and Drug Administration in particular, and when he closed it he found a bookplate on the inside front cover reading: 'Presented to Sally Atchison, a new Thousand Unit PurpleStar Dealer.'

*

When the cab let Eric out in front of Belinda's condo she wasn't home yet, so he sat on the steps of her unit and waited. For half an hour he entertained a fantasy scenario in which hours of complicated foreplay disabused Belinda of the notion that he was an inconsiderate and hasty lover.

Checking his watch he realized that this would be impossible if they were to catch Rusty's race, and after another
half hour he was wondering whether they'd even have
time for a semi-clothed quickie before they headed downtown to pick up his Volvo. By the time her car turned into
the lot a few dozen feet away and settled into its space he
was frankly annoyed with her, but determined not to spoil
the evening by showing it. She got out and stamped across
the parking lot toward him with marked displeasure.

'Have you been here all day?' she said, her expression
turning from hostility to disgust. 'You're all sunburned.'

'I left my keys and my wallet inside. My car's still
locked up over by Ruby's. I was kind of hoping I could get
a ride over there.'

'I'm not taking you anywhere, Eric. Where are your
keys?'

'I guess they fell out of my pants when I threw 'em.'

'I'll go in and look.' She unlocked her front door. Eric
stood right behind her, and she turned and snapped at
him. 'Don't touch me.'

She turned the latch and slipped in, starting to close
the door. 'Can I come in?' Eric yelled at her back.

'No.' The door shut, followed by the sound of a bolt
turning inside.

He stood there, staring at the closed door, trying to
imagine what had happened since the morning to alter
her attitude toward him so radically.

The door opened a crack and Belinda held out his keys
and wallet. 'Here. Don't come by again without calling. In
fact, don't call. Last night was a big mistake.'

'What's up your ass all of a sudden?'

'You're a fucking liar. You're broke. You're weeks away from bankruptcy court, and I have standards to maintain.' She shut the door again.

'Oh, hell, I'm not broke. Who told you that? Gary?' He knew it was, and the lack of response on the other side proved it. 'Gary's pissed off because I was screwing his wife the whole time they were married.'

'Go away,' she said from inside. He rang the bell and she swung the door open with some violence. 'I'm going to call the police if you don't leave immediately.'

'I just wanted you to call me a cab. Jesus.'

'Wait out by the street.' She closed the door again and he went to the sidewalk, his feelings of humiliation assuaged somewhat by the comforting sight of sweet cash in his wallet.

*

The Stars and Stripes was harder to pick out than Sidney had anticipated; he didn't remember the street number, and half the motels on the strip now had red, white and blue signs and names like the Old Glory Inn, the Minuteman Motel and the 1776 Motor Lodge. Despite the heat the streetwalkers were out in force, and as he slowed to look for the Stars and Stripes they moved forward one by one, trying to catch his eye. One of them, a round-faced, orange-complexioned woman with a loony, gaptoothed grin and a blonde afro wig, ran alongside the car knocking on his passenger window. Finally she tried the door handle, and as he speeded up to get away from her she started screaming something at him. He couldn't hear all of it, but it started with 'Fuck you, you fuckin' faggotty asshole,' and she was still standing on the curb screaming after him, arms flailing in wild, extravagant rage and disgust when he looked into the rearview mirror half a block away. When he got to the Stars and Stripes he parked on the street, noting the absence of hookers on the sidewalk directly in front. This was explained by a note on the door, neatly handwritten:

> *No Hourly Rentals*
> *Only Overnight!*
> *No Exceptions, please do not ask*
> *We will call the police!*

The motel's office was cooled only slightly by an underperforming window unit that buzzed urgently and constantly, a pair of white ribbons dancing frantically in the lukewarm air blowing from its vent. A young man seated at a desk looked up at Sidney's entry with a tentatively friendly smile. 'Yes, sir, can I help you?' Sidney had at first taken him for Indian, but his flat monotone was unmistakably local.

'My name's Sidney McCallum. Gunther Fahnstiel's my stepfather.'

'Oh, the old man. I was afraid you wanted to bring a hooker into one of the rooms. A lot of the johns around here think this is still the Bide-A-Wee.'

'Not me.'

'Well, I wasn't on duty last night. All I know about him is what's on TV.'

Sidney watched the ribbons flutter, feeling stupid and

wondering what he'd thought he would find in any of these places that would bring the old man home. 'Thanks anyway,' he said.

'Don't mention it. I hope you find him before he hurts himself.'

As he stepped on to the sidewalk a tall black woman approached him with a nervous sidelong look at the office of the Stars and Stripes. 'Looking for a date, sugar? That's the wrong motel for you.'

'No, thanks,' he said, moving around to the driver's side.

'Come on. Take a look at these titties.' She flashed him quickly as he got in.

'I'm not looking for a date, thanks.'

'Why not?'

'I'm a priest,' he said.

She snorted. 'A priest? In a BMW?'

'I gotta go, my child. Late for Vespers.'

'Come back if you change your mind, Padre.'

He pulled away and made a U-turn, and as he headed back toward downtown he happened to notice a thin woman in a tank top a few doors north of the Stars and Stripes, talking to an elderly john. Her eyes seemed about to pop out of their sockets and dance, and Sidney thought he recognized her as a former employee of one of the clubs, a dimwitted but cheery young woman with a hearty appetite for speed. He hoped he was wrong, but despite her loss of about twenty-five pounds he was pretty sure he was right. He was looking at her and not the john, and didn't notice when the man got into his little car and took off after him.

Half a block later the old man was right on his tail, honking, and Sidney looked back to see Ed Dieterle signaling for him to pull over.

They went through the intersection and parked in front of a church, a modern, one-story building half a block long, unadorned except for a large sign with a cross and a flame and beneath it a marquee with mismatched red, grey and black letters:

CHRITIANS ARENT PERFECT
JUST FORGIVEM

'Didn't you see me waving at you from the street?' Dieterle said, stepping out of a little Japanese car.

Sidney got out and shook his hand. 'Thanks for coming up. You getting anywhere?'

'Hard to say. You?'

'Not really. Just putting up flyers is about all I can think of to do.'

'That's good, though. Always the chance somebody'll spot him buying a coke or waiting for the bus.'

'You need a place to stay?'

'I'm at the Highland Seven on East Kellogg. Shitty but cheap.'

'You can sleep at my house for free if you want.'

He shook his head. 'Thanks, but I live in somebody else's house, it's nice sleeping in a motel for a change. Listen, do me a favor. Check in at your mom's every hour or two, would you? In case I need you.' He walked back to his car. 'See you later.'

Sidney waved and started to get back into the BMW.

'Hey, Sidney. Did you buy them an air conditioner a few years ago?'

'No.'

Dieterle seemed pleased, finally. 'Thanks.' He got into his car and drove off.

*

Loretta picked up a carryout at a Chinese restaurant a few blocks west of the office. She would have preferred Italian, but with the Chinese she could get enough for two people and if Eric didn't show it would still be good the next day.

Once again his car wasn't in its place in the garage, and this time she was happy about it. A few small household tasks nagged at her conscience; she ignored them, poured herself a glass of wine and sat on the back patio for a while to enjoy the relatively temperate early evening.

In the distance she could hear the staticky buzzing of the cicada's mating cry, a sad sound she had always associated with the end of summer. Even now, at the age of forty-two, it made her feel like school was about to start. She didn't hear them here as often or as loud as she had growing up in Cottonwood, and despite the melancholy that accompanied the sound there was something comforting about it, too.

She finished the wine and went back in and upstairs to the bedroom, where something seemed slightly amiss: the bed was made but the bedspread was considerably rumpled. Had he actually had the gall to bring one of them here? The idea of it bothered her for reasons more hygienic than sentimental, and she decided to do the sheets just in case.

In the laundry room she loaded the sheets and bed-spread into the washer and set the control to hot. As she started to leave, she saw one of her business cards crumpled on the floor next to a couple of cash register receipts. She tossed them into the wastebasket amongst the dryer lint and the cling-free static sheets.

*

Moving boxes filled Sally's entire garage except for the righthand parking space, which for the moment stood empty. Against one wall were crates full of canned food apparently dating back to the sixties, along with some five-gallon bottles of water, from which Gunther deduced that if you went and looked in Sally's old back yard in Cotton-wood you'd find a fallout shelter. Just how demented had this husband of hers been, paying to transport all this from one town to another, just to store it in a garage which would be incinerated in an atomic blast just like every-thing else above ground?

By the door was a crate filled with fishing tackle, some of it old and decrepit, some new and expensive. It looked as though the old man hadn't ever fished again after leaving Cottonwood. A large box next to it contained a stuffed moose's head with a plate on its backboard stating that it had been shot in Saskatchewan, Canada, on 20 October 1958 by Donald E. Atchison. Stacks of accordion files held old business records from an auto repair shop in Cottonwood, starting before the war and going up to 1983 when the old man had presumably retired. In a carton behind those he found a bunch of old newspapers and clippings. Something about this excited him, although he couldn't have articulated what it was.

*

'Looks like you got yourself a pretty good burn there, partner,' the cab driver said when Eric sat down. 'Don't take this the wrong way, now, but I'm gonna need to see you've got some money on you before we take off, here.'

'Why would I take that the wrong way?' he said levelly, opening his wallet and producing a fan of twenties.

'All right, then. Where are we heading?'

Eric gave him the address of the parking garage downtown and didn't open his mouth again until they got there. He paid and exited the taxi without speaking, then climbed the stairs to the second floor of the garage and got into the Volvo.

Delighted to be behind the wheel after close to twenty-four hours of walking and riding, he headed north to the freeway and opened her up, averaging ninety or so between there and the dog track. His temples still throbbed and his face hurt every time his facial muscles moved, but, with money in his pocket and a set of car keys, he was starting to feel his old swagger coming back.

He parked close to the entrance and strolled toward the admission booth. Inside he picked up the tipsheet and saw that Rusty's race started in four minutes. He got into the shortest line and bet twenty on Rusty to win at eighteen to one. With the ticket in his shirt pocket he went upstairs to the big circular bar.

Taking a seat as far from the other customers as he

could, he checked the tipsheet. Rusty looked good, with a high-percentage trainer and a good bloodline, and his times were getting faster. The morning line hadn't reflected any of this at twenty-five to one, although the odds were improving steadily as post time approached, always a favorable omen. According to the infield monitor Rusty was now going off at seventeen to one, still a nice payday if he hit.

A uniformed bartender with a ponytail served him his gin and tonic and let him alone. After the first mouthful went down Eric felt good physically for the first time since the day had started heating up, and a moment later when the bell rang and the race started, he turned away from the bar to watch through the clubhouse glass on the big monitor overlooking the infield.

The dogs shot around the track after the toy rabbit and as they took the second turn the crowd began to shout out names and numbers in joy, anger or disgust, and Eric stood up for a better view. A man in a houndstooth jacket and matching hat four stools to his left was already on his feet, fists clenched, snarling at the monitor mounted in the corner of the ceiling.

'Eight! Come on, motherfucker! Come on! Eight! Eight!'

Eight was losing ground to three and five. Five was Rusty, and Eric smiled to himself as the man to his left spat 'Fuck! Fuck! Fuck!' again and again. Eight's early lead was gone and Rusty was in front, neck and neck with number three, Prince o' Chincoteague. When they crossed the finish line it was unclear who had won, and the clubhouse rumbled with the speculative murmurs of a couple of thousand anxious spectators.

'It was Rusty,' the man in the houndstooth jacket said.

'Prince o' Chincoteague,' the bartender replied, shaking his head.

The voices started again, and on the scoreboard and monitor the words 'PHOTO FINISH' flashed. The crowd groaned collectively and then grew silent at the frustrating realization that the results and their accompanying emotional release would be delayed for a few minutes.

Eric turned back to his drink and his tipsheet, vaguely recalling having bet an exacta – or was it a quinella? – on Rusty and Prince o' Chincoteague that afternoon. He tried to remember how much he'd bet, and as he jubilantly calculated his projected winnings a simultaneous wave of cheering and booing drew his eyes to the monitor, where the words 'RESULTS OFFICIAL' blinked on and off. Prince o' Chincoteague was the winner. He stared dully at the results and ordered another drink. This wasn't a good start; maybe he'd put down a single bet on the next race and call it quits.

Looking the field over, he saw a long shot that was worth risking five bucks on and wondered what the exacta had paid; he glanced up at the infield monitor and the message it was flashing:

HAVE YOU SEEN GUNTHER?
$12,000 REWARD
FOR INFORMATION

Next to it was a picture of the naked old man from his nightmare.

Eric sat there for a second, genuinely afraid that he was losing his mind. 'He looks a little old to be robbing banks,' he said to the bartender, who looked at him with open disdain.

'That poor old guy walked away from an old folks' home yesterday. Hope that never happens to you.'

The image was gone from the monitor, replaced by the odds for the next race. The old man really had been at his house, God knew why, and really had beaten him and locked him in the closet.

'You got a phone I can use?'

'Over by the men's room. They cut 'em off at post time, so you better hurry up.'

He had no idea where the old man had gone after he left, but it couldn't hurt to put in a claim on the twelve grand. He'd already dropped two dimes into the slot when he saw the taxi company's ad next to the phone. He called the number and got the same dispatcher he'd talked to that afternoon.

'This is Eric Gandy again. Where'd that cab take me this afternoon? The first one. I lost the address.'

'Just a second, Mister Gandy. 518 Control Tower Place.'

'Thanks a lot,' he said, and headed out for his car.

*

Ed knocked on Dot's door and found her with Tricia, eating dinner. Tricia had what looked like a Caesar salad and Dot was well into a second pork chop; at Tricia's invitation he poured himself a glass of iced tea and sat down with them.

'You want something to eat?' Tricia said. 'There's more salad. That's the last of the pork chops, though.'

'I'll be fine.'

'Any progress?'

'Some. Wait until your grandmother's done eating.'

At that Dot looked up suspiciously, her mouth full of pork chop and mashed potato. 'I'm done,' she said, swallowing. 'What'd you find?'

'Where do you bank?'

'That's none of your goddamned business.'

'Sorry.'

'Moomaw.' She turned to Ed. 'They bank at the Third.'

'Who handles your account?'

Dot snorted. 'You mean who's my favorite teller?'

'I mean who handles all that money Gunther got hold of?'

'I don't know what you're talking about.'

'Ten years ago Gunther gave Sidney twelve grand for a down payment on that club.'

She'd lost a little steam. 'You're out of your goddamn mind.'

'You're going to tell me who I need to talk to or I'm going to take it to Lester Howells, and old Lester might just find that money more interesting than I do. He might want to look into where it came from.'

'That's got nothing to do with finding Gunther,' she said, her voice rising, and she slapped her palm down on the tabletop.

'You're wrong about that. Now, are you going to tell me the man's name or not?'

261

CHAPTER SIXTEEN

GUNTHER FAHNSTIEL: 20 JUNE, 1952

It had been a busy summer night of bar fights and wife beatings, and I hadn't had a chance to go and talk to Sally. When I got off duty I went home and slept for three hours, then drove over to her house. The sunrise was pretty, the birds were chirping and the drive over was nice, even though I knew I was going to catch hell when I got there.

Sally was in the kitchen drinking coffee, getting ready to leave for her shift. She wasn't happy to see me but I didn't care. It wasn't a social call. Her little girl Loretta was there, eating breakfast, and I teased her for a minute about how tall she was getting. Then her babysitter came in the front door and the girl ran into the living room to see her.

'So what do you want, Gunther? I'm running late.' Even dressed in pants and a plain blouse and flat, crepe-soled shoes for work, with her hair pulled up in a bun and her big brown eyes cold and angry, she was still about the most beautiful woman I'd ever seen. I hadn't been laid in a month and I felt like the stupidest man in the state for not picking her up right then and carrying her back into the bedroom and doing what she wanted me to.

'Wayne's in town.'

'Wayne? My husband Wayne?'

'Ed spotted him at the hospital. Somebody cracked his head open outside a roadhouse.'

'Ed doesn't know him. He's made a mistake.'

'He still sending you half his pay?'

'Not for a while now. I don't give a goddamn any more. I'm making plenty.'

'Might be a good idea to give the boys a rain check for this weekend.'

She looked at me like I was an idiot. 'Because Ed mistook some other guy for my lying shit-heel husband?' she said, a little too loud, and she glanced over at the door. She always took care not to badmouth Wayne in front of the little girl.

'Ed's not mistaken. He's checked in at the Bellingham downtown under another name.'

'And why would Wayne be using a fake name?'

'I don't know. I just think it'd be smart to be on guard.'

'Rain check. You know what that'd cost me? For one thing I'd have to set things up on one of my very few free weekends. And the girls'd have to be paid for an extra week.'

'Not if they're not working this weekend.'

'If I cancel on short notice I pay the girls anyway, that's the deal. I'd pay you, too, if that makes you feel better. The answer is no.'

'All right, then. You want me to stick around and watch the place tonight?'

'You mean here?' She shook her head. 'If you're not sticking around for me I don't want you sticking around. Ed's wrong, that's all.'

'No, he's not. There's going to be trouble. Otherwise Wayne would have let you know he was coming.'

She closed her eyes and the tendons in her neck stood out a little, but her voice was even. 'It's not Wayne, and I don't have time to worry about it anyway. I gotta go.'

Outside a horn honked, and we went through to the living room where Loretta was reading a book out loud to her babysitter. She jumped up and ran to Sally. 'Bye, Mama. See you tonight.' She kissed her mother's cheek and then mine, yelling 'Bye, Gunther,' as she raced back to her book. The babysitter, a plump old woman whose name I didn't remember, gave her a sweet smile in a way Sally almost never did.

In Sally's driveway Frieda sat behind the wheel of a brand new Cadillac convertible wearing sunglasses and a bright red scarf over her hair. Her lips were the same red and with a cigarette holder she would have looked a little bit like a homely movie star. Her cigarette dangled from the corner of her mouth, though, and it flapped up and down comically when she talked.

'Well, Gunther, imagine meeting you here at six-thirty in the morning. You two got anything to tell me about?'

If Sally needed another reason to be surly that sure was it. She got in and didn't say anything, just looked straight ahead.

'Nice car, Frieda,' I said

'Thanks. I keep telling this one she should spend a little bit of all that dough she's raking in, but she won't.'

'Can we go, please?' Sally said, and Frieda waved at me and pulled away. I watched them go to the end of the street and turn, feeling mean for being so glad I didn't love Sally the way she loved me.

*

I went over to the King's X and had some bacon and eggs, then around eight I went over to Glenn and Sonya Bockner's house. Sonya was up but still wearing her dressing gown.

'Come on in. Glenn's not here. You want some coffee or something?'

Glenn was the one I needed to talk to, and I would have said no but I could smell it perking. 'Sure,' I said and followed her inside.

When she put my cup down on the kitchen table she leaned forward enough so I could see her right nipple. She was a pretty girl when you weren't looking at her standing right next to Sally. Her hair wasn't done up, but without my seeing it she'd put on some lipstick in the two or three minutes since I'd walked in the door. She smelled nice, too. Now that I thought about it, the last time I'd seen Sonya she'd slipped me a scrap of paper with her number and the words 'CALL me.'

'To what do I owe the honor?' she asked, hands on her hips.

'I wonder if Glenn might be free for a security job this weekend.'

She shrugged. 'I don't know. I'm not on this weekend. You knew that, right?'

'Right.'

'You think there's gonna be trouble? Who won the raffle this week, anyway?'

'It's not them I'm worried about, it's another fellow. Better if there's two of us.'

Glenn was a big fellow and he wasn't afraid of a fight. In fact he seemed to like them. He liked to hang around when Sonya was working, and once he'd come in handy when both fellows decided they wanted Sally instead of Sonya. One of them already had a bloody nose when we pulled them apart, and if I'd been on my own I might have had to draw my weapon.

I never understood why it didn't bother him to have Sonya working for Sally the way she did, but from what she said it got him excited, thinking about other guys screwing her. Sometimes he'd have her bring guys home and he'd hide in the closet and watch.

'Write your number down and I'll tell him to call you when he gets home from work. In the meantime, you got half an hour, forty-five minutes free?'

'I guess,' I said, not thinking about what she was asking, and I just about spit out a mouthful of hot coffee when she hiked up her robe and sat down on me. The robe fell to the floor, and Sonya was stark naked.

'You didn't really come to talk to Glenn, did you? You knew perfectly goddamn well he's on first shift again.' She leaned her face forward and kissed me, and I kissed her back. Through the coffee and the cigarettes her mouth tasted like she'd just brushed her teeth.

I shifted around in the chair, trying to get comfortable. I was already stiff as a hound dog and against my better judgment I was pretty sure I was just going to let things happen. Then I got a picture in my head of her getting screwed by Amos Culligan, and then one of her sucking old Lester Gladwell's dick. Even that didn't manage to soften my pecker, but it sure did make me think a little clearer. I grabbed her under the arms and gently hoisted her off me, poor old John Henry throbbing along to my heartbeat. I stood up.

'Sorry,' I said. 'That's just gonna make trouble later on.'

'Come on, Gunther, bend me over the kitchen table and give it to me good.'

Damned if the way she was talking wasn't about to change my mind. I thought about the clap, about mercury treatments and sulfa drugs and still I was about to go ahead and do it.

'Come on, Sally doesn't have to know.'

That was it. 'How about Glenn?' I asked. 'How soon's he gonna know?' The look on her face gave me the feeling that he might be there somewhere, watching and beating his meat. Or maybe she was just going to tell him about it later. Anyway, I was leaving. 'Just have him give me a call, okay?'

*

Ed answered the bell looking surprised. 'What do you know. Come on in,' he said, and he opened the door up wide. Daisy was in the kitchen, and Ed had been playing with Jeff on the floor, making a large fort out of wooden blocks. Jeff got up when he saw me and ran to me. 'Gumfa!' he yelled. I picked him up and was surprised at how heavy he was now. I hadn't been around in six months or more, which is a long time when you're three.

Daisy came out of the kitchen. 'Jeffrey, come with Mommy, I'm going to make you something.' She didn't look at me. I used to be her favorite of all Ed's friends, once.

'Jeff wants to see Gunther, Daze,' Ed said, and she gave him a sharp look but kept her mouth shut. If this was the reception I got, I wondered how she would have welcomed Sally. She stood there for a minute, then turned and went back into the kitchen. I hadn't ever seen Daisy and Ed act like that; in front of other people anyway they always seemed like newlyweds, and I was sorry to be the cause of the friction just then. I suspected it came more often these days, though, with her having gotten religion and a whole new set of rules for Ed to live by.

'Who's a big boy?' I asked the little boy in the crook of my elbow.

'Me. Look, I'm making Fort Apache,' he said, and he dropped down to his blocks. I got down and helped for five or ten minutes, and we didn't say much. When we were done we'd built a wall around the fort.

'All right, now, go see your mother,' Ed said. 'Gunther and I need to talk about something.'

'Okay,' he yelled, and he ran into the kitchen, clomping with his cowboy boots.

'So what's on your mind?' he asked.

I didn't get up. 'She won't cancel or give the fellows a raincheck. She says you're wrong about him being back.'

'The hell I am.'

'I asked Glenn Bockner to come out and give me a hand but who knows if he will.'

'Maybe we should get Tommy and Rory to keep an eye

on him over the weekend, starting tomorrow night. Keep him away from the quarry, anyway.'

'On city time?'

'Unless you want to pay 'em out of your own pocket, yeah. They'll only have to step in if it looks like he's going to get violent.'

That sure came as a surprise to me from my straight arrow friend, but I was glad to hear him suggest it. 'Sounds okay to me.'

'But you know what, Gunther? This is the last time I help you out on this. It's about goddamn time you made it clear to Sally she's got to close up shop.'

'And she'll say screw you, I pay Stan Hardyway every month to keep the cops out of my hair. When you come up with an answer for that one, you're on.'

Still, we parted friendlier than we'd been in months, and between the two of us I thought we had things under control. Tommy and Rory might get out of hand with this shithead the way they sometimes did, but I guessed I could live with that.

CHAPTER SEVENTEEN

Among Sally's clippings was an item from the *Eagle* about Loretta getting a real estate award. It mentioned that her husband was Eric Gandy, the prominent local developer, though Gandy was not evident in the accompanying photo. There was a drawing of a hot rod by a boy named Tate Gandy on the kids' page, and a brief mention in the Neighbors column that Michelle Gandy had been selected for the National Honor Society. A whole obituary page turned out to include Donald's, and Gunther wondered if he and Donald hadn't known each other as children, being three years or so apart in a town as small as Cottonwood.

Digging a little deeper he hauled out some whole newspaper sections, quite a bit older than the clippings. The first was an old afternoon *Beacon*. On the front page below the fold was an article written by Frank Elting, accompanied by an early morning photo of a parking lot crawling with cops, including Gunther, and in the midst of them a sheet covering a body. The sheet had been heavily retouched so that its contours would show up in the rotogravure, and in his mind's eye he clearly saw old Gus Linderman standing there in the parking lot holding his

Speed Graphic with the flash bar on the side, trying to stay out of everybody's way and be at the center of everything at the same time.

Underneath was another edition of the *Beacon*, and when he saw the headline over Elting's story the question he had wanted to ask Sally in his dream bubbled up to the surface. This was the kind of story the *Eagle* never would have printed, let alone the headline:

DA TO FILE CHARGES IN COLLINS PLANT
SEX LOTTERY

There was no picture accompanying the article, but some of the names in it he remembered well: Lynn Furness, Sonya Bockner, Frieda Singer, Amos Culligan. Sally Ogden. He skimmed the rest of the article and dipped down into the box, pulling out another *Beacon* from around the same time:

LOVE WAS PRIZE IN COLLINS RAFFLE

Beneath that was the next day's paper:

NAB COLLINS SEX RING OPERATORS

The photo showed the five of them being led away by police, hiding their faces with their hands and in Culligan's case his hat. The unpleasant time the photo evoked notwithstanding, it was good to see the faces of the arresting officers, Lou Preston and Albert Vance, both of them dead for years and years now, the two of them grinning at the photographer like it was the funniest goddamn arrest they ever made. Gunther read down to the end of the column, then carefully opened up the section like an enormous, brittle butterfly to page 3, section A where it continued. There, buried in the middle of the article, was a description of the cabin and a vague reference to its location: an abandoned gravel quarry twenty-seven miles southwest of town, outside Pullwell.

With that, the first part of the route opened up before him in his brain as though he were driving it at that very moment: the turnpike down to Pullwell, old state highway 129 to the turnoff, and then what? Maybe if he got that far the rest would come back to him.

He left the newspapers on the cement floor of the garage and returned to the living room, where he stood on the couch looking at Sally's painting and contemplating his transportation options. He was startled out of his reverie by the sound of the back door opening, and he tiptoed into the bedroom hallway.

'Sally? You home?' The voice was familiar. 'It's Eric.' He heard keys being dropped on to a hard surface.

*

Eric entered the living room as Gunther slipped quietly into the kitchen, where a set of keys sat on the table. He walked out the backdoor with them to find the Volvo sitting in the driveway like a gift, and he took its wheel in something not unlike a state of grace. He was sorry about not staying to say hello to Sally, but they wouldn't have had much to say anyway; there hadn't been much left the day he drove her from Wichita to Cottonwood in his old Ford.

It took him a few blocks to quit pawing around with his foot for the nonexistent clutch, but he soon had the hang of it again, moving through the darkness past neighborhoods as strange and new as Sally's. He began to wonder whether the street he was on reached the turnpike or not, and when he got to a cross street leading downtown he took it, thinking the more recognizable streets would take him where he needed to go.

*

'Mr. Brown? I'm Ed Dieterle, I think Dorothy Fahnstiel called and told you I was coming.'

'She sure did. Come on in.' They passed through a dark living room and into a home office, and Brown pointed him to a chair. In the distance kids could be heard fighting, followed by the sound of their mother intervening and telling them to pipe down.

'Sorry I couldn't wait for business hours.'

'That's okay. I was just watching some TV when Mrs. Fahnstiel called. Now I can't tell you everything I could tell the trustee, but I can tell you everything I'm allowed to tell Mrs. Fahnstiel.'

'She's the beneficiary but not the trustee?'

Brown leaned back with his hands behind his head. 'One of the beneficiaries. The trustee was Mr. Fahnstiel, until he became incapacitated. Then the Trust Department took over.'

'The account was established when?'

'Nineteen eighty, I think. Might have been eighty-one.'

'And it was a big cash deposit?'

The banker's swivel chair squeaked as he leaned forward. 'Mr. Fahnstiel had a large sum of cash he'd been saving for quite a long time, and he'd suddenly become aware of the need to protect it. You see that from time to time with clients of his generation. Your generation. People who've been through the Depression and don't trust the banks, they suddenly get nervous about having all that cash around.'

'So he just had this money tucked away in a mattress before?'

'Not really a mattress as such. But I believe he kept it in his house.'

'And how much money was this?'

'A little more than two hundred and fifty thousand dollars.'

Ed asked him to repeat the sum, and he did. 'And you don't think that's a lot for a policeman and a nurse to have squirreled away?'

Brown shrugged. 'That was none of my business.'

'And the money's running out.'

He nodded. 'Dwindling, let's say. Mrs. Fahnstiel came to me just last week to see what we could do about putting her in there with Mr. Fahnstiel, and that's what got me sitting down to do the numbers.'

'But you can't tell me where the rest of the money's been going?'

'Not without a court order.'

Ed thanked the man and went outside. He sat at the wheel of the rental car for a while and tried to imagine a way Gunther could have ended up with that much money without having done something very bad.

*

Twenty minutes after leaving Sally's house Gunther, still nowhere near the turnpike, passed by the old Riverside Zoo. He recalled walking there from his old bachelor's studio when his daughters, still in their early teens, used to visit him on weekends; being in the neighborhood for what might be the last time he thought he'd swing past his old apartment, just for a quick look.

The building was still standing. It had been new then, long and narrow with apartments on either side of a central corridor, made of blond brick with thick blocks of glass instead of bricks on the front end. Being halfway underground, like Ray and Cal's Barber Shop, the studio was always a little dark even in the daytime, its windows opening out at the level of the grass. There was another floor above his, and the building was full of people like Gunther: single, or single again, working odd hours, having just arrived in town or trying to get up the courage to leave. For him it was a place to hang his clothes and to sleep when he didn't have a girlfriend who'd let him stay over; when he moved there in 1950 he was thirty-eight years old, and he'd already been married and divorced three times.

*

He pulled away and circled the block, eventually braking in front of the zoo. He thought it had been replaced by a new one, but its buildings and cages appeared intact, and people were strolling through them in the warmth of the late evening. A row of enormous bird cages still stood to the right of the entrance, one of the tropical birds inside cawing frantically. Directly behind the cages had been the big red brick Monkey and Lion House, and right in front of it the alligator pit, always his favorite part of the park. Fondly he recalled the old gator sunning himself in the circular trench with its hollow eyesockets, both eyes – so his daughters had assured him – lost to bottle caps thrown by wanton boys. During the warm months, when it could be displayed outdoors, it seemed never to move except to follow the sunlight, slinking from one end of its pit to the other, and he wondered now what possibly could have seemed amusing about such a spectacle. He almost felt like getting out to see if it was still there; instead he let slowly up on the brake and crept forward, his arm hanging out the window in the slight breeze.

Three blocks up and to the left was Daisy and Ed's old place, a small apartment complex built in the twenties; it was designed to look like a bunch of small houses attached side-by-side to one another, with a shared, sloping roof and flower beds and big windows looking out on to a central courtyard. It hadn't changed much, as far as he could see. Lights were on in most of the apartments, and someone was playing 'Stardust' on a piano.

He'd first laid eyes on Sally Ogden here, at one of the loud, boozy parties Ed and Daisy used to throw before Daisy got religion. Sally drew his attention shortly after his arrival by flinging a drink at another guest, a tipsy woman who kept playing the first bars of 'My Funny Valentine' very badly on Daisy's upright piano, again and again, faltering every time at the key change.

'Would it be too much to ask to cut that shit *out*?' Sally said just before emptying a full highball glass in the woman's direction; Gunther was stunned both by the coarseness of the act and the beauty of the woman performing it. She looked like she belonged in a painting.

While Daisy walked the weeping pianist home, Sally turned on Gunther, whose inability to stop staring at her she misinterpreted as disapproval.

'Yeah, well, you didn't have to listen to "My Funny Goddamn Valentine" twenty times in fifteen minutes,' she said.

'I didn't say anything.'

'You're thinking it.'

'I'm not thinking anything, either.'

Other people were, though; a tall, blonde pinchfaced woman passed close by and murmured 'bitch,' and Sally twisted her head around just long enough to spit 'trash' back in her direction.

She looked him in the eye. 'I've had enough of this shit. You want to go down to Jack's?'

He'd never been to Jack's but he was pretty much up for anything this woman wanted to do short of getting married. As they left the party he heard Ed Dieterle's voice bellowing over the heads of the guests, 'Don't do anything I wouldn't do.'

Now he sat in front of that same apartment building, close to forty years later, in a car he'd stolen from Sally's son-in-law. In the Dieterles' old apartment a big middle-aged man with a beard peered through the curtains at him suspiciously, and he noticed that whoever had been playing 'Stardust' had stopped. He made a U-turn away from the curb and drove.

He had been disturbed since leaving Sally's by the Volvo's failure to shift reliably, but he attributed the unpleasant sound coming from under the hood to the unfamiliar automatic transmission and left it at that. Now there was another noise, an alarming, high-pitched whine, and he noticed that the temperature gauge was edging into the red. He pulled over and looked down at the stick. P, R, N, D, D1, D2. He'd been switching back and forth between D1 and D2, unsure of which was the optimum setting.

He was a few blocks west and north of the zoo now. A block away on the corner stood Jack's; he could wait inside while the engine cooled off, and probably someone there would know the way to the turnpike.

He sauntered up the sidewalk toward the tavern, feeling very much at home. Despite the day's heat he could still see signs of yesterday's shower; between the concrete blocks grew clumps of grass three or four inches high, and the lawns he passed were all thick and past due for mowing. He halfway hoped it would rain again before he went back to the home.

Sticking out of the bricks above the tavern's doorway was a dull and fissured yellow plexiglass sign with red cursive letters so badly faded they were almost illegible even with the light on inside it: Jack's Riverbank Tavern. Approaching the door he saw as if in a dream the same old black Packard that had belonged to Jack back then, sitting fat and shiny next to the curb, and as he yanked open the battered old screen door its dry hinges let loose a grating metallic shriek.

'Hey, there, stranger,' a lady of sixty or so called out to him from behind the bar. She had a deep, unnatural-looking tan set off with pinkish white eye shadow and lipstick, short hair bleached very blonde, and stretched across her substantial bosom a tight blue t-shirt with glitter all over it read 'World's Sexiest Grandma.' In her left hand, its nails long and lacquered the same color as her eyes and lips, she held a long, thin cigarette. 'What'll you be having?'

He hadn't really thought about it. He hadn't had a drink in a long time, since before Lake Vista anyway. 'What kinda beer you got?'

'On tap I got Miller and Miller Light.'

'Miller High Life?'

'Genuine Draft. I got High Life in a bottle, though, if that's what you want.'

Gunther nodded and she pulled a bottle out of the cooler and set it down in front of him.

'Seventy-five cents. You need a glass?' He shook his head no.

He handed her a dollar, and when she gave him his quarter back he dropped it into a jar marked 'TIPPING ENCOURAGED.'

'Thanks,' she said, then returned to a conversation with a woman at the end of the bar.

He took a swig and set the bottle back down, slushing the beer around in his mouth. It was blander than he remembered, although he might have been remembering some other brand, or even another type of beverage entirely.

Across the passthrough behind the bar he saw a man his own age playing pool with a woman in her twenties. He was nattily dressed, with a bowtie and suspenders and a neatly trimmed beard, and he frowned thoughtfully at her every shot.

'Excuse me, Miss,' Gunther said, and the lady behind the bar laughed.

'Thanks, Mister. You get another beer on the house for that.'

'Thanks,' he said, though he didn't think he'd finish the first one and wasn't sure what he'd done to merit a second. 'I was just wondering about the old car out front.'

'Oh, the Packard. That's Dad's.' She jerked her thumb toward the old man at the pool table.

'Holy shit. Jack Teaberry.'

She turned to yell out the passthrough. 'Hey, Dad. Look who's here.' The young woman had missed a shot, and Jack was now lining up his. Without answering his daughter he took his shot and missed. Only then did he deign to look up at his daughter in annoyance.

'What?'

'You got a visitor.'

'Long time no see,' Jack said, obviously puzzled to see him, and for a minute Gunther was afraid he would call the cops and have him hauled back to the home. 'Didn't even know you were alive. Let me finish this game here, then we'll shoot some, you and me.'

*

Euchre had lasted less than an hour and a half, cut short by a losing streak so deep and persistent Sally could feel an outburst of pure yellow bile coming on. Reluctant to shock her card playing friends, sweet grandmotherly types

281

who mistakenly liked to think of themselves as a bunch of salty old broads, she had left early. Now she turned on to Control Tower Place and pulled into her driveway, nearly plowing into a shadowy figure who, moving into her headlights with an urgent wave, turned out to be her son-in-law. She stuck her head out the window.

'What are you doing here?'

'Son of a bitch stole my car.'

'Who?'

'The old guy they're all looking for. I tracked him down here and he stole my fucking Volvo.'

'Don't you use that language in my presence, Eric,' she said, though the word crossed her own lips a dozen times a day. 'Did you call the police?'

'Not yet. Can I borrow your car?'

'You know perfectly goddamn well you can't borrow my car, Eric.'

He turned, muttering 'Fuck,' and headed back into the house. She followed and found that while his car was being stolen he'd helped himself to the Tanqueray.

'This old man who stole your car, you figure he hot-wired it?'

'He took my keys.' He poured himself another small gin, and she didn't say anything.

Maybe it was Gunther, then. He was a man of many and varied talents, often surprising ones, but hotwiring an ignition was certainly not among them. 'What the hell happened to your head?'

He touched his purplish temple and winced. 'Guy bushwacked me back at our house.'

'You fixing to call the police?'

He shook his head. 'I'm gonna call Loretta, see if she'll let me drive the Caddy.' He dialed, avoiding her gaze, and since the bottle was out she poured herself a gin. 'Shit. Got the machine.'

'I'll give you a lift home.'

He looked at her suspiciously for a moment, trying to figure out her angle, then he shrugged and took a swig of his own drink. 'It's twelve thousand dollars to whoever finds this guy.'

'That's what I heard.'

'What was he doing here, anyway?'

Sally shrugged. 'Looking for me, I guess.'

'You know him?'

'We used to hang around a few years ago. He ran into Loretta yesterday, maybe that got him to thinking.'

'Hang around?' He raised an eyebrow.

She was annoyed by his insinuating tone, but she didn't really care what he thought about her. 'I used to keep company with old Gunther. He was real nice to me a few times when things got shitty. And I mean they got real shitty, once or twice. And he always treated Loretta right, too.'

'So how come you didn't marry him?'

'Lots of reasons, and none of 'em's any of your goddamn business. Come on, let's go before I'm too drunk to drive.'

She got up and he followed her to the garage, its door from the house standing open and its light on. She pressed the button by the door and the garage door began to lift, revealing her car still sitting in the driveway.

'What were you doing in the garage, anyway?'

283

'I wasn't in the garage,' he said.

Then she saw her storage boxes sitting open, the newspapers in a pile on the concrete floor. 'Must have been Gunther, then.'

Eric stepped forward and picked up the paper on top of the stack. 'Look at this. "NAB COLLINS SEX RING OPERATORS."' He read silently for a second, then turned to Sally, startled. 'Holy shit, it's *you*.'

'You better fucking swear you won't tell Loretta.'

'Sure thing . . .'

It was the one with the photo of herself being led away by Gunther's jovial cop buddies. She hadn't been able to look at those old papers in years, but she couldn't bear throwing them away, either.

'Bring those papers into the kitchen. You're going to have to get a taxi home, 'cause I need another drink.'

*

Loretta's lonely Chinese dinner was eaten, her suspect sheets and bedspread drying downstairs. Another glass of cheap white wine in hand, she was watching an old *Dragnet* episode about LSD. She remembered watching it years ago with her roommate Ruth in their little duplex over by WSU, both of them giggling hysterically at the show and at Ruth's boyfriend Evan, who was annoyed less by the laughter than by the fact that they were tripping and he wasn't. She remembered thinking at the time that Ruth and Evan were like a couple marrying outside their religions; eventually one of them would convert the other or they'd split up.

And so, upon getting involved with Eric Gandy, a

clean-cut, turtleneck-wearing, shorthaired juicer of the old school, she'd given up drugs of all kinds without acknowledging to him that she'd ever indulged in them. She remained drug-free until Eric discovered them himself in the mid-seventies, and when he imagined he was introducing her to the sordid thrill of pot smoking at the age of thirty, she let him think it was true.

Now, watching Jack Webb's earnest squint, she was overcome with an unexpected and intense desire to get high. It had been seven or eight years since she'd partaken, she guessed, around the time Eric stopped taking her to those kinds of social occasions. She had no idea where to buy any, nor whom to ask.

Tate had some, though, up in his room. Shortly after his last visit home, she'd gone through his drawers with the intention of boxing up some of his old comic books and monster magazines to put in the attic, and there it was, a baggieful of weed. She wasn't shocked or worried; mostly she was disappointed that she wouldn't be able to empty the magazine drawers, since doing so would mean admitting she'd found the dope. She'd opened up the baggie for a sniff, and it had smelled good and fresh, though at the time the thought of firing some of it up never crossed her mind.

*

Five minutes later she stepped through the sliding doors of the convenience store she used for last-minute emergencies. The man behind the counter knew her and smiled in greeting. He was old, maybe as old as Gunther, and that made what she was about to do feel unseemly at best.

'Zig-Zag papers, please.' She couldn't look him in the eye, and her face was hot.

'Zig-Zags. What size?'

'Double longs,' she said, and she looked up to see him still smiling in his friendly way. His white hair was slicked straight back, his nose gray from drinking, and she realized he didn't give a shit whether she smoked pot or not. Unfortunately this did nothing to stem her embarrassment.

He put a package of papers on the counter and rang it up. 'I coulda guessed. Usually the ladies like 'em good and long.' He winked and her face got hotter.

She paid him to the penny and turned to go. 'See you,' she said. Her voice sounded high and squeaky to her, and she imagined she could feel his eyes on her rear-end all the way to the car, but when she faced him again he was leaning on the counter the other way, reading the newspaper.

*

Sally and Eric had polished off half the bottle of Tanqueray. 'Even after I paid the girls their share, and Gunther, and the piece of shit shop steward, and the old farmer who owned the land, I was still clearing a thousand bucks a month above and beyond my paycheck, pure profit.'

'I always thought you guys were just scraping by when Loretta was little.'

'Later we were.' Sally got up and poured herself another two fingers. 'Want more?' she asked, already sloshing some into his glass. 'That was a pretty good shot he got in to your head, looks like.'

'He caught me off guard. I wouldn't have thought such an old guy could pack that kind of wallop.'

*

It didn't surprise Sally. One Sunday at the cabin she'd blown the alarm whistle after a big redheaded fellow named Ricky Fast had decided he wanted a little backdoor action with Sonya Bockner. The other guy that weekend, a big talker by the name of Hal Waverly, stepped in between them, and Ricky picked him up and smashed him against the wall.

'One more word out of you, Waverly, and I'll browneye all three of you.' At that the intrepid Waverly had bolted, sprinting to the safety of the trees opposite the cabin, at which point Sally blew the whistle.

Ten seconds later – she'd swear it hadn't been any longer than that – Gunther was in the doorway, and then behind Ricky, gun drawn, and then Ricky was on the floor holding the back of his neck.

'Get up.'

He did as he was told, then swung at Gunther, who slammed his fist into Ricky's big, soft gut. As he gurgled, sounding as if he were about to puke, Gunther crashed the butt of the pistol against his temple. Ricky went down with a yelp.

'Weekend's over. Pack up your shit and get out, all of you. Where's the other one?'

'He's out there somewhere. Ricky here threatened to cornhole him.'

'That what started it? Cornholing?'

Sally nodded. 'Wanted to do it to Sonya and she doesn't go for that.'

'I don't blame her. All right, you go find your boyfriend and I'll watch this bird.'

She and Sonya left to find Hal. She didn't know what Gunther had said to Ricky while they were alone, but he apologized to her and to Sonya, though not to Waverly, who steered carefully clear of him on the line after that.

*

'Hey. You listening?' Eric said.

'Sorry. I was thinking about something.' She was already drunker than she thought. 'What were you saying?'

'I said, you think he might be headed out there?'

'Where?'

'To the cabin.'

'Isn't a cabin any more. Just an old flooded gravel quarry, no use to anybody.'

'What was he here for, then? Looking for a little action?'

'He'da been pretty disappointed once he got a look at me if that's what he was after,' she said. 'Anyway I don't think that's it.'

'Tell me where the quarry was.'

'There's nothing there.'

'There's twelve grand for whoever finds him.'

'You don't need it that bad, do you?' She was kidding but his face closed up in a defensive way. Loretta hadn't said anything to her about money troubles; now she thought he might have hidden them from his wife out of pride or spite. 'No kidding, I don't see why he'd be going out there.'

'You're not the senile one, he is. Now are you going to tell me?'

'All right,' she said, just to shut him up. 'You take the turnpike down to Pullwell and get on the old State Highway 129.'

He grabbed a pen and a piece of scratch paper next to her phone and started writing.

*

Tate's *MAD* magazines were stacked neatly in two piles in the bottom drawer of his dresser, organized chronologically and protected in polyethylene bags. Loretta was sure he hadn't read them in years.

She took the bag from the drawer and into her bedroom, and after a couple of false starts rolled herself a surprisingly accomplished joint. It was long and thin, and she was careful not to overstuff it, factoring in a lowered resistance after such a long abstinence. Back in Tate's room she put the baggie back in its place between June and July 1983, hoping she'd left no indication that it had been opened and some of its contents pilfered.

I owe my only son for part of a baggie full of dope, she thought, and decided that the place to enjoy her proudly constructed joint was the bath. In the master bathroom she discovered that Gunther had availed himself of the tub as well as the washing machine. There was a ring of grime around the drain, and a wet towel on the floor next to the toilet. If her husband had done it she would have been angry, but as it was she cheerfully cleaned the tub and threw the towel into the hamper. Then she drew a hot bath and on a whim poured in some of the Mr. Bubble Gunther had thoughtfully left out for her. It frothed up pretty nicely, considering it had probably been in the cabinet for a decade. She lit a couple of candles and the joint, climbed into the tub and closed her eyes, taking a long, slow draw.

She could feel her muscles going slack in the hot water and bubbles, and within a couple of minutes she was giggling. Poor Tate must have panicked when he got back to school and realized he'd left it for her to find, never suspecting that the real danger in her stumbling upon it was that she might smoke it up.

She listened attentively to the running water, noting how different it sounded when the tub was all the way full, how rounded and deep the splashing was. With her feet she turned the faucet off and opened the drain for five seconds until the water level was just up to her sternum. Without the sound of the water she became aware of the steady monotonous drone of the air conditioner running, masking out all the other small sounds until it hit its set temperature and kicked off again. Funny how that was a sound you hardly thought of once you got used to air conditioning. They hadn't had it the first few years in Cottonwood; they'd run fans and left windows open for crossdrafts, never really cut off from the sounds of the outdoors in the hot months. A few years later, when her mother married Donald, he'd installed a window unit like the one in the small apartment above his auto parts store, where he'd lived since his first wife Cora killed herself.

It had been years since she'd thought about Cora, who had once been a subject of lurid fascination for her. She was never discussed at home, nor was the fact that Donald had been married before, but Loretta heard adults furtively mention it, and in late childhood and early adolescence she spent many hours imagining Cora's method of and motive for ending her life, even entertaining the thrilling possibility that Donald had done her in and made it look like a suicide. Eventually she got the story out of Donald's sister Norene, who'd loathed the woman: Cora had been screwing the principal of the local high school, and she knew the principal's wife was about to spill the beans, if she hadn't already. So she swallowed a fistful of barbiturates with the full expectation, Norene was sure, of Donald coming home for lunch at noon in time to call for help. Unfortunately the principal's wife had phoned him that morning. Too angry to face Cora, he'd wolfed down a bowl of stew at the Jayhawk Lunchroom that day instead of going home, and by the time he teetered in the front door at midnight, drunk and ready for a fight, the pills had done their work. Norene wasted no sympathy or grief on her late sister-in-law. 'It was the war, and there was hardly any men around anyway, and she decided one wasn't enough for her. There wasn't many single women in this town crying over Cora.'

Loretta, seventeen at the time of the conversation, was shocked that such things could happen in Cottonwood, and more so that the lover in question was Mr. Fertig, still the principal of Cottonwood High School. The image of dour Mr. Fertig trysting with the reckless, hedonistic woman Norene had described was difficult to credit, and when she said as much Norene laughed.

'She wasn't the only one, either. He's always got a little something going. Remember that math teacher, left last year? She was threatening to go away unless he left his wife and married her. Well, he sure called her bluff. She got on the bus, and he took up with the next in line.'

That was Miss Plunkett, a pretty brunette in her late twenties with a very nice figure. Most of the boys in Loretta's class were very eager to please her, little suspecting that her pleasure was coming nightly from stocky, bald Mr. Fertig. 'How do you know all this about Mr. Fertig?' Loretta asked her.

Norene's face flushed a little, Loretta remembered, and she shrugged. 'It's a small town.'

It had indeed been a small town. Even now she still didn't know exactly why they'd gone there; before they left Wichita she remembered her mother quitting her job at the plant, or was she fired? She wasn't sure. There'd been no job waiting in Cottonwood, and work was certainly scarcer than it had been in the city, with all the aircraft plants working full steam on Cold War production. Why had they moved a third of the way across the state to a town where they knew nobody at all, if not for a better standard of living?

She resolved to ask her mother about the move, and about her father, and about what really happened between her and Gunther. It was ridiculous that at the age of forty-two she still didn't know anything about her father but his name and rank, and if the old bat didn't want to talk about him that was tough shit. The joint was all but gone now; all that remained was a piece of pointy, burnt paper with a few particles of leaf nestled in it. She lowered herself a little deeper into the bubbles and closed her eyes again, smiling to herself.

CHAPTER EIGHTEEN

WAYNE OGDEN: 21–22 JUNE, 1952

It had been threatening to rain all afternoon but it hadn't started yet, the clouds so dark you couldn't tell from the sky what time of day it was. I sat watching traffic from the Plymouth for a while on Pine near Broadway, around the corner from the Crosley Hotel. After a while I got out and dialed the number from a phone booth.

'Hitching Post, Don speaking,' the bartender answered.

'Hey, Don, is Beulah there?'

'Just a sec. Who's calling?'

'Otis,' I said, picking the name from the masonry above the door of an apartment building across the street.

'Just a second, she's with somebody. Hey, Beulah.'

I hung up and walked over to the Crosley. I didn't know if she knew anybody named Otis, but I'd established that she was a good ten to fifteen minutes away from her crib; even if the call sent her scurrying home I had the time I needed.

The lobby stank as I walked in, a smell of moldy

carpets and unemptied ash trays and semi-catatonic residents sitting in the split-seamed, piss-stained armchairs of the lobby all day long, and the night manager stood behind the front desk acting like it was the goddamn Hilton. From the malevolence of his glare I surmised that he'd seen me in Beulah's company the other morning, though I hadn't noticed him.

'I was wondering if you might be able to do me a favor.'

'That would depend, sir,' he said, and when he spoke he sounded just like Franklin Pangborn in the movies, and I could hardly keep from laughing.

I pulled a fifty-dollar bill out of my wallet. It was too much, I knew, but I couldn't risk him turning down a smaller sum and forcing me to negotiate upward. 'I'd like the key to Beulah's room for five minutes.'

He looked at the bill as though it might be laced with poison, then grabbed it and handed me the key. Then he looked away like I wasn't there.

The room was tidy, the bed made and the floor swept. The glassine envelope was in the same spot behind the dresser, maybe a little lighter than the other day. I dropped it into my inside jacket pocket and left. I almost wrote her a note telling her I'd taken her heroin, but decided it would be more fun for her to discover the theft on her own.

I considered the fact that some seemed to be missing, and that got me wondering how and when Elishah got his daily shot of it. If she was already at work, she'd already supplied him with it, and I didn't want that.

*

I drove to Lincolnshire Street with the windows open, enjoying the warm, humid air blowing past my face. I parked in front of Elishah's house and went inside, and on the kitchen table I found a small envelope like the one I'd taken from Beulah's room. There was a note with it:

> *Elishah,*
> *Heres some for being a good boy.*
> *Love*
> > *B*

I took the drug and the note and left one of my own:

> *Dear inbred hillbilly imbecile,*
> *You're probably wondering where your*
> *daily dose went. Getting sweaty yet?*
> *Don't go anywhere until you see me.*
> *Your pal,*
> > *Sarge*

*

I left and headed for Sally's house – my house, really. I knew from Culligan that Sally headed straight for the cabin after work on Friday, and that the child stayed at a babysitter's house on those weekends when her mother was plying her trade. I walked around to the back door and, not surprisingly, found it unlocked. I hoped it wouldn't be necessary to turn the goddamn place upside down to find her money. Where did she used to hide things when I was here, in that short time between the end of the war and re-enlisting? I had no sense now that I was returning home; I barely remembered anything about that year except feelings of panic and entrapment, and the primal urge to flee back to the bosom of mother army.

I started with the basement. It was a mess, boxes everywhere and useless old junk that should have been thrown out years before. I was astonished to see the old bicycle I used to throw the *Evening Beacon* from twenty years ago; she must have taken it from my parents' house when my mother passed away. I thought of the telegram she sent me about Mother, assuming I'd be hightailing it home for the funeral – I had been in Japan less than a year, and she hadn't quite got the message yet – and I could only imagine her shock at the telegram I sent back:

NOT COMING STOP DON'T CARE STOP SELL HER HOUSE STOP SEND PROCEEDS HERE STOP WAYNE

I didn't really expect her to send me the entire proceeds from the sale of Mother's house, but damned if she didn't go ahead and do it; it was a great help in establishing myself within the hierarchy of the occupation forces, and I was grateful to her and Mother both for it.

In a large cardboard box sat my debate trophies, nine of them, ranging from a wooden plaque with a plate screwed to it for Honorable Mention at the 1934 Garden City Forensics Tourney to an elaborately engraved loving cup for the Grand Prize in the Regional College Invitational in Omaha in '38, at the bottom of which lay strewn the constituent parts of at least three dead crickets. Another box contained framed photographs my mother had inexplicably saved: group photos of Debate, Track and Football teams, of seven years of Student Government, of the Sales Division of Collins Aircraft Company in February

1941. There was also a casual pose of myself in Italy with a couple of close army buddies, both of whose names I had forgotten, though I recalled plainly that one of them had an unpleasant and distinctive odor. The third box I opened contained yet more worthless memorabilia, and I found myself stupidly lingering over scrapbooks and photo albums when I should have been aggressively dismantling the house in search of my money.

After a while I got hungry and went upstairs and raided the ice box. My wife hadn't left me with much to choose from in the way of protein – some slightly green-looking ham on a plate, a bowl containing three eggs that smelled ever so slightly of sulfur – so I made a peanut butter and jelly sandwich, poured myself a glass of milk and sat at the kitchen table in the dark, thinking. In the old days she always seemed to have a banknote or two hidden away for small emergencies, maybe two dollars or five. Where did she keep it? In the kitchen somewhere? When I'd pulled out the knife to spread the peanut butter and jelly the drawer had stuck a little. I got up and tried it again, and it stuck at the same place. I yanked out the drawer, sending it skidding across the floor and the silverware flying in all directions. Kneeling, I pulled out the silverware tray and punched out the bottom of the drawer and found nothing. When I reached inside the cabinet where the drawer had been, I felt paper scotch-taped to the underside of the countertop, next to the drawer's guide. I scraped at it with my fingernails, peeled it off and extracted a manila envelope, unsealed and filled with twenties and fifties and the occasional hundred-dollar bill, close to fifteen thousand dollars in cash. It was a greater sum by fivefold than I had anticipated finding, and I blessed the head of Cecil Wembly. I'd planned this detour home to defend my family's honor and maybe pick up a little working capital, and instead I found myself with a decent sized nest egg.

On top of that I had the whole weekend ahead of me; now I could indulge myself and settle at leisure my personal scores with Sally and with Elishah and Beulah.

Before stepping outside I looked around for neighbors and saw none; in fact I saw nobody at all until I got to my car and tossed the envelope into the backseat. Strolling over from a prowlcar parked half a block up were two uniformed cops, the first I'd seen close up since I got back to the States, and my first thought was how ridiculous they looked. In my mind, for a cop to be scary, he had to have a double-breasted blue tunic with a big badge pinned to it over the heart, like the officers of my youth.

'Evening, Sarge,' one of them said. 'How about a little ride? We need to talk about some things.' He was big, red-faced and stupid looking, his partner even more so.

'Muggy night,' the other one said. 'They say it's gonna rain.'

I thought the best thing to do was to pretend to be scared. 'If this is some sort of shakedown, my money's all back at the Bellingham Hotel,' I said with a lovely vibrato high in my throat, wondering what they'd do if they found out how much cash I'd just tossed onto the floor of the backseat.

'Cut the shit, Ogden.' The smaller of the two frisked me, and held open the driver's door of my Plymouth and motioned me in. After I took the wheel the first one got into the backseat and the bigger and stupider-looking one slid in next to me.

'Now turn around and start heading west on Douglas.'

I pulled away from the curb into a U-turn and headed for Douglas. At least they hadn't searched the car; my .38 was still in the trunk. They'd missed the small of my back and the knucks hidden there, but against the two of them brass knuckles wouldn't provide enough of an edge. They didn't say much until we got to Hydraulic.

'Hang a right and keep going,' the one next to me drawled.

'So how's everything over at the Crosley?' the other one said from the backseat. 'Got yourself a whore down there?'

'I was inquiring about a cheaper room than the one I have now,' I said.

'Crosley's cheaper than the Bellingham, all right. Plus you got two, three harlots right there in the building so you don't have to go out on the street looking.' They both thought that was funny.

'On the other hand, maybe the sergeant doesn't like girls. Else why'd he hightail out on a swell piece of ass like that Sally?'

The bigger one whistled. 'I'd give a year of my life for one night of that, Tommy.'

'Goddamn right,' Tommy said.

'What I hear is you can have a pretty good shot at a whole weekend of it for a two-dollar raffle ticket,' I said. 'In fact she'd probably throw you one for free if you asked her. They say she likes cops.'

Something hard hit me on the back of the head and I swerved into the lefthand lane for a second. 'Watch your fucking mouth if you know what's good for you, Ogden. Looks like somebody already gave you what for.'

'Yeah. Where'd you get the shiner?' the other one asked.

'Walked into a door.'

'The hell you did.'

'All right, that's enough. Reason we're here is we think you're looking to make trouble for Sally,' Tommy said.

'What makes you think that?'

'You broke into her fuckin' house!' the other one bellowed. 'We could've arrested you for that, you know.'

'It's my house. If you don't believe me you can check with the registrar of deeds.'

'Fuck the registrar of deeds. You know goddamn well that ain't your house any more.'

'Listen, shithead,' Tommy said. 'Things have changed since you left town. Fuck with Sally Ogden and you're fucking with plenty of other people you shouldn't be fucking with.'

'She's my wife.'

'The fuck she is. You took off on her years ago.'

'I'm telling you we never got divorced.'

'And I'm telling you I don't give a shit if you're divorced or not. You stay the hell away from her and her house.'

We were heading out toward the city limits now. The businesses were few and far between, the houses even scarcer. This was land somebody ought to gobble up and develop, I thought idly. If I didn't have an aversion to the place I might have looked into it myself.

'Turn up there at the sign,' Tommy said. 'You got the key, Rory?'

There was a big metal sign to my left:

FARRIS AUTOMOBILE SALVAGE YARD

I turned in and Rory got out and unlocked the gate, pulled it open and waved me through. I pulled ahead thirty feet or so, well away from Rory as he padlocked the gate back up. There were two quonset huts, one straight ahead and one to my left, surrounded by a half dozen or so auto bodies and a sea of cracked engine blocks, skeletal, rusted chassis, and stacks of bald tires, all of it ghostly yellow under the dim security lights. Leaning against one of the quonset huts I recognized the frame of an Indian motorcycle like one I had owned briefly before the war, cannibalized for parts.

'Now we're going to explain a few things to you about civilian life,' Tommy said. I watched Rory in the rearview finishing up with the gate and turning to walk back to the car. 'Get out.'

'Now hold on a second, officer. I have a proposition for you.'

'Don't tell me to hold on a second, you piece of crap. You're no Sergeant here, you're just a piece of shit civilian far as I'm concerned. Now get out the car like I fuckin' told you to.'

'Take a look inside the envelope on the floor, there.'

Behind me I heard tearing paper, followed by Tommy

taking in a deep breath. 'Holy shit,' he said. 'There must be a few grand in here.'

I didn't begrudge them the beating I was about to receive, but I by God was not about to let them take that money. It was mine; my wife earned it. Rory was six or seven feet behind the car, and with Tommy hypnotized at the sight of all that green I put the Plymouth into reverse and floored it. It was like hitting a moose; he thumped and fell backward, and I shifted into first, punched the gas and dived out.

I hit the dirt painfully hard, scraping my face and palms, and scrambled for the shadows. The Plymouth rolled forward faster than I'd expected and crashed into the further of the two quonset huts. I could hear Tommy cursing and trying to get out from the backseat, and I was goddamned glad I'd bought the two-door instead of the four.

In a row next to the nearer of the huts were lengths of iron rebar sticking out of coffee cans filled with concrete. I grabbed a piece of rebar with both hands and ran to where Rory sat holding his head. His uniform cap lay next to him on the dust.

'Fuck,' Rory said, drawing the word out into two syllables, the second an octave and a half higher than the first. I felt the first few drops of rain on my face, and in the distance I heard the gentle rumbling of thunder as I lifted the coffee can and smashed it into Rory's skull. The rebar made a lousy handle and I lost control of it at the last second, just before the wet, cracking sound of the impact of the concrete and tin against his skull. It wrenched out of my hands and spun off to the side as he fell over with a pathetic wheeze. I heard no corresponding intake of breath but I wasn't able to give it the attention I would have liked.

'You stand real fucking still, you sack of shit,' Tommy yelled, his revolver pointed right at my head. He was thirty-five, maybe forty feet away, and I dropped down to Rory's level to make us a single target.

As Tommy advanced I wrapped my hand in a handkerchief from my shirt pocket and took Rory's service revolver. Behind me was a big galvanized trashcan; I dived behind it and a shot went off, plowing right through the can. From the ground I aimed carefully and fired.

Rory's gun was bigger than I was used to; the power of the report and the kick threw me off a little, but the smell of burnt powder was familiar and oddly comforting, mingling delicately with the slightly electrical odor of the light rain prickling the dusty ground. Tommy yelped in pain and surprise and fired in my general direction, a wild one this time. He sank to his knees but he still held the revolver and I had no way of knowing where I'd hit him or how badly, so I fired again, aiming square at his midsection. This time he screamed.

'Jesus ... Jesus ... I'm gutshot ... Jesus, Jesus, Jesus ... in the office ... there's a phone, call an ambulance, Jesus ...' The gun was on the ground now and I sauntered over to him.

'You must take me for a fucking moron,' I said, kicking the revolver out of his reach, wincing at the appalling stench of shit and blood that began to emanate from his open gut.

Just a few feet away I examined the front end of the

stalled Plymouth. Not pretty, but not too badly damaged. I hadn't busted the radiator, I didn't think, since there was no steam escaping. I got in, started her up on the first try and backed up. Tommy was still whimpering and pleading for an ambulance when I passed by him, but Rory was already dead when I stopped to get the key to the padlock. I put the bloodied rebar and coffee can into the trunk and headed back into town. With any luck the junkyard would be closed until Monday.

*

The rain was coming down good by the time I got back to the Ogden residence. I laughed at the forlorn sight of the squadcar parked down the street, like a faithful horse waiting for its dead rider to return. Inside the house I swiped a roll of stamps from Sally's desk and addressed the resealed manila envelope to DeWayne Atwell in care of general delivery in Tucson, Arizona; it was an alias I had papers for but hadn't used yet. Neither McCowan nor, sadly, my own real name could be used safely any longer, thanks to Tommy and Rory. I stamped the envelope, going a little over what I thought it would actually come to, though not so much as to attract undue attention, and then drove down to a mail box in front of Ketteman's bakery. As soon as I was done with my business here tonight, I'd head out for Tucson and wait for the envelope to arrive. It didn't add up to what I'd left behind forever in Japan, but it'd be a hell of a grubstake for whatever I ended up doing next.

*

It was coming down in sheets by the time I got to Elishah's. I went inside cautiously; my note was still on the table, the house was dark and I saw no sign that anyone had been there since my departure.

'Cocksucker!'

The voice came out of the dark somewhere behind me, harsher and more nasal than usual. By the time I knew it was Beulah she was on my back, her legs wrapped around my hips, raking her nails down my face. I could feel skin peeling off in strips down both cheeks as I stepped backward, and it hurt like a son of a bitch. I spun, trying to knock her off, and finally toppled backwards into the kitchen door, smashing her into it. She fell to the floor, rolled away and rose again, crouching for another attack. In the feeble light from the streetlamp outside I could see her big, flushed, bony face, blood pounding in the temples, those strange little eyes bugging and angry. With her snaggly teeth bared, she looked like something from the ice age, not yet quite human. She climbed on to the kitchen table in her stocking feet, and I reached behind me and slipped the knuckles on. As she leapt at me I plunged them straight into her belly, and for just a second my hand was enveloped by cheap rayon and adipose tissue clear up to the wrist; it popped free and she hit the ground.

I turned on the light, and in the bathroom I checked my face, which was bleeding but not as badly as I'd imagined. I put on some mercurochrome and cleaned it up, hanging slightly out the bathroom door in case she got up again.

'I don't like getting ganged up on in roadhouses,

Beulah.' She didn't move. 'Elishah's going to have to go without for a couple days.' When she didn't answer I flicked the light on and went to where she lay, careful not to get too close.

Her eyes were half-open and so was her mouth, and a long trail of saliva reached from its corner to the floor. Her face was a shiny purplish red, and touching her carotid with my thumb I detected no pulse. Beulah was dead, and I had to get out of there before Snuffy Smith got home.

Slinging her over my shoulder, I carried her to a door which I correctly assumed led to the basement. I yanked on the chain and the light bulb came on overhead; I propped Beulah up in a standing position at the top of the stairs, with my left hand gripping the back of her neck and my right clenching the material of her dress at the waist. I gave her a good shove, pushing her midsection first. She fell beautifully, smacking her face on the wall with a solid splat as she went down, tumbling violently before finally coming to rest at the bottom of the stairs with a crack that I took to be vertebrae in her neck breaking. I left the door open a couple of inches; I didn't think my accidental fall tableau would fool anybody, but you never knew.

Her purse was on the kitchen counter. There was no cash, just a lot of makeup and keys and facial tissues, a checkbook with a driver's license stuck inside it. There was also a bottle of dexedrine, with a prescription label made out to Mrs. Elishah Casper, though the driver's license and the checks indicated that her name was Beulah Mae Vance.

I put everything back but the bottle of pep pills, which I left open on the kitchen countertop, beginning to think I might get this classified as an accidental death after all. I was ready to go, abandoning my plans for Elishah and consoling myself with the thought that, inadvertently, I had more than gotten even with him.

Then I heard him coming up the walk. I retreated to the living room as he entered the kitchen and listened to him, mumbling aloud to himself as he read the letter. There was a brief silence, then panic as he ran into the bedroom and started tearing the place up. Thinking he might have an emergency dose stashed somewhere, I stepped in and pointed the revolver at his head.

'Sit still, fuckhead.'

He looked up at me, more gaunt than the last time I'd seen him, a sheen of perspiration on his face. I hadn't dealt that much with junkies – narcotics was a concession I'd mostly parceled out to another outfit – but I knew he was in need.

'Where the hell's my dose?'

'Some pimp you are,' I said. 'Selling your old lady to support your habit and she ends up running the whole show, parceling out your smack every day like she was feeding a goddamn cocker spaniel.'

'I ain't a fuckin' pimp,' he said.

'You're living off Beulah's tits and ass, which is what I call pimping, whether you're doing the hard organizational work or not. Where's your straight job, anyway?'

'Night shift at Murdock Clothes Cleaners,' he said. 'Operate a shirt press.'

'Couldn't get work at the plants 'cause you got a record, is that right?'

He was silent.

'So what's that pay, a buck an hour?'

'Eighty-three cents,' he said.

'Not enough to cover the rent plus a big, healthy monkey, is it? So every night you send your mule-faced Beulah out to sell that sweet thing she sits on.'

'Don't talk about Beulah that way.'

'Don't take it so hard. My wife's a whore, too. In fact, she's the one's got your smack. We're gonna head out to see her. Come on, get up.'

Passing the kitchen table I grabbed his rig and put it back into its case and handed it to him. 'Don't forget this, you're going to need it before the night's over.'

He looked at me sadly, hoping it was true, but said nothing. He didn't suspect that the truth was even worse; I wasn't going to let him come home again at all.

*

Elishah did most of the talking as he drove, though he was distracted by the rain and the fact that I wouldn't let him slow down to allow for it. He'd met Beulah in Detroit early in the war, where he'd ended up working war production at Ford. In '43 they'd headed south, having heard that the money was better, but before VJ Day they both had arrest records for narcotics, and Elishah had spent nine months in jail in '47. That was when Beulah kicked it, and also when she started working at the Hitching Post. By the time he got out she was making close to what she would have on the assembly line; it was a touching story of stick-to-itiveness and good old American gumption that made me proud I'd fought for my native land.

We parked by the side of the road and got out. The

rain was coming down gently now, and out here it smelled sweet. I left the dead cop's service revolver in the trunk; it was still loaded and I didn't intend to hand it to Elishah for his prints until it was empty. I opened the barbed wire gate and closed it again once we were through.

In the distance was the cop boyfriend, as I'd expected. He sat on the ridge above the quarry in a bright yellow raincoat and hat, too dumb to get out of the rain, with his arms on his knees and his legs crossed at the ankles, probably brooding over the idea of Sally getting fucked by some drunken hull polisher right below him. If we crossed back into the woods directly behind the cabin, we'd stay out of his line of sight until the very second we arrived at the door, but that wasn't good enough; I wanted him out of the way first.

'Come on.' I motioned for Elishah to follow me to the east end of the ridge. If we could keep quiet enough, I intended to kill my third cop of the evening. 'And remember, if you start feeling smarter than me: you don't know where that dope of yours is and I do.'

Elishah's eyes were dry and flat like those of a dead trout, but he was listening. He nodded and followed.

We were getting close to the cop, and I had the .38 out and ready to blow him into the next world when he turned and looked right at me, his round face beaming cretinously under the yellow rainhat.

'Howdy, Mister McCowan,' he said. It was Lester Glad-well, the idiot farmer and would-be pornographer.

A moment later I felt the barrel of a gun at the base of my skull. 'Drop,' a voice said, and I obeyed. Elishah just stood there, smiling faintly and serenely.

'You're in a shitload of trouble,' the cop said. He cuffed my right wrist and yanked me to my feet, smashing me across the nose with the barrel of his revolver. I felt warm blood running down my face as he brought my left arm around a young tree about eight inches in diameter and cuffed it so that I stood facing the trunk. Then he did the same thing to a docile Elishah a few feet away. When he was done he picked up my .38 and handed it to Gladwell, who grinned moronically at me.

'Either one of these sons of bitches so much as looks crossways at you before I get back, shoot their dicks off,' the cop said, and then he went down toward the cabin.

I called out to him as he walked away. 'Am I to assume we're under arrest, officer?' He didn't answer. He had himself a dilemma; he wasn't there in an official capacity.

I smiled at Gladwell. 'Your friend got the wrong idea about us. You want to see those proofs? They're in the car.'

'Proofs?'

'The pictures I took.'

'I thought you was shittin' me, the way you left like that.'

'I wouldn't shit you. Those pictures are hot.'

'How come you bringin' proofs over this late of a Friday night?' He grinned, proud of himself for figuring that one out.

'Well, hell, I thought I'd take a look at the whore activity down there,' I said. 'Thought maybe I'd get some shots through the windows for you, but then the cop spotted us and went nuts.'

'How'd you know he's a cop?'

'You told me the other day. Or maybe it was Amos Culligan, I don't know.'

He looked at me for a long time. 'How come you took off the other day?'

'I ran out of film and I wanted to get to the lab. I thought you and Missy might be a while longer, the way you were going at it. You sure gave it to her good.'

'Right up her rear. You get some shots of that?'

'Sure did. Some good ones, too.'

Lester seemed pleased at that, thinking back on his exploits. 'Maybe we can get some more in a couple weeks with Lynn again.'

'You bet,' I said. We heard a car's engine turn over, followed shortly by another. 'So Lester, you got a hacksaw?'

He looked at the ground, furrowing his brow like he was thinking real hard.

'No, I ain't. Not for you.' He walked off, and Elishah managed a low chuckle, despite his pain.

I made fists so tight I could feel my nails digging into my palms, and that's when I remembered the nailclippers. They were in my lefthand pants pocket; if I could reach them, I had myself a file.

CHAPTER NINETEEN

Dot sat at the kitchen table in her bathrobe, drinking coffee. Ed Dieterle sat across from her, Tricia to her right.

'That money came from somewhere. It wasn't the pensions, and I know you didn't have much in the way of savings.' Dieterle's patient manner with her had begun a perceptible shift toward the interrogatory.

Dot snorted. 'Savings all went on the down for this house and that damn RV.'

'Where'd the rest of it come from?'

She sat there, looking like she hadn't heard.

Dieterle sat back. 'Let him die, then.'

Tricia was shocked, but again Dot's face was blank and she said nothing.

'What do you mean let him die?' Tricia asked.

'He's been at large what, thirty-five hours? Not many nursing home elopements last that long without ending up bad. He's in that place for a reason, honey.'

'But what do you mean let him die? It's not her fault if they haven't found him.'

'It sure is if she knows where he is and won't say.'

'Moomaw, is that true?'

Dot's expression didn't change.

'I think Gunther's out looking for some money he thinks he hid somewhere.' He turned his attention to Tricia. 'What were you looking for on that map?'

'A rock quarry,' Tricia said.

Dieterle got up. 'Thank you, Tricia.' He kissed her on the top of the head. 'You know what, sweetheart? This might be a little easier on your grandma if you weren't in earshot.'

'Oh,' she said. She stood. 'I need to go to the store anyway.'

A minute later Ed heard her car start, and he thought how funny it was that a woman her age, and about to start med school at that, hadn't objected to being treated like a child.

'He thinks that money's still hid out there,' Dot finally allowed. 'He doesn't remember it went into the bank.'

'What else is out there at the quarry?'

'Nothing.'

'There's something out there that scares the bejesus out of you, or you would have told me about it first thing this afternoon. I'm going to find out what it is eventually, and you might as well save us both some grief and tell me now.'

'There's nothing to tell.'

'You want to hear what I think? I think there's a dead man by the name of Cavanaugh, and I think it was Gunther that put him there.'

She was quiet for a few seconds, and she looked away from him. 'That wasn't it. It started with an A. He was a lawyer, I know that much. He had a Bar Association card in his wallet.'

'So it's true. I didn't really think it was.' Ed looked nauseous. 'He killed a man for the money he was carrying?'

Dot stood up and slapped him across the face, then sat back down again. 'Shame on you for even thinking that. It was an accident.'

'How come he didn't report it?'

'Why do you think? Shit. Big bag full of dirty money and there we were, up to our asses in debt. Plus Gunther could've lost his license, running a man over like that.'

Ed nodded. 'Can I have a look at that map?' His throat sounded tight.

She got it off the kitchen counter and handed it to him. As he spread it out on the table he touched his cheek where she'd hit him, and she reached out and touched it too, for just a second.

'Well Jesus, Ed, I'm sorry I slapped you but how the hell could you even think Gunther'd do something as wrong as that on purpose?'

'Just lost my head for a second.' He grabbed a ballpoint pen and leaned down a couple of inches from the map, trying to remember how to get to that quarry. 'Pullwell was the town . . .'

*

Eric walked out Sally's kitchen door with the directions to the old quarry in his shirt pocket. She watched him go with something close to affection, and for a second he looked just like his son Tate. Same jumpy gait, same slouch, same way of tilting his head to the side when he walked. For a moment she worried about the boy, coming from this lout on the one side and from herself and Wayne a generation back on the other. Then she remembered that she used to think the same thing about Loretta, and she'd turned out pretty much okay.

It didn't occur to her until he was already out of sight that the engine she heard turning over was her own. She ran outside, appearing in front of the house just as he was shifting out of reverse and heading up the street.

'You son of a bitch, you bring that back here!' she yelled, but he just stuck his hand out the window and waved. When he was finally out of sight she smashed her highball glass on to the asphalt, accompanying the attendant crash with a loud 'Fuck!' She marched back inside, not caring who'd heard.

He might at least have asked, she thought, pulling down another glass and filling it. Poor dumbass is going to drive all that way out there and find the burnt foundation of the cabin and jack shit else; be lucky if he doesn't kill himself.

She wondered about what he'd said, about Gunther coming over looking for a little action. But Gunther was married now, and he never was one to mess around behind your back. Course he was senile, so who knew if he even remembered he had a wife.

Twenty years earlier, when she heard Gunther had finally married Dot McCallum, she'd stewed for days. It figured, though; the whole time he was with her she knew he still had a thing for Dot, who didn't have half her looks.

Dot held on to him by virtue of having broken his heart, and Sally had come along too late for that.

She'd written him a few times after the move to Cottonwood, and he'd answered faithfully. When things got really bad once or twice and she'd broken down and asked him for money, he sent it immediately and refused repayment. But he never came to visit, and a few years later, when she wrote to tell him she was about to marry Donald, offering him one last chance, he didn't answer. There was no getting around the fact that without Gunther she'd likely have been put in jail. She would have lost Loretta to a foster family or the Children's Home, maybe for good, but it was going to be a long fucking time before she stopped being pissed off at him.

*

The Volvo's engine had cooled by the time Jack and Gunther finished shooting pool. Jack had been more than willing to reminisce about the old days, but he'd never been to the quarry himself and was no help with the directions, other than pointing him in the direction of the turnpike.

As he swung around the curve in the river with both front windows lowered, a warm breeze flowing through the front seat, he tried to remember Jack's directions, reflecting that he probably would have had better luck with cars if he'd been driving an automatic all those years. He had it in D now, as Jack had suggested, and the damned thing seemed to be running okay. Cut over to Kellogg and then east all the way out of town, where the onramp was; it was a waste of time since he was going to be heading west, but damned if Jack knew anymore where another turnpike onramp was. He passed through downtown and then south until he hit Kellogg.

The street had changed a lot since Gunther had last driven it; he wasn't even certain he had the right road until Calvary cemetery rose up on his right. Albert Vance was buried there, and Gunther gave him a little wave as he passed it. 'Don't take any wooden nickels, Al.'

Vance had been buried on a cold morning in November of '64 with a deep blue sky and hardly any wind. He was a popular guy, and it was a well-attended burial service. Gunther saw it now, cops in uniform and in dark suits and overcoats, and a fair number of their wives, and he could have named all the attendees if he'd been asked. The grass was almost white and crackled underfoot like straw, and the atmosphere was surprisingly light among the dead man's colleagues, if not their wives or the other women present. Al had died screwing one of his numerous girlfriends, several of whom were present and eyeing each other nastily, jockeying for position as the Official Paramour of the Deceased.

On reflection he could think of four other cops and two of their wives who were buried there, and off the top of his head he found that he could name seven local cemeteries and their street addresses, and at least two or three people he knew buried in each. His father and mother were in Hillcrest further north. His other mother, his real mother, was buried in a tiny cemetery a few miles outside Cottonwood. He hadn't visited since shortly before his first marriage, and the thought filled him with remorse. He resolved to go there before he turned himself back in at the home. Who knew if they'd ever let him out again, even for a last, short trip to his Mutti's grave.

He was off the highway part of Kellogg now, passing through a residential district on one side and a row of motels and used car lots on the other. On his left was Eastborough pond, a tiny manmade lake where one night in 1969 a man had been arrested for screwing a duck. The story made it into the next afternoon's *Beacon*, a tiny item on page three that none the less contained the phrase 'unlawful sodomy with a duck,' a first for a family newspaper as far as he knew. The perpetrator's name had kindly been left out of the story, and Gunther couldn't quite call it up now. He remembered the man's face, though, one of the scaredest guys he'd ever seen booked.

He wasn't far from Lake Vista now, and he grunted at the sight of it in the distance. Maybe they'd get their security down tighter now; God knew lots of those old people couldn't survive outside the place.

On his left was a big discount store, its lights still burning and cars in the lot. There was a traffic signal ahead and he pulled into the lefthand lane and signaled. He'd be spending the night at the quarry; he'd need a tent and a bedroll and, now that he thought of it, a shovel.

He parked near the entrance, and stepping inside he thought he'd gone into the wrong place. The store had been there thirty years and he'd been in hundreds of times, once or twice for official reasons, but nothing about the cavernous, brilliantly lit building he found himself in was familiar. There was advertising everywhere, on the walls and on the shelves and even over the loudspeaker; where before there had been only a live clerk reading off what the hourly special was, professionally produced radio ads now alternated with hysterical, overwrought singing.

Wandering toward where the sporting goods section used to be, he found instead a couple of dozen standing racks with brassieres of various colors, textures and sizes hanging above matching panties. He reached out automatically to feel the leghole of one pair that reminded him of Sally's: high-waisted, white and satiny in texture. He rubbed the fabric between his thumb and forefinger. Sometimes she wore black and sometimes white, never red, grey sometimes, he thought, and sometimes a very light brownish color. His first wife Imogene had liked nice lingerie but tended to come home lacking the bottom half of a matching set. Jean, his second wife, wore nice underwear only on special occasions like his birthday and New Year's Eve; the rest of the time it was plain cotton, purely functional and arousing as tent canvas. Number three, Mildred, habitually wore bra, panties, garter belt and stockings to bed – sometimes a gartered girdle instead of the belt – under a nightgown. He found that titillating until he realized she didn't mean it to be; they were married for nearly three years and in that time he never once saw her completely naked. Once he had blundered into the bathroom and found her sitting in the bathtub wearing her brassiere, and it began to dawn on him that he was married to a madwoman.

Then there was Dot. He tried to think what she wore underneath but couldn't picture it. In fact, he couldn't picture Dot at all for the moment, which troubled him.

He was still enjoying the smooth feel of the garment on his fingertips and was considering bringing it up to his face when he heard the pleasing sound of girlish laughter behind him.

'Can we help you find anything, sir?' asked one of two giggling shopgirls. They wore identical green vests and neither one looked older than twelve.

'Bivouac.'

'What?' asked the other, and they both erupted in a giggling fit. He waited for it to subside before answering.

'Need bivouacking gear.'

The first one started laughing again but the second worked hard to maintain her composure. 'We don't stock those. You might try Frederick's of Hollywood, down at the mall, though.'

He had only a vague idea what that was but he knew it couldn't be right, so he simplified the request. 'I need a tent and a bedroll. And a shovel.'

'A bedroll? You mean like a sleeping bag?'

'Yeah. Tent, sleeping bag, shovel.'

'Oh. Sporting goods for the first two, hardware for the shovel.'

'Where's that?'

'Way down in the corner,' she said.

Gunther no longer heard the giggling when he got to sporting goods, though he sensed it was still going on. He took the cheapest sleeping bag they had at thirty-five dollars. Tents started at seventy-five and he decided he didn't need one, but as long as he was in sporting goods he picked up a seven-dollar jackknife and put it into his pocket, intending to pull it out and pay for it when the time came. The shovel was only ten. When he checked out, the woman at the register gave him an odd look, trying to place him. She didn't say anything, though, and he got out to the car without incident and loaded his purchases in the backseat; the jackknife was still in his pocket, forgotten and unpaid for.

Gil Stratmeyer, thirty-nine years old, he thought as he closed the door and started the engine. Lived at 1136 Lasserman. Wife's name was Lorraine. That was the guy with the duck, and twenty years later he could call it up just like that. The name had a joke attached to it. Someone had asked if the duck was a drake or a hen, and Ed had piped up without hesitation: 'Shit, it was a hen. Nothin' queer about Gil Stratmeyer.' Even the poor depraved duck-fucker had laughed a little.

I'm sharp as a tack. There's no way in hell I belong in the old folks' home, Gunther thought as he got back on to East Kellogg, and a minute later he pulled on to the turnpike.

*

Eric swung Sally's Grand Am into a space in front of the Chimneysweep. Above the door was an old plastic sign with a crude rendering of a deranged looking man in a top hat, his head and a wildly bristled brush sticking out of a chimney on a rooftop. There were only six cars in the lot, which seemed like a poor tally for a Friday night. When he pushed his way through the door, though, he found it smoky, packed and loud. Either the drunks were car-pooling or the surrounding neighborhood supplied a large portion of the Chimneysweep's customer base.

He muscled his way through to a narrow space at the

bar, and one of several harried bartenders came immediately over and leaned forward, cupping her ear to hear Eric's order. 'Margarita, rocks. Is Rex here?'

She shrugged, either to indicate that she didn't know or hadn't heard; bolstering the latter hypothesis, she poured him a blended margarita from a pitcher. He took a swig anyway and dropped a twenty on to the bar, happy at least to be flush again. He pocketed the change when she slapped it down, stiffing the Chimneysweep's bar staff for the second time that day. He jumped at the touch of a finger on his shoulder and turned to see Rex.

Rex grimaced, squinting to examine the details of Eric's injuries in the darkness. 'You look worse than you did at lunchtime. What happened?'

'Fell down some stairs.'

'The fuck you did.'

'Hey, Rex, was that a quinella or an exacta I bet this afternoon? On Rusty and Prince o' Chincoteague?'

'Exacta in the wrong order. Too bad, the other way around paid pretty good.' He said it without consulting his little book, and Eric ignored the tiny voice that wanted him to ask Rex to double-check. 'You're not going belly up, are you, Gandy?'

'On one dog bet?'

'I keep hearing things. I was wondering if they were true, or if people were just talking that way because they been seeing you drunk and dirty in the middle of the afternoon.'

At that moment Eric experienced a nauseous, urgent desire to escape the smoke and voices, and he set the drink down. 'See you, Rex,' he said, and hurried for the door without waiting for a reply.

*

Sidney sat exhausted at the bar of the Sweet Cage, sipping a club soda and wishing he was somewhere else. It was his least favorite kind of crowd, enthusiastic and noisy, with another bachelor party going on around stage one. Since they were spending money he couldn't feel bad about it, but the old feeling that a fight might break out at any second made a knot in his stomach, despite his full awareness that he now paid others to deal with such eventualities. He was about to get up and leave when Francie Cherkas strode in past the doorman. She came straight over and threw her arms around him from behind, smelling of baby powder and lavender and something else, a perfume of some sort that grappled with the other two odors for primacy on Francie's generous bosom, which was pressed hard against Sidney's back and shoulder.

'Oh, Sidney, I'm so sorry about your dad, you must just be completely freaked out.' She had on one of her odd-looking ass-length wigs and a canary yellow pants suit with bell bottoms.

'He's my stepdad.'

'Oh.' She nodded solemnly. 'Hey, guess who I ran into in the Men's Department at Dillard's? Caroline.'

'That's nice.'

'I don't know, Sidney. Maybe you shouldn't have let her slip away.'

'Maybe not,' he said, unwilling to argue the point with her. Caroline was an English teacher who, in the end, hadn't wanted to share her life with a strip show promoter. They'd spent an evening at Mitch and Francie's house once; Francie had had on an avocado minidress circa 1974, and she'd served fondue and Cold Duck, the latter in jelly glasses with ice. If Caroline had had a patronizing thought all evening she'd kept it to herself. 'Isn't it sweet that two such hard-to-match people managed to find each other,' she'd said in the car afterward. Sidney, who had known Francie when she was still turning the occasional trick to make ends meet, and Mitch when he was a forty-year-old virgin, had kept his opinion of the union to himself.

'What are you doing here this late?' he asked. 'Where's Mitch?'

'It's Culligan's birthday, so we're taking him around to all the clubs.'

At that moment Mitch pushed an extremely old man in a wheelchair through the door and grinned at the sight of Sidney. He nudged the chair's occupant, who turned reluctantly from the dancer on stage two to look at Sidney and give a short wave hello. Mitch wheeled him over, to the old man's obvious discontent.

'Happy birthday, Culligan.' Culligan had been an obnoxiously faithful customer in the old days, and Sidney suspected that for him the worst aspect of old age and infirmity was the inability to get to the nudie clubs on a nightly basis.

Culligan pulled a five-dollar bill out of his shirt pocket with a shaky hand. 'Gonna be a happy birthday in a minute when I get over there to the stage.'

'How old are you, anyway?'

'Seventy-nine.'

Sidney looked at him and wondered how he could be only two years older than Gunther. In this light his skin was the color of library paste in some places and of ripe strawberries in others. He couldn't stand up any more and he didn't seem to hear too well, whereas all Gunther seemed to have lost was his mind.

Culligan's patience was gone. 'Come on now, goddamn it, it's my birthday and I want to tip the girls. Wheel me over there so's I can see the tiger jump outta that gal's snatch.'

Mitch pushed Culligan toward the stage, and Francie blew Sidney a little kiss. As they made their way to a table to the side of stage two she drew a few admiring stares, which she acknowledged with little discreet waves of the top two joints of her fingers. Mitch Cherkas drank it all in and sat down between her and Culligan's wheelchair, beaming. He winked at Sidney like the luckiest man in creation.

Over the alarmingly loud sound of 'Eye of the Tiger' blaring over the PA in Tyfannee's honor, he heard his name being called, and turning saw the bartender holding the telephone and pointing to it. He went back into the office and picked up Dennis's phone.

'Hello?'

'I need you over at your mother's house right away.'

'Hey, Ed. What's up?'

'Never mind, just get over here. I need your help.'

He left with pleasure, as a loud whooping sound rose abruptly from the crowd to comment on some unusually lewd gesture on Tyfannee's part.

*

The old woman's directions were for shit, naturally. Eric ended up getting off the turnpike in Mud Creek, just one exit before the Oklahoma border, and turning around. There wasn't an exit for Pullwell any more, if there ever had been. He drove halfway back to town and got off at Natterley, where there was an open gas station a few hundred feet from the turnpike booth. He put fifteen gallons into Sally's Grand Am and went inside the convenience store, where a longhaired kid in a baseball cap sat behind the cash register. He took Eric's money and returned his change without speaking a word or making eye contact.

'Did there used to be a turnpike exit to Pullwell?'

He still didn't look up. 'Exit's at Jockstrap, right next to it.'

'What?'

'Gilstrap. Town full of assholes. We used to kick their ass every fucking fall, and after the game we'd kick it some more.'

Gilstrap, just twenty miles south of town. He'd killed an hour and a half or more by missing it. 'Shit. Back to the turnpike.'

Now he looked up. 'Fuck the turnpike, man, Pullwell's up 83, you just go out Pike Street there, can't miss it. You can blow up there doing a hundred, nobody's gonna stop you.'

He nodded. 'Thanks.' He grabbed a six pack of Coors from the wall cooler and set it down on the counter. 'Guess I'd better get some for the road.'

'Nuh-uh, no beer sales after midnight, sorry.'

Eric pulled out a twenty. 'How about you ring it up tomorrow and keep the change.'

The boy nodded. 'Who fucked up your face like that?'

'This guy's been fucking my wife, he ambushed me right in our bedroom. I'm going to Pullman to find him.'

'Beat the shit out of him, man.'

'That's the general plan,' Eric said, opening the door.

He headed slowly up Pike toward 83, trying to remember if he'd ever been in Natterley before. It looked like a lot of other shitty places, its downtown commercial district emptied out by some mall or megastore on the outskirts of town or in the next one over. Half the storefronts stood empty, with hopeless, perfunctory FOR LEASE signs posted on their glass doors, a few with dusty displays still standing inside, advertising goods no longer on offer. At a stoplight he looked into the window of a hardware store that had managed to stay in business. A single feeble row of fluorescent lights burned in the rear, backlighting the darkened merchandise in the front of the store. It was just like Stackley, where he'd grown up, and he found now that he couldn't wait to get out of Natterley, Kansas, either.

One stoplight further down he passed another convenience store. Five or six teenagers sat out front smoking and drinking beer to the sound of heavy metal pounding out the open doors of a couple of pickup trucks. For laughs he punched his horn and flipped them off as he passed, and as they jumped into the pickups he floored it, wondering how fast old Sally's Grand Am would go. He was a quarter mile up Pike pushing eighty when he caught sight of them in his rearview mirror, gaining steadily and noticeably. This hadn't been a good idea, on balance, but with the window open the speed and the adrenaline combined with the violent airflow over and around his head to make him forget momentarily the pain in it. They were within an eighth of a mile of him, he guessed, probably less, when he saw the prowlcar lying in wait not far from a sign marking the entrance to Highway 83. He poured it on a little harder and as the first pickup passed it the cop's lights burst on. Before it was up to speed not one but both pickups had, to Eric's amazement, pulled over obediently. Entering the highway he slowed down briefly to seventy-five, thankful for providence and the respect small-town teens evidently still held for local law enforcement.

He could feel his pulse in his throat and the wind whipped through the car, billowing his shirt like a flag. He hadn't known, until he'd said it to the kid in the convenience store, how badly he wanted to get back at Gunther. The twelve grand would be nice, too, but if kicking the shit out of the old bastard meant no reward it would be worth it. One way or another that senile piece of shit was going to be sorry he'd fucked with Eric Gandy.

There was hardly another car in sight; every couple of minutes he'd pass one going the other direction, and he had yet to see one heading north with him. Accelerating again, the Grand Am hit a hundred with ease, and he decided that called for a Coors. He punched a can open with one hand and chugged half of it. Leaving Natterley behind at a hundred and seven miles an hour, at the wheel of a car that wasn't his, under a warm moonlit sky, a beer in his hand, he felt as excited and free as he had leaving Stackley twenty-five years earlier; now as then, anything seemed possible.

*

Gunther had experienced no further problems or uncertainties regarding the location of the quarry after collecting his ticket at the turnpike onramp to the state, and he spent the entire drive thinking about his first grade classmates. Their names came back with startling clarity and in order, as if printed on a sheet of paper: Herbert Albright, Myrna Friedmann, Ronald Hillburn, Ora Johnson, Alfred Ohl, Alva Ridpath, John Schnitzler, Marie Tyler, Jakob Weschler and Orma Wycliffe. Their faces stubbornly refused to appear in his mind, though, with the sole exception of Ora Johnson, whose picture had been in the *Beacon* once in the mid-thirties; she'd won twenty-five dollars in a baking competition with a fruit-free pineapple upside-down cake. It was only that adult face in the news photo that he now recalled, and apart from that incident in Ora's early life he had no idea what had become of any of them.

Their teacher's face was stuck in his mind whether he wanted it there or not. Mrs. Holmes was a stout, humorless woman whose dislike for children was said to extend to her own, a decade or so older than the ones she taught. She was the one who had brought him the news that his mother was dead, calling him inside the schoolhouse during recess to tell him. As he pulled up to the barbed wire gate, seventy-one years after that cold morning, he felt a faint residual sting on his cheek where she'd slapped him for calling her a liar.

The gate was still a simple barbed wire affair and no trouble to get through, but preparations had clearly been laid for major changes. He drove the distance from the road to the clearing, parked next to where the cabin had stood and got out to examine the property. Chainlink fencing divided various sections of the property now, and the cabin's charred foundation was gone altogether. Most of the land had been staked and parceled out, and he wondered who could possibly be obstinate or greedy enough to try and build anything on this rocky, uneven patch of leaky ground. He trudged up the rise and stood in the copse of trees that had been his shelter in the old days as he watched over the cabin.

The view was the same, somehow, despite the absence of even the cabin's ghostly outline, and when he heard a loud glub from the water in the quarry, he wondered if it had been stocked with fish. It was the sound of something coming up and not being thrown in, maybe an air bubble. He didn't think fish would survive long in that water, at least not any fish worth catching.

He passed through the trees and looked out in the other direction toward old Gladwell's house, but in its place he saw four houses in various stages of construction, situated around an asphalt cul-de-sac. The trees that had surrounded the house were all gone with it, replaced by scrawny, twiggy things so thin they had to be tethered to stakes taller than they were. It would be thirty years or more before they provided anything like the shade of those old trees.

So Gladwell was gone, the property subdivided and sold off, presumably for the benefit of nieces and nephews and cousins with no use for him when he was alive. It seemed a shame, tearing down such a beautiful, sturdy old house; then he remembered how he'd had to hold his breath against the stench from inside last time he'd been on its porch, and he wondered if they'd had any choice.

Probably the smells had permeated the beams and studs from cellar to attic.

He turned back and sat down in the middle of the trees, overlooking once again the quarry and its surrounding land, glad he'd come back to see it before it became completely unrecognizable. Probably they'd have to fill in the pit, even if it wasn't land they could build on, just as a safety consideration. He sat with his knees up and his ankles crossed and looked down. It was an odd feeling, being up there and looking down without the anxiety that used to accompany those weekends, the knowledge that at any minute he might have to barrel down there and coldcock some shithead who got out of line. Most weekends, though, that never happened. Usually it was just Sally and one of the other girls and a couple of guys having a two-day party, drinking and screwing and eating, without so much as an angry word being uttered.

He was sure as hell glad those days were gone. They hadn't ended too well for Sally, though, and he felt bad it had taken so long for her to get back on her feet. He remembered the drive out to Cottonwood, trying hard to convince Sally's little girl Loretta of what a wonderful place it was going to be. She hadn't wanted to go and leave her little friends or her school or her babysitter, and Gunther felt worse about uprooting her than he did about any of the rest of it.

He heard the gurgling sound again and, watching the water of the quarry, something about the idea of construction going on there gave him a nervous feeling. He looked back toward the cabin at the sound of Sally's raised voice, first angry and then scared, but there was no cabin, not

even the blackened frame and busted chimney there'd
been when he was out here last. He didn't see the duck-
blind either, and wasn't sure where it had been. Somewhere between the cabin and the edge of the water? He
thought of the time he came out in the RV he'd just
bought with the idea that a little travel would set Dot's
worried mind at ease. Instead it had got her fretting even
more about their debts, and on their very first trip in it
he'd backed over that poor son of a bitch with the briefcase. He didn't feel as bad about that as he should have,
and pondered the reason why he had the nagging sense
that it had something to do with what had brought him
back out here.

*

When Sidney stopped in front of his mother's house, Ed
Dieterle's rental car was there and so was Tricia's grey
Subaru.

Inside he stopped dead at the sight of Dot in tears.
'What's going on?'

Tricia, cradling her grandmother on the couch, looked
at him and shrugged. 'I just got back. Nobody'll tell me
anything.'

Dieterle stood up. 'Come on, Sidney, we got a little
drive ahead of us.' Dot didn't say anything, but Sidney
thought she looked relieved. 'Don't worry,' Ed said to her.
'Ask Gunther if I know how to keep my mouth shut.' He
turned to Sidney. 'You, come with me. You up for an out
of town drive?'

'You're the boss.' Sidney opened the door, motioning
Dieterle to go ahead of him, and Tricia discreetly signaled

that, despite appearances, she and Dot would be all right on their own. Sidney had his doubts; the last time he'd seen his mother cry he wasn't more than seven years old.

*

Loretta knocked on the kitchen door and let herself in. It was long past her own bedtime, but her mother was always up late. Sally stared at her from the kitchen table, head unsteady and eyes unfocused. 'You're lucky I don't keep a gun in my kitchen drawer any more, 'cause if I did I mighta just shot you dead for a burglar.'

'Mom, if you were worried about burglars you'd lock your door.'

'All I'm saying is don't go walking into people's houses unannounced. Never know who's gonna blow you away out of sheer surprise.' Then she smiled. 'Come on in, sit down. So what brings you all the way out here? Thought I told you I'd be playing cards tonight.'

'It's one thirty a.m.'

'So it is. Usually you're in bed before eleven.'

'Wasn't sleepy. How was your card game, anyway?'

'I was playing shitty, and getting shitty cards, and I knew before long I was gonna start acting shitty, so I came home and found your shitty husband sitting here drinking my good gin.'

'Eric was here?'

'What did I just say? Yeah, he was here. Guess who else was here? Gunther.'

'When?' Loretta asked, excited.

'I don't know, some time late afternoon. I was gone.

He stole Eric's car. And then Eric stole mine, the little cocksucker.'

'What do you mean he stole your car?'

Sally leaned forward. 'You have a bad habit of taking what I just said and asking it back to me as a question. Quit it.'

'You need a ride somewhere?'

Sally rolled her eyes. 'Now where would I be going this time of night?'

Her mother's snappishness brought back some of her earlier, stoned resolve. 'The reason I came is I have some questions I want to ask you.'

Sally shrugged. 'Fire away. Want some Tanky Ray?'

'No, thanks. I want to know what happened to my father.'

'Dead. Next question.'

'I mean why'd he stay away so long.'

'Wish I knew the answer to that one myself. Next question.'

Loretta could feel the blood rising to her face, but she stayed calm. 'All right. Why'd we move to Cottonwood?'

Sally rolled her eyes. 'Jesus Christ on a pogo stick, that was thirty-five years ago.'

'Thirty-six. There was no job waiting for you, we hardly had any money saved, we didn't even know anybody there. Why Cottonwood?'

'I felt like a change of scenery. Next question.'

'Can't you at least try to give me a straight answer?'

'That's as straight as you're gonna get. All done?'

Loretta just stared at her, and she knew that it didn't

matter how determined she was to get the truth out of her mother, it wasn't coming. Finally she stood up.

'Oh, for Christ's sake, sit down. Don't take it all personally. Have a drink.'

'I'll talk to you later.'

Loretta got up and left. She sat outside in the Caddy for a while with the engine running, listening to Debussy on the classical station and enjoying the last vestiges of her buzz. Then she pulled out of the driveway and headed for home, thinking only about climbing into bed and getting some sleep, and not at all about her mother or her father.

*

Once he'd managed to find Pullwell, Sally's directions were perfect, and when Eric got to the first barbed wire gate and found it hanging open he knew his hunch had been on the money; the old man was reliving his brief, glorious existence as King Pimp. The property was staked off for subdivision, with tiny red and white flags stuck in the mud in straight lines going off in all directions, but there was no heavy equipment on-site yet. The road was rutted and sloppy from yesterday's rains and, after the second open gate, he turned off his headlights and drove slowly, stopping at the first sight of a rise topped with trees. This would be where the cabin used to stand. A hundred feet to the left sat his Volvo. He took the last can of Coors, popped it open and drained it in a swallow, hardly even feeling drunk any more as he stepped out of the car.

'Gunther?' He tried to sound like a man attempting

to coax a whipped dog out from under a bed. 'Are you there?'

There was no answer, only the sound of crickets and frogs. In the distance he heard something plop in the flooded gravel pit, and he walked in the direction of the sound.

'Gunther? Don't be scared. I'm here to take you back home.' The whole plot was staked out, almost ready for the digging to start, and he had the vague notion that this was close to where Randy Kensington was putting up some houses. 'Come on, how'd you like a ride back to the old folks' home?' As the land rose he saw the flooded pit with the moon's reflection glowing on its surface.

Something went past his face and he stepped back. It continued low across the border of the pit before settling in the grass. A moment later another object flew two or three feet in front of him, landing eight or ten feet away, and he walked toward it. As he leaned down for a closer look there was a terrific, sharp pain in the back of his head as the third projectile hit the base of his skull.

'Fuck!' He touched his fingertips to the affected area, tears welling in his eyes. 'Come out before I find you and beat the shit out of you.'

He got no answer, and presently he discovered that his feet were wet. The edge of the water was colder than he would have expected; his pants were now wet up to midshin. He was starting to feel dizzy, and the moon in the water shone up onto his face, its own reflection distorted by his stumbling and splashing. All this he processed as the gradual slope of the bottom of the quarry steepened suddenly and gave way beneath his feet. He went under with his eyes open, finding the water below much darker than its brilliant surface would suggest.

*

Sally stood thumbing through the old newspapers on the counter. Funny how they were still in such good shape, hardly brittle at all and barely yellowed. It was a lot further in the past than it felt to her now, perusing the movie schedules and department store ads and classified ads and, of course, the sensational front-page account of the love raffle sullying Collins Aviation's pristine reputation as a morally upright place for Christian men and women to work. 'LOVE WAS PRIZE IN COLLINS RAFFLE,' shit. The whole goddamn thing was Sonya Bockner's idea, one night when the two of them were sitting around drunk and horny, waiting for Glenn to get home. It was Sonya's notion, too, that Sally be the one to run the operation, taking most of the risk and reaping most of the benefits. Now that she thought about it, it was probably Glenn who'd thought the whole thing up so he could watch Sonya getting screwed, peculiar fellow that he was. The Bockners had set the same thing up in KC a few years later and ran it themselves with no trouble from the law; just Sally's luck to be the one the roof came down on. She looked again at the picture of herself with Sonya and Frieda and Lynn and Amos Culligan, sad as she often was for the loss of her looks, and for the things the girl in the picture could have done if she hadn't hooked up with a first class prick like Wayne Ogden.

About the only thing in her life she was proud of,

really, was the way Loretta had turned out. Part of that, of course, had been knowing when to keep her damned mouth shut, no matter how self-righteous and irritating Loretta got. Sally had kept her counsel for thirty-five years, and the girl had another guess coming if she thought she was about to start spilling now. With some regret she took one last look at the newspaper picture, carried the whole stack to the fireplace and started a fire going. She wasn't going to live forever.

*

Grunting, his clothes soaked through with cold, stinking water, Gunther hauled the young man out of the gravel pit. Once onshore, he set him down and listened to his breathing. The man seemed not to have swallowed much water, for which Gunther was grateful. He'd known the guy was trouble when he first heard him calling out in that kindergarten teacher voice, but he had no desire to kill anyone.

He lifted him over his shoulders with a grunt and carried him toward the big Pontiac. Gunther would have preferred it to the foreign car he'd been driving around that evening. He wondered where he'd picked the damned thing up, anyway. He vaguely remembered a side trip to Jack's Riverside Tavern and wondered why he hadn't borrowed Jack's old car.

Thoroughly winded, he opened the door and shoved the inert body on to the front seat. He wasn't that young after all, under the harsh, yellowish dome light: probably close to fifty, his head bruised like he'd been in a fight.

Gunther closed the door and trudged back toward the

rise, pulling off his wet jacket and shirt. At the top he pulled off his pants and his shorts and shoes and socks and hung everything from the branches of a tree to dry in the wind. Maybe later he'd build a fire, though he wasn't sure he remembered how. He was bone tired, but he couldn't lie down yet because he hadn't done what he'd come here for. He couldn't remember exactly what that was, either, though he suspected it had something to do with the people in the cabin he'd been watching earlier in the evening. Gazing down in its direction now, he saw it was gone, even its foundations.

He began to worry about the man lying unconscious in the car. The last time he'd been here, bad things had happened; he was glad he hadn't let him drown, but he knew he couldn't just leave him sleeping in the car.

He headed back down the slope one more time, his legs sore. The grass was soft beneath his bare feet, but he stepped carefully none the less. He had no handcuffs, so, using the jackknife he found in his jacket, he cut several lengths of string connecting a bunch of stakes along the ground and serving no useful purpose that he could see. It was thick as spaghetti, more or less, and with it he hogtied the man on the front seat of the car. Once he was sure the man was breathing more or less regularly and that his circulation wasn't cut off, he closed the car door. Before walking back up to the rise he noticed he'd left the door to the foreign car open. Going over to close it, he found a large plastic bag on the back seat; in it was a bedroll, and leaning across the back of the car was a shovel. He had no use for a shovel, but he took the bedroll with him to the top of the rise.

He laid out the bedroll and sat on it, not willing to go to sleep yet. He could stay awake for a long time, no matter how tired he was, and he hadn't done whatever it was he'd come to do . . .

He watched the land below for a while, hearing several more unidentified plops in the water, thinking about the light of the moon and the tricks it played with color, how under it both cars appeared to be shades of gray, how the grass, lush and undoubtedly a very bright, yellowish green in daylight, looked here like the fur of a white rabbit.

He turned at the sudden, prickling sensation on the back of his neck – someone was behind him. A few feet away, her features hidden from the moonlight by the speckled shade of the trees, stood a young woman.

Her sweet voice was soft and high, the way he remembered it. 'Komm, Günther, 's ist Zeit zum Schlafengehen,' she said, almost singing.

He yawned and nodded his assent, then climbed obediently into the sleeping bag and closed his eyes, feeling himself falling asleep to the sensation of a warm peck on his cheek and a gentle, feminine hand stroking his hair.

CHAPTER TWENTY

GUNTHER FAHNSTIEL: 22 JUNE, 1952

I heard Ogden's car before he came through the first gate. He didn't allow for how quiet it normally was out there, even with the rain coming down. From the top of the ridge I could hear everything that happened at night, right down to the conversations in the cabin, though I usually tried not to pay much attention to those. I was just there to keep the peace.

After I disarmed Ogden and left him and his buddy cuffed to the trees, I walked down to the cabin and found four naked people dancing close together to a scratchy old Paul Whiteman record. Sally wasn't too pleased when I told her the weekend was over, that she'd have to give the fellows a raincheck. I made a little joke about how it really was raining, but Sally didn't laugh. From the ruckus she raised, poking her finger at my chest and shouting, you wouldn't have thought me being the only person in the room with any clothes on was anything unusual. I outshouted her and told her to pack up and get out and

I wasn't fucking around either. She didn't back down exactly, but she did stop yelling.

The two guys looked at each other and shrugged, then started getting dressed. One of them was a skinny little redheaded guy of about fifty or so, and the other was a big farmboy type with a double chin and skin trouble who didn't look as old as that record they were playing. Word must have spread about what happened to guys that didn't cooperate because they left without an argument.

They'd only been there since about four o'clock in the afternoon, but the cabin already smelled like sex and whiskey and burnt beef, and Sally said she and Frieda needed to stay and clean up. When I told her she'd have to come back the next day and do it she got snappy and wanted to know what was the matter. I was still sore at her for not listening to me, so I just told her to get her ass in the car and let me take care of it.

I headed out toward Pullwell with the raffle winners ahead of me in a light colored sedan. The car was all over the wet sandy road, and I sped up alongside with my wobbly Ford and motioned the redheaded guy to pull over.

'You,' I said to the kid next to him. 'How much have you had to drink?'

'I don't drink.'

'All right. You're driving back to town.'

'The fuck he is,' the driver said. 'This here's my car, and I agreed to drive him out here 'cause he don't have one, but I'll be double-fuckin'-damned if I'll let that cocksucker drive mine.'

'I didn't ask if you wanted him to,' I said, and I opened

the car door and yanked him out. The fat boy just sat there while I brought skinny around. 'Now scootch on over there and drive the damn car.'

He did as he was told and I shoved skinny into the passenger seat. He mumbled something I didn't hear, and I asked him to repeat it. He wouldn't, though, and I sent them on their way.

*

Back on the road, going sixty and listening to the Ford's frame rattle the whole way, I tried to think what to do about Ogden. We could have old Gladwell file against him for trespassing, or we could get him for assault with a deadly weapon. I wondered if the joker he'd brought with him might cooperate and I tried to think where I'd seen him before. Probably a narcotics beef, judging by his skinny frame and haggard face.

The clock on my dash didn't work, but it was past three by the time I got to Ed's house and I hated ringing the bell that late. Ed answered in pants and a shirt he was already buttoning, and in a minute Daisy appeared behind him in her nightgown, scowling at me, arms folded across her chest. I pretended not to notice her.

Ed put on his shoes and pulled a raincoat from the rack next to the door and stepped outside. 'Sorry, honey.'

She didn't say a word, just closed the door on us.

*

'Goddamn Tommy and Rory. I can't believe this guy gave 'em the slip.' We were almost to Pullwell now, and it was about four a.m.

'What'd you tell 'em to do?' I asked.

'Just follow Ogden around and pull him over and arrest him if he looked like he was coming out here. Shit. If I find out those guys were drinking I'm gonna tear 'em a couple of new assholes come Monday.'

'Sorry about waking Daisy.'

'She'll get over it.'

I didn't think she would, though. 'Guess this'll be the end of this whole deal,' I said, so he wouldn't have to bring it up himself. 'Ogden's sure to spill soon as he gets charged.'

'Let's not get ahead of ourselves,' Ed said. 'Maybe we can still cut a deal with him. He leaves town peacefully, we won't queer his deal with the Army.'

Back at the quarry the first thing I noticed was Frieda's Cadillac still there, next to Ogden's Plymouth. 'Goddamn it, I told those gals to clear out of here.'

I killed the engine and we got out with our weapons drawn and approached the cabin. The lights were off and the door locked, so I busted it open. There was nobody there. I opened the west bedroom and found Frieda, who sat up and screamed.

Sally came out of the other bedroom. 'What time is it?'

'I told you to get on out of here,' I said.

'Last time I looked you weren't in charge of me, so we stayed to clean up.'

A lump in the bed next to Frieda moved and grunted. I pointed the gun at it.

'What's that?' I asked, and a head came slowly up from under the sheets. It was Gladwell.

'Howdy,' he said, grinning proudly.

'Goddamnit,' I said. 'You're supposed to be watching those two up there.'

'It's raining.'

'They're dangerous, I told you that.'

'They're still handcuffed to them trees. They sure tried to get me to set 'em loose, but I didn't. I seen them other fellas leave with you, thought I might come down and help the girls clean up.'

Sally pointed at the door and damn near spat. 'You broke the fucking lock.'

'Gunther, where'd you say these men are?' Ed was standing behind me. He tilted his head toward the door.

The rain was still coming down, and halfway there I could hear the moaning of the thin one, and Ogden telling him for what sounded like the hundredth time to shut up. They were both sitting on the wet grass now, with their arms still wrapped around the trees. Their clothes were soaked right through.

'Please help me,' the thin one said in a hillbilly accent, his voice shaking. It was a nice warm night, despite the rain, but he sounded like he was freezing.

'Would one of you go to the car and get him his fucking heroin so he'll shut up?' Ogden said.

'Possession of narcotics, Sergeant Ogden?' Ed said.

'It's his,' Ogden said.

'Your car,' Ed replied. 'Doesn't matter much if you say it's his dope or not.'

'And would you open these bracelets? That idiot farmer tightened 'em up so bad when he left I can hardly feel my hands any more.'

'You're under arrest right now for narcotics possession,

for assault with a deadly weapon, resisting arrest, attempted murder. I could go on,' Ed said. 'We got a proposition for you. You never come back here and we don't pass that arrest record on to the Army.'

'That'd sure be it for my military career, wouldn't it.'

'That's the way we figure it.'

I watched the other fellow shivering and whimpering, and I'd just about drawn a bead on where I'd seen him before – not long after the war, in a shooting gallery raid – when I heard a loud crack and something slipping in the slick grass and coming down hard. Ogden was on top of Ed, the little tree snapped in two, sawn partway through.

I drew and pointed my revolver at his head. He had the chain around Ed's throat, choking him. Ed was sputtering, his face was red, and he was between me and Ogden.

'Let him go,' I said, and he didn't answer. Ed clawed at the chain while I moved to outflank them; Ogden turned with me, and I thought about shooting anyway. Finally Ogden got up and dived for the slope, and I fired after him. I missed and started running after him but slipped on the grass and landed on my ass hard.

I fired again from a sitting position. Ed groaned and got up on his hands and knees and said something I couldn't make out. I started to go after Ogden, but he grabbed my arm and repeated himself. This time I understood him.

'He got my gun,' he said.

I started running straight down to the cabin. The rise was open and unprotected, but no shots came. Then I spotted him amongst some good sized rocks next to the quarry, halfway to the cabin, and when he saw me he raised Ed's gun in my direction. I dropped to the ground but it didn't provide much cover. Like a goddamned idiot I'd come out one free weekend with a scythe and cut the grass.

He fired once and skirted the edge of the water toward the cabin. I don't think he was even trying to hit me, just keep me pinned down while he moved. I rose and ran and he fired again, and this time I could hear it hitting the ground behind me. He disappeared around the front end of the cabin and I heard screams, followed by Sally's voice, more mad than scared: 'You son of a bitch, you've got a lot of balls showing up here—'

I was close enough to hear what I took to be the sound of the barrel of Ed's revolver on Sally's face, along with a yelp from her and another scream from Frieda. I didn't hear anything from Wayne and I took that as a bad sign as I rounded the corner to the front of the cabin. I edged up to the door, thinking Wayne probably had the revolver pointed straight at it, and I crouched and poked my head in, almost down to the floor. The lights were out, but I saw Sally on the ground with her nose bleeding like hell and Wayne in the corner behind Frieda with his cuffed wrists around her throat, the barrel of the revolver pointed at her temple. I ducked back out, the gun went off and Frieda screamed one more time as the floor splintered where my head had been.

I doubled back to the room where I'd found Gladwell and Frieda. The window was open and I was pretty sure it hadn't been a minute before. Behind me I saw Gladwell hightailing it for the rise, and Ed trotting toward me. I climbed in the window as quiet as I could and motioned Ed to go around front.

'Come on out now, Ogden,' I heard him yell as he got near the front door. I landed on the bed as quiet as I could manage.

'Eat shit,' Ogden yelled back at him. I climbed down off the bed and crawled forward. Ogden still had Frieda, and Sally was still on the ground. What I noticed and Wayne Ogden didn't was that she had her hands on the handle of a big cast iron skillet.

'I said come on out, Ogden, maybe we can still make a deal,' Ed shouted.

'What kind of fucking idiot do you take me for,' Wayne yelled back at him, and he shoved Frieda forward, pulling the hammer back at the same time. As soon as he was in front of her Sally rose up, the skillet in her hand, and I thought I heard bone crack when she brought it down on the back of his head. The gun went off wild and Frieda shrieked as she and Wayne tumbled forward past the porch and down with a splash into a puddle. He didn't fight as she scrambled to get away from him.

'I'm deaf! I'm deaf!' she yelled, running away from us to the safety of her Cadillac.

I pushed past Sally, who dropped the skillet on to the floor, and I stood over Wayne, whose open eyes were rolled upward into the sockets. Ed picked up his revolver where Wayne had dropped it, and he was the one who went inside and comforted Sally and looked after her nose, which was still bleeding pretty bad.

Wayne closed his eyes, then opened them again and looked up at me. The rain was making him blink and squint, and I pulled back the hammer just to see what he'd do. He smiled, and right then I could see this bastard dogging me the rest of my damned life, and Sally's, too. He smiled because he knew I wasn't the kind to finish him off on the ground like that. He didn't even have time to look surprised.

CHAPTER TWENTY-ONE

By the time Ed had directed Sidney to the third wrong road leading out of Pullwell, neither of them had anything to say not directly related to navigation. Upon their third return they spotted Pullwell's lone police car and flagged it down. The officer riding shotgun got out and leaned over into the window of Sidney's car.

'Huh-uh. Never heard of it.' He was in his early twenties, with thin blond hair that stuck straight up when he removed his uniform cap. He turned back to the driver of the prowlcar. 'Hey, Tom, you know where the Gladwell farm is?'

'The who farm?'

'Gladwell. Glad as in glad and well as in well.'

'Who wants to know?' The driver was fiftyish and less cheerily inclined than his young partner to help out of town visitors, so Ed got out of the car, careful to keep both hands in sight. You never knew when these small town boys were going to get nervous, especially around a couple of strangers riding in a pimp car like Sidney's BMW.

'Looking for a retired police officer who walked away from a nursing home a couple of days ago.'

The driver nodded slightly. 'I saw that on TV. They didn't find him yet?' He paused. 'Gladwell's. Isn't that where they used to have those wild parties? With all the whores?'

'That's the place.'

'I remember that from when I was a kid. It was all over the paper. We called it Whore's Quarry; we used to go out there sometimes on weekends, hoping there'd still be a few of 'em around.' He chortled so hard he started to cough. 'Never did find any, though, just a burned down shack and a stinky old pond. What's the old man supposed to be doing way out there?'

'Just a hunch his wife had.'

The older cop got out with a map in his hand and beckoned Dieterle over as he unfolded it on the hood of the squad car.

*

'What wild parties was he talking about?' Sidney asked Dieterle as they drove away toward what they hoped was the right road.

'Back in the fifties whores used to use the place weekends.'

'No shit?'

'No shit.'

'You don't really think about that kind of stuff happening back then.'

'Maybe you don't. I remember it real plain.'

The moon was low enough in the sky to be seen pacing the car through the side window above the blur of the treetops, its bright face fading slowly into the canopy as the sky began to lighten at the horizon, the darker lunar seas and valleys already matching the delicate indigo of the surrounding air by the time they arrived at the turnoff. The first barbed wire gate leading on to the dirt road hung open and limp to the side of the road, and they stopped. Ed got out and examined the tracks.

He got back in. 'Looks like a couple cars to me, since after the rain.'

The low part of the sky was faintly orange and the landscape around them a dim gray as they entered the clearing. To Dieterle the place looked about the same as it had thirty-seven years earlier, despite the cabin's absence and the presence of myriad little flags, stakes and strings marking the property up. If anything it was more lush than before, with four decades of growth on all the trees, most of which he figured were slated for cutting if the stakes meant what he thought they did. Not far from where the cabin had been were a Pontiac and a European sedan.

'Either of those look familiar to you?'

'Nope.' Sidney parked and they got out. The grass was damp, the morning already warm.

'You head right, I'll head left,' Dieterle said quietly.

'Should we yell for him?'

'No. Don't want to scare him.'

Ed walked up to the Volvo and peered in. He saw a shovel and nothing else of interest. The front door was unlocked, and he dug through the glove compartment until he found the registration. The owner was an Eric Gandy, whose name meant nothing to him.

'Ed!' Sidney hissed from the Pontiac. 'There's a guy sleeping in this one, got a bunch of empty beer cans on the floor.'

Ed nodded and put a finger to his lips to signal him to pipe down. He stepped over the spot where it seemed to him the cabin had been, but the years had obliterated any visible physical trace of it. He remembered the night he and Gunther had burned it down, after Sally and the others had been arrested, the flames sparking up into the hot summer night.

It came to him that Gunther used to set up camp in the trees at the top of the rise, and he was about to head that way when he saw Sidney already making the climb.

*

Tricia was asleep on the couch in the living room, Dot having finally gone to sleep around three. The violent sound of snoring from the bedroom woke Tricia up, and she lay there for a while listening to it, watching the leisurely waltz of the dust motes in the first shafts of daylight poking through the slats of the venetian blinds. She'd slept two or three hours at the most, and she knew she wouldn't be getting back to sleep this morning. The air conditioning was already running, and she had on her shorts and t-shirt from the day before under the thin blanket.

She got up and padded into the kitchen to make a pot of coffee, then stepped outside and scooped the *Eagle-Beacon* off the driveway. The fresh warm air was pleasant on her face; standing there with the screen door propped outward with her shoulder, she opened the paper, calmed by the burbling sound of the coffee brewing in the other room. Then she sat on the porch step and rested the paper on her knees, fascinated at the number of tiny arthropods on the dewy grass this time of day, aphids leaping and spiders crawling, gnats flitting around the taller blades of grass.

The coffee pot's gurgling ceased and she listened to the birds' morning calls for a minute before taking the paper into the kitchen, failing to notice that the snoring from Dot's room had ceased.

*

The sounds of Tricia clomping around in the living room and the kitchen had awakened her, but she didn't feel like company. She sat up and took a book from the night table, *1001 Helping Thoughts for Daily Living*, the kind of thing she couldn't have had lying around when Gunther was still there. They did help her, usually, but now when she opened to a random page she found:

'In the whole history of the world God never made another you.'

What crap. She closed the book again and wondered whether Gunther was sleeping right then. He'd never cared about sleeping regularly; as a cop he was used to being up for thirty hours and sleeping twelve afterwards, and no amount of nagging on her part later could convince him that it wasn't good for him. She remembered going to bed one night with Gunther in the living room working on a jigsaw puzzle and waking up at six the next morning to find him still bent over the card table with about twenty-five pieces left of a 500-piece puzzle, a picture of a bunch of dalmatians.

They'd met at four-thirty or five one morning in September of 1942, when she was still working in the emergency ward. He came bleeding profusely from a long slice cut along the inside of his upper arm by a drunk with a carving knife; the other cop had done a good job of first aid but the wound ended up needing twenty stitches, and his aplomb had impressed her.

Fred McCallum had been called up six months earlier, and the longer the son of a bitch was gone the nicer her life got, despite the privations of the war. For a year or so, she and Gunther had a real good time and when she felt especially bad about it she went to church. Usually, though, just thinking about Fred was enough to keep any guilt feelings at bay; before long she decided that she'd look into an annulment when he got back, so she could marry Gunther.

A shortage of police officers had prevented him from enlisting or being drafted until then, the result of the drain of able-bodied men into the armed forces; most of the department's applicants since Pearl Harbor had been kept out of the services for good reason. In early '43, however, when recruitment was a little better for the department, they let him go, against Dot's vehement objections. She was so mad at him for going, she didn't tell him why she needed him to stay in the first place; he would have stayed then, she knew, but she didn't want him that way. In retrospect it seemed like the stupidest mistake she ever made in her life, stupider than having married Fred McCallum in the first place. Maybe not as stupid as taking him back, though.

She'd nearly been fired for slugging another on-duty

nurse a week after VJ day; the woman had called Sidney a bastard, and in fighting the official action which the woman had taken against her at the hospital, she realized two things: that certain people would see him as such and treat him badly for it, and that she couldn't raise him alone.

So when Fred came back in '46, forgave her and offered to raise the boy as his own, she took him up on it. She was still mad at Gunther for leaving, and couldn't risk him turning his back on her when he found out; when he got back shortly thereafter she wouldn't even take his calls at first, or let him see the boy, and they were apart for twenty-five years after that.

She swung her feet around and stood up. She could hear Tricia turning the pages of the paper, and she might as well be reading Ann Landers as sitting there on the bed trying to second-guess decisions she'd made forty-five years ago.

*

Sidney, who had not stayed awake for twenty-four hours in a row in a very long time, first attributed what he saw at the top of the ridge to a lack of sleep, wondering even if he might *be* asleep and dreaming. His own head, old and grey and smiling contentedly, seemed to be sticking out of a cheap sleeping bag on the ground, dead to the world. It was the serene smile that for a good thirty seconds kept him from identifying the head as Gunther's. He watched him for another minute or two, examining the face from different angles and finding that only from the first, upside-down point of view did Gunther's smile resemble his own. The resemblance was unsettling nonetheless, and he walked back to the edge of the trees and looked down. Dieterle was leaning into the Pontiac where the drunk lay, sleeping it off.

'He's up here!' Sidney yelled.

He turned back as Gunther sat up, squinting at him, then pulled himself out of the sleeping bag and walked over to where his clothes hung from a tree. He fingered them and turned away without putting them on.

'Got your clothes wet?' Sidney asked.

Gunther nodded and smiled again, more on the left side than the right. Dieterle appeared at the top of the rise, breathing heavily, and stopped cold at the sight of Gunther. 'Oh, Jesus.' He went and yanked the pants and shorts off the branch and handed them to him. 'How about putting these on before I puke.'

Gunther dropped the clothes then picked them up off the ground and slapped Dieterle on the shoulder, then Sidney, the lopsided half-smile still playing on his face. Then he grunted and laboriously began putting the shorts on, followed by the pants.

'Judging by that shit-eating grin I'd say he's maybe had a stroke,' Dieterle said under his breath to Sidney. 'We're gonna have to take him to the hospital. Also the guy in the Grand Am.'

'What's the matter with him?'

'Somebody, I can't imagine who,' he said, indicating Gunther with his thumb, 'pasted him a good one and hogtied him on the front seat. Head's been bleeding some and I can't wake him up.'

Sidney looked at Gunther, who sat crosslegged with

his damp trousers on, gazing down on the quarry and the three cars.

'We better go right now, I don't know how bad off this guy is.'

'Ready to go, Gunther?' Sidney said to no response. 'Come on, Mom's waiting for you.'

At that Gunther nodded, rose to his feet and, favoring his right leg slightly, started down the rise toward the car. Sidney and Dieterle followed, and Gunther gave Dieterle a little wave as he got into Sidney's car. Ed took the wheel of the Pontiac and the two cars began to crawl away toward the county road.

'You sure been keeping me busy, Gunther,' Sidney said, surprised to find all his anger toward the old man evaporated. 'What the hell were you doing out here, anyway?'

Gunther didn't answer, just stared out the window at the passing woods, staked out like the rest of the property and soon to be replaced by rows of more or less identical houses. He started to say something, then stopped.

'What?'

He shook his head.

'You started to say something. Come on.'

He tried again, stopped in apparent frustration and turned back to the window. After a second he turned back to Sidney and spoke, slowly.

'Mir ist letzte Nacht deine Oma begegnet.' He smiled again, a few gnarled teeth showing this time.

'I don't speak German, Gunther,' Sidney said. 'Didn't know you did, either.'

Gunther nodded, surprised by the admission of ignorance or maybe by the fact that he'd been speaking

German. He tried again, with somewhat more difficulty: 'To me, last night . . .' He stopped and started over. 'Last night I seen your Oma.'

'My what?'

'Your . . .' He frowned, struggling to find the word. 'Your grandma.'

'Oh.' Gunther hadn't known either of Sidney's grandmothers, both of them dead since the fifties. 'How's she doing?'

'Fine.' He nodded to himself, still looking contented.

Great, now the old woman's going to have to learn German, Sidney thought as they passed through the last gate on the way to Pullwell. Maybe Tricia can give her lessons.

CHAPTER TWENTY-TWO

ED DIETERLE: 22 JUNE, 1952

I stood there in the cabin watching Gunther stand over Wayne Ogden's body, a surprised look on his face and blood and brain tissue on the legs of his pants. After a minute he looked up at me, water dripping from his scalp on to his face. 'Am I under arrest?' he asked.

'I don't know,' I said.

Sally stayed calm, considering what she'd just watched. Once we had her nosebleed under control, she went to get the other woman at the Cadillac, trying hard to convince her to come back into the cabin, that the danger was over.

'Let's take care of this, I guess,' I said finally. After removing the handcuffs we wrapped Ogden up in some sheets from the cabin and tossed him into the trunk of his car, where we found another police issue service revolver, a piece of rebar stuck into a coffee can and weighted down with concrete, a small case full of narcotics paraphernalia and a packet containing what I assumed was the long-denied dose of heroin for Ogden's junkie pal, who'd slipped my mind entirely. We went back up the hill and found the poor bastard hurting bad, still cuffed to the tree, his hair plastered to his head.

'Your buddy sure caused a lot of trouble tonight,' I said.

'He ain't my buddy. He shoot somebody down there?'

'If he's not your buddy what are you doing traipsing around with him on private property in the middle of the goddamn night?'

'I got home from work and that cocksucker'd stoled my fucking junk, then he pulled a gun on me and made me come out here. Said he'd give me what I wanted when we was done with his business, and I don't know what that was.' He sounded like my old Uncle Merle from Arkansas. He weighed about a hundred and twenty pounds and looked like he was eighty years old.

'You ever seen this joker before he showed up at your house?'

'I seen him a couple times out at the Hitching Post. He took a liking to my wife and a disliking to me. Reckon he woulda kilt me once we was done with whatever he wanted me to do.'

'And you don't know what that was.'

He was looking at Gunther's bloody trouser cuffs. 'Look here, I didn't see nothing you all did this morning, I just want to go home and have my medicine. You take me there then you'll know where I live. You know I ain't gonna turn you in for nothing, knowing what you know about me.'

I looked at Gunther and he shrugged.

We marched him down to the Plymouth and told him we were taking him home. He was relieved but not over-joyed until I told him he'd be getting his drug back when we got there, upon which he began thanking me pro-fusely. The effort involved seemed huge and I told him to pipe down. Gunther followed in his Ford. The ladies headed for a doctor they knew in town for Sally's nose, which looked to be broken, and we told the farmer to clean the place up.

On the drive back the junkie didn't say a word the whole way home, just sat there shivering and whimpering. When I stopped to let him out he took his paraphernalia case and the little packet with him, hunching over to shield them from the rain, happy to be free, and went into his little house to do his business.

Then Gunther followed me to the Commanche, where I parked Ogden's Plymouth in the middle of the lot as though it had been there all night, the last remaining vehicle from the previous night's throng. Gunther parked around the corner and walked over to help me pull Ogden from the trunk. The sun was already up but because of the rain it was dark, and we threw the body out on to the lot and then unrolled the sheet. No one was really going to think he was shot here; most of the back of his head was back at the cabin. We balled the gory sheet up, shoved it into Gunther's trunk and drove away. We'd have to wait until the blood dried to burn it.

Neither of us said anything for a long time as he drove to my house. The thunder had started, or started again, and we listened to that instead.

'Another joint Army-Navy fuckup,' I said finally, and if he didn't exactly laugh he did give a little grunt.

*

A week after I reported Ogden's death to the Army I got a cable from the Criminal Investigations Division in Japan requesting details. The man who sent it was Lieutenant Thomas McCowan, and my requests for clarification went unanswered, despite my prompt response to the CID's cable.

Then McCowan showed up one day, expecting all of us to bend over and grab our ankles. I turned over Ogden's duffel bag and its contents and those of the hotel safe, including the cash, to him. Gunther had given Ogden's letters to Sally, so officially I had no knowledge of them. McCowan also got copies of all the official reports on the crime. I sadly informed him that we had few leads and little hope of ever breaking the case unless we got lucky with an informant. Someone had shot Sergeant Wayne Ogden at an unknown location, and then moved his vehicle and his body to the parking lot of the Commanche Club in a clumsy attempt to make that look like the crime scene. Lieutenant McCowan of the Criminal Investigations Division of the United States Army didn't think much of my skills or attitude, but he seemed satisfied that his man was indeed dead, and he left town without thanking me.

*

Sally wouldn't quit. She said she at least had to give the two fellows Gunther had chased away the rest of their weekend. Then she said if Wayne Ogden was dead and unable to spill, why stop? Gunther told her he'd have no part of it, though, and a month later I told Stan Hardyway from Vice that it was time to shut them down. He said he'd pass the word on to her, and I believe he did. I know for a fact Gunther told her. Still she wouldn't quit it.

We arrested the bunch of them at Collins on a Wednesday, the day the lots were drawn. Frank Elting and a photographer were there, and we staged it early enough in the morning for it to make the paper that afternoon. I hated to do that to Sally, but the tradeoff was that the *Beacon* never once suggested that the murder of her husband had anything to do with the lottery, in fact never mentioned that the ringleader of the notorious Collins Sex Lottery was also the widow of the Slain War Hero from a couple of months before. The more genteel morning *Eagle* shied away as much as possible from both stories.

In the end Sally's lawyer got the charges against her and the others dropped; Gunther and I helped pay for him, since she was dead broke. She and Frieda and Lynn and Sonya all lost their jobs at Collins. So did Amos Culligan, who'd claimed the union was in on it from day one and was shocked when they failed to stand by him afterward. That was the end of the raffle, although others just like it popped up at other plants and even at Collins from time to time in later years.

*

The weekend after the arrests, Gunther and I went out to the quarry with a couple of cans of gasoline. We told the farmer who lived there what we were going to do, then we trudged back over that rise, emptied the cabin of anything of use, and splashed the gas all over it, inside and out. It was a hell of a blaze, and as the night fell it was in full bloom, sparks dancing upward toward the stars just beginning to show in the darkening sky; after a while you could see through where the walls had been. When it was spent, we knocked down the smoldering remnants, except for the chimney and one beam that hadn't burned well at its base. If we hadn't been dog tired we would have knocked them down, too, but we left them up, maybe as a reminder. We poured water on the ashes, told the farmer to keep an eye on it until it cooled down, then drove back to Wichita.

CHAPTER TWENTY-THREE

At the emergency ward Gunther had trouble walking, and Sidney stuck his arm under the old man's to help him. He was still big, about Sidney's size; he was walking better by the time they got to the entrance and unaided by the time they approached the admissions desk, where they stood behind a belligerent young man with a nosebleed.

'I can't wait my turn, I'm fucking bleeding to death,' he said.

'Sir, you're going to have to wait your turn. Please go and sit down and I'll call you when it's time.' The admissions clerk was a slender black woman who was clearly accustomed to repeating this phrase many times on a daily basis, but she seemed to be wearying of the young bleeder's presence.

'This is the fucking Emergency Ward, people come here because they can't wait. It's nine-thirty in the morning, how backed up can you be?'

'Sir, please go sit.' She looked around him at Sidney. 'Yes, sir?'

'Just a goddamn minute here, I'm not done talking to you.'

'Yes you are,' Sidney said.

'What did you say to me?'

'I said if you don't go sit down like she said, right now, your nose isn't gonna be your only bleeding orifice.' He said it in a calm way, his facial muscles frozen into his most threatening bouncer's stare, and the young man retreated and sat down as far as he could from the admissions desk.

'Thank you so much. How may I help you?' the woman asked.

A few minutes later, as they sat side by side, Sidney filling out an insurance form the clerk had given him, Gunther patted him on the knee. Sidney looked over and was surprised to see him beaming at him with pride. 'You're a good boy, Sidney,' he said, very intelligibly, but that was all he managed to get out before a doctor was finally available to see him.

*

Tricia had been delighted to be the interface between the hospital personnel and her family, helpfully translating the medical terminology for her grandmother and her dad, asking the doctors questions no one else in the family would think to ask. She was aware, though, that her grandmother and Ed had more to discuss out of her earshot. It had annoyed her last night, being ordered out of the house like a child when serious matters were to be discussed, but her grandmother's emotional well-being, as well as Gunther's very life, seemed to be at stake, and so she had cheerfully trotted off for an aimless drive lasting an hour or so. Now she wanted to know what the hell was going on, but she couldn't bring herself to be insistent or impertinent with her elders.

'Mind if I take your girl to lunch?' Ed said to Gunther.

'Okay,' he said, and pointed to Tricia. 'She'll stay.' He looked at her with such tender supplication, it almost broke her heart. Poor Gunther, she thought, without that poker face you're defenseless. She nodded, and Ed walked out with Dot.

'You want to watch TV, Gunther?' Tricia said.

He shook his head. 'Ich hab letzte Nacht deine Oma getroffen.'

'Wie, bitte?' She'd never been able to get Gunther to speak more than a few perfunctory phrases of German before. It embarrassed him, she thought, but if he was having a change of heart it was fine with her.

He repeated himself, slowly, and she listened with great care.

'Meine Oma? Meine Grossmutter?' she said.

He nodded. 'Ja. Meine Mutti.'

His accent was unfamiliar to her, but not incomprehensible. Had he told her once that his mother was from Hamburg? 'Deine Mutti.' She nodded and sat down to listen to whatever he cared to tell her.

*

Ed and Dot were seated in the corner, away from everyone else. Dot had finished her hamburger and fries, and now that Gunther was safe she no longer saw Ed as an adversary.

'I talked to Rory's boy this morning about taking up the slack on Rory's bill out at Lake Vista,' he said. 'He squawked a little, but he'll pony up. He's got plenty of dough, and he'll just be making up the difference on the government's share. I'll shame him into it if he drags his feet.'

Dot shook her head. 'Poor fella. I don't begrudge him that money, it's not like he even knew about it. I just don't understand why Gunther felt like he was responsible for his upkeep.'

Ed's face was as blank as Gunther's used to be when he answered: 'Guess we'll never know.'

*

Between dealing with hospital admissions, his mother and the weasely little fucker from Lake Vista, Sidney was exhausted. He didn't want to go to sleep yet, though, and at eleven in the morning he headed for the hospital cafeteria for his sixth cup of coffee.

Sitting down he picked up an abandoned newspaper from an adjoining table. He was halfway through the racing results when he glanced up and saw the woman he'd met the day before, the one who thought Gunther had been at her house. He got up and moved to her table, leaving the newspaper behind.

'Loretta?'

She looked up at him, surprised. 'Yes?'

'Sidney McCallum.' She continued to look expectant and puzzled. 'Gunther's stepson.'

'Oh. *Oh*. Sorry. Sorry, I was off in my own little world. Sit down.'

Sitting down he saw that her eyes were bloodshot and wet. 'He's going to be okay, more or less,' he said.

'Who, Gunther?'

'Yeah. You're here to see him?'

'No. My husband.' She sniffed unselfconsciously, a loud, gurgling snotty sound that, like her laugh, fitted her in a funny, outsized way. 'You found Gunther.' She brightened.

'Yeah, this morning. Doctor says it looks like he's had a stroke. Actually this new guy thinks he may have had a bunch of small ones before this.'

'Oh. I'm sorry.'

'At least now we can get him and my mom into someplace better, where they can be together and where the medical care's up to a twentieth-century level.'

'That's good. I'll come see him when he can have visitors, if that's okay.'

'That'd be great.'

Her lip started quivering and her eyes teared up. 'Poor old Gunther,' she said.

He took a sip of his coffee. 'I didn't realize your husband was sick.'

'He was in an accident. He'll be okay, they think. Head injuries, though, so it's hard to tell.'

'Sorry. That must be tough.'

She shrugged. 'That's not why I've been crying.' She laughed and grabbed a napkin from the dispenser in front of her, dabbing her eyes. 'I was just thinking what a bitch I am for being disappointed he wasn't dead.'

He had to force himself not to laugh along with her.

*

Sally woke up on her couch in a sitting position, the remnants of a fire still going in the grate. A stack of newspapers lay next to it, waiting to be burned; she blearily recalled going back into the garage for more after dealing with the first batch.

Jesus, I'm lucky I didn't burn the goddamn house down, she thought, getting back on to her knees to poke more life into the fire. She went into the kitchen and put some coffee on, though the very thought of it made her head swim, then came back and started going through the pile. There was Wayne's Army paperwork, and the Army's side of her long correspondence trying to get Wayne's death benefits; his being AWOL at the time of his death had complicated that to the point where she'd given up trying. She held on to a few items regarding Wayne's parents and grandparents, thinking they might be of interest to Loretta or the kids, but all the rest of the paperwork and effluvia she'd been saving since Wayne's mother died she now tossed into the fire: his high school and college diplomas, group photographs and war mementos, and finally his letters.

Gunther had given her the letters after the business at the quarry, but she'd never quite had the nerve to read or destroy them. Now that she was going to do the latter she decided she might as well do the former, and she pulled one from its envelope. It was from her, written shortly after Loretta's birth, and she winced at her clinging tone, at the supplications either to come home or send for her.

The next was a crumpled and re-smoothed one from Cecil Wembly, a man she vaguely remembered from high school and maybe from Collins, too, and it was missing its first page. She had liked him, as far as she remembered, and was surprised to know that he and Wayne had corresponded, though not as much as she was at the letter's contents:

qualities as friend and classmate. Therefore what I am about to set to paper does me great pain.

Your wife, who as you know has taken a job on the assembly line at Collins, has been operating a prostitution ring right off the factory floor!

Although management is quite well aware of this, her relationship with her union is such that we cannot take steps against her. You, however, are not beholden as we are to organized labor. As an old friend I implore you not to let this slide! Your honor and that of the Collins Aircraft company are at stake.

Your Friend,
    (signed)
    Ceece
Cecil N. Wembly

She got up and leafed through the phone book until she found it: Cecil Wembly, Sr., 364 Neapolitan Street in Augusta. She dialed the number and a woman answered.

'Wembly residence.'

'Hi. Is Cecil there?'

'I'm sorry, Cecil passed away five years ago.'

'Oh. Is this his wife?'

'I'm his widow,' the woman said crisply.

'Okay, honey. I'm just calling to tell you your old man was a fucking louse.'

She hung up before the woman could respond, and burned the rest of the letters unread.

*

What, Dieterle wondered, was the idea of a skyline postcard from a place that barely had a skyline? He stood in line at the airport giftshop waiting to pay for a couple of stuffed buffaloes for his granddaughters, looking over the rack of iconic prairie images, and was shocked to see an actual news photo of a tornado looming dark over a cluster of farm buildings with the caption '*TWISTED GREETINGS From The Great Plains*.' He pulled the card down from the rack and examined the reverse and found that the tornado in the photo had killed eight people in 1982. He took them all and paid for them along with the buffaloes. Walking out he threw the whole batch into a trashcan except one, which he stuck in his inside jacket pocket, intending to write the printers responsible and let them know exactly what he thought of their attempt at humor.

He was early for his flight, and the boarding area was empty except for a little spillover from a TWA flight at the next gate. He'd toyed with the idea of staying over, just so he could get some sleep before he returned to Dallas, but he had nothing to do here, and everyone he would have wanted to see would be busy with Gunther's medical situation for the next couple of days at least. He was glad anyway that he hadn't had to waste his non-refundable return ticket.

For a while he watched the crowd pass by, harried and grouchy and none of them sufficiently dressed up, in his opinion, for air travel. He didn't know when he'd be back; maybe when Gunther was better he'd drive up and see him. Then, despite himself, he closed his eyes and fell asleep.

*

Tricia had left, but not before extracting a promise for more conversation in German. She'd seemed excited and pleased by what he'd told her, which wasn't much. He was happy to talk, though, and in German it was easy.

The old woman was there now, and she climbed up on to the bed with him, put her arm around his middle and pulled herself close to him. He could smell her and feel the warmth of her body against his as she tried to explain things to him.

'You're not even listening to me, are you?'

'Am,' he said, nodding, though he was having trouble following some of it. The gist of it, though, was they'd be together somewhere, and apart from that he didn't give a rat's ass what happened.

AUTHOR'S NOTE

The towns of Cottonwood, Natterley and Pullwell are fictional, and those familiar with the real city of Wichita will note that I have taken liberties with its geography and with the geology and topography of south central Kansas.

Though the characters in this novel are all fictional, the lottery described herein is similar to several real ones that operated at various Wichita aircraft plants after World War Two. Michael Gebert first tipped me off to them via Jack Lait and Lee Mortimer's fascinating pulp exposé *USA Confidential*; the late Jerry "Clyde Suckfinger" Clark, former head photographer for the *Wichita Beacon*, provided me with several amusing anecdotes about his former colleague Ernie Warden, the reporter who broke the story of the raffles for that paper. I owe particular thanks to Jerri Kay Smith, News Librarian for the *Wichita Eagle*, who supplied me with old *Eagles* from June 1952. My grandfather, Joe Mohr, supplied others about the aircraft plants in the forties and fifties. My father, Lee Phillips, and my friend Ed Thomas, were both generous with firsthand information on occupied Japan.

Since my considerable ignorance extends to many

fields, I am grateful to the following people for setting me straight before I wrote too far in the wrong direction: Innes Phillips, who explained the geology of Kansas rock quarries; Susan D. Snyder, who patiently corrected my misapprehensions regarding banking law; and Drs. Tom Moore, MD, and Lou Boxer, MD, both of whom devoted time and energy to my questions about head trauma cases and memory loss. My stalwart German translator Karl-Heinz Ebnet worked hard to provide me with certain German regional colloquialisms, circa 1910; Ken Hattrup kindly provided me with general information on the nursing home industry, particularly regarding the housing and security needs of memory-impaired patients.

I owe thanks to everyone at Ballantine Books in New York and Picador Books in London, in particular to my long-suffering, stoic editors Dan Smetanka and Maria Rejt; thanks are also due to my friends Paul Marsh, Abner Stein, Dennis McMillan, Charles Fischer, Sylvie Rabineau and Katherine Faussett. Finally, and especially, I would like to thank my agent and good pal Nicole Aragi for more than it would be practical to try to list here.